Currently Dead

Currently Dead

✦

A Futuristic Sci-Fi Novel

Bob Good

iUniverse, Inc.
New York Lincoln Shanghai

Currently Dead
A Futuristic Sci-Fi Novel

iUniverse books may be ordered through booksellers or by contacting:

iUniverse
2021 Pine Lake Road, Suite 100
Lincoln, NE 68512
www.iuniverse.com
1-800-Authors (1-800-288-4677)

Because of the dynamic nature of the Internet, any Web addresses or links contained in this book may have changed since publication and may no longer be valid.

This is a work of fiction. All of the characters, names, incidents, organizations, and dialogue in this novel are either the products of the author's imagination or are used fictitiously.

Cover Art: Electromagnetic Soul; Not Rollins—digital creations by Christopher Rosaferra

ISBN: 978-0-595-45784-7 (pbk)
ISBN: 978-0-595-70047-9 (cloth)
ISBN: 978-0-595-90086-2 (ebk)

Printed in the United States of America

To my wife and the men and women of the strategic attack group who gave their lives so willing at the battle of Lucifer's Crescent.

Interplanetary Literary Awards and Recognition

- Required reading Kian Military Academy

- Blue Circle Award Lalian Cultural Arts Commission

- Kaf Extraplanetary Novel of the Year

- Literary Vonus Medal Paradorian Historical Society

1

Crisis

"Run! Deena, Run!" screamed Garrett.

Deena ran down the smoke-filled, rubble-strewn corridor. Explosions behind her propelled her forward, both from the concussion of the blasts and the terror of the approaching Cylots. Garrett ran behind her, covering her retreat while firing back at the advancing Cylots. They came to the intersection of corridors that extended out to the modules at Pluto Base. Pluto Base was shaped like a spider—eight corridors extending out to eight modules from a central core. The Cylot attack had first hit the communications module, wiping it out. The life-support module had been next, and now the remaining oxygen at the base was rapidly leaking out. Deena, Garrett, and the others left alive were rendezvousing at the central core to head to the storage module, where the spacesuits were kept.

Deena tripped in the rubble, catching her ankle, and fell heavily. Garrett, firing behind, bounded over her and screamed, "Get up, Deena. Run!"

At the intersection they met Mike, Tim, and Laurie. The Cylots rushed down the corridor toward them, firing. "Where are the others?" Garrett screamed to Mike as they turned the corner.

"Dead! We're the only ones left alive."

They leaned against the wall of the central core that ran perpendicular to the one that Deena and Garrett had come down. Garrett now turned and fired back over Deena's head at the advancing Cylots. He screamed, "Come on, Deena. Come on!"

"You can't help her," Mike said. "Come on. We've got to go."

Deena lay on the ground, her hand outstretched toward Garrett and Mike, who couldn't come around the corner because of the Cylots firing down the hall toward them. "Come on! Come on!" Tim grabbed Garrett by the arm roughly. "Now!"

They rushed down the corridor into the module that housed the spacesuits and shut it, sealing in the air. They looked through the window back down the hall and saw Deena crawling around the corner, when the Cylots reached her. One grabbed her head in its pincers. She screamed as she was picked like a rag doll from the floor. With both hands she grabbed the pincer as the Cylot shook her back and forth, hitting her body against either side of the wall.

"Goddamn it!" Garrett screamed and reached for a grenade. He opened the door and hurled it at the Cylot and Deena, who was now dead, her lifeless body hanging limply from its pincers, her feet dangling just above the floor. He shut the door and locked it as the explosion ripped away parts of the wall. Garrett looked back through the windows to see Deena's body vaporized by the blast, but the Cylot's body lay twitching, half blown away, the remaining half alive.

"Christ," he said, "can't anything kill those things?"

Other Cylots rounded the corner. "We've got no chance," Tim screamed, "none!"

"Tim, we're going to take as many of those bastards with us as we can!" shouted Garrett.

They gathered the grenades in the last remaining intact module, as the Cylots hit the door. Each man held a grenade, as did Laurie, who was sobbing.

"Laurie, are you ready?" said Tim.

She nodded.

"Go, Garrett," said Tim.

Garrett opened the door as the Cylots rushed in.

◆   ◆   ◆

The TV monitor sparkled with black-and-white snow and then went blank.

"That's the last transmission we have," said Colonel McTavish, turning off the set.

"I thought you said the communications module had been destroyed first," said Razqual.

"It was," said McTavish, "but the transmission system for the monitors on the Pluto Base was at the central core. The communications modules housed the radar and telemetry to search for alien spacecraft—that's what was hit. The central system, which didn't have that, allowed transmission of this data."

"I see," said Razqual. "I'm sorry for your loss, but that is not why I'm here. I am here because Dr. Yugen is dead."

Razqual's comment brought General Stannick to his feet in anger.

"Don't you understand that our base on Pluto has been destroyed? The Cylot battle fleet is at the outskirts of our solar system. I have maybe a month before the

Cylot fleet destroys Earth," General Stannick shouted. "And all you've got to say is that some scientist is dead?"

"The attack will not come that soon. They are probing, testing your defenses. Now I say again, Doctor Yugen is dead," Razqual repeated emphatically. "And, General Stannick, Dr. Yugen is not just *some scientist*." The two stood facing each other hotly across the conference table, Stannick standing at least one foot taller than the Paradorian, Razqual.

General Stannick, a round, squat, cigar-smoking, powerful man, commander of Earth defenses, regarded the people at the table before he spoke again. They were his people: Admiral Woods, commander of the United Earth Space Fleet; Colonel Trapper, acting commander of Space Infantry; General Musashi, leader of the elite Space Assault Group (SAG); and various aides. They all watched Stannick's response to Razqual. It was explosive.

"I don't give a goddamn how many scientists you've lost. I don't think you understand our situation. I lost three goddamn outposts to this Cylot advance. I am outmanned, outgunned, and generally getting my ass kicked. If I don't get some help from somewhere soon, Earth is going to be overrun and there ain't gonna be no human race. Do you know that when the Cylots take an outpost they eat the survivors? When my men are captured alive, first their eyes are eaten, then their brains. The Cylots have powerful jaws that crack skulls like chestnuts." Stannick's shout became a hoarse whisper and his face turned red. He paused and swallowed before continuing in a more subdued voice. "It's some religious thing. Or some macho thing. Or some other thing I don't understand and don't give a good goddamn about, except I want it to stop."

"It is more philosophical than religious," said Razqual quietly. "Cylots call this ritual 'to see what they see, to know what they know.'"

"Well, I want you to know something," Stannick exploded again. "I want some weapons to blast those bastards out of space with. My men are dying and I want help now! So if you don't mind, Ambassador Razqual, I just don't care if Yugen is dead or alive or somewhere in between. I need help. You claim you're from the future. The technology you brought has only slowed the Cylot advance. It seems to me like all your help has only delayed the inevitable."

His tirade finished, Stannick sank back in his chair and energetically puffed on his cigar, the smoke clouding around the light that hung from the ceiling. The cigar tip, glowing through the haze, resembled a spark plug firing on some internal timing pattern. Supportive murmurs echoed around the table. Razqual noted them. He also noted Musashi's stillness.

Beads of sweat glistened on the general's forehead as he continued. Stannick took a cigar out of his mouth and held it between his index finger and his middle finger while pointing at Razqual. "Before you showed up I was fighting one war with the Kians and holding my own. Then, you arrived from the future. It could have been from hell for all I care. You said that wars are being fought in four dimensions instead of three. You brought weapons. And you arranged a truce with the Kians. But you also brought your enemy, the Cylots, and they are attacking your Earth's past, my present. They're more of a threat than the Kians ever were. All that happened for me is that I traded one enemy for another. Before you showed up, at least we had a chance. As I see it, now we got none. Since the Cylots entered our time space, I haven't even fought them to a draw in a single battle. The best order I can give my troops is 'If the Cylots show up in your sector, put your tail between your legs and run.' Now, you must have better weapons in the future. I want them here, or as I see it, there ain't gonna be no goddamn future. At least not for humans. Maybe your planet Parador is safe, but Earth is not"

"We all face the same problem. But allow me to correct a few major misconceptions," Razqual said coldly. "You were slowly losing to Kia. You were fumbling with the technological developments your own people had created. Earth, or what remained of it, would now be a Kian colony. Most of humanity would be slaves, mining precious metals on asteroids in the Seti-Telser system. But because in the future Kians also face a massive Cylot attack, we now have a truce with them. You know that the Kian goal is to enslave Earth. I tell you clearly that the Cylots want to destroy both Earth and Kia. While you are so willing to dismiss Yugen's death, General, I would gladly sacrifice all of your divisions to get him back. It is only scientists like him who can develop weapons systems to defeat the Cylots." Razqual shouted as he concluded, "And right now I need his research."

There was silence at the table. Stannick's uniform collar was soaked with sweat. He glared at Raqual, the short being from the future with deep-set eyes and a black belt around his waist.

Razqual spoke softly. "We allowed Yugen to take a jump belt and hide in the past."

"You mean one of those belts that allow you to travel in time?" asked Admiral Woods, pointing to Razqual's belt.

"That is correct. All our future biotech research facilities have been destroyed. Letting him go to the past, we thought, would allow him to work uninterrupted. It was a mistake. The Cylots have set up an interference pattern that isolated him from us. We know he was close to a major discovery because the Cylot activity was so intense. We are trying to duplicate his experiments. So we want to send a team back to retrieve either him or his information. Returning in force would merely expand the war and threaten our present, future, and past."

"Why did he hide in the past?" demanded Stannick. "Why did he go back there to begin with?"

Razqual shrugged. "We thought it would be safe. Our R&D facilities are prime targets. We were wrong about sending him back."

"Fine," said Stannick. "I'll arrange for a team to go—"

"There are problems," said Razqual. "Because of the Cylots' interference pattern, we can no longer travel in time freely. They know we can transfer technology from one time period to another and realize the potential power that this ability gives us, so they are jamming our ability to time travel—the way you can jam radar. Still, there are holes we can slip through."

"Keyes, arrange for a recon team," said Stannick to a major. "Razqual, tell Keyes what you need."

"I have the team," said Razqual. He reached into his satchel, pulled out a folder, and threw it on the table. Stannick opened the folder and read silently for a moment. Then the general exploded.

"You want to send a Kian to Earth's past to retrieve a scientist who could win the war for us? Why don't you just give the Kians all our military secrets? You think if we beat the Cylots it's gonna be all hunky dory with the Kians afterward? They'll eat our lunch."

"If you are saved from the Cylots, it is not my concern what happens afterward," shouted Razqual.

"What?" yelled Stannick.

"I realize," said Razqual, "that you are slowly losing the war. But the civilizations and cultures the Kians have subdued have survived, albeit in a subservient state. The Cylots are destroyers who have never lost. They are a space plague that leaves dead bodies and lifeless planets in their wake. The Kians, who are aware of this situation and must also deal with it, have reluctantly agreed to the truce."

"What's to stop the Kians from allying themselves with the Cylots?" General Musashi asked calmly. "They could combine and wipe us out. All warfare is based on deception. Hence, when able to attack, we must seem unable to do so; when using our forces, we must seem inactive; when we are near, we must seem far away; when far away, we must seem near. So I feel it must be with your commander, Ambassador Razqual. His name is …?"

"Selfridge," said Razqual. "General Selfridge. When I am from in the future, it is his leadership alone that has halted the Cylot advance."

"Excuse me," said Mctavish, "what do you mean when you are from?"

"Once time travel was established it is as common to say when are you from as it is to say where are you from. Do you understand?"

McTavish nodded.

"Before he sent me here, he told me about you, General Musashi. He wants you all to know that the Cylots have never formed such an alliance with anyone. Besides, the Kians, I am sure, have already tried that tactic. If not, they would not have allied themselves with us. We have developed some interesting new technologies. These belts represent one. From my perspective, when all looked lost, Self-ridge began to mount a successful resistance against the Cylots. He is now directing the war. I follow his orders. And so, General, will you, if you want the technology. Do I make myself clear?" Like the cigar smoke, silence pervaded the room.

Razqual continued, "There are some other complications. Since this war is now being fought in time—if you will allow such a phrase—the same battle could be fought simultaneously in different centuries and still be part of one contiguous action. Evasive action might entail changing days instead of moving through space. As the Kians are metamorphs who can change shape to resemble other species, looking like humans presents no problem to them. The Cylots have now acquired the same ability. They have developed a garment called a holo-cloak, a device that allows them to bend light to appear as humans. I don't know what else to say to convince you that our situation is almost hopeless. Only Self-irdge's forces have stopped their relentless advance. Now many flock to his cause. I have come back to tell you that the future of the human race hangs by a thread. None of you will do anything to interfere with our operation. Do I make myself totally clear?" Razqual thrust out his jaw defiantly.

"Fine," said Stannick. "Who is going back to get Yugen?"

When he was satisfied there was no further objection, Razqual continued, "I am sending a human back with the Kian."

"He better be a damn good operations guy," snorted Stannick.

"He is not trained in operations. As a matter of fact, he has very little military training at all. He is a scientist," responded Razqual. "He's the one I want to accompany the Kian."

"Are you trying to lose this war?" demanded Stannick. Veins bulged in his neck as he raised half out of his chair, barely controlling his anger. The pressure was clearly getting to Stannick. "Just who is it you are going to send back with this Kian?"

Razqual smiled for the first time. "He is called Ben Simon, one of the few people who would understand what Yugen was trying to accomplish. He will see what others will miss. He invented the technology that gave us parity with the Kians. We hope he will do the same against the Cylots."

"You just said there's a truce with the Kians," said Stannick, angry and frustrated.

"I said there is now a truce with the Kians," said Razqual. "I did not say how we got it or if it would last. General, I know this is hard for you to understand, but everyone's timeline is different. In your life, you will only go forward in time. In the future, people move back and forth in time the way you move back and forth in space," said Razqual. "The Kian and Simon will go."

"If you want this information, don't send only two operatives back. Send a reconnaissance in force," urged Stannick.

"Tell me, General," asked Razqual, "who would you rather have on your side, the Imperial Japanese Navy or Robert Oppenheimer? Only Ben Simon goes back with the Kian, whose name is Mectar, by the way."

"Cleverness has never been associated with long delays. No country ever benefited from prolonged warfare," Musashi said.

"I know," said Razqual. "Don't take what I say personally, Musashi. Take it as fact. Although Selfridge wanted you on his staff, he felt you served the cause better here for now."

Stannick's brow furrowed. "Simon, Simon, why do I know that name? He was a scientist, a famous one. Didn't the Kians murder his family?"

"You are correct about his family."

"Well, what makes you think he's going to go back to retrieve Yugen? If I were him, I'd go back and save my family."

"Selfridge won't let him. His jump belt will lock him out of that time period."

Stannick lowered his eyelids and stared hard at Razqual. "You are a bastard, aren't you?" he said, still puffing on his cigar. "Let him go back with some of my operations people, not a goddamn Kian. Do you want the Kians to get Simon's information?"

"First of all, Stannick, ten of your best commandos would not equal one well-trained Kian. If I were to bet on fifty of your soldiers or on this one Kian, I would bet on the Kian."

Despite Stannick's raw anger, Razqual continued, "Mectar will enter your space later today. His jump belt and Simon's have been delivered to your operations people. A weapons delivery will arrive here shortly for you. It is the best we can currently do. Simon is being briefed and will be here shortly also."

General Stannick's aide, McTavish, had been reading a hand-held computer. He leaned over and whispered in Stannick's ear. Stannick sat up, turned to the aide, and said, "Are you sure?" The aide nodded affirmatively.

"Am I to understand," said Stannick, "that this is the traitor Simon and that Mectar was the one who killed Simon's family?"

Razqual paused, then responded. "That information is to be kept from Simon. Is that clear?"

"No, no, I will not allow a traitor at the Battle of Bendibast and a Kian to go rooting around in Earth's past. Are you mad?"

"Do you want the weapons and technology I have in the supply ships lying just outside your time?" Stannick paused and then slumped, aware that with no help Earth was doomed. "Simon is not to know Mectar killed his family. Is that clear?"

"Oh, it's clear all right," said Stannick. "I don't care how you kill that poor bastard. Just make sure we get the weapons."

"The weapons will be there," said Razqual. "And just so you know, General, it is not my intention that Simon die. It is my intention that he kill."

2

Cutting Bait

Army Specialist Karl Gundersen, a blue-eyed, blond-haired kid from Duluth, Minnesota, waited in the spacious underground bunker. It served as the control center of the last operable spaceport on Earth.

Gundersen had his computer ready. An expert with language computers, his specialty was translation, specifically translating alien languages into English. His current assignment, a vital one, was to record and translate Kian transmissions. General Stannick considered Gundersen the army's best translation decriptor. One hour earlier, the general shocked Gundersen with news that the specialist was about to meet his first Kians.

Standing behind Gundersen was Colonel McTavish, who would read the conversation Gundersen was to record. The two tensely anticipated the Kians' arrival. They had an unobstructed view of the stairs that led down into the bunker. Gundersen sat with other technicians whose computers handled telemetry, avionics, terrestrial and solar weather, and flight patterns at the spaceport. Armed combat soldiers stood at various locations around the room.

Two hours previously, a Kian ship locked into Earth orbit. It was a War Bird K class, a small, well-protected, highly armed attack vessel that could in theory destroy Earth. It had been launched from an interstellar ship docked outside the solar system and had run the Cylot blockade. The Kian delegation it carried was now descending the stairs.

The port commander and a delegation headed by General Stannick, General Musashi, and Colonel Trapper joined Gundersen and McTavish. General Musashi was the hero of the battle of Lucifer's Crescent, where for the first time Earth had battled the Kians to a standstill.

Two civilians were also present. Razqual was one of the civilians. The other, named Simon, was sullen, armed, and clearly lacking military discipline. He stood between two armed guards, in front of the port commander. Simon captivated Gundersen. He was nearly six feet tall, with dark hair and a muscular frame. Simon, Gundersen realized, obviously did not belong.

"Ready, Gundersen," Stannick said upon entering the bunker control center. Stannick meant the statement as a question. Gundersen nodded in the affirmative, but Stannick's attention had already gone elsewhere.

From the control center window, the first Gundersen saw of the Kians was their heavy gray boots on the stairs. Studded with small silver spikes, they extended to just below their knees. Capes concealed the details of their bodies, except the silver-studded tips of their tails. What the capes could not conceal was the Kians' lizard-like faces and their huge size. Each stood eight feet tall or more.

All attention focused on the Kians as they paused outside the control-center door. "All right Simon," Stannick said in a deep, commanding voice. "Let's go meet them." Hearing no response, he looked back to where Simon had stood between his two guards. The guards stared openmouthed at each other across an empty space. Simon had disappeared.

"Shit," sputtered Razqual.

"Where the hell is he?" Stannick demanded.

"Sir," stammered the port commander. "He was here a minute ago. He was right in front of me. I turned away for an instant and he just disappeared."

"Well, find the son of a bitch," roared Stannick.

"It will do no good," said Razqual, holding up his hand.

Stannick looked out the window and saw the Kians waiting. "Goddamn it," he said. Then, turning to the port commander, he growled, "Find him now."

Razqual again held up his hand. "It will do no good. It is my failure, not the commander's. We will meet the Kians without Simon."

The door flew open and the Kians burst into the room.

"Holy shit!" said a tech behind Gundersen, as Earth soldiers nervously fingered their phasers.

Razqual stepped forward. "I welcome the first Kian delegation to Earth," he said formally in Kian. The cursor on the screen in front of Gundersen danced ahead of the letters as Razqual's statement was translated into English.

The Kian nearest Razqual was about to speak but was shouldered aside by the largest Kian, clearly a warrior. He ignored Razqual and surveyed the room. In perfect English he said, "Where is Simon?"

"I apologize, Mectar, for his absence," said Razqual. "The fault is mine. I issued him his jump belt five minutes ago and then had him escorted here." Razqual held up a belt. "I intended to lock your two jump belts together so one could not time jump without the other. I fear Simon has already jumped."

"This is a lie and a trap," shouted Mectar as he drew his weapon and grabbed Razqual by the throat. The other Kians also drew their phasers, as did the Earth soldiers. Mectar lifted Razqual off the floor so his feet dangled and pressed his phaser to Razqual's neck. Mectar stood nearly eight feet tall; Razqual was less than five feet tall. Razqual's face turned red, almost purple, as he gasped for air while his hands clung to Mectar's outstretched arm. Veins bulged in Razqual's neck. Mectar pressed his face close to Razqual's.

"Where did he run to?" The Earth soldiers looked expectantly at Stannick. "Where did that scum run to?" Mectar demanded.

A voice answered, "The scum is over here, asshole, and it will be a cold day in hell before I run from crap like you."

Simon had reappeared. Mectar turned his head to look toward Simon. Razqual slipped Mectar's grip and dropped a foot, but instead of dropping to the floor held onto Mectar's outstretched arms and kicked Mectar below the gut. Mectar exhaled quickly and doubled over. Quickly, Razqual dropped to the floor and had a dagger to Mectar's throat. "I am a king on my world; never lay your hands on me again." Mectar swept Razqual aside and Razqual slid across the floor on his back and into the wall.

Razqual lay slumped into a corner, wheezing and holding his throat, the wind knocked out of him from the blow.

Mectar strode toward Simon still bent over from Razqual's blow and thrust a finger in his face. The finger turned into a knife blade. Mectar moved it to Simon's throat. The Kian stood more than two feet taller than Simon. Simon did not budge. Instead, he pointed his own finger at Mectar's throat and said, "Go for it, asshole." The statement was barely audible yet filled with challenge. "You want me so much? Take me now," Simon demanded, smiling at Mectar's pain.

"Is he out of his fucking mind?" McTavish whispered to himself behind Gundersen.

"Do not hurt Mectar," Razqual wheezed, still holding his throat. To Gundersen, Razqual's statement sounded ridiculous. Mectar hardly seemed to be in danger.

A Kian helped Razqual to his feet and then shouted at Mectar in Kian. Gundersen watched the translation skip across the computer screen: "Your heritage and your training impel you to complete your mission. Place your mission before your desires. When it is complete, he is yours."

Mectar did not move. Razqual took two quick steps toward Mectar and stomped on the tip of Mectar's tail, which swished out of the way and then back toward Razqual, who had to jump out of its way.

Mectar's finger, which had been a knife blade, morphed into a human finger. His hand became a human hand attached to a Kian arm. Mectar slowly turned the hand over, palm up, showing that it was no longer a weapon. He said to Simon, "Before this is over I will kill you. Your head will decorate my home."

Mectar's and Simon's belts began to beep as Razqual pointed a device at them and pressed a button. "You are now locked together," he said. "There is a ten-second delay. If one of you jumps through time, the other will automatically follow ten seconds later, unless you program the belts yourselves to jump simultaneously. We have all agreed on the time and location you will jump to. You both know it is imperative that you find Yugen. Ambassador Keng, do you have anything you wish to say before they leave?"

The Kian ambassador, who had helped Razqual up, looked directly at Simon. You know where you and Mectar have to go. May you both be successful."

"I'm not going," said Simon.

"Did I not warn you of this?" Mectar demanded of Keng.

"It's a Cylot trap, asshole," said Simon. "When I jumped out of here a minute ago, where did you think I went? Running from you? Out to get a sandwich? I did a little reconnoitering." Then, Simon turned to Razqual and said, "I told you I could do this better alone than with this creep." He jerked his thumb back over his shoulder toward Mectar. "The Cylots have Yugen staked out until he dies and the little Chinese bastard is so caught up in his work he doesn't know it. They already have a disruption field around him. Yugen had the same training I got, and I know he would leave a trail, which I'm sure the Cylots don't know about. I can pick up that trail. It will be in the science. And I don't want asshole here with me."

"Do you want the war with the Kians to resume?" asked Razqual quietly. "Can Earth survive fighting two foes? If Mectar is with you, there is a truce with Kia, at least until one of you returns. You know the return point. It is on the other side of the Cylot interference field. You may need Mectar. If you don't, then do it because Earth needs the truce."

"Where do you wish to jump to, Simon?" asked Keng.

"Rahway, New Jersey, America, Earth, June 15, 2015," Simon responded immediately.

"Do you object, Mectar?" asked Keng.

"No." Mectar said, glaring at Simon.

"Then prepare yourself," ordered Keng.

Slowly, Mectar began to morph. He shrank from more than eight feet to about six feet five. His alien features softened before becoming those of a human male. His tail lifted up and he held it against his back where it was absorbed into his body, making him wider, not taller. He had a full head of dark hair, a body-builder's frame, and stunningly good looks.

"Too fucking perfect," Simon said. "Where did you research how he should look, a comic book?"

Mectar smiled, showing perfect, white teeth, which slowly yellowed. "You are right, Simon. I need to look as mediocre as you." Then, turning to Keng, Mectar said, "We are gone." He punched a button on his jump belt and disappeared into a time warp.

Simon said to Keng in Kian, "It is Mectar's head that will decorate my home. I will send you the rest of his body." Simon then disappeared into the time warp too.

A drop of sweat fell from McTavish's brow on to the translator's computer screen. He whispered to Gundersen, "That's one trip I'm glad I'm not going on."

3

Bees

"Damn Simon for having me do this experiment," Yugen thought. "He has reduced me to nothing more than a lab technician." Encased in glass, dead beehives littered his office. Still live beehives waited on his assembly line of death. Bubbling flasks of liquids gave off gasses around him and the occasional static electrical charge flashing across the solutions softly lit a dim corner of the lab. He sat oblivious to it all. Yet each time he ran the experiment modifying the infecting chemical, he got the hives to die sooner and more completely. His goal was to kill an entire hive by injecting one bee with a single dose of the chemical.

To achieve this goal he needed to create a self-replicating genetic probe, then inject it into one bee. At that point, the injected bee became the injecting agent into the whole hive.

He had chemically altered bumblebee genes as Simon had instructed. It was Simon who had given him the chemical formula to effect the change—actually a codebook of chemical charges. There were thousands of variations to try, each electrically charging the same solution in a different way. After marking each altered bee on the abdomen with a spot of dye, he returned them to their hive, noting the variant of the infecting agent. After he returned the altered bees, a chain reaction set in. Other bees picked up the genetic alteration. Then, after a little more than 55 percent of the hive's population had been altered, another phenomenon occurred: fighting among the bees. During the fight, the remaining bees also picked up the mutation. Most of the beehive then died simultaneously. His problem was that a significant portion of the hive remained uninfected.

Autopsies of the bees produced no clue as to the cause of death. Yugen did not understand how Simon achieved this result. Simon had ordered Yugen to find the most efficient death drug, but Yugen, as a scientist, had to understand. The genetic probe, comprised mostly of amino acids, was clearly not toxic. While he continued to test the efficacy of Simon's agents, he did not understand how Simon was able to do it, achieving his result. It was by changing the signature of the electrical charge that Yugen produced the variation in result. It was as though Simon was programming genetic change by writing electrical code, but the electrical code seemed to rest on a deeper, subtler, more intrinsic code. Simon kept stressing that the biology retained the electrical memory.

He began a fourth experiment and waited for the bees to die. Sophisticated instruments surrounded his new glass-encased hive—electromagnetic detectors, thermal probes, light emission monitors, radiation monitors, and thermophotographic infrared cameras. After most of the fourth hive died simultaneously, he was still puzzled.

Then came that flash of insight that separates the research scientist from the lab technician. He had been approaching the problem merely as a search for what killed the bees. But that was not the central point at all. He was not watching bees fight; he was watching an infection spread, an infection that possessed its own intelligence. Simon had Yugen tweaking a chemical virus, genetic in nature, by altering its electromagnetic memory, its code.

Every living thing has a measurable electric charge. Death is defined as an absence of that charge. A flat line. Consciousness is only present in living organisms when that electrical charge is present. But an electrical charge is not biological; it is quantum mechanical. Directly connecting quantum mechanics to biology would shake the very core of human science and religion.

Simon told Yugen that the amino acids were not the active agent. He said it was the electromagnetic message within the chemical that transmitted the change. The chemical was simply the carrier of the electromagnetic information. The underlying change occurred not at a microscopic level but at a quantum mechanical level.

Simon took the implications of this experiment to new depths. Science had been aware for years that subatomic particles continually popped in and out of existence all around us, it is the underlying basis of quantum mechanics. What Simon's contemporaries found most difficult to accept was Simon's insistent belief that the principles and effects of quantum mechanics hold true, not just in the subatomic world, but also in the observable world around us.

Few physicists denied the validity of the quantum mechanical laws, but they disagreed with Simon's interpretation of them. They restrict the validity of quantum theory to the subatomic world, but Simon argued that the theory's laws must hold at every level of reality, including human consciousness. Simon, for example, had told Yugen he thought quantum mechanics had more to do with consciousness, clairvoyance, and precognition than biology did.

Simon's work and the experiments he had directed Yugen to do involved microtubules. In the brain, human neuronal cells have a "slot" on its side called a microtubule, within which an electron exercises its normal activity during consciousness. Immobilization of the microtubule and the normal activity of the electron inside the microtubule produces a loss of consciousness. Control that subatomic activity in the brain and you control human consciousness. Modify that activity and you modify human consciousness. The physical mechanics of consciousness at the quantum level are common to all life, just as all life is subject to physical laws such as gravity.

Reducing consciousness to a scientific formula created more problems for Simon than it solved. The electron can assume many forms, or states. It can be a wave or a particle, and if it is a particle, there is only a probability it will be somewhere.

But inside the brain an electron is confined inside a microtubule in a state physicists call "quantum confinement." This process pins the electrons into nanometer-sized spaces, the microtubule. Thus confined, they behave more like trapped waves than particles.

This is where the new physics dissolved the very ground beneath Yugen's feet into particles and waves; he had no new metaphysics on which to stand. He remembered Simon quoting a New Testament verse: "The Kingdom of Heaven is within you." This may well have been where that kingdom resided in the body.

Simon's objective was to infect the Cylots with an electronic or quantum infection. Simon said he needed to inject a Cylot with an electronic genetic marker. One would do. Because the Cylots were insect-like beings, Yugen was convinced that through his bee experiments he could develop a weapon. If Yugen was right, he could use that weapon to introduce a genetic change into the Cylot species that would spread and kill them all. In other words, he believed he could electrically encode a snippet of DNA to do the same thing to the Cylots that he had been trying to do to the bees. He hoped that Cylot marker would spread across the Cylot race, as it had with the bees. But the ramifications of Simon's research were far more profound than just destroying the Cylots. Reciprocals were always possible. Why couldn't the same technique be used on humans?

Simon's theories had begun to hurt Yugen's head, which he held in his hands, elbows on his lab bench, staring at the dead bees. Simon's attack on the Cylots, if he could make it work, would end the war. Yugen was sure that the politicians of the future were currently dismissing Simon's presentation of this idea as too radical, too untested, consuming too many resources from a fight that was so perilously close to being lost, and yet as Yugen sat looking at the scientific validation of Simon's theory, one thought came to mind. It was a miserable idea, yet all others were worse.

There were still problems, however. First, he needed a dead Cylot, or a piece of one, to code the genetic DNA probe to the Cylot physiology. Then, he needed a delivery system. How do you infect a Cylot? How do you even get a living Cylot to experiment on? Before all that, though, he needed a better understanding of the bees' mass death.

Yugen held his tortured head in his hands. Suddenly the door of the dimly lit lab flew open. In the doorway, silhouetted by the light from the hall, stood the figure of a man.

Yugen squinted at the figure. Fear filled his heart, gripping his chest and throat. Finally, the image of a man morphed into a Cylot, an insectoid being with the head of a praying mantis. Its mandibles dripped saliva.

"No ...!" screamed Yugen. The Cylot approached as Yugen backed away. He passed a hive of bees, which he pushed toward the Cylot. The glass-encased hive fell to the floor, breaking at the Cylot's feet. The bees swarmed out, attacking the Cylot and causing him to back away.

At that moment, a door opened at the back of the Lab. Yugen heard someone call his name. It was his only escape from the Cylot before him. Yugen ran. The Cylot pursued, hissing at him. It reached the parking lot in time to see Yugen starting his car. The car suddenly exploded in a ball of flames.

The Cylot approached the burning car as closely as it could. It could see Yugen's body in the inferno.

Across the parking lot, in the shadows between two cinder block buildings, two concealed figures watched. The large one, whose eyes glowed red in the darkness said, "The Cylots are here, Simon. We found them in this period. If we had gotten here sooner, we might have been able to save Yugen."

"If we could have, Mectar. We could not go back one more minute in time. I tried. We are locked out by the Cylots—they put up their disrupter field first."

As Simon and Mectar whispered to each other, the Cylot in front of them, which still stood beside the burning car, ran its foreleg through its saliva on its mandibles and wiped its antennae, which protruded eighteen inches from either side of its head. Its head became erect and then tilted, as though it was listening to Simon and Mectar. It quickly turned and fired its phaser, hitting the side of a cinder block building.

"Oh shit," shouted Simon as he dove from the force of the blast. Mectar had been swifter and avoided the blast by time jumping a day ahead. Simon's force field, a type of electrical armor, protected him from the falling debris. Simon, knocked to the ground and covered with pieces of shattered cinder block, fired his own phaser at the Cylot, catching him full in the chest. Though the blast threw the Cylot back, it was uninjured and readied to fire again. As it took aim at Simon, lying on the ground, Simon disappeared into the time warp Mectar had created.

The Cylot walked to the spot where Simon had disappeared and hissed slow and deep.

4

Gomez

"I'm sorry, Doctor. I couldn't stop him. He just burst in," the nurse, Debbie, said, her voice shaking.

Dr. Ted Gomez stood just inside the door to Dr. Brad Varley's private office. His clothes rumpled, his hair disheveled, and breathing heavily, he looked pleadingly through his bloodshot eyes at Dr. Varley. "I've got to talk to you, Brad. Now," he said. Then, casting a look over his shoulder toward Debbie, he added, "Alone."

"It's all right, Debbie. Ted and I are old friends," said Varley, stepping from behind his desk and putting his hand on Gomez' shoulder. "Just close the door. It'll be all right." Debbie complied, but her face and demeanor showed she was not convinced.

Microbiologists Varley and Gomez had gone to graduate school together, after which their paths diverged. Both had focused upon medical research, but Varley had "sold out" to become an administrator while Gomez stayed in the lab. Thus, Varley became more powerful, no longer doing research but directing it. His position entitled him to an office on New York's Upper East Side. He taught at New York Hospital and was on staff at the Payne Whitney Clinic.

Gomez worked for Merck and Company and never moved off the lab bench. Still there remained an underlying bond of professional respect for each other. They occasionally spoke by phone, even if they no longer saw each other socially. Then, even the phone conversations stopped.

"Now, Ted, what—?" said Varley.

"They're after me, Brad. Listen, do you still own that cabin in Vermont we used to camp at when we were in school?"

"Yes, but who's after you?"

"I don't know. No, that's wrong. I do know who's after me, but I still don't believe it," said Gomez. He went to the window and stood beside it, close to the wall so he could see out and conceal himself at the same time.

19

Assured for the moment that no one was coming after him, Gomez sat down in a chair beside the window, put his head in his hands and his elbows on his knees. "Oh, God," he moaned. "I can't even look at you."

"For Christ's sake, Ted," said Varley, as he leaned against the front of his desk. "Just what the hell is going on?"

"Look," Gomez began. "About a month and a half ago, my boss assigned me to do a genetic research experiment. But now he's dead. He was murdered last night. He was trying to devise a formula to alter one portion of a gene. He said he was successful. But he began to have attacks like I'm having now.

"Brad, I came to you because before you got into this," Gomez said, waving his hand to indicate the lavishly appointed office, "you did some undergraduate work in molecular biology. You know those snippets of DNA? Well, my boss was using them to fingerprint various genes.

"There are two things you can do in genetic engineering. You can engineer genes either by replacing them or repairing them. He was experimenting with bees to see if his theory on gene alteration could render them more passive. He was chemically trying to re-engineer their genes, repair them, and not replace them. At least that's what he told me. But at this point, I don't believe he was doing that at all."

"So?"

"So he re-engineered some of his own genes. He—"

"You mean like Madame Curie contracted radiation sickness or like Laveran contracted malaria while trying to discover how it was transmitted? Do you know the path of transmission?"

"I think he got infected by breathing in the chemical he used as a genetic probe. At one point in its production, it gives off heavy fumes. I think he breathed a sufficient amount to trigger a biological change in himself—and I think I did too. That's how I got this way. I'm going through the same change he went through. But he opened a new world."

"Oh, now wait a minute, Ted. You should listen to some of my grad students. They also make wild assumptions based on experimental results."

"No, Brad, it's not like that. You know the guy, Leonard Javic."

"Dr. Leonard Javic, the Collier Research Foundation Leonard Javic? The guy who found the genetic marker for muscular dystrophy? The one who works for Merck?" Varley asked, now sitting at the edge of his desk.

"Yes, but his research on the bees was suspect," said Gomez. "Not that it was wrong; his assumptions were too advanced. He was onto something big and he had me working on it. Before he died, he told me that someone was giving him data. He said it was a guy named Yugen. Yugen was doing research to develop a weapons system to fight the Cylots."

"The Cylots?"

"That's what Javic said they called themselves. Look, Javic was affected by the formula he was working on to alter this gene. The chemical worked on the gene in the lab, and after an incubation period of two weeks, it worked on Javic. The genetic change does more than create passivity. It changes your electrical wiring, so to speak. The Cylots want Javic stopped, or rather Yugen stopped. His work is some kind of threat to them. Now Javic's dead, and they want me."

"Why do they want you?"

"Because I have the formula. Brad, it causes a genetic chain reaction in your body. All of you changes. You can understand it better after you've changed."

"How can you be sure that all this is really happening and that your mind isn't affected by the chemical?" asked Varley.

"I just know. Sooner or later, you'll know too. But once you know, be careful of them."

"You can see the Cylots?"

"Sometimes. Sometimes when they assume human form, if the light is right. Another thing, when they are not in their human state they're insects. Human-size insects."

"Ahh, so you see a bunch of insects walking around after you've had the transformation," said Varley. "Sounds intoxicating, not genetic."

"No," said Gomez angrily, "I see people because they look like people. They're insects who can make themselves look like us."

"When have you seen one?" asked Varley.

"The night Yugen died, in Javic's office. First I saw a person. Then, that person turned into an insect. Brad, it was horrible. It was like it took off some kind of clothing. It didn't know we were there until we all ran. Apparently it got Javic. I don't know where Eric is."

"Eric?"

"Eric Bottoms, the other research physician."

"There were only three of you at risk at Merck?" asked Varley.

"No. Beth Grey is at risk too. She probably has no idea of the danger. Bottoms and I carried out Javic's experiments. Grey had responsibility for the animals we used."

"So how come she's not running like you are?"

"She was in Dallas at another Merck site. She gets back today."

"Will she be able to tell what a Cylot looks like?"

"No, Ted. I told you—she worked with the animals. In this case, she was handling the bee populations. She wasn't in the lab during the manufacture of the chemical. Only Javic, Bottoms, and I have seen the Cylots."

"And I can't see them," Varley responded.

"That's right. Because your genes haven't been altered … I guess … I don't know." Gomez ran his hand over his head, seemingly confused.

"And yours have. You're afraid of a few bugs? Sounds like a phobia to me, Ted."

"Brad, they are six feet tall with pincers out to here." Gomez held out his hands. "God, it was terrible. I found him. I found him last night," said Gomez.

"Who did you find, Ted?"

"Javic. He died horribly, Brad. I found him in his office after we all ran. I went back there when I thought it was safe. He was lying in a pool of blood. His face and hands had been blown off by a shotgun. Looked like both barrels had been fired at the same time."

"How do you know it was a shotgun?"

"Once the trouble started, he kept a shotgun in his office. He showed it to me. He could break it down and carry it in and out of Merck in a large briefcase. Besides, you could see shotgun pellets in the wall. Some had ricocheted and were lying on the floor."

"If his face was gone, how do you know it was Javic?" asked Varley.

"Oh, I know that bastard. He was wearing those orthopedic shoes, the ones I could always hear squeaking when he came to my lab. His lab coat was soaked with blood. Even his name printed on his lab coat, 'Leonard.' It had soaked up the blood and the blue printing had turned brown from it. It was Javic, all right. He must have held up his hands to protect himself. Neither Eric Bottoms nor I liked him. Actually, we hated him. Bottoms hated him more. He was such a bastard, always willing to take credit for our work." Gomez' voice trailed off and he went quiet for a moment. Then, he continued, almost maniacally. "But this shit is beginning to affect me. I'm beginning to have headaches. It's starting to happen to me," he shouted, rising and pounding his chest.

"Calm down. Calm down," Varley said in his most professional manner.

Gomez replied slumped back into the chair.

"Do you think maybe Bottoms killed Javic?" asked Varley.

"It was the Cylots. I didn't see Bottoms after the body was found. But if he knows about this he's running just like I am." Gomez leaned forward and spoke in a hoarse whisper. "Listen. I need your help. Yugen told Javic the formula was vital, that someone from the future would try to retrieve it. The Cylots are here to stop that from happening. Promise me you'll help."

"Of course I'll help," Varley said reassuringly. "I have a question, though, Ted. What did you do with the formula?"

The door to Varley's office burst open. Debbie pointed to Gomez and said, "There he is" to three burly orderlies in white coats. They rushed in, followed by Dr. Mueller, the head of psychiatric care at New York Hospital.

"No! You'll never get me," Gomez shrieked. "Not like you got Javic." He rose and with superhuman strength tried to make it out the door. The orderlies went for him. He pushed them back. One orderly grabbed his arm. Gomez downed him with a roundhouse blow to the head. The other two orderlies blocked the door. Varley retreated behind his desk.

"Sherman, Kowalski, grab him!" yelled Mueller to the two remaining orderlies. Gomez picked up the chair he'd been sitting in, threw it through the window with a crash, and jumped to the outside ledge.

"Ted, wait!" Varley shouted.

"The formula," Mueller hissed. "Where is it?"

"Watch him, Brad," yelled Gomez. "Mueller's one of them. He's a Cylot." Varley looked at Mueller but saw nothing then looked back at Gomez, who was already on the window ledge.

"Ted, wait," Varley shouted, realizing Gomez' intent. It was too late. Gomez was gone. He jumped from the fifth-story window to the street below.

Varley and Mueller rushed to the window and leaned out over the broken shards of glass. "He was a cancer," Mueller hissed. "People like him are a cancer on society."

Varley, startled, looked at Mueller and then back out the window at the body on the concrete below.

5

Michael Leary

Michael Leary had never really found himself. His father had been a Rahway cop for thirty-eight years before retiring. Mike joined the force because he didn't know what else to do. There were times he enjoyed working on a small town police force. It was the small town politics of the job he couldn't stand. Eventually he came off foot patrol and became a detective. If there was one talent he had it was solving puzzles, so he was put in charge of homicide. On average, fewer than one homicide per year occurred in Rahway. Now, in the span of only one night, three researchers had died and another was missing. All of them except one, Yugen, worked at Merck. Yugen had died last night in the parking lot of a building just off the Merck site.

Leary, sitting alone in the patrol car, pondered the events of the previous night. Leonard Javic, head of Merck research, was dead. His face and hands had been blown off with a shotgun. Dr. Yugen, a man with no traceable past, who paid for everything in cash, was dead. He had been incinerated in his car. Ted Gomez, Javic's research assistant, died this afternoon in New York City. The TV news said he jumped out a window, a suicide. Eric Bottoms, another research assistant to Javic, was still missing. Leary assumed this was because the body had not yet been found.

Four deaths, he thought, or three deaths and a probable death. Rahway's previous four homicides had occurred over a seven-year period.

Leary got out of his car. It was parked diagonally across the parking lot from where the burned-out wreck of Yugen's car remained. Leary was five feet eleven inches. He was thin with blond hair and a scraggly blond moustache and soul patch. His sideburns, while not long, were thick and curled. He lit a cigarette and looked around the parking lot. Last night and all day today his men had combed the crime scene for clues. They had found none they could make sense of: a gutted lab, damaged buildings with fused cinder block that appeared to have been blown off them, and an incinerated car containing a body belonging to a man with no traceable past. Leary assumed "Yugen" was an alias. Or, as he would say later, "Fuck, I know Yugen is an alias."

Leary wanted to be alone at the crime scene at exactly the same time the crime had occurred the night before. His father had taught him that doing so might turn up some vital piece of information.

Walking the scene, he thought of Beth Grey, the third research assistant to Javic. She was a veterinarian in charge of the lab animals. Unlike Bottoms and Gomez, she did not deal with the experiments. He had met her at Merck this afternoon while trying to find the connection between Yugen and Javic. She had just returned from a trip to Dallas this morning. Leary had asked her why such a good-looking woman had been single so long. She answered with a cold stare.

Tonight he had walked through the lab, the parking lot, and the alleyway where the burned cinder block was, and now he stood by his car, pondering the scene. Yugen must have run from the building to his car. The lab's condition, scattered papers and scuffmarks on the floor, indicated flight. No weapons had been found on Yugen's body. Leary's ballistics people could find no spent ordinance. Still, some of the buildings looked as though there had been one hell of a firefight, almost as if ray guns had been fired. "Yeah, right," he muttered to himself as he shook his head and dropped his cigarette butt. He stared at a damaged building. Although this made no sense, a bazooka must have made the hole in its corner. Well, the FBI would soon arrive.

As he reached for the door handle of the police cruiser, he heard a grunt emanate from the alleyway. He stood perfectly still and could swear that he heard heavy breathing. He looked over his shoulder. Nothing. He still heard the breathing.

Then, he saw a soft flash of light and heard a voice say, "You are a sphincter muscle, Simon. You wasted time. You stayed to fight. Our mission is clear: get the research Yugen was doing." He heard someone scrambling to his feet. A piece of cinderblock flew out of the alleyway.

Another voice said, "Fuck you, Mectar, you gutless *pulvzar*. How often do I see a Cylot? What can I learn? What do I need to know? You know nothing about the information I need."

"I am going to get Kia the information it needs to defeat the Cylots, Simon, and to defeat you as well. I do know that if Yugen were not close to something, the Cylots would not be here."

"You know shit, Mectar. We'll jump ahead a day and see what we find. Follow me." Leary heard something in a language he did not understand. Silence followed another soft flash of light. He had already pulled out his gun and crept to the edge of the alleyway. He looked around it. There was no one there. His foot hit something. He looked down. It was the piece of cinderblock he had seen fly out of the alleyway. It was then that he saw what appeared to be the outline of a body. It looked like someone had been covered by the debris of the blast and then stood up. He backed toward the police cruiser, his gun still drawn. Then he got into his cruiser and sped away.

6

Grey

Beth Grey sat in the kitchen of her apartment. She wore a soft satin nightshirt, which came to about mid-thigh, and silver hoop earrings. At thirty-four, her face bore the first lines of age. She was five feet seven inches tall. Although she had put on a few pounds, she was still attractive. She opened her newspaper to an article about Leonard Javic's murder.

With her right hand, she brushed her shoulder-length brown hair back along her forehead. She thought about the same thing every policeman working on this case thought about. What was the common thread connecting the deaths of Javic, Yugen, Gomez, and Bottoms, presuming the latter was dead?

Beth got up and put her coffee cup in the dishwasher. She had to go to Merck to supervise the animals' care. Although lab techs did the actual feeding and cleaned the cages and stalls, a supervisor had to be present twenty-four hours a day.

The police had assured everyone the buildings were safe, and armed security had been brought in. Merck's research budget was more than one billion dollars per year, so a few deaths would not stop the experiments. Beth would review the results of the latest experiments on beagles and sheep. She also knew a delivery of bees had arrived today. Although Javic always set the agenda for the research, she did the actual work, though she was young for that responsibility.

Javic hired her because he had known her mother, an army physician. Professionally, her mother had been superior in every way. Javic had never regretted hiring Beth, who exhibited a rare combination of beauty, strength, power, and confidence. She had no desire to hide these attributes. She also retained her mother's desire for excellence in her work.

Beth's mother had met her father, a major in the military police, while serving in Vietnam. Her mother had been a captain and a doctor. Ultimately, Mom outranked Dad by becoming a full colonel. Dad retired as only a lieutenant colonel.

But "only" was not a term that ever applied to Beth's father. He was a man's man. As his only daughter, with two older brothers and two younger brothers, she was quite a tomboy. By her early teens she was on the target range with her brothers, firing submachine guns and even a shoulder-carried rocket launcher.

Beth had never married, partly because of her impatience with men, the result of growing up with four brothers. She refused to massage the male ego. She found that hard to do when her profession required her to get at the truth.

She went into her bedroom and put on some lipstick, tight faded jeans, sneakers, and a black silk shirt. She pulled her hair back into a tight braid and put various necessities into her purse: lipstick, a few tissues, her car keys, and her wallet. She thought for a second, then went to her lingerie drawer and took out her loaded .38-caliber police revolver. She hefted it thoughtfully. Her dad had given it to her for home protection. What would be the harm if she carried it tonight? She put it and a wrapped package of extra cartridges in her purse. As she checked herself in the mirror, she thought of how her father had always told her, "Use a revolver, never an automatic. It's a more reliable weapon. When push comes to shove you don't want anything that'll jam."

Andy was still lying on the bed. He had fallen asleep. She slapped his bare foot.

"Andy," she said, rousing him. "I have to leave. I won't be back until late or very early, depending on how you look at it. I want you to go home." She didn't mention how grateful she was that he had come over. Beth had arrived on the early flight from Dallas. She had gone right to Merck. She found out what happened, met with Leary, and returned home. Shaken, she called Andy to come over. But although she appreciated the company, it had been a mistake to call him. He had gotten the wrong impression. She was in the process of breaking up with him, and their getting together had only fueled his hopes and convinced her she had to move on.

She leaned over and kissed him. "You were a pleasure," she said.

"Can I see you this weekend?" he asked, rubbing his right eye.

"Call me," she said, walking out the door. "You can let yourself out and lock up."

It was the middle of June. The month had started sunny and dry, but the last week it had rained heavily. Pools of water lay in low spots on the sidewalk and in potholes in the gutter. Beth didn't seem to notice.

She bounced lightly down the stairs of the townhouse. She thought about Andy briefly and wondered if a man existed who would not bore her. It was time to move on, she thought. Andy was becoming boring. She would call tomorrow and tell him it was over. She felt no guilt. It was not as if the breakup would surprise him.

She thought of her last boyfriend, Danny. He called her callous. Perhaps. But then she was entitled to find what she was looking for, wasn't she? She got in her car and drove to the plant.

Five thousand people worked at Merck's Rahway complex, a preeminent pharmaceutical research center. Merck could trace its origins back to E. Merck and Company, established in Darmstadt, Germany, during the seventeenth century.

Beth Grey's and Javic's offices were located in Building 80. As she walked to the company entrance, she looked over her shoulder and saw two Rahway policemen relaxing in their cruiser. "Added security," she said to herself sarcastically. She took out her pass card and inserted it into the card reader outside the gate. At this time of night, the reader would signal an alarm in central security so the guard could see her on the TV camera.

"Evening, Dr. Grey. Working late?" said a guard she could not see. His voice came through a squawk box. She smiled at the camera and nodded. "Have a nice night, Doctor," said the guard as the gate clicked open.

She walked across the quadrangle, through the immaculately landscaped lawns to Building 80, where she encountered another card reader. This time the guard in central said nothing. As she entered the banks of offices, she saw a light in Dr. Javic's office. It was a flashlight. She stopped and pressed her body against the wall to listen. She heard papers rustling. The door was slightly ajar. Hidden by the poor light of the hallway, she leaned forward until she could see into the room. She saw a man whose face she couldn't make out. Sitting at Javic's desk, he held a small flashlight in his mouth and was shining it down on the papers in his hands. He was going through Javic's desk. She slid the gun softly out of her purse. She had been in Javic's office many times and knew exactly where the light switch was. Reaching into the room, she turned the light on. Then she pushed the door open and leveled her gun at him.

"Who are you?" she demanded.

The man looked up, put down the papers, removed the flashlight from his mouth, and said, "Who the hell are you?"

"Who are you is the more important question," she responded.

"Of course I'm not talking to you," he said. "I'm talking to the woman who just walked in pointing a gun at me. Why didn't you pick her up?" The man paused and then said, "Well, you should have had it turned to humans too, for Christ's sake. There are two settings on that screen. Do you know how to use it? Did you set up the disrupter shield?"

"Who are you talking to?" Beth demanded.

"Well, it sure ain't you, honey," he said.

"Put your hands on the desk, palms down," she ordered. "And don't call me honey." The man complied. Keeping her back to the wall, Beth slid along it to reach a phone on the credenza. Still pointing the gun at the intruder, she called security. The phone rang. The man had something in his palm, which he pointed at the phone. The phone went dead. She clicked the receiver, still holding the gun on him while cradling the phone between her ear and shoulder.

"Turn out the light," he said softly.

She ignored the command. "Are you the ones who've been killing the researchers?" She said. "Did you kill Javic?"

"Did you pick them up?" he said, standing up, obviously still not talking to her. "You were supposed to set the disrupter field. Did you? Goddamn it, weren't you trained for this?" He strode around the desk and turned out the light. She looked at him closely as he walked around the desk. His khaki pants hung over boots that had a military look to them, black and unpolished. His shirt was beige, with long sleeves he had rolled up to just below his elbows. It looked like a uniform that he chose not to wear like one. He was roughly six feet tall and two hundred pounds. He had brown eyes and a medium build. He was handsome in a rugged, weathered way.

They stood in dim reflected light from the courtyard outside. He looked out the doorway into the hall. She stood behind him and leveled her gun at the base of his skull. She put down the phone, stepped close to him, and held the gun to his head. He turned, clearly irritated, and looked directly into the gun barrel. He did not attempt to take the gun from her. He stared into her eyes for a moment before speaking. In that moment, his expression seemed to soften. He no longer appeared angry.

"Listen. Someone—or rather something—is killing researchers. I have to stop it. Now you're getting in my way. Take that damn thing out of my face and keep quiet. Is that clear?"

"How do you know it's not me who's the killer?" she whispered.

"Trust me. It's not you. I don't know who the hell you are, but it's not you. By the way, who are you?"

"I'm Dr. Grey."

"Oooh, Javic's assistant," he said, appraising her.

"Yes, who are you?" she asked.

"Good, keep your mouth shut," he said. He turned and looked into the hall again.

She was upset that he ignored her question, but now she noticed that he appeared to be cocking a weapon. "No, I can't leave her here," he said. "I'm going to bring her with me. I know, I know. I don't need it either."

"Who are you talking to?"

"Be quiet, he replied. Then he turned toward her. "Simon," he said impatiently. "Call me Simon, Ben Simon. Follow me closely." He began walking down the hall, which was vacant and softly lit. Beth followed him down the hall willingly, not quite knowing why. They came to the corner and stopped. The man peered around the corner. Simon held a miniature TV screen, the size of a wristwatch dial. Something or someone passed in front of them in an intersecting corridor.

Simon said to his unseen partner, "Something's not showing up." He paused. "Because something went by me and didn't register on my screen, that's how. Maybe they can jam our disrupter, or maybe you just don't know how to use the equipment you've been issued. Are you near me? Well, then something's wrong." Beth realized that this man had a partner located somewhere in the building and that she was hearing only half the conversation.

Simon looked over his shoulder at Beth, who still held the .38 in her hand. "Uh, listen," Simon said. "I want you to stay close to me. If anything shoots at us, shoot back. Okay?" She looked into his eyes for the first time. She nodded that she would, although she did not know why.

A guard turned the corner ahead of her. "It's Tom," she whispered. She called his name before Simon could stop her. The guard raised his gun and fired. Simon pulled her away. The shot just missed her, the bullet whizzing by her ear, blasting a hole in the wall behind her. Simon returned fire. Light from his phaser struck Tom in the chest. Tom fell backward, bleeding, his chest smoking from the impact of the shot. He began to get up. Simon fired again and Tom fell again, and again he tried to get up. Simon fired one more shot into Tom's head. Tom's body slumped and did not move.

Beth backed away in horror. Dazed by the shooting, she only remotely felt Simon put something on her wrist. She looked down dumbly and saw it was a bracelet with two blinking lights. The lights blinked on and off alternately, giving the impression of a single light moving back and forth. Bewildered, scared, and angry that he would put something on her, she looked up and her mouth fell open. At first, words refused to come. Then she shouted, "Look out!"

Behind Simon, someone had appeared and was about to strike him with an ice pick. "Look out," Beth screamed again.

As it came down, the pick seemed to flash light from its tip as though the metal were reflecting the dim overhead lights. Then she realized, as the pick sank into Simon's shoulder and he screamed, grabbing at it, that the tip was not metal but a spot of solidified light. Sparks flew as the weapon hit an electrical field, and Beth was not certain if the point had penetrated Simon's shoulder or not.

Simon pushed Beth out of the way, reached back, grabbed the collar and head of his assailant, and threw him over his shoulder toward her. Beth heard what sounded like cloth ripping and the head of the assailant became the head of an insect on the body of a man. The edge of the man's shoulders below the insect's head had a soft glow. Simon threw something down and it landed on her knee, which disappeared. There was no pain, just a light, fluffy feeling, but it startled her nonetheless to have her knee gone but her foot still showing. She shrieked and shook her leg, which dislodged whatever had landed on her and her knee reappeared. She was unhurt.

The assailant stood up as Simon wrenched the pick out of his shoulder and fell backward. The assailant ripped off the rest of whatever it was wearing and revealed itself to be an insect, akin to a praying mantis. It charged and Simon pushed him off with his foot. Then Simon drew a phaser from his belt and fired. A flash of light shot from the weapon as Simon's assailant dove out of the way. The shot left a large hole in the wall and one of equal size, Beth saw, in the wall of the adjacent room. The insect scrambled to get out of the way as Simon fired again.

The insect dodged the shot, moving more quickly than any person Beth had ever seen, and then leaped and grabbed Simon in a bear hug. Simon grabbed for the insect's head.

Together, Simon and the insect hit the wall and fell to the ground, the insect on top. Simon had dropped his phaser. They were directly in front of Beth, who sat against the wall, so close she could have reached out and touched the insect's face. The insect was clearly more powerful and was crushing the life out of Simon. Saliva-covered pincers moved toward Simon's neck. Beth fumbled for her gun and fired all six shots into the insect's body. It looked up at her, tilted its head, and hissed. The saliva spray from its mandibles burned her face. It swung an arm and hit her, knocking her against the wall by a fire extinguisher. In wrestling matches with her brothers when she was young, she had also been hit and tossed aside. Then as now, thoughtless of the situation but filled with anger bordering on rage, she grabbed the fire extinguisher, stood up, and swung it with all her might into the back of the insect's head. The insect was knocked forward but did not let go of Simon.

She cursed, partly in anger and partly in terror, as she reached for the fire extinguisher again. She turned it on and sprayed it in the insect's face. A cloud of vapor hit the insect. It wailed in pain but still held Simon. "I wish I had bug spray," she shouted.

The insect was bleeding at the place where one antenna had been ripped off. Still holding Simon, it raised its abdomen. Beth saw a stinger emerge from the base of its body. A viscous liquid, which Beth assumed to be venom, appeared at the stinger's tip. Simon's head tilted back and his eyes rolled back in his head.

Just as the insect was about to impale Simon, there was a flash like lightning. The insect was thrown off Simon and lay stunned while Simon lay still, apparently lifeless. Static electricity crackled over his body and then faded.

Grey had been knocked to the ground by the discharge of electricity. She crawled toward Simon on her knees and shook him. He did not move, but the insect was beginning to stir. "Oh, God. Oh, God. Benjamin wake up," said Beth. "Hurry." She softly tapped his face with her hand. Then she picked up his phaser, which resembled a small handgun. With both hands, she aimed at the insect, which was now slowly rising. Her hands shaking, she pressed the single button on the weapon's surface with her thumb. Nothing.

She heard a noise from several corridors away. Her hands shook. She heard running footsteps. The insect was stooped over, perhaps it was wounded, she thought. Then, in the semidarkness, she saw something round the corner and stare at her with red, glowing eyes. She aimed her gun at whatever it was and she shrank back in fear.

The redness of the eyes subsided. It was a man. He was about six feet six inches tall with broad shoulders and muscular arms. He had a lantern jaw and a full head of hair combed straight back. He had to have weighed more than 250 pounds, and not an ounce of it looked like fat. He was huge. Thank God it's a man, she thought. Then she realized she could not even be sure of that.

The weapon he held was unlike one she had never seen before. He fired once at the insect, which dodged around the corner with unbelievable speed. Again, a huge hole was left in the wall. Then the man pushed some buttons on his belt and disappeared—just faded into thin air. Beth crawled to the place where he had disappeared and shouted, "Wait, please wait."

She heard a hiss behind her. Turning, she saw the insect emerging from behind the corner. It moved toward Simon, who suddenly disappeared, and then it looked at her. She was alone with a human-sized insect. "Oh shit," she said softly. Then everything went black for an instant. It was a flash of black, almost as though someone had flicked the lights off and on. Suddenly Beth felt nauseous.

Powerful arms grabbed her and a rough hand covered her mouth. Terrorized, she struggled to escape, but the powerful grip immobilized her. She could not even move enough to see who held her.

"Be still," whispered the man who held her. "You are now safe." The insect was gone and so were the holes in the walls. There was silence. The man released her and she sat still, hearing the beat of her own heart and the sound of the blood racing through her eardrums.

Simon's body had reappeared. The man went to it and turned it over with his foot. He bent over and felt Simon's pulse. Then he pulled something out of his pocket. It was an oddly shaped needle. He injected Simon. Simon moaned and opened his eyes. "Where's your bracelet, you sphincter muscle?" the man asked while still holding Simon's wrist. He then threw it down with disgust. Beth looked down at the bracelet on her own wrist. The two lights blinked back and forth dimly.

Simon closed his eyes, then opened them again. He looked at his hand, which held the piece he had ripped from the insect's antenna. The man who had stood over Simon was looking down the hallway to see if anyone else was around. Simon quickly closed his hand to hide the piece of the antenna. The substance with which Simon had been injected was quickly restoring him. He sat up slowly and rubbed the back of his neck. The man who had held Beth looked at her and saw the bracelet on her wrist.

"That was a stupid thing to do," he said. "You could have been killed."

"Fuck you, Mectar," Simon said, standing up slowly and gingerly while picking up his phaser, which had somehow come along with them. "I didn't have a lot of time to make a decision."

"I accept your idiomatic obscenity for what it is—empty sounds from an empty mind," said Mectar, standing to his full height. "So, Simon fights a Cylot," he added sarcastically.

"Are you all right?" asked Simon as he helped Beth to her feet.

"I don't know. What happened?" Beth stammered, her whole body shaking. Mectar appeared to have grown larger while he argued with Simon.

"That, my dear, was a Cylot," said Simon. "Now you know who has been killing your researchers."

As Simon spoke, Beth saw him slip the piece of Cylot antenna into his pocket, out of Mectar's sight.

"This, by the way, is Mectar," said Simon. "Mectar, Grey, Grey, Mectar." Mectar nodded brusquely. Simon said, "We need to get out of here. Can you show us the fastest way?"

Beth nodded. "The back way, through the labs. Follow me."

As she passed Mectar, he grabbed her wrist and held it up to show the bracelet. The size of Mectar's hand and the toughness of his skin amazed her. "Saving her life was stupid, Simon. Gallantry has no place in what we do."

"You don't know the difference between gallantry and expediency. There's nothing gallant about it. I've got a job to do and I'm going to do it with or without you," Simon snarled. Despite Mectar's belligerence and larger size, Simon showed no fear whatsoever.

Beth looked at the bracelet and then at Simon. It was then she realized that Simon had twice saved her life, once from Tom's bullet and once from the Cylot. She wondered briefly what her life would be worth if it hadn't been expedient to save her.

"Follow me," said Beth. "I'm parked out it the parking lot."

"When are you parked in the parking lot?" Mectar demanded. "Now," she said, thinking it was a stupid question.

"She doesn't know when now is, Mectar," said Simon.

Beth turned and glared at Simon in anger. "I may not know as much as you, and I may not know what's going on, but I do know that now is now."

Simon, startled at her anger, backed up a step and smiled. Then his brow furrowed and he rubbed his shoulder. "You are absolutely right, Grey. Now is now." Then, without looking at Mectar, Simon said, "Mectar, when are we?"

Mectar read a small handheld computer. "June 16, 1998, 1:23."

"That's ridiculous," said Grey. But as she looked around, her voice trailed off. Even in the dim light she could see that the halls had the old wallpaper on them that had been removed years before.

"And when do we need to be?" Simon asked patiently.

"To reach Grey's car, we would have to go to June 16, 2015, 1:23," Mectar responded.

"Then let's go," said Simon, regarding Beth with a half-smile. There was another flash of blackness, this time followed by a sudden midday glare, and a little less nausea for Beth. She squinted at the clock at the end of the hall. They had gone from the middle of the night to 1:23 in a bright afternoon. The new wallpaper now surrounded them and the holes were back in the walls. As they appeared, seemingly from out of nowhere, a policeman sitting in a chair at the end of the hall rose to his feet in disbelief. Simon looked around and in disgust said to Mectar, "I hate it when you jump. Not day, night, you asshole."

"You said 1:23. Look," said Mectar, showing Simon the handheld device. "It says 1:23."

"One twenty-three AM," said Simon, "not 1:23 PM."

"Does your custom require you to use the same number twice to make time during your solar day? That is stupid, Simon. Why not use the same number three or four times, then?" Mectar argued.

Simon grabbed the handheld computer away from Mectar and reprogrammed it by punching in several numbers. "Didn't they teach you about AM and PM when they trained you for this mission?" Simon demanded.

"Did they teach you about knamzom when they trained you for this mission?" said Mectar. "Every Kian child knows about that."

At this point, Grey saw Detective Leary, the policeman who had questioned her about the murders, round the corner. Patrolman Jefferson was with him. Beth approached Leary and removed one of her earrings. "Michael, I need help," she said, handing the earring to him. Leary's confusion was evident as he held out his hand to receive the earring. There was another black flash and it was night again. Leary was left standing flabbergasted when the three who had been standing in front of him disappeared. He looked at the earring in his hand.

"Am I seeing things?" asked Officer Jefferson, wide-eyed, as he and Leary stood in an empty hall.

"Now, how do we get out of here?" Simon said, satisfied that he was where and when he wanted to be. With Beth leading, they walked from the building in silence. Mectar and Simon had their weapons drawn the entire time.

At Beth's car, she fumbled for her car keys and then unlocked the doors. Simon got behind the wheel as the other two piled in. Beth sat next to Simon. Mectar sat in the back. Simon put the car in reverse, hit another car behind him, and cursed under his breath. As he turned out of the parking space, his left front bumper hit a fire hydrant and he cursed again. "You can't drive, can you?" said Beth.

Mectar said, "That's not all he can't do."

"If you can do any better, then you drive," said Simon angrily.

"Fine," she said, and she was startled when he abruptly put the car into park and it jerked to a halt. He got out, ran around the car, and hopped into her side, pushing her across the seat. She put the car in gear and drove off.

As they left Merck she said, "Where are we going?" Neither Simon nor Mectar answered. As she pulled out of the parking lot, she sensed that something was following them.

7

Dr. Herman Heinrich

The knock on his office door made Varley look up from his desk. The door opened and Debbie, Varley's nurse, stuck her head in.

"Doctor Varley," she said, "Doctor Herman Heinrich is here."

By then Dr. Heinrich was already coming through the door. The two men shook hands. Heinrich was tall, thin, and muscular. His sandy blond hair was graying at the temples. As they shook hands, Varley couldn't help but notice the powerful grip. Heinrich radiated power. Varley now more fully understood why this man was professionally revered.

Heinrich worked at Hoechst as their head of research. Merck and Hoechst had done what many pharmaceuticals had done: they had formed a joint venture to pool their resources, in this case a research program. Heinrich and Javic headed their respective companies' projects.

Heinrich, however, was better known of the two. He had made his reputation in Europe before coming to America to head Hoechst's research here.

Heinrich had called Varley when he heard about Gomez' death. He had told Varley that Gomez had been one of the Merck researchers in the joint venture and since Javic was either missing or dead, Heinrich was doing all he could to find out what had happened. He had also explained the tremendous amount of money both companies had tied up in their mutual project, and he felt that by interviewing Varley himself, he might find some information pertinent to the basic research that the police might miss. Perhaps Gomez said something or exhibited some symptom that would aid in the investigation.

During their phone conversation, Varley told Heinrich what Gomez had said before jumping. He also told him about the office-taping device. "It was operating while Gomez was here," said Varley. "I just found the tape and was going to call the police about it." Heinrich had asked him to wait for him to arrive.

Now Herman Heinrich and Brad Varley watched the video replay of yesterday's episode. Heinrich looked surprised and rubbed his forehead. "My God," he said when the tape concluded. "Do you know what you've got here?" He was clearly excited. "Let me explain. The police called me in on these deaths, including Gomez'. There have been other deaths like his. They have been going on longer than you realize. What makes this tape so wonderful is that it is visual proof of this effect. I must get this tape to the police. May I use your phone?"

Varley hesitated. "Oh, I understand," said Heinrich. Without asking, he reached for Varley's phone to call the Midtown South precinct. "Detective Mueller, please. Doctor Heinrich calling." He put his hand over the mouthpiece and said, "Who was the detective who came to talk to you about Gomez' death?"

"Uh, there were two," said Varley. "One from the FBI, an agent named Cyrus. And Gilbert, a detective from the New York Police Department."

"I've met Gilbert. He works for Mueller," Heinrich answered. He continued his phone conversation. "Hello, Detective Mueller? Good news. I'm over at Doctor Varley's office and he found that he has the episode with Gomez on videotape. What? No, it's not at all uncommon to have that type of recording equipment in an office such as Doctors Varley's. With your permission, and Varley's too, I would like to bring it right over to your office. Do you need to talk to Varley? You'll call him? Doctor Varley, do you need to talk to Mueller?" Heinrich handed the phone to Varley. Before hanging up, Varley agreed to let Heinrich bring the tape to Mueller.

"By the way, have you shown this to anyone else?" said Heinrich.

"No."

"Good," said Heinrich. "Is that your only copy?"

"Yes."

Varley, attuned to people's body signs, saw Heinrich's shoulders drop to a more relaxed position. Heinrich's next question terrified him.

"You don't have that damnable machine on now, do you?" Heinrich said, chuckling and looking around.

"No, no, of course not," Varley reassured him.

Varley reached into the top drawer of his desk for his pipe and tobacco. As he did, he flicked on the hidden switch that activated the recorder. Varley didn't know why but he suddenly wanted Heinrich taped.

"Well, the quicker I bring this tape down to the police station the quicker they can look at it," said Heinrich.

Varley hesitated. "I'd like to make a copy first."

"Come, come, Varley. I'll take care of it," Heinrich chided. "And if there is a scientific find here, I'll be sure you get the credit."

Varley sensed an implied threat. He hesitated again and then relented. "Okay, then take it away."

Heinrich took the tape off the desk and stood up. "Gomez didn't give you the formula, did he?" he said.

"No, no," said Varley, puffing on his pipe. "That's everything that happened."

"No, I don't see how he could have given it to you," said Heinrich. He wrote a phone number on his card and handed it to Varley. "If you find the formula, or if it finds you, call me at this number immediately."

After Heinrich left Varley immediately opened the recorder cabinet and pushed "Rewind."

On the screen, Herman Heinrich looked normal, until he asked, "Gomez didn't give you the formula, did he?" At that point, Heinrich shimmered, as though he were backlit by the sun. Varley Shuddered. He had sat in front of an alien. Yet not once during the entire interview had he realized it. The camera had seen it, but Varley hadn't. It had to be the type of lens he had on the camera—it was sensitive to low-light recording, because during the sessions he taped he always kept the lights turned low.

"My God. What have I done?"

Varley felt as if he was sinking deeper into something dangerous that he did not understand. He cursed his stupidity for allowing Heinrich to take the only tape he had of the Gomez episode.

He then called the Midtown South Precinct and asked for Mueller, but as he was doing so, he realized that Mueller was the name of the psychiatrist who came after Gomez that day. The police operator told him there was no detective named Mueller employed at Midtown and maybe he wanted the downtown precinct. Varley then called Heinrich's office. He dialed the printed number on the card rather than the one Heinrich had written. He was told that Heinrich had disappeared five days ago. When the person on the phone asked who he was, he hung up quickly.

He had to hide. But where? Vermont, the cabin. He would leave right from the office.

8

Vermont

Varley hit rush-hour traffic out of New York City and did not get to the Massachusetts border until 10:00 PM. It was there that he gave voice to his second thoughts. What was he doing? Until then, he had thought only of the past with Gomez, and the events of the day and the past week. What about his family? Were they okay? He was confused and worried. He stopped and called home. Lois answered.

"Hi, honey," he said. "Is everything okay?"

"What's wrong, Brad?" Lois asked.

"I think the pressure of work is getting to me. You know—everybody's problems piling on top of me. It just built up to a point where I wanted to go off alone."

"Do you feel better?" she asked.

"Yeah." With relief in his voice, he repeated, "Yeah. I'll be home tomorrow."

"Good, sweetheart. We'll be looking forward to it. Suzie wants to say hi. She's in bed with me."

Suzie, his six-year-old daughter, got on the phone. "Daddy, Mr. Biggs wants to say good night." Mr. Biggs was her stuffed clown.

Varley smiled. "Good night, Mr. Biggs," he said with a playfully deep voice.

"Good night, Daddy," Suzie said with as deep a voice as she could muster while pretending to be Mr. Biggs. Then, she giggled and handed the phone back to her mother.

"Listen," Lois said. "Stay in Vermont until the weekend. Rest. Friday, Suzie and I will fly up and then we can all drive down together on Sunday night. A weekend in Vermont wouldn't hurt any of us." She went on to tell him sternly that she did not want him driving straight through. He should stop for the night.

After he hung up, he felt relieved. He checked into a roadside motel, where he slept fitfully.

He arrived in Hopewell, Vermont, at about 10:30 the following morning and stopped in town to get breakfast. He parked on the only main street. After breakfast, he shopped for things he would need at the cabin.

Martin and Martha Standish ran the Standish General Store. They were old New Englanders, descended, they said, from the Puritans. Their establishment served as general store, post office, and cracker barrel gossip center.

"Well, Martha, look here," said Martin. If it ain't Dr. Varley. When did you get in, Dr. Varley?"

"Just this morning, Martin."

"Don't see you much up here anymore," Martha chided. "Too busy down in the big city?"

"Now, Martha, don't start," Martin, said.

"Martin, a man should take care of his place."

"Now, Martha, don't go on. He knows about the hooligans who went through his place. What he don't know about is the letter."

"His being gone all the time only invites vandals into the neighborhood, Martin."

"Letter? What letter?" asked Varley.

"Got it right here," Martin said, poking around behind the counter. "Addressed to you in care of me. First one I've ever seen like that." He leaned over the counter and, with his unsteady hand, gave Varley a very crumpled letter.

Varley opened the letter and read.

Brad,

I'm only one step ahead of them and there's no place to turn. Once you thought I had a keen mind. I'm relying on that opinion so you'll give me the chance I need. I know they'll try to convince you I'm nuts.

Please do this. Copy the formula from the enclosed sheet and send it to every researcher you can think of. I know you know lots of them. Before you found your "soft" administration job, you were into molecular biology. If I'm right, and you distribute this formula, you will have saved the world. If I'm wrong, no one will know. By now, I've bet my life you will give me this chance.

Please,

Ted Gomez

Dazed, Varley looked up from the letter. His hands began to shake. Behind the letter was the sheet bearing the chemical formula.

"Martha?" he asked. "May I have some number-ten plain envelopes, a bunch of stamps, some pencils, and paper?" Then he handed her the formula. "And would you please Xerox this fifteen times?"

"Why, sure, Brad."

"Martin, if you don't mind, I'd like a cup of coffee," said Brad.

He sat down at a table near the window where the older folks in town occasionally played checkers. He looked out and realized that someone might be watching him. When Martha handed him the copies of the formula, he moved to a table in the rear, out of sight, and began to write, "Walter Harris, Chanel. Eli Simpson, Schering. Larry Livermore, Organon. Fred Rollins, Hoffman-LaRoche. Seymour Henkle, Lederle Labs," and so on—a list of fifteen names of prominent biochemists and scientists whose work he knew and respected. Some knew him. Others would have no idea who he was. But a common thread ran through all the people he sent the formula to. Their curious and analytical minds would play with it. If not them personally, their subordinates or graduate students. It would soon circulate throughout the American research community and beyond. It took him fifteen minutes to write a short note explaining who he was and how he had acquired the formula. He mentioned Javic, whom they all respected. He explained that, in the wake of Javic's and Gomez' deaths, he was the last link to what was going on. He asked them to take the letter seriously enough to make one batch of the formula and try it on someone, and then pray for that person. He understood, he explained, that trying it directly on humans was not normally done, and that he only suggested doing so because of a terrible danger threatening all of humanity.

He asked Martha to Xerox the one-page letter. When she came back with the copies, he stuffed and stamped the envelopes and handed them to her for posting.

Brad Varley walked out onto the front steps of the Standish General Store and sighed deeply. He looked at the blue sky and the puffy white clouds. He rubbed his beard and decided it was time to go to the cabin.

It looked just as he had left it six weeks before, except that the foliage had bloomed while spring turned to summer. He went inside, plugged in the refrigerator, and filled it with food he had bought in town. Behind him, he heard the cabin door open and the footsteps of someone entering the cabin. In the doorway stood Heinrich, the person who had come after Gomez in his office. Terror struck him as Heinrich approached him. His eyes looked psychotic. They both knew what this was about.

"Do you have the formula?" Heinrich demanded.

"What are you talking about?" Varley asked as he backed toward a desk in the corner.

"Don't be foolish," Heinrich said. "It'll be easier for you if you just tell me."

"I don't have the formula—I sent it to a dozen researchers. You're not going to get it now."

Varley opened a desk drawer and pulled out a .357 magnum.

"Do you think that will stop me?" Heinrich asked contemptuously, moving closer. He fired at Heinrich. The bullet had no effect.

Heinrich threw off the holocloak he wore. Before Varley stood a Cylot, its mandibles dripping saliva, its stinger coiled underneath its abdomen. Varley backed behind the sofa knocking a lamp over. He fired four shots in quick succession at the Cylot. They had no effect.

"The formula" said Heinrich moving forward.

"No," said Varley. "No." Varley then put the gun to his temple and fired one last time.

9

A Denial of Death

Beth drove out of Merck's parking lot, down the street, and onto the highway.

"Why did you bring her?" demanded Mectar from the backseat.

"Because I want better company than you, asshole. How long has it been? I'm sick of what we do; I'm sick of the fight. And I'm sick of you, Mectar," said Simon in disgust.

"I've seen five-year-olds behave better than you two," said Beth.

Simon turned his head toward her and stared in silence. Then he turned his head to look out the side window. No one spoke for a while, until Beth ended the silence. "Where are we going?" she demanded.

"I don't care," Simon responded. "Just drive."

"Fine," she said. After a few minutes, she said, "Look, why don't you both just get out here?" She started to pull over. "The two of you can continue whatever it is you're doing. I mean, I'm not your prisoner, am I?"

"No, not at all. You're not our prisoner," said Simon as Beth pulled into a gas station. "This will be fine. Thank you for the ride. Come on, Mectar." Simon opened the door and put one foot on the pavement. Still sitting in the car, he turned to look at her and said, "By the way, it wouldn't be fair if I didn't tell you something."

"What?"

"When you leave us, you'll be exposed to those creatures. They'll be tracking you, and when they find you, they will kill you. First, they will drain you of whatever knowledge they can. I don't want to tell you how, because I don't want to scare you. Then, they inject venom into you with their stinger, which attacks the central nervous system. It leaves you paralyzed with all your senses intact. You can hear and see and understand everything. You will stay alive and fresh until they eat you. They like their victims to be conscious while eating them. They will start by eating your eyes. It's a ritual—'to see what they see' they call it."

"I don't believe you," she said.

Simon shrugged. "I can understand that. But you're a scientific researcher, right? It ought to be an interesting experiment. The lady thinks I'm lying, Mectar. Am I lying?"

"No," was Mectar's disinterested response.

"I don't think I've left anything out," said Simon. "We'll leave. Come on, Mectar."

Mectar opened the door and stopped. "The brain, Simon. You have not been honest with her. You have only told Beth half the story."

"Right. 'To know what they know' completes the ritual. They will crack your skull open and eat your brain. But what the hell. You'll be dead by then anyway. Oh, can I have my bracelet back?" asked Simon, pointing at the bracelet he had put on her wrist back at Merck.

Beth looked at the bracelet. It still flashed dimly back and forth. "Suppose I don't leave you, then?" she said.

"I'll protect you as much as I can," responded Simon.

"I don't feel very safe with you."

"Honey," said Simon impatiently. "If I wanted to kill you, you would be dead already. You can take my word for this. They'll be looking for you. If they find you alone, you'll be dead." Then Simon added gently, "I will do everything in my power to protect you. Honest."

The car stood idling. Beth sat with two hands on the wheel, thinking. "Listen," said Simon. "You don't have to decide now. We're not holding you. If you would drive me to somewhere I can sleep, I'd appreciate it."

"Drive you somewhere you can sleep?" she said incredulously.

"Honey, I don't know about your schedule but it's been a long day for me. A hotel, anywhere, is fine."

Beth turned angrily and pointed at Simon. "Don't call me honey. I'm not your honey," she shouted, pointing at Simon. "I'm not his honey." She pointed at Mectar. "I'm not anybody's honey. Got it?"

Taken aback, Simon looked at her and then smiled. It was a soft smile. "Okay, Beth," he said. "You're not honey. But I'm still Sleepy and the guy behind you is Dopey. And we'd both like to go someplace and sleep."

She paused for a moment, trying to decide whether to believe their story. She was intrigued by what she had just experienced and by the mystery surrounding these two men, but the dead researchers, and the fact that she and Simon and Mectar were still alive, helped her decide. "Fine. I know a place where you can sleep—my apartment."

"Really, Mectar and I don't want to impose. We'll just be on our way," Simon said.

"Get back in," she said.

"Okay," said Simon, "but only if you're sure." He re-entered the car. Mectar, who had never left it, closed his door. As she pulled back on the highway and continued down the road, she muttered under her breath, "What have I gotten myself into?"

It was almost midnight when Simon said he needed to use a bathroom. Beth pulled into the parking lot of a TCBY Yogurt store. The three of them got out and walked into the store. Heading toward the bathroom, Simon said, "I'll be right back."

Beth looked at Mectar. In the bright light of the yogurt store he looked different. He was tall, about six feet four with black hair that was combed straight back. His rugged facial features looked too perfect. Maybe she only imagined that, she thought.

"Would you like something?" she asked, nodding toward the counter.

"I have no money."

"I'll buy," said Beth.

"You order first," Mectar said.

Beth scanned the menu on the wall behind the counter. "Chocolate, please," she said and then looked at Mectar.

"I'll have that too," Mectar said.

"Cup or cone?" the counter girl with long blonde hair and acne asked.

Beth looked at Mectar. He didn't respond.

"Would you like your yogurt in a cup or a cone?" the girl repeated.

Mectar hesitated and then said, "The first one."

"Fine, and I'll have mine in a cone. Two chocolates please, medium," said Beth.

After they received their yogurt, Beth began to lick hers. Mectar watched and began to lick his yogurt, ignoring the spoon that was stuck in the side.

"By Grundak this is good," he said.

She nodded, wrinkling her brow, wondering why he didn't use the spoon. They walked slowly to the front door to wait for Simon. A moment passed in awkward silence. Beth took a bite of her cone. Mectar took a bite of his Styrofoam cup and chewed thoughtfully. Beth, a trained scientific observer, watched quietly. Mectar ate around the edge of the cup. When he reached the spot where the plastic spoon, protruding from the yogurt, rubbed against his cheek, he bit the spoon and began to chew. He studied the broken end of the spoon sticking out of the cup.

"Is it good?" Beth asked.

"I don't like the container. But whatever this is," he said, nodding toward the end of the spoon, "it's good. It has no flavor, but I like its texture. But the choc-o-late—it is delicious."

"Do you always eat the spoon?" she said.

"Is that what that was?" Mectar responded.

"Where are you from?" she asked.

"I'll have another, said Mectar, ignoring her. The clerk went to get another cup. "No," said Mectar, "do you have a larger size?" The clerk reached for a large cup and Mectar again stopped her. "No," he said, "larger than that." The clerk this time held up the pint size and Mectar again shook his head. "Larger." The clerk put her hand on the quart size and Mectar said, "Yes, that size, but give me a cone this time."

The clerk looked at Beth and said, "Is this a joke?" Beth shrugged.

"Mectar," she said, "cones don't come in that size, only cups."

"Then give me that size cup," said Mectar. "But no spoon" he added.

The clerk looked at Beth, who nodded affirmatively, and the clerk filled the quart container with chocolate yogurt. Mectar squeezed the contents into his mouth all at once and swallowed.

"Do you always eat like that?" asked Beth.

"It does not matter," Mectar said, discarding the quart container and wiping his mouth. I can't remember having anything so delicious as this choc-o-late in my life. Wait for Simon. I'll be outside guarding the car." He walked past her and out the door.

By the time she and Simon reached the car, Mectar was leaning on the top of the car clearly in pain and holding his head.

"Mectar, are you all right?" asked Simon.

"I have been poisoned by her and this choc-o-late. The roof of my mouth aches and my head hurts." Simon looked quizzically at Beth.

She shrugged noncommittally. "He ate his ice cream too fast. He's got brain freeze. It'll pass in a moment."

"How can he get that from eating a cup of yogurt?" asked Simon.

"He downed a quart in one gulp," said Beth.

"What kind of stupid planet has food that will affect you by the speed with which you eat it?" Mectar rubbed the sides of his head.

Beth was clearly agitated now. "What's wrong?" Simon asked.

"I'm not going anywhere," she said. "I need to know what's going on. I need to know who you are and who or what your friend is."

"Why? What did he do now?"

"He just ate a plastic spoon and Styrofoam cup along with the yogurt," said Beth. "Then he ate a quart of yogurt in virtually one gulp."

"How many times do I have to tell you not to eat what the food comes in?" said Simon, turning to Mectar.

"She ate the container," said Mectar defensively pointing at Beth.

Simon looked at Beth. "I ate a cone," Beth said with exasperation. "An ice cream cone."

"Oh, Mectar," said Simon, shaking his head.

"Who are you two?" Beth demanded.

"I know," said Simon, looking at Mectar.

"Are you two communicating with each other?" she said.

"Yes. You see, we've developed a telepathic link," said Simon. "It's the first interspecies link."

"What do you mean, 'interspecies'?" she said.

"Mectar is a Kian," Simon said. "Wait. I'd better start from the beginning. I think the best way to handle you, Beth, is to tell you the truth."

"That would be nice," Beth said sarcastically. "Do you know what the truth is?"

"The truth is that I'm from the future and so is Mectar. Our planets, Earth and Kia, were at war. Now there is a truce. We have a common enemy we have to fight.

"Maybe 'enemy' isn't quite the right word. It's a disease."

"A disease?" Beth asked.

"It's a disease of awareness," said Simon.

"It's not a disease," said Mectar. "It's a race of beings."

"It's how you look at it," said Simon. He turned and looked at Mectar. "I'll tell you what. I'll answer her question first and then you can give her your answer, all right? That way we'll confuse her as little as possible. And I am going to answer her on her terms."

Mectar half-closed his eyes and nodded, indicating that he didn't agree with Simon but would comply. He rubbed his head slowly, massaging the pain away.

"What are you talking about?" asked Beth.

"Mectar is right—the race of beings we are fighting are called the Cylots. And we are losing. They have many weapons, but one in particular gives them a tremendous advantage. That weapon can inflict a disease."

"You means like the Indians that were given blankets with smallpox?" asked Beth.

"Exactly, but this is a disease of awareness. When you catch this disease, you are no longer you. You are controlled by it. It's a thinking organism. You catch this disease and you are dead. Yet your body keeps on existing. The awareness of the disease itself controls you, your body, and your mind. You may be there, but you are not in control. It tries to infect another person by using you to overcome that person. Humans and Kians have researchers working on this. Yugen, one of the researchers, fled to the past, your present. He was close to a cure, but the Cylots came after him."

"If they came after him, how can they be a disease, you *pulvzar*," said Mectar.

Simon looked at Mectar and then at the ground. Then he looked back up and said, "When is a mountain not a mountain?"

"What?" said Mectar, a confused look on his face.

"To understand what a mountain is, you must understand what it is not," said Simon. "That's why the Cylots have no planet."

"But they must have a planet!" shouted Mectar.

"Let's do it your way, Mectar. They're not a disease. The Cylots are a race that can inflict disease. From Mectar's point of view, I suppose you could say it's sort of a weapon. But it's a weapon that acts like a disease. It's not a weapon that kills; it's a weapon that controls you until they are ready to kill you. The Cylots have figured out a way to reconfigure human electromagnetic intelligence by implanting electrodes. The electrodes they put in your guard, Tom, the one who shot at you at Merck, are crude, meant for field use. When they have enough time to work in a lab, an implant is virtually undetectable. The electrical body pattern changes. It produces a new personality a new mind in the old body. The person or personality that occupied that body is gone, killed as though by a disease. The new person is completely controlled by the Cylots, who call the new person a supplicant.

"Yugen was trying to find a way to prevent all this. He was trying to develop a way to counterattack. The Cylots knew he was close to finding a cure. When he fled to the past, they came after him. He hid and began work in the Merck lab, where everyone thought he was doing genetic research trying to make bees more passive. But the Cylots got him. He's dead. That's why we're here."

Beth turned to look at Mectar again. His face had changed in an odd way. His features, which had been sharply defined, now looked as though every facial muscle had gone slack. "Am I hallucinating?" she asked.

"No, he's a metamorph," said Simon. "Metamorphs can do that." Simon turned to Mectar. "For the sake of the lady, pick a form and stick to it, okay?"

"And that's why these researchers are dying?" Beth asked, still looking at Mectar.

"There must be a common thread," said Simon. "If Yugen was trapped, he would have left some kind of trail or clue for me. These researchers couldn't have all developed—"

"Developed the same formula at once," interrupted Beth.

"Is it such a jump of logic to assume that these researchers, all dying within days of Yugen's death, have some connection to him? They must have been sent some of his research."

"Are you going to help us or not?" Mectar demanded impatiently.

"What do you want me to do?" said Beth.

"Help us find the research, whatever formula Yugen had," said Simon.

"Wait a minute," said Beth. "I want to know about these creatures that you say you are fighting. What are they?"

"I guess you could call them beings. Certainly that's the form we've encountered them in. It's the easiest way that asshole over here," said Simon, pointing with his thumb over his shoulder toward Mectar, "can relate to them. Yet, they have either weapons or the apparent ability to control humans and Kians' electrical consciousnesses. I choose to think of them as free-floating electrical consciousnesses, but either way consciousness exists where electrons exist."

"What?" said Beth incredulously.

"Simon, you have seen them, fought them. How can you say that?" demanded Mectar.

Simon explained, "They are conscious creatures that are free-floating electrical charges. Once they penetrate your body, their electrical charge takes over your physical form. If you are no longer aware, what are you?" Simon paused, but Beth did not answer. "You're dead," he continued, "but your body isn't. It is being used. You don't think a disease can be intelligent? Look at how diseases overcome immune systems. This is just a smarter disease."

Beth looked squarely at Simon. "You're full of shit," she said. "There is no such thing as a free-floating electrical consciousness."

Simon looked at moths circling the light inside the yogurt store. "Follow me," he said.

She followed him back across the parking lot to the light inside the yogurt store. He stood beneath it, watching the moths circling it. He reached up quickly and grabbed a moth. Pinching one of its wings, he held it in front of Beth. "This is a free-floating electrical charge," he said. "Do you deny that there is electricity running across the synaptic openings in a cerebral cortex?"

Beth watched the moth struggle, its legs flailing, its one free wing flapping. "No, I don't deny it. Every living organism has a measurable electrical charge," she said.

Simon released the moth, throwing it past Beth. It tumbled awkwardly in the air until its wings began to flap. "Of course you can't deny it. There are other free-floating electrical charges as well. Has your science cataloged every life form? Yes, the Cylots are quantifiable, carnivorous six-foot insects that want to devour you. But somehow they possess a psychic disrupter that affects human and Kian awareness." Simon ran his hand through his hair, now posing questions more to himself than Beth or Mectar. "From what I know, it's a machine or a machine-generated beam, but there is evidence in some victims of implants. And is every individual Cylot a single entity, or are they connected in some hive-like common mind?" Simon asked. "Either way, we can't deny is that life forms are predatory. You learned about the food chain in second grade. You haven't been able to deny that there are free-floating electrical charges because one just flew past you. You also cannot deny that they are predatory. So tell me, Doctor, why do you deny what you just saw a few hours ago?" Simon turned and walked to the car. Beth found his attitude obnoxious. She did not like being lectured to.

"Listen," she said angrily, following him. "Did you embrace every new idea you ever heard? Or did you question it first, Doctor?" She spat the words at him.

He turned around and said, "I'm not a doctor."

"Then, what are you?"

"I'm a physicist. That's my training. The biochemistry was forced upon me. I never finished my doctorate."

"Why not?" she asked.

"Other things got in the way. It doesn't matter. We've got to go." He turned abruptly toward the car and then, just as abruptly, stopped and turned back, looking squarely at Beth.

"Just who is Javic?" he asked. "What did he do?"

"Javic developed beta blockers at Merck," Beth said.

"How did he do that?" asked Simon.

"We were bringing another drug through clinical trials. But we couldn't get the results we achieved in initial experiments. We had more than a hundred million dollars invested in this drug, and it was already at the FDA, so we went back to the original research, recreating the experiment. What had happened, we found, was that our glassware distributor had substituted beakers from a different manufacturer. To him, one 800-milliliter beaker was the same as another. The new beakers were coated with a different type of polymer. The polymer blocked the reaction in our drug and gave us a whole new class of drugs, called beta blockers."

"Wait a minute," said Mectar. "How does a beta blocker work?"

"In simple terms," said Beth, "there are receptor sites in the human body that receive information chemically. It's like a lock-and-key system. Each site only accepts a certain type of chemical key. That's way aspirin works—at a pain site, the lock will be filled by the aspirin key, thereby preventing the transmission of pain through the lock, or receptor. The aspirin chemically blocks the transmission of pain across that synapse. The polymer that coated the beaker was a chemical key that blocked the reaction we wanted. If it could block that reaction in our beaker, then it could block the reaction in somebody's heart. What Javic found was a chemical key to prevent a biological reaction."

"In short, he got lucky and tripped over a piece of information," Simon snorted.

"He didn't get lucky," Beth replied. "What do you know about drug discovery and drug research? You're some commando from the future. All you know about is killing." Beth was angry, defending a man she had both liked and admired.

"Look, I'm not denying he did some hard research. But his discovery was accidental. It wasn't based on insight. I'll give him credit for being a technician, for working through a problem to achieve a good result," said Simon. "But he doesn't belong in the same category as another researcher who's alive right now, one of the most respected and revered names in all of medical research."

"Who is that?" asked Beth, her eyebrows raised in surprise.

"Dr. Jacques Benveniste," said Simon.

"The fraud who works at INSERM, the French National Institute of Health and Medical Research?" said Beth.

"Yeah, Dr. Benveniste," said Simon.

"He didn't prove molecular memory, Benjamin," said Beth. "That's what his work was about."

"Stop!" said Mectar. "Explain this to me."

Simon replied, "Dr. Benveniste discovered an entirely new way in which both physics and biology work together. What Benveniste discovered, despite what Dr. Grey says, is that water molecules store and release information not only chemically but electromagnetically. It's done through a subtle electromagnetic language, which enables one molecule to record the essence of another, much as a tape recorder records sound. What it did, Mectar, was explain why homeopathy works."

"What is homeopathy?" asked Mectar.

"Homeopathy," said Beth, "says that disease can be treated and cured using an infinitesimal amount of medicine diluted in water."

"This technique led to the medicine of our time," said Simon, much as the Wright Brothers' flight eventually led to space travel."

"That's ridiculous," said Beth.

"Honey, I'm from the future. I'm not a doctor, but I know what medicine is. Mectar, there are interactions at the molecular level that are electromagnetic, not chemical. That is the basis of the Cylot weaponry."

"If you call me honey one more time …" said Beth, raising her fist.

Simon continued, ignoring her. "His experiments were based on a few simple scientific facts. He took a human antibody called immunoglobulin E, or IgE for short, and exposed it to white blood cells called basophils. When these two interact, the IgE clamps onto receptor sites on the basophils and waits for an invading molecule in the bloodstream. This invading molecule isn't a germ but an antigen, something that causes allergies.

"In people allergic to bee stings, the bee venom wouldn't be in their bodies more than a few seconds before it set off the IgE antibody, which would cause the basophil to release a chemical called histamine, which causes the redness, swelling, and itching of an allergy attack.

"So Benveniste took human blood serum full of white blood cells and IgE and mixed it with a solution of goat's blood, he was certain to trigger the release of histamine. The goat's blood solution contained an anti-IgE antibody, which represented pollen dust, bee venom, or some other antigen. When the IgE and anti-IgE collided, the reaction in the test tube happened exactly as it would in a person with a bad allergy. Large amounts of histamines were produced. Benveniste then dilute the anti-IgE solution again and again. Every time, the IgE continued to react, even though it was well past the limit where the solution should have been chemically active. Finally, he had so diluted the solution that he knew that there was no anti-IgE at all. Mathematically, he confirmed it was impossible for the solution to contain a single molecule of antibody. When he added this solution, which was now just distilled water, to the serum containing white blood cells, the histamine reaction was set off with the same power as in his first experiment, with the full amount of IgE. In short, he got this reaction with a chemical placebo. Therefore, he concluded that the information that triggered the release of histamine had to be electromagnetic.

"Although this result seemed ridiculous, Benveniste duplicated it many times. What he found was that the molecules communicate via an electromagnetic radiation similar to the signals transmitted by a radio station to a receiver. These electromagnetic signals have specific frequencies. Each frequency prompts a specific biochemical reaction.

"His research revealed that you can separate a molecule from its electromagnetic message. He imparted to the water a memory of the electromagnetic message contained in the allergen. The next step was to give the water that contained the memory of this message to the white blood cells. When he did, the cells still released their histamine, not because the chemicals were there but because the electromagnetic memory was there. Do you know what that means, honey? The message remains in the water, just as your voice remains on a recorded tape, even when you are no longer talking. And that's how the Cylots invade a body. Their electromagnetic message causes their awareness to replace the awareness that exists in our cells, cells that, as you know, are 97 percent water."

Simon now turned to Mectar. "The problem with friends like Dr. Grey here is they have difficulty replacing their own dogmatic theories with truly insightful and revolutionary work. They prefer to cling to the idea that discovery is serendipitous rather than insightful."

"I read Benveniste's report, *honey*. A research team went to his laboratory and they proved that he falsified his data."

"What difference does that make?" said Simon. "I can falsify all the data I want. If I'm right, I'm right, and if I'm wrong, I'm wrong. For God's sake, almost every major scientist in history falsified his data. Galileo wrote about experiments that were so difficult to reproduce that many doubt that he actually conducted them. Johannes Kepler doctored his calculations to bolster his theory that the planets move in elliptical orbits, not in circles, around the sun. Just look at the math he used. That in itself can prove it. Come on, Dr. Grey. Isaac Newton fudged numbers to make the predictive power of his universal gravitational theory carry more weight. Scientists have since noted that he 'adjusted' his calculations on the velocity of sound and on the processions of the equinox so they would support his theory. Gregor Mendel's experimental results, which formed the basis of modern genetics, were so perfect that later researchers were convinced he falsified his data. But the bottom line was, he was right. So don't give me this shit that Benveniste falsified his data. I don't really care, just like I don't care that Mendel falsified his data. In both cases the theory was right, Dr. Grey.

"There are free-floating electrical charges," Simon continued. And you are an ambulatory electrical charge. Remove the electricity from your body and your heart won't pump and your brain won't function, merely because there's no electricity running over the synaptic gaps in your body. The electricity contains your awareness, your essence. Replace that electrical message with a different one and your body is inhabited by a different being."

"Fine," said Beth. "Benveniste becomes a big hero and that's why you are so in love with him."

"No," said Simon. "I have a problem with what you find when you combine what he did with my work in physics." Simon turned and walked away.

"What?" she said angrily, following him. "What?" She grabbed him and turned him. "What do you find?"

"Physical scientific evidence of the human soul," said Simon.

"What?" she gasped.

"You find the scientific basis of a separate consciousness," he said, "a disembodied form of consciousness common to every living creature. What Benveniste found was the footprint of the human soul, scientific proof that the soul exists. A consciousness free from a bodily form, provable and verifiable."

"Bullshit," said Beth.

"Human science can now put an entire library on a digital chip the size of your fingernail," he said, holding out his thumbnail. "Would you have believed that a hundred or even fifty years ago? There is science in the components of drugs and cosmetics that exist in your time that the average layperson would not believe. Why can't you make the jump in logic that says a human's entire lifetime can be encoded on a strip of electrical energy? All of Beth Grey can be encoded on one double helix of DNA. Does not the acorn contain the oak tree? Once Benveniste proved that memory was transferred electromagnetically within the cells, and that it is the electromagnetism that holds the memory, not the biochemical structure, the next jump in logic should be easy. But you refuse to accept what's in front of you."

"You want me to believe that my awareness, my consciousness, resides in the in electromagnetism within my body?" asked Beth.

"When you die, what dies?" asked Simon. "You're brain dead when you no longer have electricity running through you. Death is represented by the absence of that electricity. There is no electricity in the AV nodes, which cause the heart to contract. There is no electricity running through the synaptic gaps in your brain. According to Newton and Einstein, energy can be neither created nor destroyed," said Simon. "So your electricity is not destroyed. It transmutes. It leaves your body and departs. Once that electricity is encoded with memory, your entire life experiences can be put into it. Is it so great a jump in logic to go from a chip that can hold one hundred megabytes of memory to an electrical encoding of an equal amount of information? Memory is encoded on the electricity that's part of your body, and when you die that electricity leaves, taking the memory with it."

"If it's true that you're from the future," Beth said, "then why are you so pompous that you have to criticize the men who do the yeoman work in research here? Javic was a good man who did hard work, even if he didn't have the inspiration that the quack you're talking about did. Or maybe the quack just guessed right." Her voice rose to a yell. "Whatever the reason, for you to criticize someone who does the everyday scientific work is pompous, arrogant, insolent, and stupid."

Simon stood staring at her, not knowing how to respond. Then he turned and said to Mectar, "Guilt rays."

"You have told me this before," said the Kian.

"Earth women use guilt rays on men. You didn't know this about human physiology, did you, Mectar?" said Simon. Beth looked at him, still angry but now perplexed as well. Simon said, "Women use the guilt rays to make men do what they want them to do. There are transmitters hidden somewhere in the female body that shoot these guilt rays at men." He turned, looking at Beth. "We're just doing research work on it now in the year 5000, Grey. We think the guilt transmitters are housed in the breasts, but we're not sure." With that, Simon turned and got into the car.

"If that's the case," said Beth, "they should do research on how many penal cells are located in the cranial cavities of men. Because most of men's thinking is done with their penises," said Beth, slamming the door as she got into the car with Simon.

As Mectar got in the backseat, he asked, "Can human females really transmit guilt rays from their breasts?" Neither Beth nor Simon answered. There was a heavy silence. "Humph," said Mectar. "Simon, I have never watched an interaction of the male and female of your species before. In the time we traveled together, I thought you argued with me because you disliked me. But I know you like Beth. You protected her while putting yourself at risk. I must think on this. Was this interaction ritualistic? Was there an undercurrent of which I am not aware? Do earth males have brain cells in their penises? If it is not so, why does Beth think it is so?"

Neither Simon nor Beth answered, but they stole conspiratorial sideward glances at each other. Then they began to laugh.

10

Chanel

Walter Harris sat behind his office desk. When he needed to think about current experiments, he shut his door and threw darts at a dartboard. Sometimes the darts' configurations reminded him of how various molecular diagrams fit together. In this manner, he had designed catalysts for Chanel, the French cosmetics firm. These catalysts enabled the skin to absorb oils and collagens that made wrinkles disappear. His chemical breakthrough regarding the absorption of second-body hormones created a new class of cosmetics—and made a bundle for Chanel.

On top of his mail this morning was a letter marked "Confidential." The letter was from Brad Varley, explaining Ted Gomez' death and how important the attached formula was.

Walter Harris was a man of precision and detail. His mother once remarked to him with exasperation, "Walter, you know an awful lot about very little." Before acting or proposing a solution, he would study a problem to death. That very trait, which had helped him be so successful in his career, could also be a detriment, because it made him oblivious to the obvious.

He pondered the formula. He was lost in thought when Monica Scala, his secretary, knocked. "Yeah," he said.

"The ladies' group is here, sir," Monica said, giggling.

Harris liked Monica. She was a short, overweight Italian girl in her late twenties. "Yeah, yeah, yeah," he said, smiling. "I know."

"Have fun," she said. "Oh, by the way, Walter. There's a Dr. Heinrich in the lobby to see you."

"Tell him he'll have to wait until the tour is over," said Walter. He put on his white lab coat and went to meet the company president's wife and her group.

Sarah Clarendon, a matronly woman with two chins, was the wife of Jacque Clarendon, chief of Chanel's United States operations. Whatever Sarah lacked in beauty and youth, she made up for in money and a steadfast belief in marrying well.

Her first two husbands had left her well fixed financially. Marrying Jacque was her crowning achievement. Politics had made her marriage to him possible, the politics of love and social connections. But that was another story. For the present, she fervently wished her daughter, Abigail, would follow in her marital footsteps.

Jacque had told Sarah about Dr. Walter Harris, a biomedical researcher who was moving up in the company. The doctor's discoveries were rapidly making him wealthy. The only way to keep stars in any profession was to reward them monetarily and the cosmetics industry was no exception. His potential wealth, Sarah decided, made him a good place for her daughter to begin a career of marrying well.

Jacque had said that Harris was a little bit bookish. But after seeing his picture in the company brochure, Sarah deemed him to be sufficiently handsome.

Sarah had arranged for her ladies' club, a group of twenty "mature" women, to tour the Chanel plant, allegedly to learn how the cosmetics they used were made and what went into them. Some of the women, at Sarah's urging, brought their daughters. Sarah intended to make sure Abby met Walter. Then, as the group departed, she intended to invite Walter for dinner.

But Sarah had a problem. Abigail, in her early twenties, was rebelling. She did not want to meet "some scientific nerd." That morning, as Sarah finished breakfast, she heard the rhythmic staccato clicking of Abigail's high heels across the Italian tile floor of the foyer. As Abby entered the room, Sarah gasped, put her spoon down, and stared at Abby. The younger woman was dressed in black high heels, a short black leather skirt, and a tight sweater, all clinging to her body and accentuating her ample curves. Brown shoulder-length hair fell softly about her face. While Sarah admired her daughter's undeniable beauty, she deplored this particular presentation of it. "You're not going like that," Sarah declared.

"Mother," said Abby, "I'm certainly not going the way you're dressed. And if I change my outfit, I'd have to change my makeup. Besides, who am I dressing for? You or that nerd you want me to meet?"

Sarah sighed. Maybe she had a point. "Fine. If you want to look like a trollop, then let's go." Sarah stood up. With Abby in tow, she walked out to the waiting Mercedes.

Fifteen minutes after they arrived at Chanel, Walter met the ladies' group in the cafeteria, where they were having coffee. He was on his best behavior, since he was, after all, escorting his company president's wife and daughter. In his white lab coat he looked professional and scientific indeed. He tried not to stare at the daughter, whose ass and legs went on forever.

As the tour progressed, he discussed the company's history, the market shares of its products, and its position in the cosmetics industry. All went well until they got to the raw materials area, where he began discussing manufacturing basics.

They stood in the processing area, outside of a class-100 clean room. "This, ladies, is a clean room." He pushed his glasses back up the bridge of his nose. "It has a positive air pressure, so the air in it continually flows out through vents in the floor. The incoming air is filtered down to .001 microns. This is where we begin to process the testicles," he said matter-of-factly, "when we bring them out of the refrigerator—"

"Excuse me, Dr. Harris," said Sarah. "What do you mean 'process the testicles'?"

"Cattle testicles. We get them from the stockyards. They're hormone rich. A simple description would be that we take the testicles and put them in a larger version of what you would know as a household blender, and we puree them. We then take the slurry and put it in a centrifuge. The heavy particulates sink to the bottom, while the oils rise to the top. These hormone-rich oils are the collagens. We mix the collagens with fragrances and oils to make a face cream. When women rub the cream into their skin, it reduces wrinkles. The hormone extract is the active ingredient."

"You mean we're rubbing our faces with cattle testicles?" asked Sarah.

Some of the women blushed while others giggled nervously. Abigail moved to the front of the group. "Ooo, tell us more," she said.

As Walter, with some discomfort, tried to assess the developing situation, Sarah asked, "Why don't we move to the perfume area?" Sliding her arm into his and leading him away, she said, "How is Chanel No. 5 made?"

"Oh, do we have to leave?" said Abby as the group followed Walter and her mother.

"Come along, Abigail," said her mother, discretely giving Abby a stern look.

As they entered the perfume area, Abby stayed near Walter, her heels clicking on the ceramic tile floor. With a sigh she said, "I guess we've left the testicles forever."

"Actually," said Walter, pushing his glasses up higher on the bridge of his nose, "our creams aren't the only place where we use testicles. We use beaver testicles to make Chanel No. 5."

Abby was delighted. Either Walter didn't understand what was going on or he was playing along. "Tell us more," she said.

"Oh no," thought Sarah. "It can't be because of the hormones," she said.

"Of course not," said Walter. "Beaver testicle extract is used as a fixative to adhere the perfume's fragrance to the woman's face. The more beaver testicles we use, the longer the fragrance lasts."

"Why can't you use something synthetic? Why make eunuchs out of all those little beavers?" Abby asked, pouting. Beneath the pout was a flirtatious girl at play.

Walter smiled, happy to change the subject. "Actually," he said, "we've been going to synthetics for some time. Until about fifty years ago we used ambergris in making Chanel No. 5."

"What's ambergris?" one of the ladies asked.

"Well, basically it's pregnant whale vomit," said Walter.

"Excuse me?" said Sarah.

"How would you get it?" asked another lady.

"Well, it used to be picked up off of beaches and skimmed off the surface of the ocean. During whaling days, it was used in many different products. But one ingredient we haven't been able to get away from yet, which I'd like to, is the fecal matter of the civet cat of South Africa."

"The what?" said Sarah.

"Cat shit?" asked Abby with obvious pleasure. "Chanel No. 5 is made from beaver balls, whale vomit, and cat shit?"

"Well, actually, they're only three of fifty-seven ingredients. For instance, we also use vanilla beans," Walter said. "When we mix them in the proper quantities, then distill the mixture and mix it with alcohol and dye, we get Chanel No. 5."

"I'm sure you use only the finest cat shit," said Abby, smiling at her mother.

By now Sarah had had quite enough. "Well, thank you, Walter, for a very interesting and enlightening tour," she said. "Ladies, I'm sure we'd all like to go downstairs to the cafeteria and have some lunch."

Abby stood next to Walter as the ladies filed out. Sarah waited to thank Walter formally for the tour. But before she could, Abby said softly to him, "So with your products, I rub bull and beaver testicles on my face?"

Sarah glared at her daughter. Walter knew there was trouble ahead and wondered where the tour had gotten out of control. "Well, only in a manner of speaking," he stammered, looking at Sarah.

Abby said, "I think it would be a lot more fun to rub your testicles on my face, Walter." She smiled sweetly at him and walked past her mother, still smiling. Walter was left standing with Sarah Clarendon, wife of the president of Chanel. His mouth hung conspicuously open while her lips were pressed tightly together in anger.

"Thank you for a very enlightening tour," said Sarah stiffly. Then she followed her daughter toward the cafeteria.

"You're welcome," said Walter to her back, his voice trailing off.

As Abby sat in the cafeteria with her mother and the ladies' group, she couldn't get Walter Harris out of her mind. She had an idea. It was a filthy idea, but it appealed to her. She smiled, staring into a cup of coffee as her mother's friends talked and laughed about how embarrassed they were during the tour and how cute Walter was—in a bookish sort of way. She silently agreed. The thought she harbored made her tingle. She had had fun with him at her mother's expense and in front of her mother's group. Now she was going to play with him.

She stood up and said, "Excuse me, Mom. I've got to go powder my nose. I'll be back shortly." Every man in the cafeteria watched her walk out. So did Sarah while shaking her head.

"Well, how'd it go?" asked Monica when Walter returned to his office.

"Don't ask," he muttered as he sat down behind his desk and picked up his darts.

Monica followed him into his office. "Do you want to see Dr. Heinrich now?" she asked.

"Yeah," said Walter. "Today can't get much worse."

Monica showed Dr. Heinrich in. "Dr. Heinrich, pleased to meet you," said Walter.

"And I you, Dr. Harris," said his guest.

"Please, sit down," said Walter. "So how can I help my friends over at Rockefeller University? Is Les Brown still there?"

"May I close the door?" Heinrich asked.

"Uh, sure. Go ahead."

Heinrich stood and shut the door, then turned to Harris. "I lied to you," he said leaning against the door and blocking it. "I have nothing to do with the people at Rockefeller University. I'm looking for a formula you might have received in the mail. I want it."

"A formula?" said Harris. Then two things connected: Varley's letter and Heinrich's threatening demeanor. Harris' eyes involuntarily shot down to his desk, where Varley's letter lay.

Heinrich followed his eyes. "Have you read the formula?"

"Yes," said Harris.

Heinrich quickly stepped toward him, reached across the desk and grabbed Harris by the throat. "Has anybody else seen it?"

"Look, what are you doing?" Harris gurgled. "What are you doing?" He struggled, but Heinrich, clearly the stronger of the two, yanked Harris out of his chair and pushed him against the wall. "No, nobody else has seen it," said Harris.

With that, Heinrich crushed Harris' throat with a crunching, cracking sound.

At that moment, Monica, in response to the sounds of the struggle, opened the office door. Abby, meanwhile, was just rounding the corner to the outer offices. She heard Monica scream. Then, through a glass panel separating the offices from the manufacturing floor, she saw Monica fly violently backward. She saw Heinrich leave Harris' office and stand over Monica, who now stared lifelessly at the ceiling.

In shock and fear, Abby fell back into a janitor's closet. She tried to shut the closet door, but a mop fell and the handle lodged itself between the doorjamb and the floor. Through the space, she saw Heinrich leave the offices. To her horror, he looked at the closet. He took a step toward it but stopped, turned and walked quickly out of the building.

The police found Abby as she lay trembling on the closet floor among the janitor's supplies, dirty mops, and mop buckets. She wore only one high-heeled shoe. Her skirt was torn and soiled. Her stockings had runs. Whatever moneyed, sophisticated, polished veneer protected Abby Clarendon had been irreparably shattered.

11

Robert Joseph Cyrus

He turned away and dry heaved. The little girl's eyes had been pulled from their sockets, her skull crushed, and her brain half-eaten. Parts of her brain lay on the floor beside her head. He guessed she was no more than seven years old, but it was hard to tell. The medical examiner pulled the sheet back over her body. Leary's eyes were tearing, both from the smell and the tragedy. The body of the little girl's mother was slumped in a corner of the bedroom, shot in the head with what appeared to be a heat instrument. Her face, contorted in shock and horror, stared mutely through lifeless eyes at her dead child.

Leary had been summoned to the scene to meet the FBI agent in charge of investigating the ever-widening circle of murders. The call had not prepared the veteran detective for what he found. The child's mutilated body made the gruesome scene almost unbearable.

Leary pressed a handkerchief over his mouth and lurched out the front door of the stylish home in New Rochelle, New York. He stood on the lawn, bent over, hands on his knees, breathing deeply as the nausea faded. From behind him, he heard a commanding voice, the voice of someone in charge.

"I'm glad you didn't throw up all over my crime scene, Leary. Were the bodies at Merck like this?" Leary looked up and then stood up. "Robert Cyrus, FBI," the man said. He extended his hand to shake, then withdrew it upon seeing Leary's condition.

FBI agent Robert Joseph Cyrus was six feet two inches tall. He had thick, wavy black hair, a muscular body, and a slightly pockmarked face. He wore a gray business suit with a dark tie over a white shirt. Born and raised in Nacogdoches, Texas, he came from a long line of policemen. His great great granddaddy had been a Texas Ranger in the mid-1800s. His grandfather, a sheriff, once chased Bonnie and Clyde to the Oklahoma border. His father was the first in the family to work for the federal government. Now Robert Cyrus, in his early forties, was a respected no-nonsense agent who would drive an investigation relentlessly to its conclusion.

"Did the bodies at Merck look like this?" Cyrus asked again.

"No," said Leary, regaining his equilibrium. "Javic had his face and hands blown off and Yugen was incinerated in his car. One guard was shot in the chest and head. The wound looked something like the one in the mother's head, but I would have to look at it again, though."

"How do you know it was Javic if the face and hands were blown off?" asked Cyrus. How did you identify the body?"

"He was in Javic's office wearing Javic's clothes. Isn't that enough?"

"No." The look Cyrus gave Leary was stone cold. "Wheeler," Cyrus shouted to an agent near the sidewalk. "Wheeler, have Reynolds do autopsies on the bodies in." Cyrus looked at his notepad. "Rahway. Call them down there and tell them I don't want those bodies touched until we get there. Got it?"

"Right, BJ." It was clear to Leary that they had done this before and each knew his role. He felt there was a veteran team at work here.

"BJ?" Leary asked.

"Bobby Joe," Cyrus responded. "Get it? Robert Joseph ... Bobby Joe ... BJ. I don't care what you call me. Just get me the answers now and make sure they're right. Got it?"

"Yeah, I got it," said Leary, wiping his mouth for the umpteenth time and putting the handkerchief away.

"I understand there is some report that you saw ..." BJ again looked at his pad. "Research Assistant Grey, the day after the shootings. It's the only report we have of her or Bottoms since they disappeared. Tell me what happened."

"It was about 1:30 in the afternoon," Leary began. "I saw Patrolman Jefferson stand up and start to walk away from his post, so I came down the hall to see where he was going. There, about thirty feet down the hall, stood Dr. Grey and two Caucasian males. One was huge, about six feet, six inches tall. The other was about six feet tall. The smaller one was yelling at the big one. Grey took a few steps up to me and said, 'Michael, I need your help.' Then she handed me this earring." Leary reached into his pocket and handed Beth's silver-hoop earring to Cyrus. "Then she disappeared."

"She what?" demanded Cyrus.

"She disappeared."

"Like into thin air?"

"That's right," said Leary.

"Did she go poof when she disappeared, like in a little cloud of smoke?" asked Cyrus with a derisive smile on his face.

"No," said Leary defensively.

"And what about the two male Caucasians. Did they disappear?"

"Yes," said Leary angrily. They disappeared too. Just ask Jefferson."

"Give me a break, Leary. That dog just won't hunt," said Cyrus.

"What?" asked Leary, perplexed, wondering what one thing had to do with the other.

"I said that dog won't hunt. I mean you're full of it. I mean I don't believe you. You got it?"

"Let me tell you something, Bobby Joe," said Leary, his anger rising. "I got a dog at home and it never hunts. And I got a cat at home and it always hunts. And if I threw them both out in the backyard one night when the temperature was twenty below zero, the next morning I'd find the dog's stone-cold lifeless body on the ground and the cat would come in picking its teeth."

Cyrus looked at Leary with a deadpan expression. Then he asked, "When you northern boys talk, do you ever stop to breathe?"

"Listen to me, you cracker," said Leary with barely controlled fury. "We stop to breathe. We stop to eat. We stop to shit. And when we give a police report, we make sure it's goddamn accurate. If I can't explain it, it doesn't mean I didn't see it."

Robert Joseph Cyrus smiled a slow smile. "All right, Detective Leary. The three of them disappeared. Now this afternoon there will be a gathering at the West Orange, New Jersey, Police Department," he said, emphasizing the "O" in "police." "Officers from all municipalities who have investigated similar deaths—or any research community deaths—will be there. And so will you. Clear it with your captain. I want everyone to hear how your three suspects disappeared."

"Fine," said Leary. "I'll be there." As he turned and walked away, he muttered under his breath, "Who ever heard of an FBI agent with three first names? His mother was probably covering all the bases when trying to guess who his father was."

"I heard that, Leary," Cyrus yelled. "You be there. You hear me, boy?"

Leary kept walking and without turning around said, "Yeah, I'll be there."

12

Organon

Sylvia Walinski was finishing a phone conversation with her son as Dr. Heinrich approached her desk. "No, Stan, I won't be home until 5:30. Take the stuffed cabbage out of the freezer and leave it on the counter by the sink and we'll eat about 6:30. Make sure you shower after soccer practice. Don't come home like you did yesterday, filthy dirty. All right, dear, love you. Bye, bye." Sylvia hung up the phone. Stan was the last of her children living at home.

"May I help you?" she inquired of Dr. Heinrich.

"Yes," he nodded, "I'm here to see Dr. Livermore."

"Is he expecting you, sir?"

"Yes, he is."

"Please wait here. I'll let him know that you are here."

A crumpled letter had lain on Larry Livermore's desk for two days before he got back to his office and opened it. It was marked "Confidential." The return address said Brad Varley. Larry had met Brad some years ago at a convention of research scientists. It was actually a Lab Animal Research (LAR) Symposium. Brad had delivered a paper on the emotional desensitization of lab animal researchers as a result of killing animals for their research. Larry found the presentation mildly interesting.

Larry worked in West Orange, New Jersey, at a company called Organon. Organon was a Dutch company that had barely survived the German onslaught in World War II. Its name was derived from the fact that it processed human organs.

Larry was instrumental in developing Follistim, a fertility drug for Organon. It was the genetically engineered successor to Humegon and had made millions for Organon and its Dutch parent company. Whereas Humegon was a biological product, Follistim was synthetic. As late as 1998, Organon in West Orange had still made only three batches of Humegon. Humegon was a fertility drug for women. It was derived from the urine of post-menopausal cloistered women.

Nuns. The only community of nuns large enough to support the urine require-ments to make this drug was of course in Europe. Akzo, as its Dutch parent com-pany was now called, had made an agreement with the Catholic Church and taken tanker cars of this urine to process the drug. A kilo of Humegon, barely more than one could fit in a couple of coffee cups, was worth in excess of a mil-lion dollars. Prior to Humegon, in the 1940s and '50s, the fertility drug that Organon produced was Primarin, made from the urine of pregnant mares.

Using human urine as a component of a manufacturing process went back at least as far as the American Civil War, when Southern women would save their households' urine for the nitrates that would then be used in gunpowder.

While using nuns' piss as an ingredient in anything might seem perverse, there was really keen and insightful logic to it for all parties. When harvesting any bio-logical byproduct, the animal population has to be controlled. This applies whether harvesting tissue from pigs or urine from pregnant mares. To extract the estrogen from the urine of human females successfully, it could not be contami-nated by either menstrual byproducts or testosterone, which was usually injected in the form of sperm. The large, elderly nun population of Europe was a socially acceptable population that fit these criteria. It was one that would police itself. It also was a drain on the Catholic Church's resources. An income stream, so to speak, to help support their elderly women was beneficial to both the church and the women who had given their lives to it, and Akzo obtained the raw material source for a new and more powerful class of fertility drug. The drug's use was also philosophically consistent with the church's dogma.

As age took its relentless toll among the nun population, the urine supply gradually diminished. Akzo needed a replacement product for Humegon. It was Larry who led the team to synthesize Humegon, and it was to him that the rewards fell.

Still, he couldn't help thinking about the initial conversation that must have occurred between Akzo and the Catholic Church after upper management had seen proof positive that the science was absolutely correct and a new more power-ful fertility drug could be produced from nuns' urine: "Monsignor, we would like to make a large donation to the Catholic Church. However, there is one thing we would like in return." Even now, years later, that image in his mind made Larry smile as he opened up Brad Varley's letter.

The letter was brief and to the point.

Dear Larry,

You'll find attached a formula for one of the most powerful drugs on human psychology I have ever encountered. The man that developed this, a Doctor Yugen, is now dead, as is the man who gave it to me. My knowledge of this formula may make me the next candidate. There is a group, and I won't go beyond that, who doesn't want this drug developed. What benefit to humankind it has you will have to discover. It may make you very wealthy or very dead. You can throw this letter in the garbage as the ramblings of somebody who's become a crackpot, but the fact that I've sent it to you means that I've exposed you to the dangers. Your best defense may be to develop it instead of ignore it.

Good luck.

Brad.

Larry flipped the letter over, and there was the formula. He found one fact particularly interesting: when the batch was being made, it was subjected to an electrical charge. It energized the electrons in the various molecules to the higher end of unstable levels. That would mean, of course, that the drug would have a very short shelf life and be difficult to mass market.

Larry put the letter down and continued his work, but that night he thought about it. The whole idea bothered him.

The next morning, he called Brad first at Payne-Whitney, which was connected with New York Hospital. The receptionist gave him Brad's office number, which she said was across town on Park Avenue. It was by calling Brad's office that he had found out that Varley had committed suicide.

As he put down the phone, Sylvia Walinski came into his office with a copy of the daily newspaper in her hand. Placing it on his desk, she said, "Shall I send Dr. Heinrich in?" Livermore looked at the front page and there, in the upper right hand corner, just under the main headline, was a sub-headline: "Eric Bottoms, Researcher at Merck, Found Dead."

It was at that moment Larry put it all together. "Oh my God," he said, standing up and rubbing his hands across his forehead. "Oh my God, oh my God, oh my God." Realizing he was probably on someone's hit list, he wanted to flee, to hide. But before Livermore could do anything, a tall, thin man with narrow eyes opened the office door.

"Excuse me," said the man. "Dr. Livermore? May we talk for a second? I called you to make an appointment," he said, now walking into the room. "My name is Heinrich. I'm here about a formula a fellow named Varley may have sent you."

"Sir, you should have waited outside by my desk," said Sylvia, amazed at Heinrich's breach of etiquette. She was equally amazed by Livermore's response.

"Oh, God, oh, God," said Livermore very agitatedly. "Here, here, take it."

"Have you read it?" asked Heinrich.

"I only glanced at it," said Livermore.

Heinrich took the paper and said, "That's a shame." He then pointed a weapon at Livermore and fired. Livermore flew backward, hit the wall, and slumped to the ground dead.

Heinrich then turned and pointed the weapon at Sylvia.

Before Heinrich left, he picked up the copy of the formula Dr. Livermore had been sent and replaced it with one he had brought.

13

The Metamorph

Simon, Beth, and Mectar ended up at Beth's apartment just as the sun was coming up. It was a one-bedroom unit on the second floor of a garden apartment building in Parsippany, New Jersey.

Both Simon and Mectar were tired, Simon especially so. He was coming down from the injection Mectar had given him at Merck. They did not tell Beth where they had been prior to meeting her at Merck, even when she had asked.

Beth entered the apartment, followed by Simon and Mectar. She pointed at her living room sofa. "That pulls out into a sleeper the two of you can share. If you need food, it's in the refrigerator. I'll be back in a minute."

Mectar nodded and headed for the refrigerator. "Do you mind if I use the bathroom?" Simon asked.

"No. Follow me."

She pointed to the bathroom and then entered the bedroom, flopping on her bed. From the bed she could see the door of the bathroom. She heard Simon running water in the sink.

She could see his double reflection in the two mirrors, one on the medicine cabinet and one on the bathroom door, which was half-closed. She watched him pull up his shirt, which hung loose about his waist concealing a black belt. The belt looked like something a policeman would wear, with a small holster for his phaser and various canisters she could not identify. She watched him remove one such small canister the size of a tube of lipstick. He took the antenna of the Cylot from pants pocket and stuffed it in the small black canister and then sealed it. Then he took what looked like a small calculator from the belt and pushed some buttons. The canister disappeared. He waited for a few seconds and then the canister reappeared. He then returned it to his belt.

As she watched this, she thought about the events of the night. It was all so strange. She thought about the adrenal rush she had felt during the night with Simon and Mectar. In her research she always reached beyond her ability to break new ground. This was a turn-on for her. That's why she enjoyed working for Leonard Javic. He excited her too.

She experienced that with Simon tonight. She had even enjoyed her argument with him at the yogurt store. His take on science was so different from what she was accustomed to. She decided to get more information and make the terms her own. She would pull the information from him. She felt challenged.

She sat cross-legged on the bed and looked at the closed bathroom door. She heard him moving in there.

The bathroom door opened. Simon stepped out and looked around for the kitchen. "Can I ask you a question?" Beth said from the bedroom.

He looked at her on the bed and stepped into the bedroom doorway. "What?" he asked tiredly.

"What is a Kian?" Beth asked. "How do they metamorphosize?"

Simon stood in the doorway. In a formal voice, he recited as if by rote, "Metamorphosis: (a) a change of physical form, structure, or substance, especially by supernatural means, (b) a striking alteration in appearance, character, or circumstances, (c) a marked and abrupt change in the form or structure of an animal, as a butterfly or frog, occurring subsequent to birth or hatching, (d) an abrupt change in color, as a chameleon or octopus, or a total change of color and structure, as a Kian."

"I know what metamorphosis is," said Beth. "I want to know what a Kian is."

Simon again spoke by rote: "The creature known as a Kian appears in Webster's Dictionary, circa 2850, as the definitive metamorph. However, before I can explain how a Kian metamorphosizes, it is necessary to describe a Kian anatomically. Exteriorly, a Kian's skin has the texture of leather and the consistency of putty. It rides on a layer of gelatinous material, which surrounds a cartilaginous spinal core. Nerves emanate from the core. These nerves are connected to the putty-like skin. The skin can contract or expand and, through a process of dehydration, can harden almost to the consistency of concrete and hold a form the size of a man. The gelatinous material on which the skin rides acts as a digestive system, much like that of an ameba. Waste products sink through the gel and are excreted through an opening in the Kian's posterior."

As the information spilled out of Simon, Beth shook her head in amazement. "Where did you get all of this?" she asked.

He ignored her question and continued, "At the top of the spinal column, which houses the central nervous system, sit the cranial cavity and the brain. The two have to be discussed separately, because there are instances in which the brain vacates the cranium and moves into the body. It has been theorized that during the evolution of the species this was a defense mechanism.

"Early Kians tended to decapitate each other, the head being most vulnerable during battles. The Kians who were decapitated were the losers and had to find a sanctuary to wait for their heads to regrow. This process is not unknown in nature. Certain worms, when caught, shed their tails so they might escape, only to regrow their tails later. In many ways, Kians exhibit reptilian tendencies.

"The byproduct of the web of nerve endings that run through the gelatinous interior of the Kian give the race a specific psychic ability. Kians can communicate with each other telepathically and read the minds of simpler or unwary creatures. If an Earthman is unaware of this capability, a Kian can not only read his mind but also make psychic suggestions that the Earthman will think are his own thoughts. The Kians, in order to go undetected in this endeavor, must be sure not to suggest a thought or action contrary to that individual's social or moral imperatives.

"So then, now you have taken the first step in understanding a Kian." Having finished the explanation, Simon took a deep, tired breath.

"You sound like you have that memorized," said Beth.

"Beth, I have the ability to remember every bit of science, every bit of politics, every bit of anything I have ever read. It's been a blessing and a curse. It's kept me alive, and it's made me a target. What I just told you about Kians is absolutely accurate."

Beth knitted her brow. "Benjamin," she asked, "if Kians are metamorphs and they can look like humans, then are Cylots metamorphs too? How can they look human?"

"They use a device we call a 'holocloak,' which projects a holographic image around an individual to give them an appearance other than their own. In order for this to be successful, the species using the holocloak has to have the same size configuration as the one they're trying to imitate. For instance, a Cylot or a Lalian could use a holocloak to resemble a human being, but a swift could not."

"A swift?" Beth asked.

"A bird-like species, highly intelligent, about the size of emperor penguins. The reason they're nicknamed swifts is because—"

"They're swift?" Beth asked.

"Yes," said Ben, smiling, "they move swiftly and erratically. They're a friendly species, adaptable to many environments. They ran from the Cylots and befriended Selfridge. They work for him now."

She stared at him and smiled. "I'm almost afraid to ask my next question," she said.

He smiled back at her. "What question?" he asked. "Mind if I sit down?"

"Please," she said holding out her hand in invitation and gesturing toward a large armchair near the bed.

He sank into the chair with a luxuriating sigh. Both were relaxed, she sitting on the bed holding a pillow in front of her, he with legs out and head back, sunk into the overstuffed armchair.

"Tell me about the future," she said. "Are humans and Kians friends, now that there's a truce?"

Simon leaned back in the chair and shook his head. "No. As I said last night, Earth and Kia were at war when the Cylots attacked both planets—if you prefer Mectar's version. Actually, he's right. On the surface, the Cylots attacked us. I take my position to give him a hard time and to make him think beyond the obvious.

"We first heard of the Cylots when they attacked other races that bordered our space. Then we heard that the Cylot onslaught was heading in our direction. In any event, planets that both our races had colonized were wiped out by the Cylots—wiped out in a most horrific way. We realized that we faced a common enemy. A truce was declared between our two worlds, but it's an uneasy truce. That's how I wound up traveling with Mectar ..." Simon's voice trailed off as he stared blankly at the floor in front of him. There was a momentary quiet.

"How old are you?" she asked. Dropping the pillow she'd been holding in front of her, she began unbraiding her hair. Simon watched her. She felt his gaze fall on her breasts. At least one thing hasn't changed in the future, she thought.

He smiled and shook his head. "Does it matter?"

"No."

"Thirty-two. How about you?"

"Thirty-four. Is there anyone in your life?"

"Aside from the space crustacean that I'm traveling with ..." He stopped himself. "Why?" he asked.

"I want to know if there's someone in your life. You know, a love," she said, raising her eyebrows, jutting her jaw out slightly, gently insisting on an answer while feigning a lack of interest. She rearranged herself to sit cross-legged on her bed. Her long brown hair fell to about her shoulders as she continued unbraiding it.

He leaned his head back and closed his eyes. There was a pause. She wondered if he had fallen asleep. "No," he said, slowly opening his eyes and looking toward the door. He spoke quietly and she sensed he did not want Mectar to hear him.

"What do you mean?" she said.

"I was in a battle in the future. My family was killed in an explosion. I wish I could get back to them," he said.

"What do you mean?" she asked.

"If I could go back to that time and stop that explosion, or get them out of there before it happened, then I could begin to have a life," said Simon, looking uncomfortable. He raised his head to look at her.

"How long ago was that?" Beth asked.

"Three years" he said. "My mother, father, sister, and two brothers. A sister-in-law, a niece, and a nephew. My family."

In his eyes she saw old anger and a flash of hardened determination. "I'm sorry, but why can't you go back to that time and save them?" she asked.

"I'm locked out of that period," said Simon. "We travel in time with the use of jump belts. They allow Mectar and I to jump from one period to another. We each have one. Mine is registered. That means there are certain periods I can't jump to. One is the period my family died in. In short, the period of their life."

"Why?" Beth asked.

"Because of a son of a bitch named Selfridge who is running the war from the future," said Simon. Beth sensed he lacked conviction in what he said, that he was disinterested and saying this by rote, much as he had recited the definition of a Kian.

"What do you mean," she asked.

"All this, this chase. What do you think is going on? In the future there's a war. Look. In your time, wars are fought progressively. They occur on land or on the ocean and progress from moment to moment. But the landscape for wars of the future is time. Selfridge is the one with overall command. I've never met him. But if I ever get my hands around his neck, I'll kill him."

"Aren't you working for him?" Beth asked, perplexed.

"That's beside the point. It has been determined that my going back and getting my family would be detrimental to the future," said Simon. "It would make me vulnerable, make me an easier target."

"And Selfridge won't let you go back and get them?"

"That's right," said Simon. "Whether it's detrimental to the future is not really my concern. My concern is to find a way to get to that period to save them. Do you understand?"

"I think so," she said. "Where have you been during the last three years?"

His head fell into his hands, his elbows on his knees; he rubbed his face with both hands. "I've been in deep space with aliens for the last three years. Look.

Can we talk about something else? What about you? Are you involved with anybody?"

Beth shook her head. "No. Not as far as I'm concerned." She reached over to her nightstand, picked up her hairbrush, and began to brush her unbraided hair.

"You really are beautiful," he said softly. "I didn't realize it earlier. I must have been preoccupied." He smiled.

"Why thank you, Benjamin," she said coyly and smiled back.

"Has there ever been anybody special in your life?"

"No," she said, "Although once I nearly got married."

"Oh, really?" he said.

"Six weeks before the wedding I canceled it and then moved in with a new guy, Thor."

"Thor?" Simon asked, raising his eyebrows. "A blond, blue-eyed Norwegian who carried a hammer, no doubt?"

"No," she said. "He was about six feet tall and he had dark hair. I lived with him for nearly two years."

"And?"

"And he wanted the same thing that every man wanted—for me to be a good little girl and follow exactly what he said. I had my own life, my own desires. I simply acted on them."

"Well," said Simon. "I bet all this pissed your fiancé off."

"I don't know," said Beth . "His name was Richard Lancaster"

"Ricky Lancaster?" he asked with a smile.

"Dick Lancaster," she said. "He was too regimented—or he wanted me to be in his regiment. I just didn't want to be that confined."

Mectar came to the doorway. "Grey, you said this choc-o-late comes in other forms. Do you have any here?"

"Yes, but it's probably stale."

"I will try stale choc-o-late. What is stale? Is it as good as cold choc-o-late?"

"Yes," she said, rolling her eyes at Simon while shaking her hair so it fell past her shoulders. "I'll get it for you."

After she walked out of the bedroom with Mectar, Simon looked at Beth's empty bed. He stood up, lay down, and was asleep before his head hit the pillow.

Beth went to the kitchen. As she entered it, Mectar sat at the table. "You don't need the chocolate, do you?" she asked.

"No," said Mectar disdainfully. "I will take it, but I wanted to talk to you. Do not mate with Simon. Do not even think of it."

"I don't see that what I do or think is any of your business," said Beth, going to the sink for a glass of water. Her hand trembled slightly as she reached for the glass. She hoped Mectar would not notice.

"It is my business. My planet needs him. You will never keep him. Besides, there is another, his wife, called Kathy." She turned her head abruptly. He smirked at her. "He did not tell you about her, did he?"

"He told me his family died in an explosion."

"He lied. His family did die, but so did his wife. He is trying to reach her in time," said Mectar. "The ones from the future won't let him."

"So, she's dead," Beth stated flatly.

"I know," said Mectar. "I killed her and his family." Beth turned, startled, and took a step back. "Do not tell him it was me. He does not know."

"Why?" she asked. "Why did you kill them?"

"I had no intention of killing them. I had the intention of killing only him. I missed, accidentally killing his wife and family. He and I were then separated. Events took their course and brought us back together. One day I will have another opportunity to kill him. And this time I will not miss."

"But why?" Beth asked.

"Because I must prevent him from destroying my planet. My problem, Dr. Grey, is that I need him to protect Kia from the creatures he is fighting for Earth's benefit. I need him to develop better weaponry for Kia. I need him much more than you do. But, for that reason, he is a threat to my planet and I will kill him when this is over."

"Oh," Beth said, her eyes narrowing. "You're using him. Why does he travel with you?"

"Because as long as he's with me, Earth is safe from Kian attack, said Mectar. Understand this, Beth Grey. He's not yours. He's mine. I need him and Kia needs him. When I'm done with him, I'll kill him as I killed his wife and family. If you stand in my way, I'll kill you too."

"Maybe I'll tell him you killed them," Beth said.

Mectar shook his head. "If you don't want to end up like them, you won't tell him," he said. The Kian stood up belligerently. "If you tell him, regardless of what happens, I will kill you. I will make sure yours is a painful death. That is a promise."

"Why tell me at all if its critical he does not know?"

"Because I want you to know I am watching you, because some day I do want him to know if I don't kill him now. And last, simply because I want you to know."

Mectar began to change shape, becoming distinctly lizard-like. She could feel him probing her brain, and terror began to creep in. But she felt anger as well. The anger overcame the terror. "You need me now," she said.

"For now," said Mectar.

"Then for now, I'm safe because you need me." She turned and walked back to the bedroom where Simon was.

Mectar then stood and followed her back into the bedroom. Simon was sound asleep. She stood in the doorway. "Will you please bring Simon out to the living room so I can go to bed?" she said.

Mectar walked in, and put a blanket on him. "Simon will sleep until the drug I gave him wears off," he said. "It is more important that he get his rest than you get yours, Grey. Sleep wherever you want."

"Well, then you sleep in here with him and I'll sleep in the living room," said Beth.

"I don't sleep on a mission. When I return to my planet I may sleep for several months. Now I will stand guard." He turned, walked into the living room, and turned on the TV. Beth sat down on the chair in the bedroom. For a while, she watched Simon sleep. Soon she was asleep.

14

A Fasting of the Heart

Beth Grey awoke with a start to find herself lying with her head on Simon's shoulder. She sat up abruptly and quickly backed off the bed. He felt her get up, so he rolled over, sat up, leaned on one arm, and smiled.

"Good morning," he said, even though it was clearly mid-afternoon.

She pulled her hair back from in front of her eyes. "What do you think you were doing?" she said accusingly.

"I was letting you sleep."

"How long have you been awake?" she demanded.

"About twenty minutes."

"Don't get the wrong idea, mister," she said, pointing a finger at him.

"I don't have the wrong idea," he said, a tinge of hurt in his voice.

"Why didn't you wake me?" she asked.

"Frankly, I enjoyed watching you sleep. It's been a long time for me, Beth."

"I'm not that kind of girl. Don't think you can take advantage of me."

"I never thought you were that kind of girl. And I'm not the sort who would take advantage of you." He got out of bed, not angry but clearly hurt.

She was about to say something but stopped. His back was now toward her. He had slept in his jump belt and undershorts and was naked from the waist up. She gasped at the sight of a long scar that ran between his shoulder blades down the middle of his muscular back, ending at the base of his spine. The scar's jagged, red outlines showed that his skin and flesh had been violently torn. It was still a fresh wound.

"I'm sorry. I didn't mean it," she mumbled.

"What?" he asked.

"I'm sorry. I didn't mean it," she said more loudly. "Cut a girl some slack, huh? It isn't every day someone runs into the likes of you two."

"No, I suppose not," he said, lacing up his boots. She sat down on the bed beside him. Their thighs were touching as they sat. He stopped what he was doing and looked at the pictures on her nightstand. There was a picture of everyone in her family, but the picture he picked up was the one of her parents when they were younger and in the service. The two young people in the picture wore combat fatigues and had their arms around each other. They stood in front of a tent. There was a fifty-five-gallon drum at the right side of the tent. He stared at it and then put it back down. "You must have a very hard life," she said softly.

He responded softly, slowly, pausing between words: "You ... have ... no ... idea." His voice was almost inaudible, his face only inches from hers.

Their conversation over, Simon stood up and began to move. Beth stared at the space he had occupied. She was startled at what she had found in him, and in herself. She knew she was falling in love. No, that's not acceptable, she thought. I will not.

Looking half-human and half-lizard, Mectar barged into the room. Grey snapped out of her reverie and stood up. "Mectar!" she said, appalled at his effrontery.

Oblivious to her feelings, Mectar said, "Grey," mimicking her inflection. "I'll never get these Earth greetings right," he said to Simon, who smiled.

"Ohh," said Beth in exasperation. "Give me a minute." She stomped angrily between them to the bathroom. Simon responded to Mectar's questioning look by shrugging.

When Beth emerged from the bathroom, she found Simon and Mectar foraging in her kitchen. She pushed them out and prepared eggbeaters and bacon for them. Mectar had several large glasses of milk.

As Beth began to clean up, she turned on the radio. Simon immediately perked up. He stood and turned up the radio. "That's Howard Stern," he said excitedly.

"You know who Howard Stern is?" Beth asked surprised.

"Oh, yeah, I listen to him all the time," said Simon.

"How do you know who Howard Stern is if you are from the future?" she demanded, immediately suspicious.

"The classics man, some of the funniest stuff I ever heard. It's like listening to live history." Beth looked at Simon skeptically.

"Listen Beth, in space there are no radios to listen to because the distances are too great. You can't watch video and pilot a ship but you can listen to audio. How many songs can I hear? Do you know what a Koim quartet sounds like?"

"A what?" asked Beth.

"Exactly," said Simon. You can pick up the local music when you are on planet like Koe, but there is nothing like Earth music, and how much of that can you listen to? I heard some of Howard's classic stuff, but it was centuries old. So one of the first things I did when I was experimenting with time travel was drop a recording device in Earth orbit that looked like a piece of space junk. NASA had no idea. Then I jumped thirty years ahead and ran it through a filter, and bang—I had thirty years of fresh listening. It was the best. When I am alone on a space flight I can listen to human instead of alien transmissions with all the twisted humor I like. I credit Howard Stern with helping me keep my sanity," said Simon conclusively.

"Didn't work," said Mectar.

"Mectar, is he telling the truth?" asked Beth.

Mectar looked at her and paused. "Unfortunately, yes. When I was in flight with Simon, he listened to this Howard Stern constantly. No, Simon has not retained his sanity."

"Did you like Howard Stern?" asked Beth

"He was weird," said Mectar. "I liked Robin Quivers more. She seemed rational. But I will tell you what I did find interesting. Last night while you were asleep I watched your TV. There is a channel that calls itself Discovery that did a program that reports what it calls science. There was a story about a place called Sedona, Arizona. The story claimed they had recorded paranormal activity there and that there was evidence of interdimensional travelers." As Mectar went on to mock the science of the report, Simon stared at the now blank TV and then at Beth.

"Beth, have you ever been to Arizona?" he asked.

"My dad was from there, not Sedona but Phoenix." As she said the word Phoenix, Simon choked on his coffee and began to cough. Mectar looked toward him, but Simon held up his hand and wiped his mouth with the napkin in the other hand. "I'm okay," he said.

"Are you sure you're okay?" Beth asked.

"Seems like a good place to rise out of the ashes" said Simon cryptically.

"What does that mean?" Beth asked.

Simon shrugged as Mectar changed the subject.

"I went out and got a paper," he said. "A researcher died at Organon last night. The map indicates Organon is near here."

As Simon and Mectar discussed the murder, Beth read the article about the murdered researcher, Larry Livermore. "Larry's dead?" she said, shocked.

"You knew him?" Said Simon.

"Yes. I met him at several conferences."

Simon sighed deeply as he read the article. "Well, Organon is where I'll be tonight," he said.

"We," corrected Mectar.

"We," agreed Simon. "Beth, I'm afraid you've got no choice. You must come with us."

She was putting the dishes in the dishwasher. "You don't hear me arguing, do you?" she said.

"No, I don't," said Simon.

"Beth, the guy who marries you is going to be one lucky guy," said Simon, now carrying his dishes to the sink.

She looked up at him with a puzzled look now that he was standing next to her. "Why?" she asked.

"I feel I intuitively understand you," said Simon.

"Do you really?" said Beth disdainfully, even though she sensed tenderness in him. "And what about Kathy?" she whispered so Mectar could not hear.

"Beth, there is no ..." Simon looked toward Mectar. "Are you comfortable out here, Mectar?" called Simon.

"And if I'm not?" asked the Kian.

"Tough," said Simon. "I'm going back to bed. It's 3:00 PM. I'll be getting up around 8:00 PM. We'll do this in the dark."

Simon walked back into the bedroom, leaving Beth with Mectar. The Kian sat silently looking out a window. After several minutes, he turned to her and spoke: "I need you to understand that I have no desire to kill you."

"And I need you to understand that I have no desire to be in the middle of this," answered Beth. "But I think I understand you. You see Benjamin as a threat to your entire planet, to the entire Kian race."

"And yet his alleged discovery protects us. That is why he is a focal point in time," said Mectar. "So, if he gets a few minutes of pleasure with you, I am not bothered."

"I don't imagine much bothers you," said Beth.

"Not much does," said Mectar, "although one thing did. His wife was with child when I killed her." Beth said nothing. As Mectar resumed staring out the window, she heard him mutter, "That bothered me."

I should hope it would, she thought, walking back to the bedroom.

Simon was asleep again. She stood in the doorway and watched him sleep, trying to envision his future. She felt compassion, pity, and fondness for him. She sat down in the bedroom chair and began reading a magazine. As she read, she couldn't help looking over the top of the magazine at him. She finally put the magazine down and crawled into bed with him. She gently ran an index finger along his scar, surprised at how hard it felt. She thought of the pain he must have felt when whatever caused it tore his flesh. Then she noticed an angry black-and-blue mark at the base of his neck. She lay there quietly with him for some time, going in and out of sleep herself.

Suddenly an explosion outside shook the apartment. Mectar screamed, "Cylots!" A brilliant flash blinded Beth temporarily. The smell of burning metal permeated the room. Mectar kicked the bedroom door open, stood inside the doorway, and fired back toward the apartment entrance. "The window," Mectar shouted. "Get out through the window."

Beth threw on pants and a sweatshirt. Grabbing her sneakers and leaving her purse, she climbed out the window onto the fire escape. Looking back, she saw Simon hopping on one leg while putting on his pants. "Go. Get her out of here," he shouted. Mectar and Beth raced down the fire escape ladder. Pulling on a shirt, Simon climbed out the window.

When Beth and Mectar reached the pavement, she looked up and saw Simon standing on the fire escape, firing back into the bedroom. Then, rather than come down the fire escape, he jumped the fifteen feet to the ground. Before jumping, he threw something into the apartment. As she watched his body hurtling toward the ground, the explosion of the grenade he had thrown followed him in flame and debris, completely gutting the apartment and, she was sure, killing or destroying anyone or anything in it.

Beth had been running with Mectar, looking over her shoulder at Simon, when the explosion occurred. She stopped and began to run back toward her apartment, screaming, "What have you done? What have you done to my home?"

Simon stood up halfway and said, "Beth, I had to." She swung her fist at him. He ducked under her blow and then sprang at her, catlike. Coming up with his shoulder at her waist, he picked her up and carried her.

She pounded on his back. "Put me down, you jerk!" She looked back at the flames leaping from her windows. They almost seemed to be alive, reaching out to grab her and Simon. "Run, goddamn it, run!" she yelled.

As Simon lumbered passed Mectar, the Kian fired something that emitted a force field. The field quickly formed a protective sphere around Beth, Simon, and Mectar. The flames hit the sphere, licked at it for a second, and then dissipated. The three ran to Beth's car.

"Range!" Simon screamed as he opened the front door of the passenger side and pushed Beth in. Beth tried to get up, but Simon pushed her back down into the seat and slammed the door.

Mectar pushed buttons on a handheld device. "I have no reading. We must be out of range momentarily." He climbed into the backseat, all the while facing the burning building. Simon jumped in the car, started it, and they sped out of the parking lot.

As they pulled away, Heinrich stepped out of the flaming apartment onto the fire escape. He was unscathed except for a few burning spots on his leather jacket. Looking up, he noticed a small flame flickering on his shoulder. He brushed his hand across it casually, extinguishing the flame. Then he took out his contact lenses and threw them to the ground. "Run, Simon," he muttered. His cold, ice blue eyes glared at the disappearing car. "This is between you and me now." Then he walked to the car he had come in, climbed in, and drove off in pursuit of Beth's car.

"Whatever humans the Cylots controlled, I'm sure you killed them all, Simon," said Mectar.

"How did they know where we were?" Simon asked Mectar.

"How in Grunduk's name do I know?" snapped the Kian.

"Let's not involve Kian mythological warriors. This is confusing enough already," responded Simon.

They both looked at Beth, who said, "I don't know."

As they turned a corner, Simon said, "Damn. I sure hope you had insurance, Beth."

"Not enough. Did you have to destroy everything I owned?" she asked angrily.

"Don't worry," he said. "If you live through this, some movie company will buy your story."

"If I live?" she asked.

"Mectar and I will do our best to make sure that happens. Don't worry. You're in good hands," said Simon. "Isn't that right, Mectar?" His cavalier manner told Beth that Simon, despite what he said earlier, loved what he was doing. He reveled in the fight and the flight. She looked at Mectar, who smiled craftily.

"Absolutely," he said. She noticed that his canine teeth looked larger than they had before.

As she turned away from him, Mectar set up a small apparatus on the narrow shelf behind the rear seat. Beth watched him in the rearview mirror. "What's that?" she asked as a small scanning dish on the little unit moved back and forth.

"A scanner. I think we are being followed. But I can't get a clear reading. If anything is there, it is at the edge of our range."

As Simon turned to look at the scanner, Beth noted that the motion made him wince. He began rubbing his neck and shoulder around the same area where she had seen the black-and-blue mark that morning. Looking closely, she saw that the mark had grown. It had crept above the collar line.

Meanwhile, Mectar disassembled the scanner and slipped the parts into a compartment of his jump belt. "I see nothing, Simon," he said, "but I am sure they are following us. We should have jumped."

"They won't catch us, Mectar," said Simon.

"Why don't we just jump? If a group of Cylots catches us, we're dead."

"To do this right," replied Simon, "we must stay sequential. We could miss something important if we don't—like the newspaper we read this morning, for example. Besides, if we jump, Grey is dead."

"What does she offer except physical pleasure for you?" Mectar demanded.

Simon glared at Mectar. Neither said anything.

"What's the matter, Mectar?" asked Simon. "Are you a little too close to the flame? Does it burn a little too hot for you? Then save yourself. Time jump. Get out of their way. But remember: you can't find the cure by running from the disease."

"I want to fuck you!" Mectar replied.

"Oh, Mectar, I didn't know you cared," Simon said, smiling.

Mectar, confused by Simon's amusement, looked at Beth Grey, whose head was down, shaking back and forth, her eyes closed. "I cursed wrong, didn't I?" said Mectar.

"Yes," she said.

"How do I curse at him correctly?"

"Tell him to go fuck himself," said Beth.

"Simon, go fuck yours …" Mectar stopped abruptly. "That's not possible. He cannot possibly fuck himself. Your species is incapable of that act."

Simon, laughing, said, "What difference does it make? Tell me to go fuck myself. If you want to curse at me, tell me to go fuck myself."

"Go fuck yourself, Simon," Mectar shouted, saliva forming around his mouth.

"That's it, Mectar. Say it with feeling," said Simon, barely restraining his laughter.

Mectar was quiet for a second. His face hardened. "Fine," he said. "We'll do it your way."

"Just how much trouble am I in?" she asked.

"If we leave you," Mectar answered, "you will die, horribly. They know who you are and they will kill you."

Simon took her hand. She looked into his brown eyes, whose pupils were nearly black. "I will not leave you until you are safe. I promise," he said.

"Can I believe you?" she asked softly. He smiled and nodded, his eyes communicating sincerity.

"Where are we going?" she asked.

"Well, first we need some clothes. I could use a jacket."

"I don't have any money. I didn't have time to grab my purse," said Beth. "Oh. Wait a minute." She rummaged in the glove compartment. "Damn it. I thought I had my MAC card in here."

"What's a MAC card?" asked Mectar.

"It's for a MAC machine. I can access my checking account from any machine by simply inserting the card."

"A MAC machine contains money?" asked Mectar.

"That's right," said Beth.

"Great," said Simon. "Let's go find a MAC machine."

"But I don't have my MAC card," she protested.

Simon said, "It's only a machine. Don't worry about it."

They found a MAC machine in a supermarket parking lot. Simon laid an electronic device on top of the machine and began to press numbers on both it and the MAC machine.

"Crap," he said. "I can't get my own damn machine to work. There must be something wrong with this intervector."

"Let me try," said Mectar. He placed an instrument on the console of the MAC machine, next to Simon's device, and began to press numbers on the MAC machine.

"Benjamin," said Beth. He didn't respond. "Benjamin," she repeated more emphatically.

"I'm sorry," he said, smiling.

"I have a question," said Beth.

Smiling warmly, he said, "You're just full of questions, aren't you?"

"Doesn't changing the past change the future? I mean, what happens if you go back in time and kill someone who has already lived?" asked Beth.

Simon snorted disdainfully. "Let's put that fable to rest once and for all," he said. All dimensions are totalities. All dimensions are simultaneous. All of up exists now, and so does all of time. Yesterday, today, and tomorrow all exist right now. You just don't have the physical receptors to see yesterday and tomorrow.

The only reason you see time the way you do is that we are sequential beings. It's called the arrow of time. You see three dimensions as totalities and the fourth only sequentially. Because humans are sequential, I'm here because I've lived to reach this point. If someone goes back in time and kills me in my past, then I never existed beyond that point. So what you are proposing is a null loop."

"So the universe is infinite and all four dimensions exist totally, right now?" asked Beth.

"Hard question. I think there are eleven dimension, some of which are quantum in nature."

"What does that mean?"

"Some are macro, like the universe, and some are micro or quantum, like a particle."

"How do you know there are other dimensions?" asked Beth.

"Two reasons. One: subatomic particles don't go in and out of existence; they go in and out of our plane of reality. Two: black holes suck matter out of the universe. Things leave this time space in a macro and a micro manner. Black holes suck matter out of the universe. But to where?" Simon asked. "Where is nowhere? Where does the matter go when it leaves the four-dimensional plane I live in? Maybe I'm not a dimensional creature. Look at it like a child's fable. There once was a little soul. He lived in a place with all the other souls. His teacher came to and said he needed to learn but to understand you must feel. How do you learn about food without tasting? So the little soul left for the class. The class was a narrow place for the soul—it was confined in just four dimensions, and to get there he had to go through a tunnel, small at one end and small at the other. But air and sky and taste and feeling didn't exist in the little soul's dimensions, because they were quantum in nature. These things existed only in the macro dimensions. It was like a ride, and at the end the little soul came back to his teacher and said, 'I know what fun is. Also, I know sadness and love. But when I am there, I want to learn more.'

"Now look at it from this side. You say you have a soul—how does it look to you from your tube of life, from the confining four dimensions you are in instead of the eleven your soul lives in? What are you learning, acceptance or hate? If the myth and the science are right, this is happening. All religions then reduce to a mathematical formula—one formula, one God. The language of God is math. Where do I go when I die? Where was I before I was born?"

Suddenly Mectar said, "Got it!" as the MAC machine's screen flashed on. "How much cash would you like?" Mectar punched a few more buttons on the gadget he had placed on the MAC's console. "This machine contains $44,283," he said. "How much do we need?"

"Hell, take $44,200," said Simon. "Let's leave eighty-three bucks. Why be greedy?"

"Done," said Mectar, punching still more buttons.

The MAC machine whirred and clicked, depositing bills in its console. Mectar opened the console, removed handfuls of money, and shoved them at Simon. Twenty-dollar bills poured out of the machine. "Here," said Simon, handing Grey about $15,000. "This should cover your furniture." Money dropped on the floor as they filled their pockets.

"It's too much!" she protested. He ignored her. She stuffed the bills into her pockets. The machine went silent, its screen flashing, "End of transaction."

Mectar walked back to the car, but Simon hesitated. He said, too quietly for Mectar to hear, "I'm sorry about your home. Paying for the damage with stolen money is not a good way, but right now it's the only way I have to help you," he said.

"It's all right Benjamin," she said.

As he turned to follow Mectar, he muttered, "It hasn't been all right in a long time." She followed him in silence.

Fifteen minutes after Simon, Beth, and Mectar drove away, Heinrich drove up and got out of his car. Holding a weapon in one hand and a tracking device in the other, he scanned the area around the MAC machine. He walked across the money scattered on the ground, ignoring it. Putting the weapon inside his coat, he got back in his car and drove away in the same direction taken by the fleeing trio.

15

The Stakeout

Leary drove down the ramp from Route 280 and inched his car through the reporters, news-channel vans, and onlookers clustered around the entrance to the parking lot of the West Orange Police and Criminal Justice Building. A patrolman moved the barricades, admitting Leary to the parking lot. His unmarked car blended in with the other municipal vehicles.

Leary climbed the back stairs and followed the arrows to the police desk. The sergeant on duty sat behind two inches of bulletproof glass.

"Can I help you?" the sergeant asked. His nametag said Doyle. Doyle was a powerfully built man, about five feet ten inches tall, with a full head of dark hair and a neatly trimmed mustache on his round face.

"Lieutenant Leary, Rahway Police, to see Bobby Joe," said Leary, smiling to himself.

"To see who?"

"Agent Cyrus, FBI task force."

Doyle found Leary's name on a clipboard and said, "The task force is meeting in Room 302. The stairs are on your left."

On his way into the conference room, a patrolman handed him a set of papers. Cyrus was seated behind a desk at the front of the room, calling the meeting to order and straightening a sheaf of papers by tapping them on the desk. "Gentlemen, can we take our seats please," he said, nodding acknowledgment of Leary's arrival. Leary looked around him. The room was filled with plainclothes and uniformed officers from various New Jersey municipalities. They were all investigating the murders of researchers at large pharmaceutical companies. Two plainclothes men sat in the corner behind Cyrus. Leary recognized Wheeler, whom he had met with Cyrus on his visit to Varley's house.

After a few welcoming remarks, Cyrus plunged ahead in his no-nonsense fashion. "As you all know," he said, "our resources are being stretched almost beyond our ability to handle these homicides. So it's important for us to coordinate our efforts.

"The MO in most of the incidents is identical." He paused, then added, "and disturbing. In the last five days, we have, in sequential order, as best as we can make this out, the following:

"On the evening of June 15, a researcher who goes by the name Yugen at a lab just off the Merck campus in Rahway is murdered. That same night, on the Merck site itself, a man originally presumed to be Leonard Javic is also murdered. His hands and face were blown off by a shotgun and he is wearing no socks or underwear. Javic is, or was, head of a research project and a known associate of Yugen's. Eric Bottoms, a research assistant of Javic's, was missing. We have completed DNA testing of the corpse presumed to be Javic's. We now know that corpse is that of Eric Bottoms," said Cyrus, looking at Leary. "It is Leonard Javic who is missing. Also missing is Beth Grey from the same facility, another of Javic's research assistants. We have reason to believe that she may still be alive and in the company of two male Caucasians who right now are prime suspects in this case.

"Ted Gomez, the last one of Javic's research assistants, commits suicide the next afternoon at a psychologist's office in Manhattan. I would have liked to question that psychologist, but he blew his brains out in Vermont the next morning. As near as we can tell, his family predeceased him by a few hours at their home. The little girl's eyes and part of her brain looked like they had been eaten. We are dealing with a real sicko here, people.

"We have one witness to the murder of Walter Harris and his secretary at Chanel. We are trying to stabilize her now. Her name is Abigail Clarendon. She alleges she saw a perpetrator who was not one of the two male Caucasians. He was using the name of Heinrich. There is a description of him in your information packets. Abby Clarendon is under sedation and we were not able to get much more out of her.

"Last night, Dr. Livermore, here at Organon in West Orange, was murdered. His secretary, Sylvia Walinski, was murdered at the same time. I will briefly mention other peripheral murders in the same period, aside from Varley's wife and daughter, which we assume was probably to get to Varley: Livermore's secretary, two guards at Merck, and three research workers at the Payne Whitney Institute, in New York.

"All these researchers had their brains blown out with a weapon we cannot identify. The West Orange coroner's report stated that while Livermore's head was blown apart, the wall behind him was unmarked, and no projectile passed through his brain.

"The cause of Livermore's secretary's death was the same. Her brain is burned internally, as though someone took a red-hot poker and pushed it through the forehead and out the back of her head.

"We are dealing with something we have never seen before. Forensics has no clue, either. I've heard theories about ultrasound or microwave radiation powering some form of new weapon. But as I understand it, such weapons would take too long to build up a large enough modulation or frequency to inflict this type of injury."

As Cyrus spoke, Leary pored over police reports he had been given.

Leary sat in the back of a large training room. Cyrus and his assistants sat behind a table at the front of the room. Behind them on the blackboard was the sequence of events and possible lines of investigation.

One by one, the officers in charge of the individual investigations discussed the unique features of each case and presented their findings to date. Finally, Cyrus asked Leary to stand and describe the events at Merck.

Leary explained that after the murders at Merck, Javic's lab was burglarized and several guards were killed in a gunfight. The weapons used in the gunfight left burn holes that went right through the guards' bodies, as though someone had shot them with twenty thousand volts of electricity. There was no apparent reason for the guards to have had a shootout with anyone.

An interior wall on the first floor of Building 80, site of the shootout, had been severely scorched. Also, a hole had been made in a concrete block exterior wall of the same building.

"At this time," Leary said, "the Rahway police cannot figure out what made the hole in the concrete blocks. There was no rubble or debris. The damaged concrete seems to have been pulverized into dust. The scorch marks on the interior wall look like those made by an electric arc welder, rather than a flame."

Leary surmised that other labs in which researchers had been killed might have been broken into after the murders, and he recommended staking them out. With that, Leary thought he had finished his part of the presentation.

"You're not telling us everything, are you, Leary?" Cyrus asked in a bored monotone voice, as though suffering great fatigue. "Tell us about Grey." Leary looked down at his feet and then out the window. He reddened as though deeply embarrassed. "Don't be ashamed, boy," said Cyrus loudly in a thick southern accent. "Tell us what you saw."

"I saw Grey the afternoon after the murders at Merck," Leary said, now looking at the ceiling.

"But she's still missing," said Cyrus. "She has been since the night of the murders. When did you see her?"

"I saw her in a corridor of Building 80 at about 1:30 in the afternoon. I rounded a corner and there she stood with two male Caucasians, one six feet tall, 190 pounds, the other at least six feet six, 300 pounds. The smaller one was yelling at the larger one about what time it was. Whether it was 1:30 AM or PM. Grey walked toward me and said she needed my help. Then she handed me an earring." Leary stopped.

"And then what happened, Detective Leary?" demanded Cyrus.

"Then she disappeared," Leary said.

"Did she go poof when she disappeared?"

"No," said Leary, now staring at Cyrus angrily.

"What happened to the two male Caucasians?"

"They disappeared too."

"Did you see any little green men?" Cyrus asked derisively. Laughter permeated the room at Cyrus's question and Leary's obvious discomfort.

"All right, people, now settle down," Cyrus shouted, now all business. "Fact of the matter is there is another witness, an Officer Jefferson, who saw the same thing Detective Leary did, and Leary has the earring to prove it. Whether it is true or not, whether these two male Caucasians disappeared or whether it was some hypnotic trick, is yet to be determined. Has anyone else had a similar experience?" Cyrus asked. The room became silent. "Only Leary, huh? Well, Detective Leary. Thank you for your observations.

"That brings us to Beth Grey. Her picture is in your information packets as well. It is possible that she is being held prisoner by the two male Caucasians and has information crucial to this case. The importance of her capture—alive—cannot be understated. If any contact with her is made, notify me personally, immediately." Cyrus broke the last word in two for emphasis.

"We will be staking out every facility where there's been a murder or that might be connected to this ... crime wave. We have already cleared with your superiors your participation in this." Leary was handed a sheet that showed he was to stake out the Merck facility in Rahway. Leary approached Cyrus as the meeting broke up.

"Yes, Leary?" Cyrus asked, anticipating Leary's question.

"I don't want to stake out Merck. I think there may be some activity at Organon tonight."

"And just why is that?"

"Because I think there is something going on."

"How long did it take you to reach that conclusion?" Cyrus asked sarcastically.

"I mean," said Leary through tight lips, "that at each of these facilities, someone is looking for something. I think someone will be looking for something at Organon tonight."

"Fine, Leary. You want to stake out Organon tonight? Go ahead. You might as well make yourself useful. Arrange it with Wheeler."

"Did you read the coroner's report I gave you?" asked Cyrus.

Leary shook his head. "No, I just got the papers. I haven't been allowed near the bodies since your crime lab boys got there. There's more you're not telling us, isn't there?"

"Those cops at Rahway all died of sudden brain trauma," said Cyrus.

"I thought you said that electrical shocks or gunshots killed them?"

"They were shot, but they were dead before that happened. They all had some kind of damage to the central nervous system. It was as though they were electrocuted before they were shot, by electrodes hooked up to their bodies."

"Then what's the cause of death?" asked Leary.

Cyrus shook his head. "Take your pick. Either they were shot while dead, or they were able to move after they died. We don't know which," said Cyrus. "We found this in some of the bodies." Cyrus held up a small Ziploc bag containing what looked like a two-inch needle. "We have several of these now, pulled out of the bodies of some of the dead. They were found in the back of the neck. We don't think they are enough to cause death by themselves, but they are highly electrically active. We don't know what they are. There's another problem that has us baffled. The researchers are being shot in the head. But we've found no bullet holes in the walls and none in the bodies."

"Then how are they being shot?" asked Leary.

"We don't know. So far I've heard two theories, neither of which I buy."

"What are they?" asked Leary.

"One says they were killed by a laser, the other by ultrasound. But police pathologists tell me that a laser would leave a scorch mark on the wall and that ultrasound wouldn't blow the heads apart from within. Whatever the weapon is, it leaves scorch marks through the brain, and the center of the brain is virtually routed out."

"Are we dealing with some pathological criminal?" asked Leary.

"No, everything's much too precise scientifically," said Cyrus.

As Leary and Cyrus finished talking, Patrolman Murphy came up to them, followed by a man who stood about five-eleven, had dark hair, glasses, and a big nose. His blue rumpled suit looked as though he had slept in it.

"Agent Cyrus," said Murphy, "this is Dr. Mueller, from Rockefeller University. The one I was telling you about."

"Dr. Mueller, pleased to meet you," said Cyrus. Mueller shook Cyrus' hand.

"Lieutenant Leary, Rahway Police," said Cyrus. Leary shook Mueller's hand.

"I was there when Simon died," said Mueller. "I'm here to help you in any way I can. How is your investigation proceeding?"

"We can use all the help we can get," said Cyrus.

"I understand that you are going on a stakeout tonight," said Mueller.

"Actually," said Cyrus, "we'll do several stakeouts, at every pharmaceutical plant where there's been a murder."

"Well, I'd like to join you," said Mueller.

"I have no problem with that, but I think the best thing you can do is stay here at the command center. Use the time to go over the records this afternoon, and if there's any action, we'll contact you and you can go right to the scene."

Cyrus stopped speaking and looked over to a group of agents who had just appeared in the hall. "Wheeler," Cyrus shouted, motioning for him to come over. "Al, you met Leary here the other day. This is Dr. Mueller."

"Al Wheeler, FBI," said Wheeler shaking hands with Mueller and Leary. Wheeler was as tall as Leary but a bit heavier, about 250 pounds. He had piercing blue eyes, which looked over Leary from the gold rims of the glasses perched on the end of his nose. The soles of his shoes, Leary thought, were inordinately thick. When Wheeler spoke, the lights from overhead reflected off his scalp through his thinning hair.

"I want Leary at Organon tonight. Set him up with that surveillance crew."

"No problem," Wheeler said, motioning with his head for Leary to follow him.

"If you'll excuse me," said Leary, "I've got some things to do. Nice meeting you, Dr. Mueller." Leary followed Wheeler down the hall.

"I'll see you in about twenty minutes," Cyrus said to Leary as he walked away.

"We'll open up our complete files to you," said Cyrus to Mueller as they walked down the hall. "They're downstairs in the office. Agent Wheeler will debrief you. Perhaps you can help Wheeler find something we have missed. Stay as long as you want tonight. The stakeouts go right through 'till dawn."

"I'd like to see everything," said Mueller. "You never know what might be helpful."

"No problem," said Cyrus.

Wheeler came running up. "Boss," he said breathlessly. "Big explosion in Parsippany at some garden apartments. In Beth Grey's unit. She's the missing Merck researcher."

"Wasn't anyone staking out her apartment?" asked Cyrus.

"We just don't have enough men," said Wheeler.

"Shit! You've got Mueller," Cyrus said to Wheeler. Then Cyrus rushed out to a squad car and headed to Grey's apartment.

16

The Microphysics of Biochemistry; Where Does Consciousness Reside?

After driving the short distance to West Orange, they parked near a group of stores on a hill behind Organon. Behind the stores was a school with a playing field they would have to cross before they got to the Organon property. Between the stores and the field was a small hill.

Before they began what Mectar called "The Operation," he wanted to "scan" it. As Beth waited for Mectar to set up some equipment, she turned to Simon and said, "I have a question."

"Another one?" asked Simon, waiting for Mectar to finish setting up the scanner.

"How does time travel work?" Beth asked.

"Time has mass," said Simon.

Beth thought for a moment and then said, "That's impossible."

"Oh no, my dear. It isn't," Simon asserted. "Space tells mass how to move, and mass tells space how to bend. There is no action without an equal and opposite reaction. If time did not have mass, it could not react with mass. Mass slows time. You know that. How can mass force a concept to respond? Time only responds because it is a thing, matter. Time is matter. That is what makes the universe you see finite. If mass bends timespace, which is what the theory of relativity is all about, then timespace itself must have mass."

Simon fumbled with a device Beth didn't recognize. "Think about it, Beth. Time has to have mass. Newton said every action must have an equal and opposite reaction. You agree with Newton, don't you?" Simon asked rhetorically. She nodded her compliance.

"Einstein said that mass bends timespace and that timespace tells mass how to move. That was proven during your time. Think how your scientists use gravitational lenses, the bending of timespace by large masses in space such as stars or planets, to determine a star's size, brightness, and distance from our solar system. If time is a component of timespace, and mass bends timespace, and every action has an equal and opposite reaction, then timespace must have mass. You can't move something that doesn't have mass. Also, mass slows time—you weigh anything down and it slows down."

"Space is made up of reacting particles," said Beth. "It's the particles that react."

"So time must have its own subatomic particle. I call it a time-on." Seeing her confusion, he continued, "Let's look at it from the subatomic point of view. According to Neils Bohr's quantum probability theory, you can't locate a subatomic particle. You can only tell where it probably is located. If you interpolate, and look at ten events, in three of those ten events, the particle isn't even there." Giving Beth his full attention, Simon continued, "In short, the particle goes in and out of existence, in and out of our time space. Einstein said that subatomic particles' behavior indicates that not all events occur in our reality plane. Bohr and others agree with him. If timespace is indeed a finite matrix, then things occur outside the matrix. That's why time has mass. It's totally consistent with macrophysics, microphysics, and the findings of every physicist worth his salt."

"It can't be," said Beth, bewildered. "Timespace is a dimension. It can't have mass," she said, pumping a clenched fist up and down for emphasis. "It's like saying up and down have mass."

"They do," said Simon tiredly. "First, let's dispose of the scientific beliefs you once held as true." Simon sighed, closed his eyes halfway, then paused as though trying to remember something. Then he said, "'The doctrine that the Earth is neither the center of the universe nor immovable, but moves, even with daily rotation, is absurd and both philosophically and theologically false, and at least an error of faith.' Those were the words of the Roman Catholic conclave against Galileo. In spite of clear evidence to the contrary, the church clung to a false idea. This is not debatable. It's fact. So don't you, Beth, cling to an old idea."

"But time is a dimension," Beth said hesitantly, as though trying to assimilate Simon's assertions. Her brow furrowed.

"Fuck it," he said. "This is not a physics class, okay?" He walked away abruptly.

Mectar, having completed his scan for Cylots and satisfied that none were close, leaned against the car with his arms folded. He looked uncomfortable and then burped. "There's no way you could know who Simon is," he told Beth.

"What do you mean?"

"In his time, he redefined physics not just for Earth but for my planet as well. If he has a scientific idea, I suggest you listen to it."

"Why doesn't he have a bunch of degrees?" Beth asked.

Mectar shrugged. "How can I say it to you, Grey? He does not take the classes; he writes the textbooks. When he talks about science, to be honest with you, I don't always understand him."

"He's crazy. Time doesn't have mass," she said. "It can't. Time is a dimension."

"No," said Mectar, shaking his head. "I don't understand it. But all the best minds centuries from now agree. Time does have mass. He proved it to them and laid the groundwork for time travel. His research catapulted him into a time beyond the period he and I come from. He became a focal point, and his intellect makes him as tough an individual as I've ever met. Things aren't as they appear. No one would argue that Kians are not the fiercest warriors." Mectar changed his shape as he spoke. Before Beth's eyes, he became a Kian in full military configuration, with four arms, scales, and lizard-like eyes. "But Simon is tougher than anything I have ever encountered. If Simon seems to relent, he is simply choosing not to fight. I have never seen him back away from a battle he considered worth fighting."

Beth backed slowly away from Mectar until she bumped into a parked car. "Yes," she said meekly, stunned by the Kian's transformation, as though she had never realized just what Mectar was. The change in Mectar seemed to cause discomfort in him, as though he had an upset stomach. He burped again then, licking his lips, continued.

"I'm sorry if I surprised you," Mectar said, returning to a human shape. If Simon says time has mass, then time has mass. Yet he so often says things that are clearly untrue, lies, that I occasionally cannot separate lie from truth."

"I guess I understand Simon better now," said Beth.

"Do you?" Mectar asked contemptuously and then he hiccupped.

"Yes. The night he saved my life, he fought one of those creatures you say are after you, the Cylots."

"They would have killed him if you'd had the bracelet on," said Mectar. "It controls a force field around him. If you had been wearing the bracelet, you would have been protected by that field instead of Simon."

"But I did have the bracelet on."

"What do you mean?" asked Mectar.

"This creature came out of nowhere and stabbed him with a dagger made of light. He threw the creature to the floor and fired at it. Then it disappeared," said Beth.

"The Cylot stabbed him?" Mectar asked, incredulous.

"Yes. In the hallway at Merck."

"That's impossible," said Mectar.

"What did you just tell me about Simon?" asked Beth. "Is he human?"

"That has been my impression," said Mectar. "My impression has also been that nothing about Simon is quite what it seems to be." Mectar stopped as though catching his breath.

"Are you all right?" asked Beth.

Mectar bent over, his hands on his knees. "Yes," he said. "Let's go."

Mectar and Beth caught up with Simon, who was at the edge of the building setting up a disruption field.

"This, Mectar, my operations lizard, is how to set up a disruption field before entering a building." Mectar bent over suddenly and threw up.

The attack was as quick as it was unexpected. One minute Beth was discussing science and the next she was in the middle of a firefight. Only Mectar's bending over to throw up saved his life. Rough hands pulled her down as the shots flew. What looked like two humans were trying to subdue Simon, who was fighting for all he was worth and getting beaten up for his effort. Beth struggled to get up but was pushed down and held on the ground. A voice with a thick accent she did not recognize said, "Please, for your own safety be still."

An explosion ripped off the edge of the building by the manicured berm. She turned to see Simon reach for his phaser, get hit in the gut, and double over, his force field not protecting him. He was then kicked in the back of the knee and fell to the ground. She heard one of the men attacking him say, "Sir, please stop and listen."

Simon was pinned to the ground when one of the men holding him down said something softly in his ear. Simon went limp, no longer resisting. She then heard someone shout, "Clear," and she was released.

She stood up to see dead Kian bodies and a little man directing nearly everyone in a quick cleanup. He was no more than four feet nine inches tall, but with the stacked heels on his black boots he stood nearly five feet tall. He had a flowing black beard and long, curly jet-black hair. There were three humans and three Kians working to clean the dead Kians from the scene of the attack. They would throw thin sheets over the body parts, point something at the sheet that looked like a small flashlight, and it would disappear.

Simon was trying to stop his nose from bleeding. He was cut over his eye. Mectar, as sick as he had been a moment ago, was in a rage. The small man who Beth was not quite sure was human was trying to placate him when a bird of a species she had never seen before flew in at a speed she thought impossible. It landed on the small man's shoulder and chirped in a strange way. The small man nodded and the bird flew off.

"What do you mean *I* was their target?" Roared Mectar to one of the Kians. Mectar grabbed the Kian by the throat.

"Stop. It is true. Selfridge found out about the plot to have you killed and sent us to stop it."

"How did Selfridge find out about a plot to have me killed?"

"He is on Kia," said Razqual. Razqual watched Beth tend to Simon's wound but said nothing. She was dabbing at a cut over his eye with a tissue trying to stop the bleeding.

"Kia is under attack?" Mectar asked.

"No," responded Razqual, "he came alone with better technology so Kia could fight the Cylots."

"Then why am I a target?"

"Because there was only one thing he wanted in trade for the technology."

"What was that?" demanded Mectar.

"When you returned from this mission you be named the head of the Kian military," said Razqual.

"What?" Mectar was incredulous.

"Some in the Kian army plotted a coup to take the technology and kill you. They did not want to give up power. Did you think that you would be sent out with Simon and not be as well protected as possible?" asked Razqual.

Mectar stared at Razqual digesting this information. Simon asked Mectar if he was okay and Mectar silently nodded, wiping his mouth.

"Who are you?" asked Beth.

"Yes," said Mectar, "who are you? You show up at an interesting moment with strange information. Simon, do you know him?'

"Let him tell you," said Simon.

"My name is King Razqual the Twelfth, from the planet Pardor, in the double star system we call Sfnar." He said this with a flourish and then he bowed low, as though he'd given her a formal introduction. "I owe a debt to Selfridge," he said, straightening. "The payment of that debt is to guard him," said Razqual, pointing at Mectar, "until I don't have to guard him anymore."

"When is that?" asked Simon.

"When I say so," said Razqual.

Beth's brow knitted, her eyes narrowed, and she stared hard at Razqual. "What sort of debt do you owe Selfridge that needs to be paid with your own life?" she asked.

"You have no understanding," said Razqual with contempt. "I am a king. I have a king's obligation to my people. If that obligation requires my life, so be it," he said with a flourish.

"If you are a king," said Mectar, "who sits on the throne in your absence?"

"My brother," said Razqual.

"And couldn't your brother usurp your power?"

"You do not understand my race, my people, and certainly not my brother. Let me first tell you of my brother. He was a general in the army during our war with the planet Dardia. Both of our planets revolve around the sun Kronos. Theirs is the larger planet. Ours, Pardor, is the smaller. Our people have a long history of commerce. The Dards coveted our wealth, and so they began their attacks. They launched an expeditionary force that landed on our planet, and city by city they began to take control of our world. They were barbarians, slaughtering our people. We went to our trading partners for help but received little, for they feared the Dards as well.

"My brother led a force that was holding the town of Tormono. His son was captured by the Dards in the fighting. What do you call your communication devices here in this timeperiod?" said Razqual.

"What do you mean?" asked Beth.

"If you were to make long-distance communication, what would you call it? What device do you use here?" he said, waving his finger at Beth.

"You mean the telephone?"

"Yes. Then, by telephone, the Dards contacted my brother, who was in charge of the defense of Tormono, and said they had captured his son, and that if he did not surrender the town they would murder his son. My brother asked to talk to his son to verify that they indeed had him. When his son got on the telephone my brother said to his son, 'Be brave, my son. Tormono must not fall.'"

Tears welled in Razqual's eyes. "My brother listened to the shots that killed his son, my nephew. He was a good boy. Tormono did not fall. This event led to a victory for us at Tormono and we began to push the Dards back. Our trading partners brokered a peace conference, which I attended.

"It was then that I fell captive to the Dard expeditionary force, at the spaceport. Another deal was then brokered, as my people wanted me back and the Dard army wished to evacuate. I would lead the Dard expeditionary force through our defenses, so they could escape and leave our planet. My life guaranteed their safety.

"Again they lied, and I remained their captive after their safe escape was granted. My people called me Razqual the Great after that. Now I am known by them as Razqual the Absent."

"But what about Selfridge? How then do you owe him a debt?" said Beth.

"I languished in a Dard prison. To be perturbed in the face of vicissitudes befits jackals. Caged monarchs can acquit themselves well only by showing contempt for the dungeon and the jailer. The fighting had weakened our planet—factories were destroyed, homes ruined. Do you know what it is like to be exiled from your homeland, remote from your family and loved ones? You compose yourself and endure patiently the torments of days and nights. I was ridiculed by those Dard weaklings who vanquished me by virtue of their numbers, not by their individual determination.

"The Dards were making plans for a greater attack upon us when Selfridge's fleet, if you can call it that," said Razqual with disdain, "came through our sector of space on their way to fight the Cylots. We had heard of the space plague that the Cylots were. We had also heard of Selfridge, yet his fleet seemed insignificant. Just a few black ships. They were undetected until they contacted us. Selfridge heard of my plight and asked to see me. The Dards refused. I am told that he was amused at that meeting as they threatened him. Then one day he stood in my cell. The guards did not even know he was there. He just appeared. I did not know where he came from. I know now."

"Where was that?"

"His jump belt allowed him full access to me, he ignored the Dard order that he could not see me. I told him my story. He listened and asked me if I would like to return to my planet. 'Of course,' I said. But I did not think he could help. He told me I should be careful not to become trapped by my own conceptions. He admonished me that I should not allow my desire to cloud my understanding. Then he handed me a jump belt and said, 'Let's go.'

"For a mere moment I was on the bridge of his ship. Then I was back in my own throne room on my own planet. He announced he was imposing a peace on both our worlds, and he needed the resources of our planetary armies for his fight, which we would give freely. If we gave nothing that was acceptable, but we were not allowed to fight. He freed me, and then he claimed that he would fight both of us, Pardor and Dardia, to keep the peace. Then he said he had to leave and he would leave an emissary in one small ship to keep the peace.

"Months passed. Dardia continued to build a force to attack us again. The emissary warned Dardia and told them that if any ship crossed a certain demarcation line in space, that ship would be destroyed. Then he told us the same thing.

"My generals wanted to attack Dardia in a preemptive strike. We knew through our spies the date they would launch their invasion. We assembled our fleet in space, and as we did so, the emissary came to me and warned me not to cross the line of demarcation or my fleet would be destroyed. I remembered Selfridge's warning not to be trapped by my conceptions. I felt if there was so little shown, there must be much hidden. So with caution I followed his suggestion.

"The emissary was in space as well, in his own ship, broadcasting a warning to both of us. The Dardians disregarded it and crossed the line of demarcation. Before our fleet could attack, the Dardian fleet was destroyed by Selfirdge's force.

"They came like a whirlwind, out of nowhere, and showed no mercy. They were not on any of our scanners. I tell you, they did not exist in our time space." Those who retreated behind the line of demarcation were not pursued or touched. My generals recommended strongly that we attack the Dardian fleet, now that they had been dealt such a blow. My brother demanded it as well, hoping to avenge the death of his son. But my instinct, and my instinct alone, was not to pursue. Some called me Razqual the Coward that day. My order was obeyed.

"One of the wings, a young commander named Petri, whose family had perished in a Dard attack, charged a vulnerable flank of the Dard who were on the other side of the line of demarcation. The destruction of his battle wing by Selfridge was merciless. Then, others among my people called me Razqual the Wise. When the battle was over, my brother summed it up best: he called me Razqual the Realist.

"Selfridge plucked me from a Dardian prison hole, restored me to my throne, and imposed a peace—not a perfect one, but there is no bad peace. You would not understand, Grey."

"There is no good war and there is no bad peace," said Simon. Razqual nodded.

"My people, my planet was safe. When I finally saw the emissary after the battle, I demanded to know the cost of this protection, what tribute Selfridge demanded. But the emissary told me there was none and offered me a standard constitution that my planet could be a signatory to, a standard galactic constitution whose signatories would benefit from and be obliged to support. This meant I would have to support, with troops and money, the fight against the Cylots. For that, I would be protected with the force and money of the combined federation from Cylot attack. Dardia was offered the same constitution.

"Any domestic policy on my planet was to be my purview alone. Democracy, theocracy, dictatorship—it mattered not to Selfridge. But galactic politics there were stringent rules. If I did not sign, he would simply vacate this sector of the galaxy, exposing it to possible Cylot attack, a policy of benign neglect. I was forced to sign, in the best interest of my people. If I did not sign I would be open not only to Dardian attack but to Cylot attack as well. If I did sign, there would be no tribute. It was not a tax but my contribution, my planet's contribution, to protecting the whole. And who was to run that whole? Selfridge was dictatorial in his power. We agreed, and we signed. But we had incurred—rather I had incurred—a death obligation.

"As king, within the social mores of my world, my life was forfeit to Selfridge. He had saved me from a Dard prison. How could I remain on my throne? So I went to him and explained that I could not stay on my throne as long as this debt remained unpaid. He had given me my life back. He had saved my planet. So I came to his court as his equal and as his petitioner. So that I could continue to rule on my world, I needed relief from this debt.

"If you are a king and you search the faces of the least of your subjects and courtiers as they petition you for your favor, some are rabbits in their faintness of heart, some foxes in their cunning, and some are snakes in their vileness." Razqual looked hard at Beth. "So I asked him for relief from this debt. It was in this vein he told me of Mectar and constructed a concise repayment plan. Protect Mectar from all threats, with my life, if necessary."

"Why wouldn't Selfridge have sent his best soldier? Wouldn't that have been more effective?" asked Beth.

"One soldier versus the resources of a King?" Razqual raised one eyebrow. "Clearly you have no idea of the scope of what I have been asked to do."

"I need no protection from the likes of you," Mectar blustered.

"Yeah right," said Simon.

"I have said my good-byes to all in my family. I will see or speak to them only if I complete my mission. My last will has been filed on my planet. There I am considered dead. And so here my payment is being made, Grey."

"I need no protection from you or Selfridge," Mectar burped. He made a face as though he had tasted something vile.

"What the hell is wrong with you?" asked Simon. Mectar ignored him.

"So, is my debt paid, Simon?" asked Razqual.

"Yes. Tell Selfridge I said your debt is paid. You can go home."

"It is good to know I am free of debt, but I cannot go home. I am trapped by the fight, like you. I cannot escape this until it is finished, because if I leave, all I love will die. Isn't that so, Simon?

"Yes," said Simon softly, and then he turned back to the disruptor to make sure the field was still in place.

Razqual turned to Mectar. "There are weapons, Mectar, that attack our very essence. That is why your mission is so very important."

"Wait, Simon," said Mectar. Simon stopped and turned toward the Kian. "Grey said that a Cylot stabbed you the other night at Merck," said Mectar. "Is that true?"

Simon looked disgustedly at Beth.

"Listen," she said defensively, "Mectar is just trying to save his planet. He is just trying to save his family, like you are trying to save yours."

Simon snorted disdainfully. "Being around you, Grey, has been the best and worst thing to happen to me in the last ten years, but Mectar doesn't know shit. Yes, Mectar. A Cylot tried to inject me. If it had been successful, I would have been dead."

Then, turning to Beth, Simon said, "Now I have two of you to deal with. He still thinks this fight is between Earth and Kia. I used to think that too. I was wrong. This fight isn't about physics, either. It's about the microphysics of bio-chemistry. It's about awareness." Razqual nodded.

As Simon spoke, Mectar stared up at the night sky. It was brilliant with stars. Slowly, Mectar raised his hand and pointed to a star. He said, "There is Kia, Grey. It revolves around that star." In his voice, Beth thought she heard a tinge of nostalgia, perhaps caring. "And there," he continued slowly, majestically sweeping his hands to both right and left, "is our empire. Nothing has yet stopped us. And now we have come here to Earth. Earth won't stop us either." He looked squarely at Simon. "The fight isn't about physics. It isn't about biochemistry or awareness. It's about Kia defeating Earth." He jabbed his finger toward Simon's chest. "It's about the space between Earth and Kia and who controls it."

"You're wrong," said Simon. "The fight isn't about the space around us but the space within us. Because within us, the change in biochemistry, the change in awareness, changes the entire universe. To threaten you, all I need to do is change your awareness. If this is the most damage I bring to your world, Mectar, who can say what is good and what is bad? If I bring a change of awareness to you, Miss Grey, who can say what is good or what is bad?"

"You sound like Selfridge," Razqual said with a smirk. Simon ignored him.

"Where does consciousness reside, Mectar?" Simon demanded. "Is it in your brain, or is that just the organ that houses it? Where does consciousness itself come from? Beth Grey here has replaced every cell in her body in the last two years. Science has proven that human bodies do that. Yet if every atom of the Beth Grey that existed two years ago is different from those of the Beth Grey who is here before me now, how does she remember the taste of choc-o-late?" said Simon, mocking Mectar's inflection. "Consciousness exists where electrons exist."

Beth interjected, "You know, he's right, Mectar. Radioactive isotope studies done in Oak Ridge Laboratories during the 1980s showed that humans can replace 98 percent of the atoms in their bodies in less than a year. We make a new liver every six weeks and a new skin once a month. The configurations of our bone cells remain somewhat constant, but atoms pass freely back and forth through the cell walls. So, a human acquires a new skeleton every three months. The brain cells we have now weren't there last year. Even our DNA, which is genetic material, comes and goes every six weeks."

"So where does consciousness reside, Mectar?" asked Simon, smiling approvingly at Beth for her contribution. "Is it simply a function of the chemicals in your brain? Is your brain different from your mind? If not, then when you're dead and your brain remains in your body, what becomes of your mind, of your consciousness? The only thing that's missing is the electricity that travels across the synapses of the brain. If energy can be neither created nor destroyed, then where did that electricity go? Is consciousness the chemical manifestation of your body, or the electrical manifestation of your soul?"

"You are an asshole, Simon," said Mectar. "We have been over this ground before. Are you going to talk to me about God again? There is no God. There is here. There is now. There is you. There is me. That is all."

Beth looked puzzled, Razqual intent. "Explain," she said. "Help me to understand."

"A disruptor field prevents Cylots from getting inside where we are. Think of it as a cap. They cannot penetrate our immediate space. But these disruptor fields operate on certain frequencies. I did not set up the disruptor field to keep Kians out, or Mectar could not have followed." Then Simon turned to Beth. "Now I'll give you the rest of it. I'll give it to you in simple steps, in your timeframe," he said.

"Number one: Benveniste proved that electricity retains memory."

"All right," said Beth. "I'll accept that."

"Number two: Death is defined as the absence of electricity in the body. Your brain is still there, but without electricity there is no mind. There is no electricity going across the brain's synapses. Your heart is still there, but the AV nodes don't pump because the electricity is gone. Right?"

"Right," said Grey, nodding.

"Number three: Energy can be neither created nor destroyed. Both Newton and Einstein support that bit of science.

"Number four: Electrons—the electricity that has to be there for one to have a mind isn't there all the time; they pop in and out of our existence.

"Number five: They keep the same characteristics as particles when they are not in our four dimensions. This means our minds exist outside our plane of reality, the four dimensions we live in.

"So then," said Simon, "electricity contains your memory. But it's not housed biologically. The cells go in and out of existence within a two-year period. The electricity leaves when you're dead, and electricity containing your memory can be neither created nor destroyed. If consciousness is contained in the electricity and those very electrons go in and out of our four dimensions, doesn't it stand to reason that your consciousness exists in the other seven dimensions? Now, what have we just proved, or agreed to, Grey?"

"A scientific basis for consciousness after death," Beth said softly, as the explanation sank in. She was beginning to realize the depth of Simon's science. She looked at him in awe.

"Jesus," she said, stepping backward. "You mean you can measure a quantifiable out-of-body awareness, a soul?"

Simon nodded. "The continued awareness can be verified scientifically. What kind of world are we entering when we die? Is it a dimension outside timespace? A place that creates the particles that pop into existence? And if such a place exists, what is its name? Heaven? Nirvana?"

"So that's what you and Yugen were doing, looking for an entry to that other dimension?" asked Beth.

"No," Simon snorted. "I'm trying to find a way to prevent the human race from getting slaughtered. Listen. Do you know how engineers build a tunnel through a mountain? They start digging on both sides and meet in the middle."

"Yes," said Grey.

"Well, Yugen was a biologist. You know how a biologist describes life, a combination of chemicals and such." Beth nodded. "Well, I'm a physicist, and we are looking for the bridge between biology and physics. Can we connect biology to quantum mechanics? If you ask a biologist what life is made up of, he says chemicals. If you ask a quantum field physicist what life is like, he will tell you it consists of atoms, and that these atoms consist of subatomic particles, and that these subatomic particles are not material objects but fluctuations of energy in a field of energy. In short, the biologist sees matter and the physicist sees energy. What did Einstein say about energy?"

"That it can't be destroyed," said Beth softly.

"Then the perception we have of our bodies is wrong. Our bodies are not material objects. We only perceive them that way. They are fields of energy that we perceive to be our bodies. Your perception of the human body is that we are made up of molecules. As these molecules move around, they produce thought. But the human body is not a physical machine that has learned how to think. You know what I see, Grey? If we were to look at the atoms in your brain, and then the particles within the atoms, we would find that they are moving at lightning speed and are fluctuations in energy located in a huge void. That is because the space between the atoms is analogous to the space between the stars. A great void. If you could look at an atom under a microscope you would initially see an empty void. Then a fluctuation in energy would appear, dance around, disintegrate, and be gone. So we are not physical machines that have learned how to think. We are thought processes that have learned how to create physical machines that we call bodies. Consciousness creates matter. Your soul creates your body."

"Wait a minute," said Beth. "What do you mean consciousness creates matter?"

"Can I kill you?" Simon asked turning to Mectar. "Maybe I can destroy your body, but if your consciousness is not destroyed upon death, because it is different than your brain, and consciousness indeed creates matter, then what have I done? Let's get to the root of consciousness, because that's where the Cylots attack is. That's where we have to fight back, Mectar. You know what I'll find there?" asked Simon.

"What?" demanded Mectar.

"God," said Simon.

The answer made Mectar wince. "Is that why you put that thing on her?" he said, pointing to the bracelet on Beth's wrist. "Is that why it now protects her instead of you?"

"I gave her the bracelet because she is beautiful," said Simon, looking at Beth.

"Stop," said Razqual. "I must leave and so must you. My men are done here." As quickly as Razqual and his force had arrived, they departed.

As Razqual was disappearing into his time jump the door to the building burst open and the West Orange Police force appeared.

"Shit" Simon muttered. "Humans." His shoulders slumped and he said this more to himself than anyone else. "A disruptor field cannot be set to keep out humans if I am there."

Two policemen aimed their shotguns at him, while four others burst out of another door at the corner of the building, all aiming their weapons at Simon and Beth.

Simon raised his hand in a mock salute and said, "I am from the planet Zim-barf and I come in peace. Take me to your leader." Then he chuckled softly. A policeman roughly shoved him against the wall. Beth saw that the officer's nametag said Murphy. He was a handsome young man with thick black hair. Then another cop pushed her against the wall. She and Simon stood spread-eagle side by side as the two officers frisked them. Mectar was likewise pushed against a wall and frisked. "Stay calm, Mectar. I need to get inside the building." Mectar nodded.

"Now stand still, buddy," said Murphy as he reached into Simon's coat pocket and pulled out a wad of bills. "Jesus, Comstock, look at this," said Murphy. He handed the money to another officer. Continuing his search, he felt Simon's jump belt.

"What you got on, buddy?" asked Murphy.

"It's a belt."

"Take it off."

Simon said, "It can't come off."

Murphy reached around Simon and opened the belt buckle of his jeans, then pulled up Simon's shirt to expose the jump belt. Simon's pants dropped to knee level as Murphy continued to look for a way to unfasten the jump belt.

"He's right, Sarge. I don't see any catch on this," said Murphy over his shoulder.

"Pull up his pants and take him to Wheeler."

Murphy handcuffed Simon's hands behind his back while Comstock held Simon at the elbows to keep his hands away from the jump belt.

Comstock frisked Mectar. Suddenly a thorn-like growth sprang from Mectar's side, slashing Comstock's hand.

"Ouch!" yelled the wounded officer. As quickly as it had appeared, the thorn-like growth disappeared into Mectar's body.

"Knock it off, Mectar," said Simon.

"How did he do that?" asked Murphy.

"Beats me," said Comstock, sucking the wound. When the bleeding slowed, he continued to pat Mectar's sides, but more carefully.

"Hey, Sarge," said Comstock. "Look at this." He handed Doyle the money Murphy had found.

"Any weapons?" asked Doyle.

Comstock shook his head. "Just a weird belt that won't come off."

"Come on," Doyle said. "Let's go." With Comstock and Murphy bringing up the rear, Doyle led the prisoners into the building and down the corridor to an office with two glass partitions and two solid walls. When the prisoners were seated he left them with Comstock and Murphy standing guard. Before he left he said, "Wait here for Wheeler. I'm going back to the station to pick up Mueller. Cyrus wanted him out here if we caught anyone."

17

You Mated with an Alien?

While Simon, Beth, and Mectar waited, Patrolman Murphy told them to sit down. Murphy put the money he had taken from them on the table. He shook his head and said to Comstock, "There must be $50,000 here." Officer Ignatello opened the door and looked at the money. His eyes widened and he whistled under his breath.

"Forty-three thousand seven hundred," said Mectar.

"Perhaps a little less," said Simon, winking at Beth.

"Exactly $43,700," said Mectar emphatically. He glared at Simon. "And why do you wink at Grey?"

"We dropped a bunch of bills by the machine," said Simon, "and I have something in my eye." He winked at Beth again.

The door opened wider. Wheeler and Leary entered past Ignatello. Leary looked surprised to see Beth.

"Hello, Beth. Are you okay?" asked Leary.

She nodded. "Can we take her cuffs off?" Leary asked Wheeler.

"This is Beth Grey? Javic's assistant?" asked Wheeler.

"One and the same," said Leary.

"The one who disappeared?"

"Yeah."

"Leave the cuffs on. I don't want her to disappear again, Leary." Leary looked at Beth and shrugged apologetically. "These are the two you saw at Merck?" Wheeler asked. Leary nodded his agreement.

"Now, what have we got here, Murphy?" asked Wheeler.

"Well," said Murphy, pointing to Mectar and Simon, "Each have belts we can't remove."

"What about this money?" asked Wheeler.

"They had it," said Murphy.

"There's an awful lot here," said Wheeler.

"Comstock and I guess it's about $50,000."

Mectar looked up again. "Forty-three thousand seven hundred, I said."

Simon rolled his eyes toward the ceiling but said nothing.

"And where did you get this money?" asked Wheeler.

Mectar said, "We took it out of a machine."

"What kind of machine has this much money?" asked Wheeler.

"The MAC machine in the plaza in West Orange," answered Beth.

"Comstock, go ask Sergeant Doyle if a theft has been reported. Tell him a MAC machine's been knocked over."

"There won't be any report," said Simon.

"We took the money out of it," Mectar said disdainfully. "We didn't knock it over. It was bolted to the wall." Simon closed his eyes and shook his head.

"And why not?" asked Wheeler.

"Because the MAC machine thinks it was a legitimate withdrawal," said Simon.

"How did you do that?" asked Wheeler.

"With an intervector," said Mectar, staring at Wheeler.

"What's an intervector?" asked Wheeler.

"It's a device that interfaces with the machine's computer. It digitizes the signal the computer uses to issue the money and then inserts its own signal," said Mectar.

"What?" said Wheeler.

"The intervector can talk to other machines, like a MAC machine," said Simon.

"Where did you get one of those?" asked Leary.

"Radio Shack," said Beth, giggling. Mectar and Simon both scowled at her.

"This is starting to get to you, isn't it, Grey?" said Simon.

"I'm sorry," said Grey, composing herself.

"What's your name?" asked Wheeler.

Grey noted how tired Simon appeared.

"My name is Simon," he said.

Wheeler looked at Mectar, who said his name before Wheeler could ask it.

"Where do you come from?" asked Wheeler of Simon.

"Earth," said Simon.

"Listen, wise guy," said Wheeler threateningly.

"Ask me *when* I come from," said Simon.

"What?" said Wheeler.

"When do you come from, Simon?" asked Leary, smiling.

"I come from the future," said Simon.

"And I'm Little Bo Peep," said Wheeler.

"Do you want the information or not?" demanded Simon.

"Are you the ones killing the researchers?" asked Wheeler.

"No, the Cylots are," responded Mectar.

"What's a Cylot?" asked Leary.

"The Cylots are an alien race at war with both Earth and Kia," said Simon.

"Kia?" asked Wheeler skeptically.

"Another planet, currently an ally of Earth. They are a race of metamorphs. Mectar here is a Kian."

"A metamorph. You mean they can change shape?" asked Leary.

"Yes," said Simon.

"What bullshit story is this?" demanded Wheeler. "I'm supposed to believe that you're from the future? You're just a crook, or maybe a murderer. Don't give me this crap that you are from the future. And this cretin," said Wheeler, gesturing at Mectar, "can no more change shape than I could jump a hundred feet in the air." With that he turned his back on Mectar and stood threateningly in front of Simon.

Simon looked at Mectar and shouted "No!" Mectar understood and did not change shape.

"What's a cretin?" asked Mectar.

"It's a misshapen, stupid human," said Beth.

Mectar's features hardened, his anger showing.

"Wait," said Simon, "Later." Mectar glared at Wheeler.

"There will be no later for you," said Wheeler. "You are all under arrest for the murder of Lawrence Livermore." He proceeded to read the three suspects their Miranda rights. When he finished, he said, "Take them down to the station."

"No," said Simon, "I am here for a reason. I think there is a formula here, one that holds the answer to Livermore's death. That is why I came into this building," said Simon.

Wheeler leaned against the desk with his arms folded in front of him.

"Is that why you are here tonight, at Organon?" asked Wheeler.

"I need that formula," Said Simon

"Why?"

"The Cylots. You could say they are consciousness parasites. They can control humans as if they had infected them or taken over their bodies. Once this happens to someone, that person is effectively dead. But asshole over here doesn't understand that," said Simon, motioning toward Mectar.

"What the sphincter muscle doesn't understand," said Mectar, angrily nodding at Simon, "is that there is no such thing as consciousness parasites. Cylots have a planet and they are attacking both of us. I don't know how. And, frankly, I don't care as long as I find a way to kill them."

Leary looked confused.

"Let me lay this out for you," said Simon. "Mectar and I have come back from the future to find a doctor called Yugen who, like me, was working on a formula to counter a disease or device—we don't know which—that the Cylots, our common enemy, are using on us. In the war in the future, most research facilities have been wiped out in Cylot attacks, so the plan was to do clandestine work at research facilities in our past, which is your present. Problem is, the Cylots have entered Earth's past to wipe out the remaining researchers. The researchers are close to a solution, a formula that could wipe out the Cylots, and the Cylots know it."

"What does this do to humans?" asked Leary, "this so-called infection?"

"It kills them, Leary. It kills them. After Cylots infect bodies they can use them. If they infected you, Leary, they could make you kill me. Because I carry defense mechanisms, such as a force field, they can't use most conventional weapons to kill me. They are trying, though."

"So this is like a virus infection?" asked Leary.

"Right," said Simon. "But this is a more intelligent disease. The Cylot disease has a quantifiable mentality. You can talk to the germ after it takes over the body. So if it infects you, Leary, I could talk to it. If I threatened it, it would try to kill or infect me. Biologists, like Yugen, were working on the problem but the solution seems more rooted in physics. I haven't found a way to kill the disease yet. Just the host," said Simon. "The only solution is to kill anybody who gets it. That's why I need the formula. Until I get it, when I destroy a Cylot host, I don't even affect the Cylots themselves. I merely kill some poor bastard who was unlucky enough to get infected."

"We have found some ways to slow them down. We use a bracelet like the one Grey is wearing," said Simon. "It emits an electronic frequency that impedes infection."

"Why doesn't the bracelet protect against Cylots totally?" asked Leary.

"Because there are only so many frequencies. Isn't that right?" said Beth.

"Exactly," answered Simon. "We can distort our electrical frequencies. Ultimately, though, they counteract the distortion and can reconfigure themselves. So you must change the frequencies. When you do, the odd chance exists that they can get lucky and connect with you. If it spirals out of control, all of humanity can be infected. In short all humanity can be wiped out. Infected individuals can contaminate uninfected individuals by removing their bracelets and enabling other Cylots to infect them. You got it now?" asked Simon. Wheeler looked at Leary skeptically.

"It's about electrical biochemistry," said Simon. "It's about where biology and physics operate at the most minute levels of consciousness. The essence of man is consciousness. If you attack the biology, which houses consciousness, you destroy the man. You don't destroy the energy constituting the awareness of the man, however. The Cylots understand this. They attack man's essence, his consciousness. They attacked me because I invented time travel. I'm a threat to them, just like Yugen. We are pretty sure we know how the disease is transmitted. And we think we have the formula to identify who is infected. Yugen was working on a cure. Before we could find one, the Cylots started to attack our past."

"So by attacking our past they can change the future?" asked Wheeler.

"No," said Simon. "Time is a matrix. It has mass. The future exists simultaneously with the past." Simon stopped abruptly. The blank stares from his audience told him he was not getting through.

He sat back heavily and said, "Oh, fuck me!"

His comment clearly confused Mectar, who asked Beth, "Is he cursing at himself?"

She opened her mouth to respond but said nothing. She shook her head no.

"An invitation then?" asked Mectar perplexed. Beth shook her head no again.

Simon began again quietly, "The Kians, who still want to control Earth, began to catch the disease. I'm one of the guys who has to figure out how to stop the Cylots. Once I do, that Kian," he said, nodding at Mectar, "will want me dead. Additionally," Simon continued, "when Cylots take over bodies, we can't tell which bodies are infected. That's part of what Yugen was working on when he ran to the past with this formula. He was close to the answer, but the Cylots were after him. To escape from the battle of the future, he had to go further back in the past. They found him anyway. At his lab there was nothing. I know; I went there. But he left me a trail. It died at Varley, because the Cylots got to Varley before I did. They know something I don't, because there are researchers dying all over the place. I have to stop this infection of humanity. This disease has its own consciousness. It develops strategies. It—"

"This is bullshit," said Wheeler. "You want me to believe that there is some space virus infecting people, and it can think?"

"At least in the sense that it can outwit a potential host's defenses," said Simon. "The Cylots merely take things one step further. They use their consciousness to facilitate, or speed up, that invasion. That's why Lynth was so instrumental in helping me," Simon continued, addressing Beth. "She was hiding. The Cylots had annihilated the Lalians. The last few remaining Lalians were unable to help their comrades. Those who knew they hadn't been infected left their planet and spread across the universe. But Lynth had information concerning the Cylots."

"What?" said Mectar.

"You think the Lalians didn't learn something from Liud's death? Asked Simon.

Leary rubbed his head confused. The information was coming too fast for him.

"Look at what I'm saying," said Simon. "My purpose is to destroy a sentient organism. Do you think that organism will allow that without a fight? That's what happened to the Lalians."

"Who are the Lalians again?" asked Wheeler.

"The Lalians," said Simon. "You know, the creatures, the humanoids, that lived on the planet Lalia."

"I know the Lalians," said Mectar. "And I know Lynth, the one you had an affair with."

"You had an affair with an alien?" said Beth Grey in surprise.

"It wasn't an affair," said Simon. "Our sexes are not compatible."

"You mated with her," said Mectar emphatically.

"No, I didn't," said Simon.

"You had sex with her and I know it," accused Mectar, standing and pointing at Simon.

"You had sex with an *alien*?" asked Beth.

"No, it wasn't sex," said Simon.

"Then what was it?" demanded Mectar. "You are as contemptible a creature as I have ever seen, Simon."

"She had lost her husband and her world and needed comforting." He paused. "But we couldn't have had sex."

"You had *sex* with an alien?" said Beth Grey again, not comprehending and looking bewildered.

"Goddamn it! We didn't screw each other, all right?" shouted Simon. "Anyway, my past sexual practices have nothing to do with this. We're talking about a danger to the human race and to Kia. We're talking about a disease that's already wiped out one culture we know of. We're talking about eliminating the most deadly disease that mankind has ever encountered. Do you understand?" Then

Simon laughed. "Think of it as field research, Grey. Perhaps you can relate to it better."

"That's it. I want out of this. Forget it. I'm not going to help you," said Beth angrily. "I thought you were different. I thought you were special. My shortcomings always seem so nonthreatening, harmless, amusing, actually, when I examine them. Much different from your stark deficiencies."

"Honey," said Simon, "right now my stark deficiencies are all that's keeping you alive. The minute you are open and exposed, they would hit you so hard that it would be the end of Beth Grey. So regardless of what I am or what I'm not, you'd better understand something fast: I am the person protecting you."

"I'll protect myself just fine!" shouted Beth. "You arrogant, pompous, bed-hopping son of a bitch. And another thing. Don't ever call me honey—"

"All right, all right, calm down," said Leary.

"Shut up," shouted Wheeler. Startled, Beth stopped. "Now sit down." Beth sat. There was a momentary silence. Then the building shook as though someone heavy were jumping on the roof.

"Jesus, what the hell was that?" said Wheeler. Simon just looked at the ceiling and then Mectar, who nodded as though they had spoken and agreed on something. Then Mectar belched again. A quizzical look came over Simon's face and Mectar responded with a look that said, "Just forget it." Beth knew they were talking.

"Let me understand this," said Leary. "You want me to believe Yugen was a biomedical researcher who came back from the future and tried to develop a formula to identify and combat people who are infected by the Cylots."

"Why do you even listen to this crap?" Asked Wheeler of Leary. "This story is ridiculous."

"You didn't see them disappear like I did," responded Leary. "People don't just disappear or time jump or whatever the hell they did. Jefferson was with me, he saw it too. Let Simon talk." Leary nodded to Simon to continue.

"Essentially," said Simon. "That's why Yugen was working with bees. What is the beehive if not the microcosm for a brain? The queen is the cortex. The brain's synaptic gaps are the spaces between the bees. I understand why Yugen was working on those bees—because the hive possessed a collective consciousness."

"So Yugen discovered the formula, but before he got it back to the future the Cylots found him and killed him. Except before he died, let's say he gave the formula to other researchers from this period and they sent it out among the research community. The Cylots are on the trail of the formula, killing these researchers. And you're the ones who came back from the future," said Leary, pointing his finger at Simon and Mectar, "trying to find the formula. Because once you can identify who's been infected with the parasite, you can at least know how far it has spread. Or, if Yugen found a solution, be able to control it."

"That's right," said Simon, "and then maybe we will be able to treat the victims."

"By killing them?" asked Beth.

"By at least trying to quarantine those who have it until they can be treated," responded Simon.

"Now the reason you are with him," said Leary to Mectar, rubbing his forehead, "is because if he discovers how to treat the disease, then you also benefit."

Mectar looked in disgust at Leary for stating the obvious. "A brilliant deduction," he said.

Simon added, "Except that as soon as I find out how to treat the disease I remove the one plug that prevents the Kians from attacking Earth again.

"Kia is an expanding military empire," he continued. "One thing they do well, though, is use their conquests. They enslave the people they've conquered. If those people have an area of specialty, they make them work at it for the benefit of the Kian race. They found that biology seems to be a specialty of Earth. Mectar is getting a chance to see how the basic research work is done. Kians can overcome any kind of adversary except one that infects their own body politic. Isn't that right, Mectar? Isn't that why you need me?"

"I don't need you at all," said Mectar, glaring at Simon. "I've got my orders. You've got yours."

"That's where you and I differ, asshole," said Simon. "You've got your orders, I've got my imperatives. I act from my own mores, not from an ordered hierarchy. You're afraid of the Cylots, Mectar? Be afraid of me. I am the disease."

Mectar's skin started to harden. Sharp spines began to grow out of it. The handcuffs that he wore snapped. "When this is over," he said, "you and I have something to settle, Simon."

Simon looked at Mectar unflinching and unafraid. "For all your posturing, you asshole, you're impotent. To kill me would mean you've violated your orders. It's the one thing that you can't do. You wouldn't be able to go home, because if nothing else, a Kian is honorable. Isn't that right?" demanded Simon.

"Something Earthers lack," spat Mectar.

Simon stood in his handcuffs. Officers Murphy and Ignatello had their drawn guns, pointed at Mectar. Mectar let out a belch like a lion's roar and then bent over and stood back up.

"What the hell was that?" asked Simon. Beth who had been standing closer to Mectar than Simon, moved to the other side of Simon, further away from Mectar.

"That was hideous," she said.

Simon saw the officers back away, obviously nervous. These policemen were seeing a true alien, a hostile one at that, for the first time in their lives. "Put the guns away," said Simon with a smirk on his face. "He's impotent. He's bound by the chains of his own orders."

"Your day will come, Simon," said the Kian. "And I will be the instrument of your death."

"Killing you, Mectar, will not be creative enough. I will not get the satisfaction I want from just killing you. I am going to destroy Mectar the warrior in a way you can't imagine, in a way I will enjoy."

"Individuals like you should be stamped out for the benefit of the universe," said Mectar. "You see, Grey, what he is? He is the disease." Then he shouted at Simon, "You fucked!"

Leary blinked as Simon smiled. "No, no, no, that's not how you curse," said Simon amiably. "Tell me to fuck myself, or say 'fuck you' as an imperative. You don't mean I fucked, because then you'd have to say who."

"Stop playing games, Benjamin," said Beth.

"You're on his side now?" asked Simon. "I'm hurt."

"You made it with an alien?" she asked.

"Oh, stop with the alien already," he said.

"You went to bed with an alien?" said Beth Grey again. "That's perverted."

"You know it's not perverted, Grey. Kinky, maybe, but not perverted."

"You wouldn't know the difference," said Beth disdainfully.

"Oh, I absolutely do," said Simon. "Kinky is when you use feathers when you make love. It's perverted when you use the whole chicken." Beth laughed in spite of herself. Simon smiled at her with genuine warmth.

"Simon," Leary said. "Kinky or perverted, that's a little strange. Why did they send you? Of everybody, why did the people of the future send you to get the formula back? From what you're telling me, you're a scientist, not a detective, and certainly not a soldier, according to Mectar here." The roof shook again as Mectar belched and then doubled over.

"I'll answer that," said Mectar still bent over and wiping his mouth with the back of his hand. "It's because wherever they send him he sees a different science. He is the father of time travel. He discovered it and he developed the mechanism that makes it work. He is the one person who could see the whole of Yugen's thought from the fragmented pieces. He will see what others will miss."

"Tell me," said Simon to Leary, "which researchers have been killed?" Leary hesitated. "Listen," said Simon. "If I knew who I was going to kill next, I wouldn't need you to tell me. So I'm not the one killing these researchers. We both have the same interest—stopping these murders."

Mectar belched again.

"What the hell is wrong with you?" demanded Simon as he looked at Mectar. Mectar shook his head and did not answer.

Leary looked at Wheeler. "Al, what do you think?"

Wheeler shook his head and shrugged as if totally overwhelmed. "What could it hurt?" he asked.

Leary recited the list of names. At the end, he paused and asked Wheeler, "Is that everybody?"

"As far as we know."

"Do you have any clues as to what connects them?" asked Simon.

Leary shook his head. "No, they were all working on different things at different locations."

"But they were all doing research that required them to have an LAR department," said Beth.

"LAR?" asked Leary.

"Yes, lab animal research," said Beth.

"Who hasn't been hit?" asked Simon.

"How do I know?" Wheeler said.

"I can't say for sure, but I can make a pretty damn good guess," said Beth. "Look. Organon and Merck have been hit. What about Schering, Novartis, Hoffman-LaRoche, and Berlex? If the Cylots killed Javic, they're going after people like him at the other LAR facilities."

"Javic is not dead," said Leary. "It was Bottoms in Javic's lab coat."

"Leonard's alive?" said Beth, excited.

"Missing," said Leary.

There was a knock on the door. Officer Ignatello, his uniform tight around both his ample stomach and his bulletproof vest, opened it. Comstock stuck his head in. "Mueller's outside. Says he won't come in."

"Can't come in," said Simon. "Mueller's a Cylot."

"Bullshit," said Wheeler ducking involuntarily as the noise crashed above his head. "Why can't he ... what is that?" Wheeler said, referring to the noise.

"Disruption field," said Simon. "What you hear is the Cylots trying to break through our disruption field. It won't hold up forever. Do you have the goddamn formula?"

"Show it to him," said Leary. Then he said to Simon, "Yeah he's got it. What could it hurt? If he's lying it won't mean shit, and if he's telling the truth it's important."

Wheeler hesitated, then handed a paper to Simon. "Is this it?" he asked, looking at the ceiling.

Simon looked at the formula, "Yeah," he said. "It's a formula. Is this what Varley sent him?"

"It was in an envelope sent by Varley."

"We have got it," said Mectar, who looked as if he was in pain. "Let's go."

Simon stared at the formula and then handed it to Mectar. "Go ahead," he said. "It's a setup. That's not any formula worth having."

Mectar crumpled the paper in his hand in anger. Mectar belched, then belched again. Simon looked at Mectar quizzically. Then he dropped the paper to the floor. The sound of the bouncing intensified over all their heads. All the cops looked at the ceiling, as did Beth. Only Simon continued to look at Mectar. "Find out what the hell that is," demanded Wheeler. Comstock nodded and left.

"Doyle says they've sent two patrolman outside and neither has come back. He can't raise either one of them on their radios," said Ignatello, who walked over to a corner with a radio to one ear and his hand over his other to continue his conversation with Doyle.

"Simon, I don't feel well," said Mectar.

"What's wrong?"

"The liquid we had for breakfast."

"Milk? The milk on the cereal?"

"The liquid, Simon. I do not like the liquid." Mectar now leaned against the wall to hold himself up.

"You're lactose intolerant?" asked Simon. "That wasn't in your dossier."

Mectar groaned softly. He belched again and his head went in and out of form—a human face with reptilian features.

Beth, watching Mectar, asked Simon, "Would you drink the water in Mexico? Even if it's okay, the local bacteria may be something your system would not tolerate."

"Beth, we're getting out of here now."

"Oh no you're not, buddy," said Murphy pointing a gun at him.

"Oh yes we are," said Simon walking into the gun on the way to the door, challenging the Murphy to fire point blank. Murphy grabbed Simon's arm as Mectar's tail flopped from his back onto the ground, ripping the back of his clothes. Beth could see the metamorph skin separate, and Mectar sighed in relief.

"Ohaahhh."

Simon pushed the door open past Murphy, whose expression was a mixture of wonder at what he was seeing and revulsion at what he was smelling. That was followed by the sound of flatulence. Mectar's tail decreased in size as Wheeler, Leary, Murphy, and Ignatello ran for the door. As the last cop exited, Simon shouted, "Shut the door."

From the room came the sounds of Mectar groans of relief accompanied by musical emanations of his reptilian body. It sounded like someone learning to play the scale on the tuba for the first time.

"What the hell is that?" asked Ignatello.

"That is a Kian with intestinal distress, and speaking of distress, we have a problem. Here," said Simon, handing the closest cop the handcuffs.

"How did …?" said Murphy, looking at the handcuffs being proffered by Simon.

"Go. They're yours. Take them." Murphy reached out and took the cuffs.

"Oh, Mectar," said Beth, putting her hand to her mouth to hide her laugh. Mectar had come out of the room, the relief evident on his face. He was dragging his tail behind him, leaving a slight liquid trail on the tile.

"Sanitize the room," said Simon. With his blaster, Mectar vaporized his scat, but the room burst into an acrid flame. That was immediately followed by the sprinkler system going off. As they looked up at the sprinklers, everyone then heard a final bounce, which was accompanied by a ripping sound. The ceiling then split open, and two Cylots fell to the floor through the ceiling.

"Christ!" said Ignatello. He fired, causing the rest of the cops to open fire at the Cylots, who immediately returned fire. Leary dove to the right, firing as he slid away from the Cylots on his back. Wheeler dropped to one knee, took aim with his Glock extended in front of him, and did not stop firing until his clip was empty. Murphy slipped into a doorway and fired at the Cylots partially shielded by the door. Ignatello was hit in the chest and flew backward down the hall past Mectar as Mectar also fired at the Cylots. Simon then dropped a sensory grenade and grabbed Beth. The instant the sensory grenade exploded, all the cops fell to the ground in convulsing nausea. Beth doubled over and Simon grabbed her. Pulling her with him, he disappeared into a time jump.

Mectar remained another instant before he too was pulled into the jump.

That left the insectoids in a hallway raining water from the ceiling, fighting the impact of the sensory grenade. Having seen Simon and Mectar time jump from the hallway and having no one attacking them, they too jumped into their own time jump. Nothing remained except the hissing of the sprinklers putting out the fire and the retching of the men on their hands and knees.

When Mectar came out on the other side of the time jump he found Simon trying to administer the antidote to the sensory granade to Beth while ranting to himself. "He puked and crapped throughout our mission. I am with a lactose-intolerant lizard. You can't make this stuff up. Reality is stranger than fiction."

18

Would You Even Know the Truth If You Heard It?

The Park Diner is located near Organon on Route 10 in Livingston, New Jersey. Since Beth was still groggy from being drugged, Simon stopped to get her coffee. Mectar additionally needed solid food, having emptied his system at Organon.

No one talked during the drive from Organon to the diner. The silence continued during dinner, until Beth, who sipped her coffee and felt better, said to Simon, "So, you two have traveled together before?"

Simon nodded. "Yeah from Earth to Zingx."

"What were you doing there?" she asked. "It seems so far away."

"Zingx was a moon in the Bendibast system and was behind the main defensive line Earth and Kia had formed to meet the Cylot advance. I was delivering a weapons system I had developed and Mectar was traveling with me as part of the truce. He was there as an *observer*. Mectar had met me on Earth's moon, where I had had the weapons system packed and ready to go. We traveled from there to Zingx. It was there I met up with Jerry."

"Karlson," said Mectar. "Another Earther, Jerry Karlson."

"Who is he?" asked Beth.

"He's a dust control salesman. Old guy. Bald. Bushy eyebrows. A real piece of work," said Simon.

"A dust control salesman in outer space?" Beth asked, raising her eyebrows.

Simon put down his spoon. He had been stirring his coffee and staring down into the cup.

"Dust control systems are, perhaps, among the most important pieces of equipment on any spacecraft. The filtration of air and recirculation of water and oxygen are paramount for sustaining life in a spaceship. Karlson ran a company that repaired this type of equipment. The motto of his company was, 'We Lust for Dust.'"

"You're kidding."

Simon shook his head.

"The second time was when Mectar caught up with me on Gongrn."

"That's when Mectar—" said Beth.

Simon finished her sentence. "Said I made it with *her*."

"They were in the same bed holding each other," said Mectar. "Just like he was with you."

Simon nodded. "We were in bed and I was holding her. But she was crying." Compassion and pain filled his eyes. Beth knew that Mectar had misread the situation.

"Don't be fooled," Mectar said. "He lied to me then. He's lying to you now."

"He lied to you then?" she asked.

"When we were coming into Zingx," said Mectar, "Simon and I didn't know each other well. I had my assignment and had just met him. As we were traveling into Zingx at sub-light speed, Simon asked me how Kians procreate. 'Are you Kians bisexual?' he wanted to know. 'How is it determined who is the child's primary caregiver?' 'By mutual consent,' I told him. Although the mother, to use your term, does not suffer or, rather, give the most.

"In our culture, the father would be the *znec*. But 'father' is not a good word to use," said Mectar. "A *znec*, a provider and protector, is more than a father." Mectar leaned back and imitated Simon's voice. "Hey," Mectar said indignantly. "In the human race a father is all of that too. That is what you said to me. Isn't it, Simon?"

Simon nodded. "I said no, Simon. He is not like a father, because our physiology is different. You see, when Kians conceive a child and bring it to term, the member of the partnership, uh, marriage, who bears it loses nearly half her body and brain mass during the delivery. The mass passes directly into the child. The partner who is the mother, or the *liat*, regenerates the lost portions of the brain and body by the time the child reaches adolescence at age fourteen. This is why a *znec* is more important than a father: he raises both the child and the *liat*. Then do you know what he said to me, Grey?"

Beth was sitting back in the booth, amazed at Mectar's description. "I have no idea, she said."

"He said our races aren't so different. You see, when a human child is born, half the female brain comes out in the placenta. This causes human females to be very emotionally unstable during the child's early years." Beth's mouth fell open. She turned to stare at Simon, who looked innocently out the window. Mectar continued, "I said, this is not what I've read about your race, Simon. He said,

'We try to keep this human biological characteristic to ourselves.' Then he told me that you incarcerate your children within things called playpens. The word pen derives from penitentiary."

"Is that what you said to him?" Beth asked, making no attempt to hide her disapproval.

Simon shrugged and shifted uncomfortably. "I guess," he said. "I really don't remember."

Beth shook her head. "There's more that this *pulvzar* said," said Mectar.

Beth's brow knotted. "What's a *pulvzar*?"

"It's a Kian shit-eating mole," said Simon. "It's what he likes to call me."

"Of all the animals on Kia, it is the most disrespected. Do not get the wrong idea, Grey. Simon has called me Earth names when we were in a shootout. It happened on Zingx when we were attacked by the Cylot hit squad. He called me an 'asshole.' Karlson was there. I didn't know what an asshole was. Karlson told me it is a sphincter muscle. I asked if I had been insulted. He said yes. He said this sphincter muscle controls the flow of human excrement. So I told Karlson that I expected as much from a race whose females' brains fall out in their placentas. Karlson didn't know what I was talking about. I told him what Simon told me. He said that it doesn't happen that way. I asked if I had been lied to. Karlson said that either I had been lied to or there was something about human females he didn't know. Karlson then considered the new information and said that maybe that's why his wife left him after his third child was born. He explained that she did get a little strange after the birth. At that point, she probably had no mind left. Or, apparently, her mind was set on getting rid of him. That's what he said. Do not be fooled by Simon," said Mectar to Beth sincerely. "His lies can deceive other humans. Karlson believed Simon's explanation. Simon is an asshole."

"Well?" Beth said. "Is this true?"

"Is what true?" Simon said indignantly. "That I'm an asshole?"

"No, Benjamin," Beth said sternly. "Is Mectar telling the truth?"

Simon didn't answer immediately. Then he said, "I suppose. But I don't have a monopoly on lies in the relationship, do I, Mectar? Didn't the Earth/Kia truce extend to us? Wasn't that our agreement? Tell me, when are you supposed to kill me? When do your orders say you break the truce? Or, how you are going to kill me? Will you do it in the traditional Kian fashion: decapitate me from behind?"

"When the time comes, Simon, I'll do it the way I enjoy most. I want it to be by my hand." He spread his fingers into an arc before curling them into a fist. Then the skin on his hand hardened.

"Better be sure you do it at the right time if you want the formula. I've got most of it." Mectar's eyes hardened into thin lines.

"I don't have the catalyst, though. I have most of the ingredients. Yugen had the balance. I think I can make it powerful enough to be effective. So, can you kill me at just the right time, Mectar? Can you kill me at the exact moment I solve this puzzle and prevent Earth from getting wiped out? If you guess wrong, you bring back nothing to Kia."

"If I guess right, Earth dies."

"If you guess right, Mectar, Kia may also die. If you guess wrong, Kia may live."

"Aaaakh," said Mectar sitting back in disgust. "Your games mean nothing to me. When the time comes, we'll both know. I will be right back."

Beth waited until Mectar was well away from the table.

"Mectar said you stole a fighter and before you ran from the battle you destroyed the weapons system on the heavy cruiser you were on. Is that true?"

"Mectar told you the truth."

"Why, Ben? I could see you running if you were scared or had a reason to, but why destroy the weapons they could have fought with before you left?"

"Why," he said slowly, "should I tell you anything?"

She returned his stare. There was no weakness in her. Her strength matched his, but while she was exceptionally smart she knew he was uniquely brilliant. She was making it clear that that his brilliance did not relieve him of the responsibility of being honest. The concession she would rightfully extract from him was that brilliance was only one facet of a personality, yet she was far stronger than him when it came to interpersonal relationships and emotions—those areas a woman leads a man without ever relinquishing her strength and intelligence.

"Because you need to give the honesty you ask for. You did what you did for a reason. Are you afraid to tell me your reasons? Do you expect me to believe you acted out of fear? The man I spent the last few days with wouldn't have acted that way regardless of the spin you have put on it. My God, you have Mectar spinning like a top. He thinks you are a coward. You want him to believe it. You act psychotic telling him you are going to kill him and Selfridge. You know what I think, Ben? I think you're full of shit. I think you are the most calculating son of a bitch I have ever met. My God," she said in sudden revelation, "you're like that goddamn commercial—you're an army of one."

"What are you talking about?"

"The commercial for the army on TV—be all you can be, be an army of one. That's what I think you are. Now you have two choices, Benjamin," she said throwing her napkin on the table. "You can tell me the real reason or you can continue to feed me your line of bullshit. But if you feed me the bullshit, don't expect me to eat it. You may be able to bullshit an alien, but neither you nor any other guy can get past my bullshit detector."

"You didn't answer my question."

"What question?" asked Beth.

"Why?" said Simon.

"Because I could never like a man who wasn't honest with me," said Beth, staring directly into his eyes.

"You like me?"

"Not yet—I might when you give me the truth," said Beth, keeping her eyes locked on his.

"Suppose the truth was dangerous for you to have?" asked Ben.

"You're an idiot, you know that, Ben? How many other women have even stopped to ask about you or cared or had an interest. Look, I've had enough," said Beth, now glaring at him.

"No, wait … all right," he said. He lowered his eyes as if to collect himself. Simon paused and let out a deep and troubled sigh. "I have to start with what Mectar got right. I was a weapons specialist on a heavy cruiser with a new weapons system that could fire conventional weapons from outside of time space; it was before I developed the jump belt. Because we had to leave the time space of the battle, the commander of the cruiser felt it would weaken the fleet to be less one cruiser—and one of the newer ones at that. That rendered the weapon and the advantage useless. The fleet was taking a beating. He had at his disposal the one thing to change the outcome of the battle. I knew how to use it—I had developed it—and it could have turned that entire fight around if I had been in command. But I didn't have command, and after my … tantrum, if you want to call it that, I was escorted from the bridge under guard while being restrained. Mectar rightfully saw the whole thing.

"In the drop shute on the way down below deck our ship was hit and I was separated from the guards. If our ship was boarded and captured that weapon would fall into the Cylots' hands. I can assure you they would know how to use it. I had to destroy it to prevent it from falling in to enemy hands. So I blew it up."

"That easy?" she asked.

"Don't you think I had to prepare for that outcome?" He shook his head slightly. "It's about preparing for outcomes. I did take some componentry out before I destroyed it, then I simply stole a fighter and ran from the battle. I couldn't change the outcome of the battle, but I could change the outcome of the war. I ran until I had to stop at a free port to refuel."

"A free port?"

A free port is just that, a free port. It can be on any rock, asteroid, moon, or planet. A gas station in the dessert where cons, thieves, crooks, and cutthroats ply their trade. A place where beings pay a lot for fuel, arms, food, or passage. At that moment, it was a place where the refugees of the planets the Cylots had been attacking had washed up. The free port I was at was called Gongrn."

"It was there I met Lynth, a young queen of the Lalians. Her was husband dead, her planet destroyed, and her people scattered. There was a Cylot force after her, intent on killing her. I also had a Cylot force after me and Mectar.

"The clan who ran this free port demanded she leave or they would kill her themselves. What stopped them was the small Lalian force traveling with her, who would have destroyed the free port if their queen had been killed. They could have easily done that before the Cylots got there. Once she left that free port, the trailing Cylot force would destroy her. Once I heard about her, I sought her out.

"I told her that if she left with me the way I said and did what I told her I would defeat the Cylots. She wanted to know my price. Nothing, I told her, just do what I say in the battle. The clan refueled us so we could leave—-at too high a price I might add, which she paid. I painted my fighter black and docked it under her larger spacecraft so her craft was empty and visible while the fighter was occupied with just us and almost invisible because of its stealth capabilities.

Once we left the Gongrn a small group of Lalian light cruisers and assorted transports joined us unaware of me. They were going to follow their queen to her death. So while the main part of the Cylot battle fleet was kicking ass against the joint Kian and Earth force, a smaller Cylot force was going to destroy the Lalian queen. Mectar had caught me, but the Lalian guard caught him."

"Why would she believe you?" Beth asked.

"I moved my ship in the space port with her in it. It was the only ship like it—it was the only way. Up to this point, the Cylots had never been defeated in a battle. But in my arrogance and determination, I knew that they had never faced a weapon like the one I possessed. What I did not know is why they always won. Apparently, they had a pulse weapon that did not attack the enemy ship but rather its occupants, disabling them at a subatomic level. It could disrupt your consciousness and render you vulnerable to their attack. I saw the Lalian ships being destroyed while doing heroic things, and because we were in my fighter below Lynth's unoccupied ship, I was only sickened by the pulses, not disabled.

They were firing at her ship above us, not at us directly. This allowed me to capture an electromagnetic signature of their weapon on my instrumentation and chart their positions for my firing resolutions. While I did that, half of her force was destroyed.

"Then I disengaged from her ship and for the first time in battle time jumped completely out of time of that battle. She and I were in the same space but in a different time. That made us totally safe. She started to talk to me and I simply said, 'Lynth, shut up and keep your word.' She's a great lady. She did. It took me a week to fight that fight. I would jump into the time space of that battle, fire a few shots before they could get a firing resolution on me, and then jump out of that time space. To the Cylots it looked like they were fighting fifty ships, yet it was just me coming in and out of the time space and firing at them. I had all their positions recorded at a certain point in space-time. I fuckin' destroyed them all, no survivors, except the ones I let escape. To them I broadcast in Lalian: Tell them the Lalians are coming. Tell them you have angered Lynth, queen of the Lalians, who takes her revenge upon you.

"Since I had slave control over Lynth's ship, which I was focused on defending, I went back to the free port that monitored the battle and robbed them blind. I took their fuel, food, and money, while the Lalians took anything that wasn't nailed down on my direction. It was at this point that Mectar escaped from Gongrn, as some of the clan had run and he had left with them.

"Then I suggested to Lynth that we get the hell out of there, and we ran. The remnants of the Lalians who had escaped began to flock to her. I was made her commander in chief, and I began to outfit her ships with my weapon designs and train her people. They called me a great general and said I was a great weapons specialist. But I knew I was nothing more than a lucky asshole, because if they had fired their disrupter weapon at me and hit me, they would have won. It wasn't because I had hit them but equally because they had missed me.

"Now I had a bigger problem. I had a Cylot target tattooed on my ass and I had to find a device to deflect their disrupter. It was easy enough to develop the jump belt—all I had to do was miniaturize what I had in the fighter—but I needed a research lab to find out how their disrupter worked on human physiology and I couldn't put that research lab in a space fleet running for their lives. So I left Lynth and time jumped and came back to a calm period in Earth's past.

"Do you know how Edison built the record player?" he asked.

Beth had been silent, letting Simon spin his tale. "No," she said.

"He drew a diagram on a piece of scrap paper and handed it to an assistant and said, 'Here, build this.' I did the same: I put researches in the past at various research companies and said, 'Here, do this.' New Jersey has the biggest concentration of pharmaceuticals doing research in the world. I used that group of companies to bury my researchers in. They did clandestine research in the past unknown to the host companies.

"But Cylots are no fools, and they are trying to find these researchers—and me. My jump belts and weaponry has leveled the playing field so they are no longer invincible. If I crack their disrupter code I am going to take it and shove it right up their ass."

Simon leaned back and stared at her as though he were starring right through her. Then he smiled and said, "That's my story and I'm sticking to it. Actually, Beth, aside from the spies, stolen plans of jump belts, false plans of jump belts, failed alliances, traps, treaties dealing with threatening aliens, misguided Kians, the jealousy of Lalian sub generals, incompetence of our own Earth forces, and needy Lalian female queens, a complete lack of human female company, and occasionally getting drunk, that is the whole story. Now, what girl wouldn't just die to take a guy like that home to her mom? How's that for honesty?" Simon said sarcastically.

Beth nodded while looking at her hands in her lap. "I'm thinking that's probably pretty honest."

Simon reached softly into her lap and put his hand on hers. She looked up into his eyes. "Listen," he said. "If I ever thought it would be safe to ask a woman to share my life, I would ask. I ache for it."

She put one her hands on top of his, holding his hand now between hers. "And when that time comes if it ever comes, and I could find someone as neat as you …"

"Neat?" she said smiling and wiping away a tear.

"Wonderful, beautiful. From the moment I saw you that's what I felt. And what have I brought you?"

"Neat?"

"High praise indeed," he said.

"Look Mectar is coming back," she said, pulling her hand away from his and picking up the napkin from the table to blow her nose. Mectar was staring at them as he approached. They could sense that he could sense that something had occurred between them. Simon's face turned deadly serious, as though he had seen something across the room. Mectar followed Simon's gaze as Simon turned his back to Mectar to hide his face. He smiled at Beth and with a wink said, "Watch this."

Simon nodded and stood up. "I'll pay the bill." Mectar and Beth followed.

After Simon finished paying, he grabbed Mectar abruptly. "We've gotta get out of here," he said.

Mectar reached for his phaser. "Why?"

"See that man over there in the corner?" Mectar saw an unusually obese man eating with a napkin around his neck. "He's committing suicide. He's going to explode." Mectar looked at the man, whose chin seemed to merge with his neck. Brown suspenders held up his pants. He gobbled a salad soaked in dressing. A piece of lettuce fell from his fork, landing on his shirt. He wet his napkin and dabbed at the stain.

Beth realized that Simon was lying to Mectar.

"What do you mean he's going to explode?" asked Mectar, immediately suspicious. Beth started to say something to stop Simon, but he held up his hand so Mectar could not see it and Beth stopped. She sensed Simon wanted her to watch something.

"That's how some humans commit suicide," said Simon. "People like him overeat until they explode. Let's go. It's not going to be a pretty sight."

Mectar pulled his arm free and walked toward the man. He looked at him squarely. "Are you in the process of committing suicide via explosion?" Mectar demanded. Simon watched gleefully.

"What?" said the man. When he lifted his head, the fat on his chest and stomach jiggled.

"Explode. Are you going to explode?" Mectar demanded.

"What are you? Some kind of idiot?" said the man angrily.

Mectar threw his end of the table in the air. "No, I'm not mentally deficient," Mectar said. He was now standing directly in front of the man while poking his chest. "Are you eating until you explode as a method of suicide?"

The fat man swung at Mectar. Mectar caught his fist in the palm of his hand and held it. Then Mectar's hand enveloped the fat man's fist as he began to squeeze it.

The man began to whimper. "Let go. You're hurting me."

"Tell me," said Mectar. "Do humans explode?"

The man could not get up. "No, you jerk. Of course not!" he shouted.

Mectar was seething. Simon stood in the diner doorway, laughing.

"Excuse my friend," Simon said to the fat man. "I have to get him back to the institution soon." Mectar screamed and charged at Simon, who fled into the parking lot.

"You're the asshole, Simon," said Mectar.

"I know, I know," said Simon laughing. "Just calm down. You fucking Kians don't have a sense of humor."

"This is not humorous," Mectar said.

"Then what would you call it?" asked Simon.

"You're a total asshole. An imbecile. A *pulvzar*."

"I agree with you, Mectar."

"Have you no self-esteem?"

"Have you no desire to explore altered states of perception?"

"What's that got to do with it?" demanded Mectar.

"If humans can't explode, timespace can't bend," said Simon.

"What?" yelled Mectar.

"Unless you accept what isn't you can never accept what is."

"What are you talking about, Simon?"

"In order to understand what a mountain is, you must be a mountain, but before you can be a mountain, you must understand what a mountain is not."

"Have you gone insane?" Mectar demanded.

"I'm trying to get you to understand timespace. You can only see the parts. When you understand the entire idea, you understand what it isn't. It's not sequential. It's a whole entity. And you're a part of it. Forever. As a sentient being, you are part of a cosmic consciousness. Your hatred and warlike attitude interfere with your pursuit of that truth," said Simon. "When will you understand that? When will you understand what isn't?" said Simon, answering his own question. "Humans don't explode. And they're not sphincter muscles. And Earth and Kia aren't at war. As a matter of fact, Kia isn't even trying to expand its empire."

"Of course we are," said Mectar.

"No. See the whole picture, Mectar. Although you are a warrior, you lack a warrior's gaze."

"A what?"

"A warrior's gaze. Sight and perception. Perception is strong; sight is weak. It's strategically important to take a distant view of close things and a close view of distant things. See without looking. Know where your enemies are located because you know where they are not located. You see me, your enemy, in front of you. But I'm not your enemy. I am your ally. Perception is an evolving interaction between consciousness and reality. I see a fat man committing suicide via explosion, Mectar. You are the fat man. You choke on conquered worlds you cannot digest. It's better to abandon this hopeless fight between us. There is nothing that is hidden from the `not I.' There is nothing that is visible to the `I.'

If I look at something from the viewpoint of the `not I,' I do not really see it. The `not I' sees it. If I see it as `not I,' it may also become possible to see it as someone else does. Our disputes continue to affirm and deny the same things they have always affirmed and denied. They ignore new aspects of reality that change the present. Instead of proving this point by logical disputation, see all things intuitively. Don't allow the limitations of the `I' to imprison you. Every argument includes both right and wrong. In the end, they can be reduced to the same thing." Beth caught up with them and listened. Mectar became calmer.

"When the wise man understands this turning point, he stands in the center of the circle while yes and no pursue each other around the circumference. I stand at the pivot, the center, where all affirmations and denials converge. Once we understand this center, we can abandon all thought of imposing limitations and taking sides. Therefore, I will abandon this fight with you and the Cylots. I will seek the truth, the light. Only if I become a Cylot can I identify and defeat a Cylot. I must be what I am not before I can be what I am."

Police sirens wailed. Mectar and Simon stood transfixed.

"'How can a mountain be not a mountain,' the disciple asked the master," said Simon. "The master replied, 'How can light not be a particle? How can light not be a wave?' Light exhibits characteristics of both wave and particle. We only perceive half of this natural duality. Light therefore is a 'wavicle.'" Simon smiled, clearly enjoying himself. "You must practice gazing with sight and perception. You must realize that the reality surrounding you constitutes only half the duality of life. The only way you can prove consciousness exists after death, Mectar, is to die. I say there's a God. That means consciousness exists after death. You say this is not true. That means there's nothing after death."

"If you are right about the relationship between consciousness and death, that does not mean there is a God, Simon."

"That's true," said Simon. The only way to know for sure is to die yourself. Are you ready to die to find the truth?"

"Then here is my truth," shouted Mectar brandishing his fist. "I must kill you. I must kill you as soon as I have protected my race from Cylots. If you are lying to me, Simon, then I must kill you to protect my race. And if you are not lying to me, then I must kill you anyway," said Mectar. Spines sprung from the middle of his back. His face changed to resemble that of a menacing lizard.

"Fine," said Simon. "Fine. So kill me now. Or kill me later. I don't care. You know what? You're anal retentive and so are the rest of the Kians. You're stuck in a mental loop. I am going to destroy Mectar the Warrior. When I am done with, you will laugh about it."

Mectar glared at Simon, his arms at his sides and his fists clenched. "Oh, you are such an asshole, Simon," said Mectar.

"I agree," said Simon. "Come on. We've got to get out of here before the police or more Cylots show up."

Mectar, now calmer, took his human form again.

"Okay, Mectar," said Simon. "I'll try it another way. You're on a boat in the middle of a river. A mountain is located in the distance. Is the boat or the mountain moving?"

"The boat, Simon. What do you want me to say? That the mountain is moving? Is that the answer you want?"

"No, Mectar. Neither one is moving."

"Then what is moving?"

"The mind, Mectar. The mind. If reality is a construct of the mind, it only exists in consciousness. The mind moves, not the boat or the mountain."

"You never answer questions. You just confuse me with scientific riddles. You make nothing clear. Whatever you allege to have discovered will be of no use to the Kian race. You show no logic in anything you say or do!" shouted Mectar. "Why is she with us?" he demanded, pointing angrily at Beth.

"How about it, Grey? Why are you with us?" Simon said. "Where's Javic?"

"I don't know where Javic is," she said.

"Can you find a piece of Javic?" asked Simon. "Can you find his wife? She's gone too. The cops went through their home. Does he have any family?"

Beth was silent for a moment and then answered, "I was invited to his grandson's bris. His daughter had a child four days ago. The bris will be held at the end of this week."

"Is Javic going to be there?" asked Simon.

"I don't know. His daughter, Judy, is a friend of mine. She hasn't been answering her phone."

"Why are you telling us this now?" asked Mectar.

"Well ..." She looked at Simon. He smiled.

"Well?" demanded Mectar.

"Because now I believe you. I believe in what you're doing. That's why," she said. "I agree with Mectar. You do talk in riddles. You appropriate my science and you don't give science back. Instead, you offer convoluted stories about logic. Explain what the Cylots are about! Explain what you're doing! Give it to me in hard science," said Beth while pounding her car's hood. "Give it to me so that I can understand and hold it. You want me to be part of this? Then make me a part of this! Make me understand. Give me the whole story, Benjamin."

"All right," said Simon. "Get in the car. Before I leave, I'll give you as much of my science as I think you can handle."

A crowd had gathered outside the diner. They had heard the argument and seen Mectar change form.

Beth got in the car and started the engine. Before Mectar got in, he glared at the gathering crowd. Using his physic ability, it took only seconds to immobilize them. Feelings of anguish and fear flowed from his mental synapses into their minds, his face contorting hideously in the process.

When Mectar got in the car, Simon saw in the rearview mirror that the Kian's face had returned to normal. Mectar smiled at what he had just done. Each person in the crowd would find and relive their deepest fears. Mectar stared at Simon with narrowed eyes and said nothing.

They sped out of the parking lot moments before the police arrived.

19

The Fear of Trust

After leaving the Park Diner Simon, Beth, and Mectar went to Berlex labs. Simon and Mectar now followed Beth's lead trying to locate clues Yugen may have left. They found nothing there. Beth drove east on Route 46 toward Hoffman-LaRoche as the sun was coming up. They had been riding silently for ten minutes. Simon was looking out the window. Mectar sat in the backseat, looking at the ceiling of the car, bored and indifferent to his surroundings.

"So let me put all this together. Kia," Beth said to Simon, "was an outward-expanding empire, and when they discovered Earth they tried to defeat and envelop it as a kind of colony. Am I right?"

"Essentially," Simon replied.

"And this fight was going on between Earth and Kia when each planet was attacked by the Cylots."

"That's about it."

"Kia defeated everybody they ran into until Earth and the Cylots?"

"Not quite," said Simon.

"What do you mean?" asked Beth.

"I mean the Barcini kicked their ass," said Simon.

"The Barcini," said Mectar from the backseat, "did not kick our ass. No one has kicked our ass. The Barcini simply have nothing we want."

"Bullshit," said Simon. "What the Barcini have is the technology that prevents you from defeating them."

"Who are the Barcini?" Beth asked.

"The Barcini, my dear," said Simon as Beth changed lanes, "are a mentally and technologically superior race, although I would say they are impoverished emotionally and genetically. Their morality is one based on science. They were the first race to make contact with Earth."

"What happened," said Beth, "when Kia attacked the Barcini?"

"The Barcini easily defeated the Kian fleet but did not attack Kia after they repulsed the Kian attack. They became independent, nonaggressive. They wouldn't align themselves with anyone from anywhere and would trade with anybody, no matter how hostile or ethically bereft the species was," said Simon, turning and looking at Mectar.

"Fuck you," said Mectar.

"Congratulations," said Simon. "You finally cursed at me properly."

"Well, why don't you ask the Barcini to help you fight the Cylots?" asked Beth.

"The Barcini don't help anyone," said Simon, suddenly getting very serious, his face turning dark. "I'm pretty sure the Lalians went to the Barcini to help them fight the Cylots. It's kind of the way the national park service takes care of your forests. If a forest burns down, the park service doesn't mind. It's part of nature. That's how the Barcini look at it. We humans are on our own. Just like any other species on Earth or in the cosmos. It's the competition of survival."

As they turned off Route 46 onto Route 3, Simon asked Beth how far they were from Hoffman-LaRoche. "It's only a few miles up the road," she said.

"Good. Let's pull into this restaurant. I need to make a phone call." Beth saw the golden arches of McDonald's ahead and followed his instructions. They pulled into the parking lot. The restaurant was built into the side of a hill.

"Who do you need to call here?" asked Mectar.

Simon responded, "I want to call Leary."

"The cop?" Mectar asked.

"One and the same," said Simon. "I want him to do me a favor."

"What do you want from him?" asked Beth.

"I need to know where Mueller came from. That's the site of infection. But you already know that, don't you, Doctor?"

"You know," she said, "I understand the site of infection and its path, but I never thought about it in terms of the human population. Not relating to a disease like this one, anyway."

"I won't be long." Simon walked into the restaurant and left Beth and Mectar standing in the parking lot. As Simon walked away, Beth saw him rub the back of his neck where it was black and blue.

Beth looked at Mectar and said, "Come on." She got back into the car and drove through the drive-up window to buy hamburgers for Mectar and herself. Then she parked the car and got out.

Mectar got out of the car and stood beside it. He took out the scanner and placed it on top of the car. It showed no activity, but he left it on. They stood quietly for a moment and then Beth said, "Mectar, when we were at the Park Diner last night, I saw Simon coming after you. I saw you go to strike him and then you didn't. It seemed like you were afraid of him."

Mectar removed a hamburger from its paper bag and bit through both the wrapper and hamburger itself. Beth watched, smiled, and said nothing. She unwrapped her hamburger.

Mectar looked sullen. "It was pointless to strike the blow," he said.

"What do you mean?" she asked.

"Simon is not what he appears to be. He has an electrical charge as part of his body's defense mechanism, similar to that of an electrical eel. Truthfully, striking him would hurt me more than it would hurt him. The strength of his electrical charge is proportional to the strength of the blow. Therefore, if I struck him hard enough, I might have killed myself. No, my dear," said Mectar, looking first to see if Simon was coming and then back at her. "He is not what he appears to be. You must understand. For the good of my planet, I must kill him. He is the greatest threat my planet has ever known."

The scanning device suddenly began to beep. The beeping increased and then decreased. "They passed us," said Mectar. "They're out looking for us," he said, looking up and down the highway, "but they don't know exactly where we are."

"The Cylots?" she said. Mectar nodded.

After the beeping subsided, Beth asked, "Did Kia ever defeat Earth? How did the war begin?"

Mectar replied, "If you ever have a chance to study planetary sociology, Beth, you will find that as a race matures it is natural to form a planetary government. Earth was just forming their planetary government. There was one world council that every nation sent delegates to, and the head of that council was called the general speaker.

"We inserted an agent who posed as the general speaker's aid. His purpose was to subvert the government and cause chaos until a Kian fleet could formally attack. The general speaker, with our agent's help, became a dictator. He used us as we used him. We were more technologically advanced than Earth at that time."

"Instead of subverting the Earth government, why didn't you first attack?" asked Beth.

"Our resources were elsewhere. Besides, it was cheaper to win by subversion than by frontal attack. In any event, our fleet was preparing to attack," said Mectar. "Then, out of nowhere, Simon appeared. They say he arrived in a crude time ship and he was disoriented. They say he organized the resistance and overthrew the general speaker. In the five Earth he overthrew the government, brought Earth to parity militarily with Kia, and fought us to a draw."

"Why didn't he rule the government of Earth, then?" asked Beth.

"It was at that point," said Mectar, "that a traitor to Earth, a man named Dirkin, sold the technology of time travel to Kia. Then the Cylots attacked us both, and from the there the story gets much more complicated."

"Well, Benjamin doesn't seem like such an asshole to me, Mectar. He seems like a hero," said Beth defiantly.

Mectar gulped the last bite of his hamburger and said, "Hero? He is a *pulvzar*. If I called another Kian that, there would be blood. It is the worst insult a Kian can hurl. And do you know what Simon did, Beth, when I called him that? He laughed. I expected a fight and he found it humorous. So I vowed to curse at him in his language. Do you know what that is like? 'Fuck you' and 'I want to fuck you' are totally different. But when I took the English course before this assignment, I was told every sentence must have a subject. So 'Fuck you' means 'I want to fuck you,' which is not what it means at all! You call this a language? And what does 'Fuck me' mean? Are you cursing at yourself? Is it an invitation? And 'go fuck yourself' cannot be physically accomplished by your species," explained Mectar as if talking to a child. "And of what use is it in a sentence like, 'I drove the fucking car'? It makes no sense, Beth. And when someone says, 'You are a real fuck,' is that a compliment? And I have no idea what it means when someone says, 'Fuuuuuuck.' Once Simon said to me, 'Fuck you and the horse you rode in on.' And I wasn't even near a horse," said Mectar with obvious frustration. "Why do you use one word to describe awe, sex, love, hate, and anger? It does not make sense. He helps me curse at him correctly. How do you fight such a being?" Mectar said mostly to himself.

Beth did her best not to laugh and nodded. "I agree," she said. "It doesn't make any fucking sense." Mectar stopped and glared at her. "Oh relax, I'm just fucking with you," she said, and then she laughed.

Then Mectar continued angrily, "But I tell you he is an asshole. All of you are assholes. I know what that means." Mectar lowered his voice again as he saw Simon coming out of the restaurant. "He is the muscle that controls the flow of excrement. Say no more." That was how Mectar ended the conversation.

"Let's go," Simon ordered angrily as he reached Beth and Mectar.

"What's the matter?" asked Mectar.

"You know, after a while you just get callous to people dying," said Simon.

"Who's dying?" asked Beth.

"Two cops are going to die and there's not a goddamned thing I can do about it," said Simon.

"Well, didn't you tell them? Didn't you warn them?" Beth asked.

"Of course I did," said Simon getting into the car. "You think they're going to listen to me? Do you think they trust me? Shit, you don't even listen to me. Do you trust me, Grey?"

She stared at him hard. "No," she said quietly.

"Mectar trusts me. Don't you, Mectar?"

"Not at all, Simon."

"I trust you, Mectar. I trust you will try to kill me."

"You can trust me to do that, Simon!"

"You think two strange cops are going to listen to me when I tell them not to do something or how to do it? Goddamn it!" he said, slamming the door. "Take me to Hoffman-LaRoche!"

20

To See the Future: Darkly

Tom Jenkins was sweating and his heart pounded as he searched his house for his two little boys. He finally found them huddled together in a corner in one of the bedrooms. They were seven and nine.

Then they ran down the hall, passing door after door until they reached the back stairs. As they reached the bottom of the stairs, flames blew into the hallway. A creature, evil and loathsome, glared at him and hissed, "Tom Jenkins, we want you."

He ran back up the stairs with his family, going into the bedroom whose window overlooked a lower porch roof. Creatures came at him from both ends of the hallway, and this was the only escape. His wife climbed onto the porch roof. He handed the seven-year-old through the window into her waiting arms.

Before his eyes, the porch roof collapsed into a fiery inferno. His family fell into the flames. "No!" he screamed as he ran to the window.

He sat bolt upright in bed, sweating. "What's the matter?" his wife asked. He put his head in his hands. "Another headache, dear?" she said as she sat up and rubbed the back of his neck.

He opened his mouth to speak but then shut it. "Yes," he said." A headache." He didn't want to tell her about the dream. He looked at the clock on his bed stand. It was 5:45 AM. "I've got to go down to the lab," he said, swinging his feet down off the bed onto the floor. Then he sat on the bedside, his hands gripping the side of the bed. "Darling …"

"Yes, babe?" she said, placing her hand reassuringly on his back.

"I love you and the boys, you know," he said.

"I know, dear. Maybe you should take a break. Maybe you should take some vacation time."

He was quiet for a minute and then shook his head. "No," he said. "I can't do that. I've got to save my vacation time so we can visit your mother in Florida."

"It's okay if you take a couple of days, dear," she said.

"I'm going to take a shower," he said.

"I love you," she said, putting her head back down on the pillow.

"I love you too," responded Jenkins as he walked from the bedroom. But before he went to the bathroom to shower, he checked both of his children's rooms. When he finished getting dressed, he drove to his job as a Schering-Plough chemist.

21

The West Orange Police Station

The West Orange Police Department was very active, as two policemen had been killed at Organon during the previous night. While officer Ignatello was relatively new to the force, Doyle, a popular sergeant, had been there for sixteen years. Whenever an officer dies in the line of duty, a special effort is made to apprehend the killer. During the mobilization, Patrolman Murphy found Sergeant O'Toole seated at Doyle's desk.

"Hey, Sarge."

"What?" asked O'Toole. O'Toole had red hair and a strikingly fair complexion despite his chiseled old face. Murphy, a nice young man who joined the department during the previous year, had dark hair. O'Toole constantly kidded him about being Black Irish. He explained to Murphy that his Irish coloring derived from the Spanish sailors who had washed up on Irish shores after the English defeated the Armada. O'Toole never would have thought of expressing the explanation in terms of gene pools.

"There's something you ought to see, Sarge," said Murphy.

"What's that?"

"We've got people out here from the Park Restaurant. There was a fight there last night. The Livingston police sent them here for questioning. They questioned them and said we should look at what they had. I mean, Sarge—"

Take their statements," said O'Toole disinterestedly. His disinterest was a façade, though. Because of their common descent, O'Toole held Murphy to a higher standard. He wanted him to be not just a good cop but a very good cop.

"Sarge, I think you ought to look at this," persisted Murphy.

O'Toole grunted as he got up from his desk and walked impatiently out the door. "What is it?" he asked approaching the group.

"Sarge, these people say two guys and a girl started a fight before they left the restaurant. The Livingston Police couldn't catch them. Seems one guy told the other that this man here was going to explode," said Murphy, pointing to the fat man.

O'Toole, seeing the bulk of the man in question, grunted. He sure looked fat enough. "So what?" said O'Toole.

"Then they argued because the first guy believed him," said Murphy.

"So, there was an argument," said O'Toole impatiently.

"Sarge, the second man changed his shape. This happened in front of twenty people. This ain't normal," said Murphy with certainty.

"Take their statements, Murphy." O'Toole took the pictures. "Have you seen Leary here yet?"

"Yeah. He's upstairs with the FBI guys."

"Keep these people separated. I don't want them mixing their stories," said O'Toole. "I think Cyrus ought to know about this."

"Right, Sarge," said Murphy.

"Oh, Murphy?"

"Yeah, Sarge?"

"Good work, son."

Murphy grinned in response.

As O'Toole searched for Cyrus, he did not see the girl who entered the reception area. Murphy did. She was beautiful. The grin never left his face. He recovered with a start and said, "Can I help you?"

This was not the first time Abby Clarendon had received that response from a man. Although not fully recovered from having witnessed a murder, she smiled appreciatively. "My name is Abby Clarendon," she said. "Detective Wheeler had me come in for questioning. I was at Chanel when Walter Harris was murdered."

"Oh, yes," said Murphy.

"I'll take care of this, Murphy." Murphy turned and saw Tom Comstock. Although Comstock was the senior officer, Murphy and Comstock acted as partners. He would, in all likelihood, replace Doyle as sergeant.

If Murphy had been slightly awkward when he encountered Abby, Comstock was professional and suave. "Right this way, Miss. Detective Wheeler asked me to take your statement. Can I get you a cup of coffee before we begin?"

"No, thanks," she said as she followed Comstock down the hall.

"Lucky son of a bitch," Murphy murmured as they departed. His attention focused on Abby's posterior and shapely legs. He noticed his buddy Comstock rubbing his right shoulder. A black and blue mark was becoming visible above his collar.

◆   ◆   ◆

As the group from the Park Diner was being questioned, Leary drove to the West Orange Police Department. Whatever had exploded the previous night at Organon was still affecting him. He felt like he needed a shower and three cups of coffee.

On his way to the station, he mulled over the previous night's conversation with Simon. Could Simon prove that he was from the future? Even if could, the situation seemed ridiculous. Yet he had seen Simon using technology so advanced it could only be from the future. He saw the Cylot and two dead police officers. He decided for one day to suspend his disbelief and accept what he was seeing as the truth. "Okay," he said to himself, "Simon is telling the truth."

Leary drove into the station's parking lot. A moment later, he walked past Desk Sergeant O'Toole. Leary nodded at him as he walked toward the coffee pot. "Morning, Sarge," he said.

O'Toole didn't return the greeting. "All you've got time for is that cup of coffee," O'Toole said. "Get right upstairs. Cyrus is waiting for you."

Leary gave O'Toole a weak two-fingered salute and thanked him.

"God, you look like hell," detective Longo said as he saw Leary.

Leary ignored Longo's comment, got his coffee, and made his way to Cyrus' office.

"You wanted me?" Leary asked as he entered Cyrus' office.

Cyrus looked at him and said, "You look like hell—you know that?" Leary nodded wearily. "Wheeler will be in soon," Cyrus continued. I have an APB out on the fugitives. I want Simon and Mectar stopped and brought in. That should end the killings. At least now we know who's committing the murders."

"Simon didn't kill anyone last night. I know who did it now," said Leary.

"Oh, do you?" said Cyrus.

"Yeah," said Leary at once smiling and wincing. He knew what was coming.

"Who, pray tell, who murdered Livermore?" asked Cyrus.

"The Cylots," said Leary

"Who are the Cylots?" asked Cyrus.

"An alien race."

"What?" said Cyrus.

"That's why Earth and Kia aren't at war right now. They have a truce."

"Huh?" said Cyrus, now thoroughly confused.

"Listen," said Leary. "Earth and Kia are at war in the future. Cylots attacked both planets with a kind of infection weapon. A Kian, named Mectar and a human, named Simon, are working together to stop them.

"A researcher named Yugen was working on the project. He came back to hide in the past, but he was killed. Either he or someone who got their hands on the formula mailed it to a bunch of other researchers, presumably in hopes of exposing the Cylots. Now at least we know that Simon and Mectar don't have the formula. They're tracking it. Since Yugen is dead, they can only hope to get it from the researchers who received it in the mail.

"The Cylots have a list of those researchers and have been killing them. That's why we have to find a researcher who has the formula and is still alive."

"I see," said Cyrus, nodding. "Earth and Kia are at war and Simon and Mectar are working together. When did Simon find out?" Cyrus raised his eyebrows questioningly.

"Last night when he broke into Organon," said Leary.

"Why was Simon at Organon last night?" Cyrus asked.

"Because," said Leary impatiently, "he's looking for the formula that exposes the Cylots. Dr. Yugen created it. The Cylots can infect a human body and control it. Simon is working with a research assistant from Merck named Grey."

"You mean the Cylots are like body snatchers?" asked Cyrus through tight lips.

"Sort of," said Leary.

"Listen, Leary," said Cyrus standing up. "Maybe you've been working a little too hard. Maybe you should take some time off."

"Bobby Joe," said Leary, "I'm not kidding."

"Listen, I'm not asking you to take time off," said Cyrus. He approached Leary in a fatherly manner, putting his hand on Leary's shoulder. "I'm telling you to take time off."

"No." Leary looked directly at Cyrus.

"I'm going to suspend you until you are evaluated by an internal affairs psychiatrist," Cyrus said flatly.

"I'm not coming off this case," said Leary.

"Oh, yes you are."

Leary removed his badge and gun and slid it across Cyrus' desk. "I resign," he said with finality.

Cyrus stared at the badge and gun in front of him.

"Ask Wheeler to describe what he believes and what he saw last night. If he doesn't completely back me, then throw me in jail for all I care," said Leary. "But the fact is that two police officers were killed last night. I was there. Whatever the hell it was, we were there with our guns drawn. They threw something and none of us could move for about two hours. I feel like a piece of shit, but I'm not going to quit this case. The trail is still warm. I'm staying on it."

Cyrus stared at Leary. "You know what you sound like?"

"I don't give a shit what I sound like."

Cyrus sat down, then lowered his head and leaned forward. Cyrus grabbed the gun and shield Leary had placed in front of him. He slid them back across the desk toward Leary. "Since I can't control you, I've got to support you. You report everything. Is that clear?" barked Cyrus. "And if Wheeler doesn't totally agree with you, I'm throwing your ass in jail."

"Yes, BJ," chuckled Leary. He returned his gun to his holster and snapped his belt.

"Or a sanitarium. You understand, boy?"

"Bobby Joe?"

"What?" said Cyrus now obviously irritated.

"I promise to write."

"Get out of here," said Cyrus.

As Leary turned to leave, Wheeler, Longo, and a forensic toxicologist named Reggie Dennin walked in.

"Wait, Leary," said Cyrus. "I'm glad you're here. You already know Wheeler. This is Reggie Dennin. Al," said Cyrus, "Leary just told me—"

Wheeler held up his hand for Cyrus to stop. "Whatever he told you, just go with it, BJ. We'll hash it out later. Listen to this first."

Reggie shook Leary's hand. He had a thin mustache, a paunch, a friendly smile, and dancing eyes. "Hi, how are you?" he said.

Leary shook his hand and nodded.

"This is Jerry Longo, West Orange Police," said Wheeler.

"Jerry and I have already met," said Leary. He noted Longo's thick shoulders and heavily calloused hands, his round, pudgy face and flat, passive eyes. Cyrus went through the same conversation with Wheeler that he had with Leary, in spite of Wheeler trying to delay the conversation. Wheeler, while not accepting the explanation Simon had given as easily as Leary had, did corroborate Leary's version of the events.

When that was done, they all sat down to listen to Dennin's report.

Leary sat down with his coffee. Cyrus said, "Reggie here has done the pathology reports and the autopsies on everyone that was killed. This includes the policemen murdered at Merck."

"I also had a chance to examine the bodies of the two policemen killed here last night. What happened to them resembles an electrical accident," said Dennin.

"You mean Sergeant Doyle was electrocuted?" asked Wheeler.

"Oh no," said Reggie. "He was shot, but he died before he was shot. Like the police officers at Merck, they were dead for several hours before they were shot. Deterioration begins at death."

"Are you saying they died and then walked around?" asked Leary.

"All the cops who died at Rahway had brain or central nervous system damage. Sudden and traumatic," said Dennin.

"I thought you said electrical shock or gun shots killed them," said Cyrus. "You're not making sense."

"The reason I'm giving you contradictory information is because that is what the results were. There are several indices that we use to determine time of death. The primary ones are body temperature, food digestion, blood coagulation, lividity, and eyewitness reports. There is another sub-group of indices, such as enzymes and protein deterioration, but we couldn't use those in this instance. We could determine the time of death at Merck because we had videotapes of the guards entering Building 80. We know when the bodies were discovered, so death had to occur during that window of opportunity between 11:00 AM and noon. However, the body temperature loss indicates that they died at least five hours prior to that time; their bodies were at ambient room temperature when they were examined at 13:30. So the body's heat loss is inconsistent with the eyewitness reports.

"We next explored digestion. One guard, Atkins, had stopped digesting two days earlier. The others had all clearly stopped digesting at least six hours earlier. Frankly, gentlemen, I've never seen anything like this. We next tested lividity."

Wheeler held up a pencil to indicate that he wanted to ask a question. Dennin held up his hand. He wanted to finish his statement before answering questions.

"Lividity, as we all know, is how blood pools in the body after death. If the victim is face down, with the left side of his face on the ground, more blood will be pooled in the left cheek than the right. If he is found on his back, more blood will be found along the dorsal side of his body than the frontal side. Regarding Atkins, we found that blood had pooled in the bottom of his feet. It seems he died standing up. The examination yields the following information: Atkins died two days ago standing up, but he was not actually 'dead' till he was shot at Merck. The other guards also died standing up, at least six hours earlier. They were not 'dead' until midnight that night."

"Then what was the cause of death?" asked Leary.

"Let me provide an analogy," said Dennin. "Suppose we go outside, remove your police cruiser's battery, and empty the gas tank, and return. Then later we find your car two blocks away. Now, clearly, the car has moved when it could not possibly move. How did it move? My response to you, sir, with all due respect: Beats the hell out of me."

Cyrus slammed his pencil on the desk and emitted an exasperated sigh.

"I know," said Dennin, waving at Cyrus as if to calm him. "But there's more. There's the electrical burns on the back of the neck. It's as though somebody hot-wired these people and was controlling them."

"They were zombies?" asked Wheeler.

"No," said Dennin, "a zombie is still alive while under the control of someone else. These people were dead."

"Was it anything like what happened to the murdered researchers?" asked Longo.

"No, but that's interesting. I've never seen a weapon like that," said Dennin.

"Nobody has," Wheeler muttered load enough for everyone to hear.

"They were clearly shot in the head with an electrical charge entering the brain," said Dennin. "And there's one fact that ties them together."

"What's that?" asked Cyrus.

"A particular part of the brain was destroyed."

"Which is?" asked Wheeler.

"The hippocampus," said Dennin.

"The hippo what?" asked Leary.

"Look," said Dennin. "There's a whole new field called brain cartography, brain mapping. According to it, the hippocampus consolidates recently acquired information and turns short-term memory into long-term memory. It's the brain's epicenter."

"Are you trying to tell us that the murderer or the murderers specifically wanted to destroy each victim's hippocampus?" said Cyrus.

"I'm not telling you anything," said Dennin, leaning forward with palms outstretched. "All I'm telling you is how they died. I can't tell you why anybody would want to prevent the hippocampus from functioning. I can't tell you why they are killing researchers. However, They're doing it. They're doing it in a way I never thought of before. All I can say is that these people are very, very dead."

"We knew that already," said Wheeler.

"Yeah, I thought you did," said Dennin, smiling.

O'Toole knocked and leaned into the room. "Agent Cyrus, we've still got some people downstairs. One of you should interview them," he said. "It sounds like your guys from Organon."

"Leary, why don't you interview them?" said Cyrus. "You seem to have the best handle on this guy Simon. See what you can get out of them." Leary nodded and followed O'Toole downstairs.

"The waitress is in here for questioning," said O'Toole, pointing to a closed door.

Leary opened the door and entered a small retaining room. Inside, he saw a black-uniformed waitress looking out the window and smoking a cigarette. "Ma'am?" said Leary, nodding at her. "I'm Lieutenant Leary. Can you tell me a little about what happened last night?"

The waitress began to tell her story. As she began, she nervously put out her cigarette and lit another one. As she was finishing, she described the man who was the last to enter the car. Leary realized she had described Mectar. "I ain't seen nothing like it," she said, cracking her gum. "His face just melted. You know what I mean? I was a hideous … thing!" She spread her fingers. Still holding her cigarette, she slowly drew her hands downward to indicate Mectar's melting face.

O'Toole entered the room and stood quietly while the waitress finished.

"Thank you, ma'am," said Leary. He rose to leave.

"Well, what are you going to do about the thing?" she asked.

"I'll get back to you, ma'am," Leary said rising with a nod.

Back in the hallway, O'Toole handed Leary a file and pointed to another closed retaining room. Leary swiftly looked at the file, then entered the room. Inside, Edna, and Louise Laufner sat at a table. Sisters, in their late seventies, they did not want to be separated.

"Would you mind telling me what happened when the car pulled away, ladies," Leary asked.

"Well, Edna and I were just talking about that," said Louise. "We both agree that his face melted. I'd say it looked like that thing from that movie. You know the one that jumps out the closet at you?" As she said that, she reached out to Leary, her hand gestures punctuating her words. "But Edna won't say where it's from. I think it was hideous."

"Edna," Leary leaned down, "I need to know, Edna. It threatens other people," he said kindly. "What did it look like?"

With her lower lip trembling, Edna looked Leary in the eye and said, "It looked like Uncle George."

The other interviews ran the same way—each observer seeming to connect the event with his or her deepest fear. Afterward, Leary came back upstairs with another cup of coffee. He didn't know what to think. As he entered the conference room, Wheeler and Longo were on their way out. "See you later," Wheeler said to Leary.

"We're going to check out Mueller's boss, a guy named Heinrich at Rockefeller University in New York. His name was on the visitors' register at Chanel the same time Harris was murdered there. Cyrus here wants to debrief you. I'll be back later this afternoon. Take care of yourself."

"Hey, if you meet any aliens, don't antagonize them," said Leary. Wheeler gave him a mock disgusted look.

"Well?" said Cyrus.

"It was them, all right. But they're doing things I can't describe," said Leary. "A witness said one of the guys looked like her Uncle George."

"Then how do you know it was them?" asked Cyrus.

"Trust me. I know. Apparently, Simon argued with Mectar. Their fight concerned some fat guy that Simon said would explode and Mectar chased him out of the restaurant."

"Huh?" said Cyrus in disbelief.

"Look," said Leary with exasperation. "It doesn't make any more sense to me than it does to you. Frankly, Simon's story, as ridiculous as it sounds, is the only one I've heard that ties all this together, and it's real hard to believe him."

"Was Grey still with them?" asked Cyrus.

"Yeah, and she went with them willingly too."

"Did you get a plate number? Can we track them?" asked Cyrus.

"No, they covered their tracks. Nobody can remember anything about the getaway car. They just remember being frightened by Mectar."

"Great," said Cyrus, throwing his pen on the table. "Okay. Write it up in a report. We'll meet back here this afternoon when Wheeler returns with Longo. In the meantime, I'll have the medical people examine the bodies."

After leaving Cyrus, Leary got another cup of coffee and went to the office he was sharing with Wheeler. As he typed his report about the Park Diner interviews, O'Toole walked in.

"We've got an anonymous tipster on the line for you," said O'Toole. "Says he'll only talk to you. Claims he's got something about your—"

Leary rose with a pained look on his face. "Okay, Sarge. Where should I take the call?" The sergeant pointed to a small room at the end of the hall.

Leary walked into the office and picked up the phone. "Leary, homicide," he said.

"Leary? This is Simon."

Leary immediately perked up. "Yes?" he said calmly while signaling frantically to a patrolman to trace the line.

"I need some help," said Simon.

Leary chuckled, "What kind of help do you need from me?" he said slowly, to facilitate the trace; he wanted to keep Simon talking.

"I want you to find out everything you can about Mueller. Where does he come from? What was he working on? Who is he ... or was he? Get as much as you can for me. I'll get back to you."

"Wait a minute! Who the hell do you think you are?" demanded Leary.

"Consider it a professional courtesy. By the way, how are you feeling?" Simon asked, referring to the sensory grenade Mectar had thrown.

"I feel like shit. How do think I feel?" asked Leary.

"Next time I see you, remind me to give you the antidote. If this ever happens again, you can use it."

"What professional courtesy do I owe you?" said Leary.

"Consider me a cop from the future," said Simon.

"I don't really know what to consider you," Leary said.

"It really doesn't matter. Good-bye ... Wait! I've got to tell you what we're looking for. Mueller's body was taken over. I don't know how recently. So talk to his wife and children. But most importantly, find out who he worked for. Not just his boss, but who directed his actions. Mueller was not in charge of this Cylot operation."

"How can you be so sure Mueller was a Cylot?" asked Leary.

"Does it make a difference?" Simon asked. "If you visit his home, don't bring weapons."

"Why?"

"Because you should not make yourself more of a target than necessary. Besides, any weapon you carry isn't going to stop them or prevent you from getting the disease. They will want you if they think you're a threat."

"Let me tell you something," said Leary. "Wheeler and Longo are on their way to see Mueller's boss. They're carrying their weapons. As a matter of fact, they're bringing him in for questioning."

"No!" shouted Simon. "Don't do that. If you try to push the Cylots too hard, your men will wind up dead."

"Listen, Simon. Don't try to tell us how to do our job."

"Fine," said Simon. "I'm merely suggesting ways to limit your exposure. By the way, I also need to know what you found so far. And are you near a fax machine?"

"Yeah," said Leary.

"I need the number. I'm going to fax you a list of names of researchers in danger. Grey told us that all the people who died were connected with lab animal research colonies. Even if this information doesn't connect them with the Cylots or the formula, it does link them to each other. There are only a few lab animal research colonies in this area. We need to go to every LAR colony that hasn't had a murder to find out what the Cylots are searching for. She even gave me the names of doctors who head departments for these facilities. I need to track them down. If you find the formula, get it to me. And Leary, you had better hope that I get it before they do. No, I'm wrong. Your children had better hope that I get it before they do. I'll get back to you."

As Simon hung up, the patrolman entered.

"Where is he calling from?" said Leary.

"Lieutenant, there's no trace on that call. Somebody scrambled the conversation. It seems that your conversation knocked out every call on the cellular network."

"Shit," said Leary. "Send O'Toole in here, will ya?"

"Yeah, Leary?" said O'Toole as he walked in.

"I want you to find out everything you can on Mueller. He's the guy who was here the other night, then he disappeared. And get me Wheeler."

"The radio's broken in the car that Wheeler took. We can't get a hold of him," O'Toole said.

"Shit," said Leary.

When Leary received the faxed list of researchers, he noticed immediately that there was something wrong with it. He gave it to Cyrus.

"I want to go up to Novartis," said Leary. "Can you spare a car?"

"Why?" asked Cyrus.

"There's a doctor there who I think is a target. He's on that list Simon faxed us."

"Did you call him?" asked Cyrus.

"I got his secretary. She says he's not in his office but somewhere in the plant. I want to go to talk to him."

"Fine. O'Toole will give you a driver and a car. But keep in touch," said Cyrus. "In the meantime, I'll try to contact the other two doctors and get a hold of Wheeler. There are only two left, right? One at Hoffman-LaRoche and another at Schering Plough?"

"Right," said Leary. "And I'll cover Novartis right now."

22

The Orangetown Police

Lederle Laboratories, a division of the American Cyanamid Company, is located in the town of Pearl River, New York. In 1991, Lederle built a quarter-million-square-foot pharmaceutical research facility there. It is known as Building 200.

Dr. Seymour Henkle's office was located on the first floor of Building 200. He sat back in his chair and read the formula attached to the sheet behind Varley's letter. Since interoffice mail at Lederle was exceedingly slow, it had arrived late. Henkle remembered that Varley had given an interesting desensitization lecture at the last LAR symposium.

Henkle put the letter down in the middle of the desk and stared at it thoughtfully. The formula was interesting, but he wondered why Varley, a respected professional, would write him such a letter. Obviously, the man had gone mad. Beings wandering around eating consciousness? He shook his head. He turned the letter over and looked at the formula again. How many other researchers had received the same letter? Then he wondered if this letter was connected to the deaths of so many researchers he had read about. He again took up the letter, then put it on the side of the desk and began to do some paperwork. Then he stopped and flipped the letter over to look at the formula again.

He began to call the police and then stopped. Then he put the letter in his inside coat pocket and left his office. "Michelle," he said to his secretary.

The young girl looked up from her word processor. "Yes, Doctor?"

"I'll be back in an hour. If anybody needs me I'll be down at the police department."

"All right, sir."

Dr. Seymour Henkle had been gone for fifteen minutes when there came a soft knock on his secretary's door. A smiling man appeared in the doorway. "Can I help you?" said Michelle.

"Is Dr. Henkle in?"

"I'm sorry, no. He won't be back for another forty-five minutes," she said.

"Any idea where he went?"

"Yes. He said he was going to the police department. Can I help you?" Michelle asked.

"Here in town?" the man asked.

"Yes, who shall I say called?" she asked.

Heinrich stepped into her office, leaned over her desk, and gently touched her hand. She never felt the static electrical charge, which jumped between his hand and hers.

"Here in town?" he repeated. Her eyes momentarily went blank.

"I guess," she said. "He really didn't say. I think that he went to the Orange-town Police Department."

"I'll try to catch up with him there," said Heinrich.

"Excuse me, sir. Should I say who called?"

"Dr. Heinrich," the man said. "Tell him a Dr. Heinrich was looking for him."

"Would you like to leave a number?"

"No. That won't be necessary. I'm sure I'll track him down."

Michelle absentmindedly wrote on a piece of paper: "Dr. Heinrich stopped in" and left it in Dr. Henkle's box. Then she returned to her work, not fully aware of what had just transpired.

Dr. Henkle had walked out of Building 200 and into the parking lot. Deep in thought, he didn't say hello to the staff who waved hello to him as he walked to his car. Could he be on the target list too? He began to drive toward the Orange-town Police Department, which had jurisdiction over both the town of Pearl River and Lederle Labs.

A radio newscaster was talking about a sadistic ritual killer who had struck again in New York City's Greenwich Village, killing a woman. He found himself involuntarily looking in the rearview mirror.

The Orangetown Police Department was having an addition put on the municipal building. As Henkle walked into the building, he passed a backhoe, and a front-end loader. Both machines sat next to an excavation. The hole already had concrete sides and rough stone at its base. Henkle walked across the muddy parking lot. He entered the municipal building through a side door. As he walked through the open lobby of the first floor, looking for the police department, he passed several offices with clerks sitting behind desks.

In one corner, there was a lady with no title sitting behind a desk. She had her hair in a bun and disinterest in her eyes. Henkle asked her where the police department was. She pointed toward the basement. He descended the steps into the cellar and saw that the police station entrance had a coded card entry that said, "Authorized Personnel Only." However, in the little basement lobby there were several items. One was a phone on the desk with a sign that said, "Police. Pick up the phone. Dial 10. Police Department personnel will answer." Henkle picked up the phone, dialed 10, and waited.

A voice said, "Orangetown Police, Officer Dellaluna speaking."

"Ahh, yes," said Henkle diffidently. "I'd like to talk to a police officer."

"In regards to?" said Dellaluna.

"I received something in the mail that I think you should see."

"Take a seat and someone will be out to pick you up in a moment." Henkle heard the phone clunk down. He stood in the dank area and looked at the many doors that led out of the small lobby. He looked at the walls. There were signs posted randomly. "Say no to drugs," said one. Another over a door with a card reader on it said, "This room has been designated for the questioning of juveniles as approved by the Appellate Division, Supreme Court."

Finally, the door at the end of the hall opened, under the sign that said, "No Admittance, Authorized Police Personnel Only." A secretary stuck her head out of the door. "Dr. Henkle?" she said. "Come right in." He walked past her down a short hallway. Behind the main police desk sat Police Officer Carmine Dellaluna.

Carmine Dellaluna typified the popular derisive image of a policeman. Prominent on his desk were a half-eaten Old New England pecan fudge brownie and a cup of coffee. The buttons on the shirt around his waist appeared to be under such stress that if they popped, they would fly with enough force to put a hole in the wall across from him. The police belt he wore held his gun, handcuffs, keys, and a small flashlight in a sheath. The belt looked thick enough to hold a saddle to Dellaluna's back.

Dellaluna held a pen and a newspaper. Henkle waited for a moment at his desk. As Dellaluna put the paper down, Henkle saw that it was opened to a half-finished crossword puzzle. "Can I help you?" Dellaluna asked.

Henkle studied the officer's face for a second. Heavy jowls, bags under his eyes, not from fatigue but from age. A receding hairline, yet in the middle of his forehead there was a prominent peak of hair shaved into a long crew cut.

"Yes, I'm Dr. Henkle," he began. "I work at Lederle. I received something disquieting in the mail this morning that I believe is connected to the deaths of other researchers."

"May I see it?" said Dellaluna holding out his hand.

Henkle hesitated, then handed Dellaluna the letter. Dellaluna nodded, looked it over, and handed it back. Then he held up a finger to indicate one minute and dialed the phone.

"Hi, Leo. Carmine." Henkle distinctly heard two words: "Car" and "mine."

"Is the lieutenant there?" Dellaluna asked. "I've got a doctor here from Lederle. Says he's got some evidence connected with all those researchers dying." Dellaluna looked up at Dr. Henkle. "Anyone die at Lederle yet?" he asked.

Henkle shook his head. "No, not that I know of."

"He says no," said Dellaluna. "You want to talk to him? All right, I'll send him up. That way you can start filling out a report by the time the lieutenant gets back." Dellaluna hung up the phone and pointed down the hallway. "Down the hallway, second door on your left. Up one flight of stairs and first door on your right."

Henkle followed the directions to the second floor. When he entered the detective's office, he stopped, startled. Leo Dellaluna smiled at him. "Carmine's my twin," Leo said in answer to Henkle's unasked question. "The way to tell us apart is that he eats those New England pecan fudge brownies and I eat Twinkies."

"Sit down, Doctor. What have you got for us?" said Leo, putting Seymour Henkle at ease.

"Well, I got this letter in the mail," began Dr. Henkle, handing Brad Varley's letter to Leo Dellaluna.

◆   ◆   ◆

Heinrich had no trouble finding the Orangetown police station. He knew the danger he faced; certainly, if governmental agencies knew about the formula, it would become public. He had to retrieve it, and now. He walked into the police station, dialed 10, and asked if Dr. Henkle had arrived yet. "Yes," said Carmine Dellaluna. "He's here."

"I'm his associate," said Heinrich. "He asked me to meet him here."

"Okay. Sit tight and let me check," said Dellaluna.

"Wait," said Heinrich.

"What?" said Dellaluna. The phone line crackled with a static electrical charge. Had Dellaluna been able to see it, he would have seen a blue electrical glow surround the phone and his hands, and even penetrate his ear.

"Why don't you buzz me in?" said Heinrich.

"I'll buzz you in," said Dellaluna.

Heinrich walked through the door and down the same short hallway that Henkle had come through just a few minutes before. Carmine had not yet finished the crossword puzzle or the Old New England pecan fudge brownie.

"I'm looking for Dr. Henkle. He told me to meet him down here," said Heinrich.

Carmine nodded. "He's upstairs in the detective's office."

"How do I get there?"

Carmine pointed down the hall, "Second doorway on the left, up one flight of stairs, first doorway on your right."

Heinrich walked into the detective's office. He saw Henkle sitting on one side of the desk and someone who looked distinctly like the gentleman downstairs sitting behind this desk with a form in the typewriter, typing. Heinrich paused briefly and recorded in his memory that humans had the ability to clone themselves. "Dr. Henkle?" Heinrich asked.

"Yes," said Henkle.

"I believe you received a formula in the mail. Do you have it with you?"

"Who are you?" said Henkle.

"I'm Dr. Heinrich from the National Institute of Psychiatry. I believe you have been the victim of a terrible hoax."

"Why is that?" said Henkle.

"You received a letter from a man named Varley?"

"Yes," said Henkle.

"Do you have it with you?" asked Heinrich.

"It's right here," said Henkle, holding it up.

"Has anyone else seen it?" asked Heinrich.

"Just Officer Dellaluna," said Henkle.

"Are you certain of that?"

"Why do you want to know?" asked Leo Dellaluna, swiveling around in his chair.

"I need to know who has been exposed to this hoax," said Heinrich.

"Well, no one else," said Henkle.

"Good," said Heinrich, drawing a phaser and pointing it at Henkle's head. He fired the weapon.

Henkle fell backward. His brains preceded him to the floor.

"Aww, shit," said Leo Dellaluna. He fumbled for his gun, which he hadn't had out of his holster since last month at the firing range. It was no contest. Heinrich turned and fired again.

Leo Dellaluna fell back over the chair and onto the floor. Heinrich picked up the letter and walked toward the door. Before stepping into the hallway, he looked both ways. He heard footsteps coming up the stairs he had come up, so he turned and swiftly went down another stairwell.

Carmine Dellaluna was first in the room. He saw Henkle lying on his back in a pool of blood, his eyes open, staring at the ceiling. Then he saw his brother, Leo. He pushed aside the chair, knelt down beside his twin brother, and cradled him in his arms. When the other policemen reached the door they found Carmine Dellaluna cradling and rocking his dead brother in his arms, crying, "Leo, Leo, Leo …"

Heinrich walked quickly out through the building and into the parking lot. As he pulled out of the parking lot, he passed two officers in a patrol car pulling in from their shift, unaware of what had just occurred. He pulled out of the parking lot and onto the Palisades Parkway South. He would head back to the office in New York to sanitize it. He was nearly done here. Then he would head toward his rendezvous with Mueller at Schering-Plough.

23

The Memory Molecule

Hoffman-LaRoche, located in Nutley, New Jersey, has two primary entrances. One is located at 340 Kingsland Drive. The other is situated on Route 3, which parallels Hoffman-LaRoche's north side.

Simon, Beth, and Mectar arrived at the guardhouse near Route 3. Beth called Dr. Rollins' office from the sentry's phone.

"LAR," the secretary said.

"Hi, is Dr. Rollins in?" Beth asked.

"No, he isn't," said the secretary.

"Who is this?" Beth asked.

"Cheryl."

"Hi, Cheryl. This is Beth Grey from Merck."

"Oh, hi. We haven't heard from you since the symposium. How are you?" Cheryl said.

"Fine, thanks. It's important that I get a hold of Fred right away. Can you page him?"

"I can send one of the techs out to look for him. He's with Dr. Terino, the FDA inspector, out in the vivarium," said Cheryl.

"Oh," said Beth. "You mean The Terror." Cheryl giggled.

"Isn't that the truth?" Cheryl said. "He always gives us a hard time."

"Listen," said Beth. "It's very, very important. Can you find him? Can you get us in?"

"Hang on a second," said Cheryl. Grey heard Cheryl talking. "Beth?" said Cheryl, coming back on the line. "I just got a tech to radio Dr. Rollins. He's in the primate area. He said he'd see you, but not until he's done with the FDA inspection. Do you know where the cafeteria is in Building 76?"

"Yes," said Beth.

"Go over there and have a cup of coffee. I'll have the guards let you in. Wait about a half an hour. Then be at the office at about 11:30. Okay?"

"Fine," said Beth. She handed the phone to the guard. He talked with Cheryl for a minute and then let them enter Hoffman-LaRoche.

As they walked toward the cafeteria, Simon said, "Tell me a little about Rollins, Beth."

"Fred was a researcher at Harvard Medical School before he came to work at Hoffman-LaRoche. He told me he did it for the money. I suppose that may be true, but it wasn't the whole truth. The real reason he came here was that he was allowed to work on anything he wished with virtually unlimited funding. His work on Alzheimer's disease and his progress toward a possible treatment made him attractive to Hoffman-LaRoche. You may think you have academic freedom in a university, but actually grants control your funding. Once you receive a grant, you are locked into a particular type of research. As a Hoffman-LaRoche director, he could pursue multiple lines. That's probably why he ended up on the list of researchers."

The cafeteria in Building 76 was large, empty, and filled with the smell of institutional cooking. It reminded Beth of her high school lunchroom. She got a cup of coffee and the trio sat down. Simon looked impatiently at his watch. "Why can't we just interrupt Rollins?"

"You don't interrupt an FDA inspection," said Beth.

"You think the Cylots will feel that way?" asked Mectar.

"Just be patient for another twenty minutes or so. What did Leary say when you spoke with him?" said Beth.

"He was with a forensic toxicologist," said Simon. "The toxicologist alleged that the hippocampus was the area of the brain being destroyed. It's the area which turns short-term memory into long-term memory."

Beth shrugged. "Maybe that's happening. Maybe the Cylots can read the brain's neurotransmitters as they process the formula. They want to destroy that portion of the mind before the formula becomes recallable as long-term memory."

"Do you really believe that?" he asked incredulously. "I don't buy it. You think you only remember things in your brain? Every cell has a mind. Information, though, has a longer lifetime than the solid matter with which it is matched. As atoms of carbon, oxygen, hydrogen, and nitrogen come and go through our DNA; the bits of matter change. They even go in and out of existence in a very microphysical sense. Yet, the DNA structure is always there and never moves. This fact alone means that memory is more permanent than matter. Once you have that view of reality, the entire environment reinforces that view so you can configure your physical shape to reinforce that view of reality," said Simon.

"Reality only exists in the mind. If you read a book and you think it happened, then that's your reality, Mectar, whether it occurred or not."

"I'll show you reality, Simon," said Mectar as he held up his fist.

"I'll give you an example," said Simon, dismissing Mectar's threat. "You're sitting in your apartment and you hear your bedroom window opening and you see a shadow of a man on your wall. You run out your front door terrified and get your next-door neighbor. Although you both are scared, you set out together to confront the intruder. When you get there, you find not an intruder but the sweater you hung on a coat hook. The wind was causing the hanger to hit the window, causing you to think the window was opening, and you saw the shadow move. What you thought was happening was not, but whether it was happening or not, your fear was still real. All our fears emanate from just such a delusion. In fact, nothing real can be separated from what we tell ourselves is real. The real fear that we feel is valid even when the threat is not. Reality only exists in the mind.

"This is the problem with Grey's explanation regarding Cylots. An infection by the Cylots is not a chemical reaction involving neurotransmitters or physical parts of the body. Rather, it is an electromagnetic one. Human memory is electrically encoded. The Cylots' consciousness electro magnetically takes over a human consciousness within a cell or cells. That's how the Cylot disease differs from a biological disease."

Beth said, "I don't understand how you connect those two ideas. How does reality only existing in the mind mean that the Cylots take over electrically and it's not a disease centered in the brain?"

Simon rubbed his eyes and began again, slowly, as if teaching a dull child, "Since information is stored throughout the body, the mind exists throughout the body. Like a hologram, each part contains the whole. The whole body/mind must be controlled, and the only way to do that is with an electromagnetic infection."

"Electromagnetic infection?" asked Beth disbelievingly.

"Yes. Infections were thought to be strictly bacterial until viruses were discovered. Now this disease adds another type of infection: electromagnetic. It can electromagnetically change memory in a memory molecule. The cell is a puppet of the electromagnetism. What controls the electromagnetism? The thought of fear and the neurochemical, which it becomes, are somehow connected. This connection involves transformation of non-matter, a thought, into matter, a neuropeptide. What is the difference between the thought and the neuropeptide? If I want to move my foot, any physiologist can trace the neurotransmitter, which activates the impulse that runs down the axon, causing the muscle cell to contract. However, nothing physiologists can describe explains how thoughts turn into the neurotransmitters, how thoughts turn into chemicals."

"What you are saying," Beth said excitedly, "is that in order to understand life, we should stop examining the physical machine and examine the charge which the machine has. The electricity is present in the beginning but absent in the end."

"The old paradigm states that consciousness is a product of matter. This means that until there is matter you cannot have consciousness. The new paradigm, Mectar, is that matter is a product of consciousness. First, there is consciousness, and then matter."

Mectar silently shook his head to indicate disbelief.

"My science is telling me that my consciousness exists without my body," Simon continued. "The disease of Cylotism, or the weapon they use, erodes that consciousness. It is at that point, biologically or microphysically, that the Cylots have a weapon to attack us. They are attacking our very soul. Your electrical engrams are virtually pirated. You lose yourself. The body is an irrelevancy. Your awareness, your soul, is electrical engrams etched on biological matter. When the electricity leaves the biological matter, the biological matter dies. Life and the soul depart with the electricity. Since Benveniste proved that memory is transferred electromagnetically, then, what is lost to the Cylot disease except your soul?"

"How do they do it, Simon?" Mectar asked sarcastically. "With a computer chip?"

Simon shrugged. "My guess is some type of biochip."

Mectar snorted his disbelief.

"You're kidding," said Beth.

"Am I?" said Simon. "There was a Chinese philosopher, Li Po, who Yugen once told me about. Po dreamed that he was a butterfly. Upon waking, he didn't know if he was Po who dreamed he was a butterfly or if he was a butterfly dreaming he was Li Po. Nietzsche said, 'I think, but it is equally possible that I am being thought.' Where is the mind, Grey? Some say it's the brain. Some say it's the body/mind. Some say it is in electromagnetism. But your example shows that different personalities can manifest in the same body. There is a change in the amplitude in the electrical current that causes all cells instantaneously to know that a different presence is there. I need to quantify that field, Grey. You want to do something remarkable in physics and medicine? Then measure that field for me. Quantify it. Identify it. Take the electromagnetism of the body into the laboratory and you'll find the soul.

"What do you think an out-of-body experience is?" asked Simon. "Some ethereal apparition? It's your electromagnetic awareness projected somewhere. Until that's measured scientifically in terms of electromagnetic biochemical psychology and physiology, you are in the Stone Age. A hundred years ago, if you told somebody that you could measure an aura coming off the body by means of infrared or thermo-photography, would they have believed you? No. If you couldn't see it, it didn't exist. If you can't measure it, it doesn't exist. But I'm telling you it does exist. Measure that electrical personality. Develop the instruments to record it."

"A personality has no molecules in it. It's composed only of memories and psychological tendencies," said Beth. "But these tendencies are more permanent than the cells, which are replaced every two years. Electromagnetism, though, is constant throughout life, isn't it?"

"You got it. The quantum particles that go in and out of existence are within these cells, and that's what's important," said Simon. "Some part of the human self or soul is not subject to the laws of space and time. Patterns in nature repeat themselves. The whirlpool you find in a bathtub is the same as the whirlpool you find in a black hole. Atoms follow the same physics as the stars. The reason it's important that subatomic particles may cease to exist is because it offers proof that you do the same. What is that if not life after life after life? You know how a beta-blocker prevents a reaction in the heart, Grey? It's simply a polymer blocking a reaction. Then what kinds of blockers are in me to prevent me from remembering my past lives? How does a clairvoyant configure himself to see into the past or future? What I need is a clairvoyant," said Simon. "That's what I need. I need a clairvoyant!" shouted Simon as if stumbling onto some important realization.

"For what?" asked Mectar sarcastically. "To tell you what is going to occur?"

"No," said Simon. "To study. To figure out how their physiological/electrical wiring differs from ours and how it allows them to access the future. I can change my world by changing my reality. I can change your world, Mectar, by changing your reality. Grey, you work in the medical research field. All around you, you see how drugs and disease change us. But there are anonmolies. How someone with faith is cured miraculously and unexplainably. Primarily, that cure rests on their perception that they will be cured."

"The power of positive thinking," said Beth.

"Right," said Simon. "Perception creates a reality. Perfume is believed to make a woman more attractive regardless of its ingredients. If you believe you will be cured, you will be. These events occur at a deeper level than your biologists examine. They occur at the level of microphysics within the human body. It is the microphysics of biochemistry. In microphysics, the quarks and so on that make up your cells are not measured by mass but by energy, and energy can be neither created nor destroyed. People don't connect that thought with the statement that you are immortal, but it is the scientific explanation for the religious dogma and exactly the place the Cylots are attacking us. This is a crisis of your very soul. You die, your energy and memory depart, you live on, but are you or a Cylot puppet? Do you lose your soul to this enemy?

"It is, Mectar, the common denominator that unites human and Kian, and why the war between us is irrelevant. We are the same. The electrical charge in a Kian is no different than in a human. What causes Tommy to have multiple personalities? Whatever electronic mechanism in him causes matter to have one personality is somehow defective. Cylots change this electrical order purposefully."

As Simon spoke, Mectar became intensely angry. Finally, he slammed the table with his fist, breaking the pressed board and the laminate. "No!" he shouted. "Humans and Kians are not alike. We are different. Our physiology is different. Our planets are different. Our mores are different. We are a stronger race. We are a better race, Simon."

Beth, shocked by Mectar's intensity, did not move.

"You are anal retentive," said Simon with quiet menace. "You either cannot see the facts in front of you or refuse to see them because you so dearly hold the old ones. Change is difficult for all of us. My biomedical explanation of the Cylots is the only possible one, Mectar. The old paradigm is that humans and Kians are different species. The new paradigm, Mectar, is that both are biologically the same. Different cell colonies are being manipulated by the same electromagnetic pulses."

"Carl Jung said we possess the memory of ourselves and the memory of our ancestors within our molecular memory," said Beth to support Simon's argument.

"Yes," said Mectar. "Maybe he'll remember his ancestor, Simon. Did you know Simon is a *Jew*?" he spat. "If he has any molecular memory at all he'll remember how Shimon, in the Old Testament, lied to his father, sold his brother into slavery, and slaughtered the Sheikemites after lying to them. The Shimon of the old testament is a liar, a murderer, and the leader of Simon's house in his *religion*," said Mectar while pointing at Simon. "That is the molecular memory of Simon, Grey."

Simon glared at Mectar. Beth sensed a deep anger, bordering on psychosis. "You better remember my ancestor, Mectar, and hope that I don't remember him, because my family line will then have killed two peoples: the Sheikemites and the Kians."

Mectar blinked in surprise. Then his eyes hardened. Green scales slowly began to cover his face.

"First the Old Testament Shimon lied to them," said Mectar. "Then, he murdered them while they slept. Kians will not be sleeping, Simon. We will not be duped by an inferior, lying murderer."

Simon glared at Mectar without blinking. His teeth were bared. It was a quiet, deep threat. "Then, Mectar, that bloody event is in my collective consciousness, and I have it within me to do the same to another race."

"Truly, Simon, one of us will be dead by the time this is over. I promise you." The green scales receded quickly. "A Kian never breaks a promise."

Simon smiled and looked at Beth. "A Kian never breaks a promise," he repeated. With that, Simon turned and walked out the door of the cafeteria.

24

Schering

Eli Simpson Jr. was the son of a famous father. Simpson Sr. had made one of the breakthroughs that established Schering-Plough as a preeminent pharmaceutical manufacturer. Prior to the beginning of World War I, Schering-Plough had been a German corporation.

Although Simpson Sr. discovered antihistamines, he wasn't looking for them. He was, instead, seeking a drug to treat intestinal infections. When he asked his human guinea pigs if the drugs he was providing helped their stomachs, they replied negatively. They did say, however, that their breathing had greatly improved. He recognized that he had found a method to open up nasal passages. With that insight, he provided Schering with a drug that would ultimately generate hundreds of millions of dollars.

After making this discovery in the late 1940s, he remained with Schering until retirement in the mid 1970s. His son did not have his father's good fortune. Simpson Jr. was involved in some minor discoveries, which he stole from other Schering researchers who then left the company in disgust.

When his father retired, Simpson Jr. was politically well connected within the Schering research community. He was active in many research society programs that occurred outside Schering. During one of these programs, he attracted Brad Varley's attention. One day, a letter with a formula arrived on Simpson Jr.'s desk. It was sent by a man whom he hardly knew.

While Simpson Jr. was not a scholar, he was aware that speed and nimbleness led to market share and prestige. So without delay, he entered the laboratory of one of his clinical assistants, Thomas Jenkins. Jenkins was a tall, gangly young man. He had hair Eli felt was too long, an unkempt beard, and piercing eyes. He was adept in biochemistry and creating new drugs. Eli liked Tom because he would never advance in the Schering hierarchy. Tom preferred the lab bench to the boardroom.

Eli found Tom in the lab. He noticed his tee shirt, which pictured two round hairy objects, each with sneakers. They were running. Underneath the objects was one word: "Go-nads."

Eli ignored the obvious breach of etiquette in Tom's attire, "I want you to make a batch of this drug. Then, I want you to run some trials on some monkeys of your choice."

"No problem, boss," said Tom, looking at the formula. Tom stopped Eli from leaving. "Eli, I'm going to need some new equipment to make this."

"Why is that?" said Eli.

"Because I have to charge it electrically. You can't make this stuff in a pot. You need electrodes to run through it. You need current to activate it."

"What's it going to cost?" Eli asked.

"Ah, with the test batch and equipment I'll need, it can't be more than $20,000 or $30,000."

"Go do it," said Eli while walking out. He was confident that soon he would be testing a revolutionary drug. He had read in the letter that the person who made this batch would be placed in danger. He had not given the letter to Tom. He sincerely hoped that Tom would not be in too much danger, but Eli wasn't the sort of man who would let endangering someone's life stop him.

25

A Visit with Heinrich

Wheeler and Longo drove through the Lincoln Tunnel on their way to visit Heinrich at Rockefeller University. When they reached Park Avenue, they turned uptown heading toward Sixty-eighth Street. The ride had been quiet. They were both tired from the night before. Rockefeller University is on York Avenue, adjacent to the corner of Sixty-eighth on Manhattan's East Side. They parked in a lot on York Avenue, which was lined with Sycamore trees. A guard directed them to the lab animal research area.

As Wheeler got out of the car, he looked back at the entrance and at the wrought iron gates through which they had come. "Old place, huh?" he said to Longo.

"I think I saw a sign up front," said Longo. "It said this place was founded in 1901."

Wheeler nodded and looked at the imposing buildings. They walked across the quadrangle to the lab animal research facility.

A pretty older woman wearing a white crepe blouse sat behind the lobby reception desk. They waited for her to finish her phone conversation.

"May I help you?" she said.

"We'd like to see Dr. Heinrich please," said Wheeler.

"Do you have an appointment?"

Wheeler indicated that he had no appointment and produced his badge. "We'd like to see him now please. FBI."

"Oh," she said, startled. "One moment, please."

Wheeler and Longo waited while the receptionist called Heinrich. "How do you feel, Al," Longo asked. "Last night still bothering you?"

"It was a bitch. I don't know what that stuff was that Mectar threw. I've never felt anything like it. How about you?"

"Tired, but nothing like you," said Longo. "My son got me up early this morning."

"Okay, gentlemen," said the receptionist. "Go on up. Dr. Heinrich will see you. Take the elevator to the third floor," she said, pointing with her pencil at the elevator. "Turn left, Room 307."

Longo nodded and said, "Thanks."

Heinrich met Longo and Wheeler at the door to his office. "Come in gentlemen, come in," Heinrich said.

"Dr. Heinrich." They shook hands. "I'm Al Wheeler, FBI, and this is Detective Longo. We'd like to ask you a few questions."

"Certainly," said Heinrich, turning his back on them and leading them into his office. Heinrich continued around his desk and sat down in his swivel chair.

As he did so, Longo appraised Heinrich. He was five feet eleven, of medium build, and in his early thirties. He had sandy blond hair and a muscular frame. He surprised Longo and Mueller with both his youth and strength.

"What can you tell us about Dr. Mueller?" asked Longo.

"Mueller, Mueller," said Heinrich, rubbing his chin thoughtfully. "Well, I don't know an awful lot about his personal life. He's worked here for several years. I'm pretty sure he lives in Queens. I do know that he got his undergraduate degree at St. John's and went on to graduate school at NYU. May I ask why you are asking?"

Longo said, "He killed a policeman last night."

"Oh dear," said Heinrich. "Do you know why?"

"We only have one theory," said Wheeler. "And it's not even a theory. Somebody said his body had been taken over by a Cylot." Longo noted that Heinrich blinked slightly.

"What's a Cylot?" asked Heinrich.

"It's a space disease that can take over bodies, from what I hear," said Wheeler, "although I don't know if I believe it."

"And where did you hear that?" asked Heinrich.

"It doesn't matter," said Wheeler.

"How much do you know about this disease?" asked Heinrich.

"Why do you want to know?" said Longo.

"As a doctor, I'm interested. Perhaps I can help," said Heinrich.

"You can help me by telling me what happened to Mueller."

"A sad story. He was under a great deal of stress."

"Stress doesn't make people kill innocent individuals," said Longo.

"Who can say when someone can snap?" asked Heinrich innocently. Wheeler stood up. "Dr. Heinrich, I'm afraid that we're going to have to take you in for questioning. How can we be sure that you aren't suffering from the same kind of stress?"

Heinrich smiled. "I really can't go with you, you know. I'm much too busy."

"I don't think you understand," said Longo. "This isn't a request."

"You mean I'm under arrest?" asked Heinrich disbelievingly. "Is that the law? You can just take me into custody?"

"That's correct," said Wheeler. "Once the FBI gets involved we can cross jurisdictional lines. If you are unwilling to come voluntarily, we can arrest you. We are bringing you in for questioning for the murder of Sergeant Doyle of the West Orange Police Department as well as for an ongoing investigation ..."

"Oh, I'm really sorry, but I can't do that," interrupted Heinrich.

Then Heinrich reached into the top drawer of his desk. Wheeler's hand involuntarily moved to his revolver. Heinrich produced something resembling a child's squirt gun. It was metallic and had no opening at the muzzle. Wheeler relaxed.

"You see," Heinrich said. "I've got other appointments to keep." Then he fired at Wheeler. Wheeler's brain burst from the back of his skull. The gun made no sound. Its electrical charge caused Wheeler to fly backward. Longo reached for his revolver but in the last instant realized that he was too late. He dropped to the floor to dodge the shot. A hole appeared in the wall behind him. Heinrich missed. The miss only delayed the inevitable. As Heinrich aimed at Longo's head, and just before Longo died, the detective uttered his last words.

"Oh Jesus."

26

A Dream within a Dream, a Nightmare within a Nightmare

Beth turned on Mectar. "Why can't you leave him alone?" she demanded. "Why do you have to threaten him? Do what you have to do. But stop shoving it in his face."

"You don't understand, Grey," said Mectar. "Simon is not what he seems." Mectar paused and then said, "Here, I won't hurt you. Close your eyes." Then he touched her shoulder. Beth closed her eyes. With her eyes closed, a scene emerged.

She saw a tribe of Jews moving westward in wagons on a grassy plain. She did not know how she knew they were Jews. She guessed they were situated somewhere in Russia sometime between 1890 and 1895. This was the tribe fleeing pogroms Simon and Mectar had traveled with after their crash in Tunguska.

Beth saw Mectar noting the dust cloud just beyond the hilltops. The Cossack band crested the hill and stopped their horses. Twenty or thirty of them, with billowing shirts, beards, and braided hair looked down at the Jews. At first, Simon looked at the Cossacks without realizing that they posed a danger. Then he realized a slaughter was about to begin.

The women ran to protect their children. The men grabbed shovels and axes that hung on the sides of the wagons. They would do anything to defend themselves against the Cossacks, who rushed down the hill at full gallop brandishing their swords and screaming. Although Mectar tried to push Simon out of danger, Simon headed directly toward the charging Cossacks.

Everyone's roles were clearly defined, except Mectar's, but the battle-hardened Kian could not resist participating in this fight. In part, he fought because he needed Simon alive, in part because it was what he was trained to do, in part because he loved what he did. His flexible skin hardened to the consistency of concrete. Brandishing a sword in each hand, he waded into the charging Cossacks, stabbing and slashing horses as well as horsemen, slitting throats and torsos, severing hands, arms, legs, and heads.

Half the Cossacks went down as they passed Mectar. The other half, who faced Simon wielding one sword, found him to be simply unhittable. She saw how time jumping in a fight could be such an advantage. He seemed to anticipate all their moves as he dispatched the Cossacks one by one. When Mectar saw Simon fight, he realized the type of adversary he faced. Before long, only three Cossacks remained. Those three slashed at the Jews, who fought back. One Cossack struck the rabbi's little girl, Basya, who fell, bleeding profusely. Before the remaining Cossacks could flee, Yakov, the butcher, with help from the others, finished the job Mectar and Simon had started.

The Jews stared in awe at the two beings who had stopped the Cossack charge. Standing among the dead and wounded Cossacks, Simon and Mectar faced each other. Their blood was up, and each knew soon they would fight each other. Each also knew only one would live. Some mortally wounded Cossacks groaned. Bleeding horses writhing in pain on the ground whinnied and tried to get up.

Mectar, brandishing his swords, took a few menacing steps toward Simon. Simon turned to meet him. Both were ready to fight. Basya's mother screamed, distracting Simon. He ran back to the caravan, followed by Mectar.

Basya lay on the ground in front of her mother, bleeding to death. As blood gushed from a severed artery, her mother cried in anguish. Mectar pushed past Simon and put a part of his hand in the girl's wound. The hand metamorphosed into human tissue and became one with the girl's body. The bleeding stopped and the wound healed completely.

When Mectar finished with Basya, the rabbi looked at her. "Now we can go to Poland."

"No," Simon said, "you can't."

"We have people in Poland. We're going to Poland," said the rabbi emphatically. "Now."

"You can't go to Poland. You can't go to Germany," Simon said.

The rabbi's wife, Rochel, a plump and pretty woman who wore a babushka over her long hair said to Simon, "We have to go where the rabbi says we go."

"No!" screamed Simon. "It is wrong."

Itzak said, "It's time for you to leave." He began to tie bags to the cart with a rope.

Simon grabbed the rabbi by the shoulders, spun him around, pushed him against the cart, and put a knife to his throat. "Then I'll kill you now. Go to America."

"We go to Poland," Itzak said defiantly.

Mectar had been disinterestedly watching this drama unfold. One of the congregants, Yankel, a hulking blacksmith, moved to attack Simon. Mectar stopped him with sword drawn. Mectar now stood with his sword drawn and his back to Simon and the rabbi, preventing anyone from coming to the rabbi's aid. The group knew that they could not successfully oppose Mectar. They had seen his frightening ability. They were helpless, and their rabbi was in danger. Simon, his face just inches from the rabbi's face, held a knife to the rabbi's throat and said through gritted teeth, "You cannot go to Poland. America or Jerusalem are your only choices."

"Are you a prophet? How do you know what is best for us?" the rabbi asked sarcastically.

"I know," said Simon grimly. Simon, still facing the rabbi, had pushed him against the cart. The people of the group stood in a semicircle behind Simon with Mectar still holding them at bay.

Simon let go of the rabbi's collar. Still holding the knife to his throat, he pulled Mectar backward, catching him off balance, and pinned him against the cart. Mectar reeled in anger and raised his sword to strike. Mectar then felt as though a brick had smashed into the middle of his mind. He saw horrible images and realized that Simon wanted a psychic bond with the rabbi. Acting as a conduit, he used his Kian psychic ability to bond the three minds into one.

They momentarily did not speak. Images of concentration camp deaths, piles of dead Jewish bodies, orphaned children, gas chambers, and crematoriums flowed from Simon's mind to Mectar's, and then into the rabbi's. The rabbi, horrified, stared at Simon, who waited for him to understand why he could not bring his people to Poland, or anywhere else in Europe.

No one moved. Mectar slowly lowered his sword and stared in shock at Simon.

Horror replaced the rabbi's look of defiance as he finally understood Simon's revelations. At first frightened by being connected to another mind, he began to grasp the horror of the obscene pictures he saw: corpse-filled ditches, piles of bodies bulldozed by huge machines, famine-racked bodies pushed into open graves. Ovens. Smoke. Bones. Death. Simon then placed one last future image into the rabbi's mind: his daughter, Basya.

People of all ages were getting off trucks and were then forced to strip by order of an SS officer wielding a horsewhip. They undressed without a cry and stood together family by family. They kissed each other, said good-bye, and waited for a signal from another SS man, who stood near the trench. He, too, was armed with a whip.

There was not a single complaint or plea for mercy. The image focused on a family of eight: a husband and wife in their forties accompanied by three young children and two grown daughters. An old woman with snow-white hair held their one-year-old child while singing to it and tickling it. With a shock, the rabbi realized the old woman was Rochel. The wife was Basya, who had grown into a beautiful woman. The image was of his family, his grandchildren. He, though, was not there. The child in his wife's arms laughed. Basya and her husband tearfully watched. The father, holding the hand of his ten-year-old son, spoke to him gently. The child tried to hold back his tears. The daughters were clearly angry and stood apart. The father, pointing toward heaven, stroked the child's head and appeared to be explaining something to him. Then the SS man near the trench shouted to his comrade, who ordered twenty people to move toward the other side of the trench. The rabbi's family was among them.

The trench was two-thirds full. It held about a thousand people. A soldier sat on the narrow edge of the trench with his legs dangling inside. A submachine gun rested on his knees and he smoked a cigarette. He began shooting into the trench, murdering those held captive within it. The rabbi, tears streaming down his face, witnessed his family's death.

He then looked past the images of the concentration camp and back through Simon's mind. He saw Simon slumped, dead. His eyes were lifeless as they stared into space, his legs severed from his body. The psychic connections broke during this image of hell. They had all seen their own private hells.

The rabbi thought he saw Simon's death, or at least his punishment. Mectar, viewing the images through his own alien perspective, glimpsed something he could not define, what the Kians call *chasdrote*—suspicion about something when the truth is not available. Their mental connection then broke.

The rabbi collapsed on his knees, sobbing. Mectar pulled away from Simon with disgust. Simon turned with anger to face the people, who were now themselves angry and fearful. Simon jabbed his knife into the cart that held all the bags. Then he walked away from the sobbing rabbi, pushing his way through the crowd. The rabbi collapsed on the ground leaning against the wheel as his wife and daughter ran to him.

Simon picked up his haversack and walked away from the people. The adults seemed relieved, but the children were sorry say farewell to their friend who had traveled with them for six months. Mectar had brought Simon to them after their ship crashed. While Simon's broken legs healed, he stayed in the carts with the sick and lame. The medicines he provided cured many people. The children liked Simon. He had truly bonded with them. Yet they were anxious because someone they loved so much had made their parents so afraid.

The adults saw a killer, not someone who had changed their direction and saved their lives. As someone who had threatened their beloved rabbi, Simon was now a pariah.

Simon mounted a Cossack horse. Without saying good-bye, he rode south. Mectar mounted and looked back at Basya, who was now in her mother's arms. Tears streamed down the rabbi's cheeks. Mectar wheeled his horse around and galloped after Simon.

The rabbi stood with tears streaming down his cheeks took a few steps forward and screamed, "Simon! God waits for you, Simon, at the end of your path. He will be there."

Simon looked back. His tears and the pain in his heart caused the image to cloud. As he turned and rode away he heard Yankel mutter a Russian proverb, "The tears of strangers are only water."

Beth saw Mectar questioning Simon.

"Are these images true, Simon?" Mectar asked as they rode away.

"Oh yes, very true, Mectar."

"What kind of God is yours that allows such things? What kind of people are you who would do that? You come from a sick planet, Simon."

Simon did not reply.

The scene faded, and Mectar released Beth, who was now mentally exhausted, as though she had watched a film for hours. She glanced at the clock. Two minutes had passed.

Beth stared at Mectar. His eyes were glazed. As he talked about the fighting, saliva dripped from his teeth.

"Simon fought, so I fought. I needed to kill. It was good killing humans, but it was Simon I wanted. Do you understand, Grey? He is my prey, not yours. Do not tell him I showed you this," said Mectar as he walked away from her. Simon was unaware that anything more than conversation had passed between Mectar and Grey. She looked at the clock for reassurance that this image had lasted for only a few moments. She had seen Simon's past as Mectar's memory had recorded it.

"Are you coming with me to see Rollins or not?" Simon asked. Beth followed Mectar. As they approached Simon, he turned and walked out the door of Building 76. They walked across the street and entered the LAR facility. As they stood in the clerical offices located outside the doctor's offices Cheryl approached them them and said, "Dr. Rollins will see you now. Omar will take you to him."

◆   ◆   ◆

Mueller was arriving at the Hoffman-LaRoche main gate. Like all visitors, Mueller, after parking, entered the guard shack. In accordance with Hoffman-LaRoche's regulations, the two uniformed guards inside were unarmed.

"Can I help you, sir?" one of the guards asked.

"I'm here to see Dr. Rollins," said Mueller.

"Do you have an appointment?"

"Yes, with Dr. Rollins." The guard stared at Mueller. A flash of light seemed to emanate from Mueller's eyes. The beam of light contained information that traveled from Mueller's eyes into the guard's retina and to his brain via his optic nerve. The guard was mesmerized. The light flashed again.

"You have an appointment with Dr. Rollins," the guard said. His inflection was now flatter.

"I have an appointment with Dr. Rollins," said Mueller again. The guard began to do paperwork.

"Your name?"

"Dr. Mueller."

"And you are here to see Dr. Rollins?" he said, filling in the form. "Have a nice day, sir," the guard said while handing Mueller the visitor's pass.

Mueller left the guard shack. The other guard, who had been directing cars to the visitor's parking lot, saw his colleague standing as if in a trance.

"You okay, Joe?"

"Huh?" said Joe while shaking his head and blinking his eyes. "Yeah, I guess. Where was I?"

"You ought to wake up, pal," said his companion. He stepped outside the shack to continue directing traffic. Mueller receded into the distance as he walked toward Rollins' office.

He knew that Rollins was at the facility today. He also knew that Rollins would not live much longer. He walked toward the LAR building, which was a quarter-mile down the road.

27

An Open Mind Will Be Rewarded

Beth led the way into Hoffman-LaRoche's Building 34, which housed a large lab animal research department on its first floor. She went right to Cheryl, the department secretary, who sat at the reception desk. "Listen," said Beth. "It's very important that I find Dr. Rollins, now."

Cheryl said, "No problem, Dr. Grey. Hubert." A middle-aged Hispanic man wearing scrubs came over. "Please take Dr. Grey and her party back to the micro-pig area. You'll find Dr. Rollins over there with Dr. Terino."

Hubert nodded at Beth, Mectar, and Simon. "Follow me," he said. He had them gown up before entering the lab animal area. They found Dr. Rollins in a corridor, deep in a heated discussion with Dr. Terino.

Dr. Rollins was an older man in his early fifties. He was six feet three and very lanky. He had a full, well-trimmed beard and a mustache. Other than that, he was bald. He was leaning over Dr. Terino, nodding his head with a stern look on his face as Dr. Terino explained in a nasal twang why he felt Dr. Rollins' lab animal area was not in compliance with section 2.31 of the FDA code. Dr. Terino was five-seven and also very thin. He had a full head of dark hair and a neatly trimmed, heavy beard. Over his white shirt and tie, he wore a white lab coat borrowed from Rollins, instead of a suit jacket.

Dr. Rollins saw Beth and her companions approaching. He and Beth were good friends. They were both associated with local, regional, and national lab animal research groups. Both were part of the Institutional Animal Care Committee. He did not acknowledge her presence because Terino was speaking.

"Listen, Fred," said Terino. "I'm not asking you to comply with section 2.31. I'm telling you your standards aren't up to FDA levels. You must have a stronger psychological enhancement program for your monkeys."

"Listen, Luis," said Dr. Rollins. "We already take drilled PVC tubes and fill them with peanut butter mixed with raisins for our primate colony. This serves as a substitute for foraging. Our primary feeders are all puzzle feeders now. It takes my technicians an hour to fill the damn things and the monkeys empty them in minutes. We even have a technician bring in a handheld video game. One of the baboons does better on it than the technician. As far as I'm concerned, our psychological enhancement program for monkeys is second to none."

"I know how you feel," said Dr. Terino, "but you're not adhering to the regulations, which clearly state you need a written program to describe how to address every specific issue of your entire program. For example, let's say you have a hair picker. You have to have a clearly defined program describing how you treat that type of primate."

"Or a nitpicker," said Beth Grey to Simon out of the corner of her mouth, motioning toward Terino.

"You also have to clearly define your methods of euthanasia," Terino continued. Regardless of how well you perform them in the lab and colony environment, without a clearly written program, you are not complying with FDA requirements."

"You can't have a written program for everything you face," said Rollins. "You can't document everything. All major occurrences, absolutely. All policies, absolutely. But some of the things you want me to do are ridiculous, like describing how to fill a PVC tube with peanut butter."

"Fred, it's something that you are simply going to have to do," said Terino.

There was nothing left for Rollins to say, so he finally acknowledged Beth, Simon, and Mectar. "Beth, what brings you here?" asked Rollins.

Simon noted that both Terino and Rollins were wearing lab coats stitched with the name "Dr. Rollins."

"Fred, this is Dr. Simon and Dr. Mectar," Beth said.

"How do you do?" said Rollins, shaking their hands.

"It's very important that we talk to you. We'll wait wherever you say," said Beth.

"Well, I think that Dr. Terino and I are about done. Don't you think so?" said Rollins.

"For now," said Terino.

"I'll see you soon. You don't need me to show you back to my office?" asked Rollins.

"No," said Dr. Terino. "I'll pick up my briefcase there. Nice to see you, Dr. Grey. Gentlemen." Terino departed.

"Well, Beth," said Rollins, "didn't I read in the paper that you were missing? Welcome back. And what brings you all the way to Hoffman-LaRoche?"

"Listen, Dr. Rollins," said Simon, "did you receive a letter from a Brad Varley containing a formula?"

"Yes," said Dr. Rollins. "I got it."

"What did you do with it?" asked Simon.

"I think I threw it away," said Rollins.

"Why?" asked Mectar.

"A disease that takes over your consciousness? It was a joke, wasn't it?" said Rollins. Mectar grunted and looked at the ceiling.

"No, it wasn't a joke," said Simon. People are already dying from this disease. Do their deaths make it serious enough?"

"My dear Dr. Simon," said Dr. Rollins. "Self-awareness *is* a consciousness disease." Rollins said this in a clearly unapologetic manner.

"Oh, Fred," said Beth quietly.

Mueller was sitting in Dr. Rollins' office when Terino entered wearing Rollins' lab coat. Terino saw Mueller sitting there and nodded his acknowledgement. Then Terino took off the lab coat, hung it on the coat rack, and started to take his briefcase off the desk.

"Excuse me, Dr. Rollins?" Mueller said. Terino was about to say that he was not Dr. Rollins. He stopped as Mueller raised and pointed something at him.

Shots and screams erupted from Rollins' office. Simon and Mectar ran toward the shots. Beth and Rollins followed. Cheryl was not in the office. Terino lay on the floor with his brains blown out. Rollins' lab coat was next to him.

"How much of a joke is it now?" Simon said to Rollins.

"Fred. Please. Listen," said Beth. "You were at a meeting with Brad Varley at the LAR symposium, "and now every doctor who attended that meeting has been murdered."

"Except you and Javic," said Simon.

"But Javic wasn't at the symposium," said Rollins.

"Are you sure?" asked Beth.

"I'm sure of it," said Rollins. "He wasn't there."

"Then where did Javic go and why?" Simon asked Beth.

"I don't know."

"Was anybody else at that meeting who hasn't been killed?" Mectar asked Rollins.

"I don't know," said Rollins.

"Think, Rollins. Who is usually at such a meeting?" asked Simon.

Beth read aloud the list of dead people. "Bottoms, Livermore, Harris …"

"There was also Henkle and myself. Wait a minute. Eli Simpson was at that meeting," said Rollins.

"The only ones who haven't been killed are you, Eli Simpson, and Henkle," said Beth.

"Wrong," said Rollins. "I heard over the radio that Seymour Henkle died this morning."

"What about Javic?" said Beth. "Are you sure he wasn't at the meeting?"

"No," said Rollins. "I'm sure of it."

"We've got to get out of here," said Simon. "Whatever you do, Rollins, don't tell the police about Simpson or that we were here."

"I can't do that," said Rollins. "When they come, I've got to tell them."

"Don't you understand the danger? We must get that formula," said Simon. "The police will only get in our way."

"I don't care. I don't know who you are. I'm going to damn well tell the police that you were here. Beth, I don't know who you're traveling with …"

Rollins collapsed.

"What did you do to him?" Beth demanded of Mectar.

Mectar put something back into his pocket. "He will not tell we were here," said Mectar.

"Did you kill him?" asked Beth.

"No, but when he awakens he'll wish that he were dead. His head will hurt for many days," said Mectar. "I left him alive out of respect for your sense of morality. Let us find this place Schering and this Simpson now."

"Fine," said Simon. "Let's get out of here."

Beth took a last look at Rollins and the body of Terino before hurrying after Simon and Mectar.

28

Novartis

Tom Peschi was a laboratory animal technician and a caretaker of the animals. He fed animals used in lab experiments and carted away their excrement.

While most people had jobs that were interrupted by weekends, his work never was. Animals ate and crapped on weekends too. He was pushing the three-sided bulk truck filled with bags of animal feed down the corridor when Chris Zurimski, the lab animal supervisor, came rushing around the corner. His eyes were wide and he was out of breath. Chris was clearly out of breath and even more clearly excited.

"What's the matter, Chris?" Tom asked.

"Somebody's fouled up the experiments running in the A Block. Max was down there and the next thing I knew the environmental alarms are going off. The rooms are wide open, the experiments are contaminated, and I don't know who has been in 'em," Chris rambled. The Max Chris referred to was Dr. Maxwell Innis, head of lab animal research.

"Leave that here and come on with me," said Chris, pointing to the bulk truck. "We've got to shut A Block down and find out how Max wants to handle this." Tom and Chris raced down the hallway and up the back stairway to Max's office.

Dr. Max Innis' office was located on the second floor of the lab animal building. His secretary sat in an anteroom, where the lab animal supervisors had office cubicles. Chris Zurimski had his desk there. As Tom and Chris entered the anteroom, it was clear that a struggle had taken place. Some of the modular partitions had been knocked over. Alarms now sounded in the general building.

A ruined experiment could cost millions of dollars. Lab tests often ran for more than a year. Time as well as money was lost. This was drilled into all the researchers. Max's door was slightly ajar. Chris pushed it open and stopped short. Tom, who was thinner and slightly taller, bumped into Chris as he stopped short behind him. Dr. Max Innis' body lay face down in a pool of blood. His skull was reamed out front to back.

"Oh, shit," said Chris quietly. They heard someone running down the hall toward them and they turned. A man burst into the room and crouched down. His gun was drawn.

"Freeze!" he said. Chris and Tom stepped backward and raised their hands. Their movement exposed Innis' body to the man's view. Mike Leary stood up and lowered his gun.

"We found him this way," Tom blurted out. Several police officers now gathered at the door.

"Too late," Leary said to the officers. "Too late."

More people were heard running down the hall. A breathless police officer ran up, out of breath. "Detective Leary," he said. "We got a message from headquarters. Agent Cyrus said to meet him at Schering and said you'd better hurry."

"Stay here and take their statements," Leary ordered. Chris and Tom watched as Leary sprinted down the hallway.

Leary left the Novartis lab animal area and ran to the police car. The Summit police force was now arriving at Novartis. Lieutenant Lowell was the head of homicide. Lowell was a short man with a beard and clear, bright blue eyes. Lieutenant Lowell now caught up with Leary to question him.

Leary sat in his car talking on the radio with Sergeant O'Toole of the West Orange precinct.

"O'Toole, this is Leary."

"Where are you? Over," said O'Toole.

"I'm up at Summit. Dr. Innis is dead. Is Wheeler back? Over." The receiver went silent except for static. Leary said, "Do you read me, O'Toole? Over."

As Leary waited for O'Toole to respond, he saw a policeman standing at the gate. There was a radio on his left hip, a gun on his right, and a whistle in his mouth. He was directing traffic out of the parking lot. O'Toole's voice on the radio broke Leary's reverie.

"Jesus, Leary, I've never seen anything like it. I don't know what's going on. The Orangetown police lost a guy this morning. We lost two last night and now Wheeler and Longo are dead. What the hell are we fighting? Cyrus wants to talk to you. Hang on."

"What?" asked Leary in shock. "Wheeler is dead?"

"That's right," said O'Toole. "He went to see Heinrich, Mueller's boss in New York. They found his body in Heinrich's office at Rockefeller University. Longo is dead too."

Leary was stunned.

"Lieutenant," said Lowell, the police officer from Summit, who stood near Leary's car. "I'd like to ask you a few more questions as to why you came up here. How did you know that Dr. Innis was going to die? You were the first one on the scene. In fact, plant security told us that when you burst through the card reader at the main gate—"

"You wouldn't believe it," Leary said. "You just wouldn't believe it."

"Leary? This is Cyrus" came over the radio.

"Yeah?" said Leary.

"Get to a landline now. Now. Call me on my private number. You got it?" said Cyrus.

"Let me get a pen," said Leary. As he fumbled for a pen, Lowell handed him one. Leary wrote down the number, stood up, and said, "I need to get to the nearest phone. Now."

Leary ran into the Novartis lobby and found a phone. Cyrus answered after the first ring. "Leary?"

"Yeah?" responded Leary.

"Wheeler is dead," said Cyrus. "He was killed a little while ago at Rockefeller University. Dr. Rollins at Hoffman-LaRoche has been in a coma and we can't figure out why. An FDA inspector there is dead. Simon and Grey were there. The only one left on that list is Eli Simpson at Schering. I want you down there now. Meet me there. I want this guy Simon found and I want him brought down. Is that clear? I want that bastard brought down. Wheeler and Longo went to Heinrich's office, but I think that Simon had something to do with the killing."

"Bobby Joe, you can't do that," said Leary.

"What do you mean, I can't do that? I've got cops dropping left and right," said Cyrus.

"It's not Simon who's killing the cops," shouted Leary.

"Well, who is it, goddamn it?" demanded Cyrus.

"It's the Cy …" Leary stopped. His voice dropped several decibels. "It's the Cylots."

"Give me a break, Leary. You buy that for even a second?" asked Cyrus.

"Yes, Agent Cyrus, I do," said Leary.

"Seven guys saw Simon last night. Four of them are now dead. You, Comstock, and Murphy are the only ones who can recognize him. Murphy is going to be with the SWAT team and you're going in with me. Get down there now. Is that clear?"

"You are making a mistake, Cyrus," said Leary.

"I've had you transferred to my command. I've called your captain. You are assigned to me. I'm giving you a direct order. Now!"

"Yes, sir," said Leary. "I'll get down there. But BJ, you've got to hold off. If I can get to Simon, we can do more good than harm."

"I'll meet you at the Garden State Parkway Kenilworth exit. I'll be sitting just off the exit on Galloping Hill Road," said Cyrus.

"I'm on my way." Leary hung up and ran to the patrol car.

As he ran down the steps to the front building of Novartis, the young lieutenant from Summit said, "I have a few more questions for you, Leary."

Leary ignored him, hopped in his patrol car, and sped off.

29

Simian, Simian, Simeon

Tom Jenkins left his house that morning and drove to Kenilworth on the Garden State Parkway. It took him twenty-five minutes to travel from Montclair, his home, to Schering-Plough. He never minded rush-hour traffic. In fact, he used the pleasant commute as a quiet time to think.

He drove through East Orange, where the parkway traverses a cemetery. The road was flanked on both sides by gravestones. When the parkway was under construction, many bodies were exhumed and reburied in other parts of the cemetery. The drive through the cemetery always gave him a new perspective on life, but today other things were on his mind.

The headaches, which first occurred soon after he started the experiment for Simpson, were growing more severe. Instead of traveling to his office today, he was driving directly to the plant health center. He wanted to consult a doctor. He was also going to ask Simpson for some vacation time. His mother-in-law would have to understand that he and his wife would not be able to spend as much time as she wanted with her in Florida.

Jenkins drove along the outside of the plant until he reached Building K-15, which was actually six separate buildings connected by atriums. Each building was four stories high and filled with labs. Together the buildings formed a one-million-square-foot complex. Jenkins, who had toured the site several times during its construction, was told that the building, completed in 1992, had cost $250 million. Jenkins moved in during January 1993. He inhabited the world's newest, largest, best equipped research facility of its kind.

Tom went directly to the plant health center to meet Dr. Lynne Avery. She was a Schering staff MD who handled the plant population's medical problems. Her short blond hair was cut in a mannish style. Lynne did not know Tom, but she had seen many work-related medical problems that affected Schering's employee population. Researchers like Tom generally suffered from stress, which she usually treated with rest and drugs.

However, Tom's examination was disturbing. The psychological and physical data indicated a real problem. His blood pressure was exceedingly high and he had an irregular heartbeat. His anxiety bordered on psychosis. Tom sat on the examination table with his shirt off. "Listen," she said. "I want to send you for more tests."

"What's wrong?" Jenkins asked.

"I'm not sure," she said. "All I'm sure of right now is that I'd like to send you to the hospital for some blood work and an EKG."

He nodded. "Fine. Listen, I need to talk to Eli Simpson for a few minutes. I won't be gone long. I'll just take the elevator upstairs."

"Okay," said Lynne. "I'll make the arrangements. Be back down here in ten minutes." He nodded and started to button his shirt.

Simon parked in the lot and then, with Beth and Mectar, walked across the access road into the lobby of K-15. Grey approached the receptionist. "We need to see Dr. Simpson, please. Can we go up to his office?" said Beth.

"I'm sorry, you can't go up. I'll have to call."

Simon pushed Beth aside. "I'd prefer if you didn't do that," he said.

"I'm sorry, sir. We can't admit anyone without calling first."

Simon held something under her nose. Her head pulled back involuntarily as she smelled it. Then she looked at him blankly. "What office does Dr. Simpson have?" Simon asked.

"His office is A-402."

"And where would that be?"

"Take the elevator to your right, fourth floor," she said.

"Is there a pass key I can have? I don't want him to know we are coming and I don't want you to remember that we've been here. You've never seen us before, have you?"

"No, sir," she said.

"You'll feel better in five minutes. Do you understand?"

"Yes," she said.

Simon started toward the elevator. Beth and Mectar followed. Beth caught up to Simon and grabbed his arm. "What did you give her?" she whispered.

"Sodium Pentothal's great-great-grandson." He ran the passkey through the reader and pushed the elevator button.

As Tom Jenkins entered Eli Simpson's office, Simpson sat at his desk reading a file.

"Eli?" Tom said diffidently. Two men were seated at a conference table. Tom did not recognize them.

At first, Eli did not recognize Tom. A broad smile then crossed his face. "Tom, Tom, come in," he said, magnanimously waving his hand for Tom to enter. Even though Tom was suffering from drug-induced migraine headache, he found it out of character for Eli to be so warm. "Come in, my boy. Sit down," said Simpson.

Jenkins approached the chairs in front of Simpson's desk. He collapsed into one and looked at the two men seated at the table. Simpson said, "Oh, don't mind these fellows. They're busy doing something for me. Heinrich, Mueller, this is Jenkins. I was telling you about him. Now, son, what can I do for you?"

"Eli, I need a break. I got some of that chemical on me and I'm just exhausted. I don't feel well."

"You mean the formula?" said Simpson.

"Yes," said Jenkins. "Whatever that shit is, it's potent. I've had headaches. I haven't been able to sleep. I have nightmares."

"Does anybody know about this formula? This batch that you made?" asked Simpson.

"No. I made it in my private lab. I have it wired up in A-423. It's just a small batch. It gives off heavy fumes, though. I think that's how it got me. I didn't expect it to."

"I want you to destroy it," said Simpson.

"Destroy it? Why?" said Jenkins, now really looking at Simpson for the first time.

"We've decided not to go ahead with the project," said Simpson.

"Eli ..."

"What Tom?"

"Never mind," said Jenkins.

"Listen," said Eli. "Here is a formula that I want you to add to it. Simple compounds, really. It will render it totally inert." He wrote the formula down and handed it to Jenkins. Jenkins took the paper and then looked at Heinrich and Mueller. Heinrich's holocloak was slightly askew.

"You're glowing!" cried Jenkins, springing to his feet. "My God. You're glowing! Simpson, do you see this?"

Simpson stood up. "Now calm down," he said evenly.

"My God. It's not you! Who are you? What are you?" said Jenkins, backing away and knocking over his chair. "My God!"

"Come back here," Simpson ordered.

"My God," said Jenkins, backing out of the office as Heinrich and Mueller stood up. Then he turned and ran out the door.

"No, no!" Jenkins yelled as he ran down the hallway. Simpson came to the office door and said, "Wait."

Simon, Beth, and Mectar were in the elevator when Jenkins escaped from Simpson's office. As the elevator doors opened, Jenkins ran by screaming.

"No, no," shouted Jenkins.

"Come back here," said Simpson.

Simpson drew a phaser and fired at Jenkins. The shot passed the opening elevator doors. Simon saw Jenkins run and saw the shot. He fired at Simpson and hit him in the chest. Simpson collapsed. The black and blue mark of a Cylot implant was clearly visible on the back of Simpson's neck.

"Shit. Cylots," said Simon. "Let's catch that guy," he said, motioning toward Jenkins. Simpson lay dead in front of Beth. Almost automatically, she started to follow Simon. Suddenly, Mueller ran out of the office and fired at them. Mectar, the last to leave the elevator, fired at Mueller. Anticipating the shot, Mueller ducked back into the doorway. Heinrich appeared in the doorway and fired at Mectar.

The building's A Block contained a dual parallel hallway. Two corridors connected the lab to the administrative offices. Mueller ran down the west corridor and Heinrich followed. Jenkins, Simon, Beth, and Mectar ran down the east corridor.

Jenkins finally reached his lab and entered it from the east corridor, followed by Simon. When Jenkins ran through his lab, he encountered Mueller, who emerged from the west corridor. "My God, you're glowing too! Leave me alone!" screamed Jenkins. As he turned and ran to the east corridor, he paused by the vat containing the chemical formula he had mixed. He screamed, "They're trying to kill me! They're trying to kill me." Mueller fired at Jenkins but missed. Simon returned fire and ran across the lab to try to get Jenkins down. Jenkins stared wide-eyed at Simon and screamed, "You're one of them. You're one of them." He stood up to run, exposing himself to the line of Mueller's fire. Simon heard two thuds as two shots hit Jenkins. Black and red fluids spouted from his chest. He pitched forward, dead. Drops of blood spurting from his chest hit Beth's sleeve.

Simon fired at Mueller but missed. Mueller drew a grenade from his pocket, pulled the pin, and dropped the grenade. The explosion rocked the lab and destroyed everything in it, including the vat of formula. Simon, anticipating the blast, had dived out the door, pulling Beth with him and lying on top of her to shield her with his body.

Beth heard distant sirens. The explosion had blown the windows out on one side of the building. Fire and smoke engulfed the other side. Dust and smoke filled the air.

Mectar ran down the hall. "We've got to get out of here," he said. "There are two Cylots present."

Simon stood and helped Beth to her feet. "No shit, Mectar," he said. "Did you think of that all by yourself?"

As Mectar surveyed the blast damage and the back of Jenkins' body, Heinrich darted around the corner and fired at Simon, aiming not at Simon's body but at the phaser Simon held.

The phaser was not contained within Simon's force field, as Simon could fire it only from outside the field. When Heinrich's shot hit the phaser, it exploded and ripped away part of Simon's force field as well as two of his fingers. Thrown backward, he cursed in pain. With Simon now fully exposed Heinrich fired again.

Beth was still stunned from the explosion. Mectar, stepping between her and Simon, fired at Heinrich and then dragged Simon by the back of his collar along the hallway to another lab. Simon moaned and left a trail of blood. Mectar literally threw Simon into the lab. Then he grabbed Beth by the front of her shirt, pulled her down, and tossed something into the hallway. The explosion was deafening. Mectar threw Simon over his shoulder. He grabbed Beth, kicked out the lab's far door, and ran down a different hallway. While following Mectar, Beth heard Simon saying, "Put me down, you fucking ape." Mectar did so when he reached the end of the hall.

"Are you all right?" he said to Simon, who was applying something to his hand. The bleeding would not stop.

"No, that won't do," said Mectar. He grabbed Simon, pinning him to the wall with his shoulder. Mectar held Simon's injured hand and, with a low-intensity blast from his phaser, burned the wound closed. The acrid smell of Simon's burned skin filled Beth's nostrils. She wretched as Simon screamed.

Keeping Simon pinned to the wall, Mectar said, "Injection." Beth watched the Kian inject something into Simon. Instantaneously, the wound completely healed—the severed fingers were still missing, but otherwise Simon seemed completely normal. Mectar turned to Beth and said, "The fastest way out of here. Now!"

Although she had been to the site before, she was not sure of the fastest escape route. She pointed down the hall into the lab animal wing, which she had once toured with Leonard Javic. They stopped running down the hall when they reached a sign that read "Primate Colony." They entered a transgenic room located in front of an examination room that bordered other wings.

The primate colony in G Block was housed in two wings. Each had its own door into a common transgenic room. An examination room was located behind the transgenic room. These rooms opened out from the central access hallway. Two wings were perpendicular to the transgenic room and examination room. Each wing housed 138 lab monkeys.

Simon, Mectar, and Beth stopped to catch their breath in the examination room. "What do we do now?" Beth asked.

Simon opened a door to a wing and looked at the monkeys. "I'm going to release the monkeys and stampede them. Then I'll set off a sensory grenade. That ought to hold off the Cylots until we get to the car." He then added, "I hope."

"You're out of your mind," Beth said. Simon reached for the first cage. "Don't!" she said. "These are old-world monkeys. If they bite, they'll kill you."

"A monkey bite will kill me?" asked Simon.

"Yes," she said. "They may carry herpes B, and there is no cure for it. You'll die in about six weeks. Conversely, if you carry herpes simplex and you bite a monkey, the monkey will die in about six weeks."

"I'll be careful not to bite any monkeys," said Simon. He touched his jump belt. A dull electric glow seemed to surround him. "If a monkey bites me, he'll get an electrical shock."

As Simon reached into a cage, a monkey backed into a corner. Simon grabbed the animal by the nape of its neck and pulled it out. The monkey fled to the far end of the room. "Get in the cage," he said to Beth.

"What?" said Beth.

"Get in the cage," ordered Simon.

"Are you out of your mind?" she said.

"I don't have time to argue, Grey," said Simon. "This is the only place you'll be safe. Once I get all these monkeys in here, I don't know what the fuck they'll do. Do you understand? That bracelet will protect you from Cylots, but it sure won't protect you from monkeys."

Beth got in the cage and Simon locked it. "Hey, wait a minute. I don't like being locked in a cage," she said.

"I am not going to have you die in six weeks because you just got bit by some monkey. Not after everything I've done to keep you alive. And I'm not going to go traveling in time to get the anitidote. So shut up."

Meanwhile, Mectar, following Simon's lead, was releasing monkeys in the other wing. Monkeys were chattering all over the room. Mectar looked at his monitor. "Cylots are getting closer," he said.

"I wonder if they can see what we are doing?" said Simon. He fired his phaser at the floor to herd the screaming monkeys into the transgenic room. One monkey jumped on Simon's back. He shoved it off.

"They're getting closer," said Mectar as he fired his phaser to herd the monkeys. He too had surrounded himself with a force field.

The transgenic room was now filled with monkeys. Many hung from overhead lights; others sat chattering on cabinets. Those that tried to bite Simon and Mectar recoiled from the taste of the force fields. Even the four baboons could not threaten them. "Feel right at home do we, Simon?" said Mectar. Simon made a face in imitation of a chimpanzee. Mectar smiled in response and continued herding.

Simon approached Beth's cage. He unlocked it, allowing her to push the bars open. He unlatched the rear door and held it ajar. Then he fired his phaser to drive the monkeys away. This diversionary tactic enabled Beth to open the cage and dash from the transgenic room to the examination room.

"Listen," Simon said. "They know where we are. They don't know I have a monkey army. I'm going to send 276 terrified lab monkeys right at them as soon as I drop this sensory grenade. Now you go first. When we fire, you move the hell out of here. If you get hit by any part of the sensory grenade, I'll carry you. You got it? You just make it down those stairs and run like hell, because I'm going to pass you." She realized that he had every intention of doing so.

"Give her an antidote now," said Mectar.

"Do you want it, Grey? I'll have to inject you."

"Will I feel nauseous like I did at Organon?" asked Beth.

"No, you won't."

She thought for a moment and said, "Do it."

Simon reached for the injector gun located on his belt. It resembled the one Mectar had previously used on him. As he loaded it with the antidote and began to inject Beth, one of the monkeys jumped on him. Already fumbling due to the loss of his two fingers, Simon lost control of the injector. Only a part of the dose entered Beth's body before the injector fell to the floor. Simon took another dose, loaded it into the gun, and injected Beth again. She stood up.

The door suddenly blew off its hinges and Heinrich charged into the room. Mectar and Simon fired their phasers at him. Simon threw the sensory grenade and then fired at the monkeys. Screaming, the monkeys stampeded through the door away from Simon and toward the Cylots in the rear. Simon opened the back door. Beth ran through it and rushed down the stairs. Mectar and Simon followed. Simon lingered to drop a time-delayed sensory grenade in front of the rear door. Then he too ran down the stairs.

The explosion occurred at Heinrich's feet, knocking him down and making him convulse momentarily. Meanwhile, escaping monkeys jammed the doorway, making it impossible for the Cylots to pursue the fleeing trio.

When they reached the parking lot, Mectar, Simon, and Beth raced toward her car. Beth slowed down and laughed. She turned and said with slurred speech, "They're not following us."

Simon stopped to look at her. "Are you all right?"

"Of course I'm all right," she said as she tripped and fell on her face. She lay on the ground laughing.

"My God," said Simon. "She's drunk."

Mectar stared at Beth, who was now trying to stand up. "You overdosed her, you sphincter muscle," said Mectar.

"That's asshole, asshole," said Simon.

Beth, still lying on the ground, giggled. "Asssssssssssshole," she said. "What is this stuff you put in me, and how do I get more of it?" She stood up.

Mectar threw her over his shoulder and ran to her car. Simon entered the driver's side. Mectar opened the back door, threw Beth on the seat, and then climbed into the front passenger seat. They sped out of the parking lot toward the back entrance of Schering, just past the K-15 loading dock. As they were about to pass the guardhouse, they skidded to a sideways halt at a police blockade. Officers stood with shotguns at the ready.

"Give yourself up and nobody gets hurt," came their instructions from a bullhorn.

"Oh shit," said Simon.

Heinrich and Mueller exited the building and saw them slide to a halt, and they were now racing for their own car.

"Get out of the car now. Hands up," Bobby Joe Cyrus said through the bullhorn.

"What's this?" Mectar demanded. "Who are these people?"

"They're cops, Mectar," said Beth.

"Tell them to move," said Mectar.

"Mectar," said Beth. "I don't think they want to, all right?"

"They'll have to," said Mectar while stepping from the car. The police all cocked their weapons.

"Throw your weapons down. Give yourselves up and no one will get hurt."

"Are you talking to me?" said Mectar.

Cyrus looked at Leary questioningly. "Tell him," said Leary.

Cyrus said, "Yes, I'm talking to you."

"I will give you no weapon," said Mectar as he walked toward them. "You will move the cars out of our way."

Cyrus removed his hand from the bullhorn switch and said to Leary, "Is he crazy?"

"I don't think so," Leary responded. "I think we ought to let him by."

Cyrus was incredulous. "Doyle, Longo, and Wheeler are dead. Policemen are dropping all over the place and you still say that?"

"You will move the cars now," said Mectar, still walking toward the blockade.

Leary stood up, exposing himself. He also placed his revolver in its holster. "Mectar," he shouted.

"Leary, you understand that there are Cylots in the building and that we must flee. Fighting them will be futile. There will be much death. Simon has been injured. We must escape."

Cyrus dropped the horn and took a shotgun from one of the officers. He pointed it directly at Mectar's chest. "You are under arrest for the murder of Al Wheeler," said Cyrus.

"I killed no Al Wheeler," said Mectar.

"Put up your hands," ordered Cyrus.

"Bobby Joe, don't," said Leary.

Mectar reached for the shotgun muzzle. Cyrus fired point-blank into Mectar's chest. Nearby officers winced and were then hit with that spattering shotgun pellets that ricocheted from Mectar's force field. Mectar stepped backward. He was uninjured but surprised that he had been fired upon. Mectar grabbed Cyrus' gun, twisted the barrel, and threw it aside.

The shotgun blast also surprised Simon and Beth. Simon, still feeling the effects of the painkiller, was not alert. He barely realized that Beth was leaving the car. She walked drunkenly toward Cyrus. "Lishun," she said. "Don't you fire at him. He'll throw one of those 'thingies' at you. Now get out of the way," she said, waving her hands at the police officers. "We want to get out of here now. Don't we?" she said to Mectar. "Come on, Mectar, make 'em get out of the way."

Cyrus looked at Leary. "Who the hell is she?"

"I'm Dr. Gay," she said and then giggled. "No, I'm not Dr. Gay. No. No. I'm Dr. Grey. No, I'm not gay. I mean there's nothing wrong with it. But, I'm heterosexual. Well, once I had an experience," she said.

"Are you all right, Dr. Grey?" Leary asked.

"Of course, I'm all right," she said. "Can't you see I'm all right? Get out of the way, Leary."

"I say again, move the cars," said Mectar. He reached into a pocket of his jump suit and produced a sensory grenade.

"Oh shit," said Leary. "Don't, Mectar. We'll move them."

"What are you talking about?" asked Cyrus.

"It's a sensory grenade. You don't want to know, Cyrus. Murphy," ordered Leary. "Move the cruiser." Murphy had already started the engine.

Mectar's grenade exploded at Cyrus' feet. Nauseated, he doubled over. Beth saw police officers dropping all around her. They held their stomachs, convulsed, and vomited. Surprisingly, she felt euphoric. She laughed and said, "What is stuff you put in me?"

"It's the antidote for the sensory grenade," said Mectar. He lifted the front of a car to move it aside to create an opening. "We told you that already."

"Geez, this stuff is great," she said, laughing. "God, where did you get it? Can I get some more?" She turned to Simon.

Simon told her to get back in the car. She stumbled into the backseat and Simon drove through the opening created by Mectar. He shouted out the window, "Inject Leary." Mectar nodded. He injected Leary in the back of the neck. Leary coughed, rolled over on the ground, and looked up at Mectar. Mectar smiled villainously. "Feel better?" he said. Leary nodded. "Tell the sphincter muscle who fired into my chest that if we ever meet again I will kill him. We will be in touch."

Leary slowly lifted his head. Mectar climbed into the car beside Simon and the car drove off. Though his vision was blurry, Leary tried his best to record the license number.

As Leary tried to stand and reorient himself, another car raced through the hole in the blockade. It contained two individuals. Leary knew they were the Cylots.

30

I Have Outlasted All Desire

After Beth, Mectar, and Simon left Schering and drove west toward Parsippany, they stopped at the Tara Sheraton, a four-star hotel. "I need two rooms that adjoin each other," Simon told the receptionist.

"I'm sorry, sir," the receptionist said. "The only available room which fits that description is the Presidential Suite. It's $425 a night."

"No problem," said Simon, extending a roll of bills. He fumbled with them because of the loss of his two fingers. Beth, even in her state of euphoria, felt his pain.

The receptionist blinked in surprise as Simon took five one hundred dollar bills from the large roll of hundreds.

Simon and Mectar shepherded Beth up to the room trying to attract the least amount of attention possible. Simon shut his room door and made sure the connecting door to Mectar's room was locked. Beth, who had kicked off her shoes, lay on the bed singing, laughing, and giggling. She was clearly still under the drug's effects. The painkiller Mectar had given Simon was effective and acted as a stimulant. Simon made sure the disruptor field was set for the night.

Beth, exhausted, was coming down from her drug-induced high. Simon sat on the end of the bed, got undressed, and spoke with her. "You know," he began. "Javic was a great researcher."

She looked at him with compassion and surprise. "You said he was a mechanic," she said good-naturedly.

Simon hung his head. "We're all mechanics. I said he was lucky too."

"Serendipitous," she corrected him.

"Serendipity. Luck. Fate smiling at you. Everyone needs that. He needed it. I need it. I wonder if his body got beat up as much as mine during this research."

She took his injured hand in hers and she stared at it. "It's amazing," she said, "it looks as though you've healed." She touched the skin on top of the area were the fingers had been severed. "What is this?" she asked, rubbing her hand over the rough skin.

"I don't quite know how to describe it," he said. "The product is a kind of liquid skin that grows by itself."

"It's amazing," she said. "It looks like your own skin."

"It becomes my own skin—it actually becomes a part of me," said Ben. "I guess in your time you still use skin grafts for burn victims and such."

"Yeah," she said, nodding.

"This is like skin in a bottle. I'll get a more permanent repair when I get back." He struggled taking off his shirt.

She rolled over toward him and put her hand on his back. "Let me help," she said while rubbing his back and tracing his scar. "How did this really happen?" she asked.

"I already told you. The Tunguska event," he said.

"That 1910 meteor crash in Siberia?" she asked.

"Yeah."

"Yeah?" she said.

"It wasn't a meteor. It was our shuttlecraft, Mectar's and mine. We were running from the Cylots and we put the reactor on overload and then ejected. Let's say we've gotten a little more sophisticated in escaping from the Cylots, but we still haven't evaded them."

"My head is spinning," she said. And today at Hoffman-LaRoche I had an ankwar with an alien. How did you see the future when you were traveling across Russia?

"He told you that?"

"Yes," she said.

"How did you see the future?"

"I didn't. I remember everything, as I told you. I simply have that ability—that gift or curse—whatever you want to call it. Everything I showed the rabbi and Mectar came word for word from a picture and description at Dachau. Well I recited that description verbatim. I had visited there as a young man. I suppose if I ever write a book I can be sued for plagiarism for using that," he said more to himself.

"Actually I want to publish a book in your time, but not under my name. I need a contact in your time." Ben said.

"Why?" asked Beth

"My God, woman, do I have to tell you everything? I need a contact in your time. That's all."

"I know someone who called on us at Merck. He's a small independent businessman. He was a helicopter pilot during Vietnam. He's got a good sense of humor and he stands on his own. He's very independent. If I were to recommend anyone, it would be him."

"Well why didn't you go out with him?"

"My God, Ben, he's thirty years older than me." Ben seemed satisfied with Beth's response.

"Mectar thinks you are descended from Shimon. He fears you. How can that be true?" asked Beth.

"It isn't. I want him to think that. Kians are bullies and they are superstitious. I want to play on that weakness. They believe in 'signs' and omens. It is historically how the Kian race evolved, and while they don't believe that, it is still a part of their psyche. I want to play on their collective fears. What if it is true? If I am descended from Shimon? Who the hell knows? And what's the point anyway? But if Mectar thinks I am then he'll be a bit more cautious, move a bit slower perhaps. I could never beat a Kian in a fair fight, but when has fighting ever been fair? I want to level the playing field."

"Come to bed," she said. "I'm exhausted."

He stood up and turned to look at her. His depression was evident. "I'm not ready," he said quietly. "I'm just going to read for a little while." He opened a device the size of a piece of paper, something she had not seen before. Had she not been recovering from her drug-induced state, she would have been curious about the device. He sat in a chair and looked out through the double windows, then down at the device. Beth turned out the light next to the bed. Before putting her head on the pillow she said, "Wake me when you come to bed." She soon fell asleep.

She woke early the next morning resting between soft sheets. Feeling wonderful, she reached out for Simon. He wasn't there. He had fallen asleep in his chair. She walked across the carpeted floor. Simon's device remained open. She picked it up and saw that it was a poem by Pushkin. She read it.

I have outlasted all desire,
My dreams and I have grown apart;
My grief alone is left entire,
The gleanings of an empty heart.

The storms of ruthless dispensation,
Have struck my flowery garland numb;

I live in lonely desolation,
And wonder when my end will come.

She began to feel sad for Simon. She reached down to touch him. Before her hand contacted his skin, she received a static electrical charge.

"Ouch," she said, pulling her hand away. His eyes immediately opened. "You keep a force field on when you sleep?" she said.

"Doesn't everybody?"

"No," she said, a bit angered by the shock she had received. Her anger receded when she looked at his shoulder.

"Your shoulder looks different. It looks like that small wound is festering, Benjamin," she said.

He brushed his bare shoulder and then quietly said, "Oh shit." He reached into his jump belt's pouch and took out what looked like a small funnel, three inches long. Holding it toward the light, he pressed something and activated its electronic system.

Looking at Simon's shoulder, Beth saw a pin prick in the middle of the black and blue mark. Simon handed his electronic device to her. A small casing that held a microchip was embedded in its point. "Push it into my shoulder," he said. "Put the point directly on the pin prick, the center of the wound. But don't guide it. It'll guide itself. That's it." He winced as she pushed the point into his flesh. "When it beeps, stop," he said.

It whirred and beeped. Simon gritted his teeth. "Okay, now pull it out," he said. As she did, a cutting device fractions of an inch wide came down from the point of the conical device and extracted a small core sample from his shoulder.

Beth pressed a handkerchief to his shoulder to stop the bleeding. The wound did not bleed much. He ejected the device's contents on a sheet of white paper. It was a small piece of metal that looked as though it had melted and resolidified. He separated the blood and tissue from it. "A Cylot control device," he said. "They must have put it in me at Merck."

"Why didn't it affect you like it affected everyone else?"

"My guess is that my defense mechanism against Mectar, the electrical pulse, protected me here, too, by fusing the metal. Look." Simon took the needle and held it up to the light. "There, Grey. You can see where the metal melted and re-fused. It's more than a guess. I know. Why didn't you tell me about the bruise on my neck sooner?"

"Benjamin, I thought you knew."

"Look," said Simon. "I should be dead. This was an accident, a fortunate one. I'm alive. If you see another human with a mark like this from your period, they're already dead. Destroy this device and you destroy the Cylot control of that person."

"Destroy it now," she said, pointing at the device.

"No. It's much too valuable." He used another sheet of paper to clean the device. "It's probably how the Cylots were tracking us. After it fused, it couldn't control me, but I'll bet they still can receive a signal from it." He taped it to the paper, folded it, and put it in his pocket.

"You got lucky with that electrical charge. Suppose you fought the Cylot and it won, and Mectar hadn't come," Beth said.

"I would have died," answered Simon flatly.

"Don't you care if you die?" she asked.

"I don't think you understand, Beth. I'm not involved in this. I'm committed. Do you know the difference?"

"Why don't you tell me," she said sarcastically.

"At breakfast, the chicken is involved; the pig is committed. It's my ass in this, and I don't come out of it until it's over."

Beth felt goose bumps on the back of her neck and the base of her spine. "The only other man I've ever heard say that, Benjamin, was my father. He led a team that rescued downed fliers behind enemy lines. That's why my mother loved him. But he scared her. Not that he threatened her; he loved her deeply. He understood commitment and was committed to her. He scared her because when he made that commitment she never knew if she was going to see him again. He always held himself to a higher standard of integrity than most."

Beth took Simon's face in both her hands gently and kissed him. He looked into her eyes. "I ..." he stammered. "If things, if circumstances were different. I just wanted to say thanks."

She felt he wanted to say he loved her. "Why did you want to say that?" she asked, trying to assuage his awkwardness.

"I ... I ..." he stammered and stopped.

"You poor man," she said. She straddled his lap, sitting on it and facing him. She leaned her forehead against his and draped her arms over his shoulders. He felt her hair brushing against his cheeks. Slowly and softly she kissed him, then kissed him again.

"I need to know where they are," said Simon, trying to change the subject. "For now, I need them to follow me. I need to have access to them."

"I ..." he said.

"Shhh!" she ordered, gently. Finally he did. He felt a soft, quiet, peaceful comfort. They ended up on the bed, where their soft intimacy turned hot. They found a refuge in each other. They expressed physically for each other the word neither dared to speak: love.

Afterward, Beth lay naked in Simon's arms. "Was I as good as the alien you made love to?" Her head rested against his shoulder and her eyes twinkled. "All right, all right. You didn't make love to an alien," she said.

"Let me ask a question," Simon said. "Was I as good as Thor?"

"Oh, yes. You were just fine. Did you love Lynth?" she asked finally.

"No, I stayed with Lynth. And yes, I loved her and do love her, but not like you're asking. I felt sorry for her. I needed information from her. Lalia had been annihilated by the Cylots.

"So what made Lynth sp special?" asked Beth.

"Her husband," responded Simon.

"Her dead husband?" asked Beth.

"It wasn't that he was dead—it was how he died. The Cylot army was advancing across their planet, destroying everything in its path. At the spaceport, near where Lynth and Liud lived, there were frantic preparations to get as many Lalians off the plants as possible. Women and children mostly. They were running the Cylot blockade in space. Liud began broadcasting a message to the Cylots. A challenge. An acceptance of defeat, not a surrender but an acknowledgment of it. The reason they had won, he broadcast to them, was better technology, not that they were superior beings. To prove it he would gladly meet any Cylot in mortal combat using traditional methods. In this case a Lalian broadsword."

"Lynth told me he hoped that the mass of information that he was broadcasting would attract attention away from the fleeing Lalian ships. He did much better that that. He brought the entire Cylot advance to a dead stop. Fighting ceased along the entire front. They responded to him. They accepted his challenge. He would fight one Cylot to the death, and if he lost the Cylots could prove conclusively to themselves, the Lalians, and the universe that they were indeed superior. It became entertainment for the Cylot troops.

An individual Cylot, because of its insect physiology, is ten times stronger than a man. Liud knew this. They met for battle in an open park, and the event was televised for the entertainment of the Cylot troops. Liud knew he was going to die.

Simon paused and gazed transfixed at the carpet before him, as though he were seeing it again.

"Well," she said.

"Well," said Simon, looking up, "he died slowly and horribly."

"They killed him like that?" Beth asked. "Made an example of him?"

"No, he chose to die like that."

"I wasn't being funny," said Beth.

"Neither was I. I'm telling you honestly. The longer he stayed alive, the more time he bought for his wife, child, and every other Lalian trying to leave the planet. He extended the battle as long as he could. Every bit of guile he could bring to the fight, he did—from the ceremony he claimed that every Lalian goes through before a combat like this (which didn't exist) to the way he fought the battle. The Cylot he fought killed him slowly. Liud was a brave Lalian."

Beth heard his voice tremble as though something were caught in his throat.

"So that's why you went to Lynth? To comfort her?" Beth now said, her voice full of compassion.

"No. Not at all," Simon replied matter-of-factly. "I did not know this when I first met Lynth."

"Why then?" she asked, perplexed.

"I needed to know everything about Liud and what he did. I needed to know what he said, why he said it, when he said it, how it occurred, what their initial response was, what their second response was."

"Their?"

"The Cylots," said Ben, talking faster now. "I wished to learn about my enemy, about their weaknesses. Every bit of information I have makes me stronger and them weaker. Lynth understood that, but in reliving it, she collapsed, sobbing in my arms. How was I going to leave her then? Pull the information out of her and leave her an emotional wreck. Of course I stayed with her."

"Well, surely Mectar has to understand," said Beth.

"The less Mectar knows, the better," said Ben. "This isn't about teaching and understanding, Beth. It's about surviving."

"You got it now?"

"Yeah," said Beth, "I understand."

"So," Beth stammered, unsure where to go next, "were the Lalians able to recover his body? Did they bury him?"

Ben stared at her, his mouth half-opened for just a moment too long. "You simply don't get it," he said flatly. "They ate him. After they killed him they ate him. They also ate his son, his older boy, who had stayed with him. His older boy was still alive when they began. And they broadcast it to the departing Lalian ships when they realized what Liud had done. You don't get it. You just don't get it."

Both angry and revolted at what he had told her, Beth grew defensive. "No I don't get it," she said. "I live here, on Earth, in the twenty-first century. I don't get aliens that want to eat you. I don't get the wars you are fighting in. You're right—I don't get it—but there's one thing you don't get, Benjamin."

"What's that?"

A softness seemed to come over her features like a passing cloud. "How much I feel for you and what you've been through. The admiration and respect I have for you." Her voice was quiet, soft. And with that softness she deflated Simon's anger.

"I'm sorry," he mumbled, and then he added more distinctly, "I'm sorry. I apologize." He turned his head away.

She took both his cheeks in each of her hands and turned his face back toward her. "I'm sorry too," she said. And then she kissed him.

"Lynth was alone and afraid. I held her, a lot like I'm holding you now. Mectar thought we mated, but it wasn't anything like that. She had lost her husband and her family. She had nowhere to go. She was running from the Cylots as much as I was. She was someone I was willing to fight for."

"Did you love her?" He shook his head no. "But you do love Kathy," she said.

"Very much," he said. "She also saved my life, but in a different way and in a different time."

"How?" she asked.

"I had a cancer. There are more virulent diseases ahead. Ultimately, when I reached her time—"

"You mean she lived in a period ahead of you?"

"Yeah," he said, "she lived five hundred years ahead of me and I time jumped to that period. It was the first time jump, and I jumped into the time of the general speaker and the Kian War. By then, a cure for my cancer had been developed. She risked her life to help conduct the operation. Don't you see? I owe her that much. Whether I love her or not, I owe her that much."

"You're an honorable man, Benjamin Simon."

They talked for a while. Then he rolled over and placed his back against her. She spooned him and they fell asleep together.

Beth awoke to sounds of Simon showering. Naked, she stretched languidly and listened to his indecipherable singing. She had had a good night's sleep. She felt sensual and happy.

She remembered how excited old Mom became when she told her about shelling operations. She knew what her mother must have felt. And she knew what her mother saw in her father. Even though he was more forceful than her father, Simon had this same power.

The knob on the door connecting the two rooms jiggled. It was Mectar wanting to enter. The knob continued to turn but the door would not open. Beth thought that Mectar was being obnoxious. After all, the door was locked. She heard Simon turn off the shower. The connecting door suddenly flew open on its hinges and slammed against the wall. The doorjamb and metal were torn. With a satisfied look, Mectar entered the room. "Is Simon ready?" he demanded.

"Don't you know how to knock?"

"What's knock and how do you do it?" asked Mectar.

"You rap on the door before you open it."

"Rap? What is rap?"

"You hit the door. It's a polite Earth custom," Beth said with exasperation.

"What is the point?" asked Mectar, perplexed.

"The point is to let other people know that you are coming into the room."

He looked at Beth blankly. "I'm coming in," he said.

"You're here already!" she said, sitting up and pulling the sheet in front of her breasts.

"I know that," he said. "And you're there. And you should be out of bed, because we have ground to cover, Grey." Mectar paused and then added, "I give you a Kian promise to respect this custom that seems so important to you."

Simon emerged naked from the shower and vigorously dried his hair with a towel. "Why does your water ritual last so long?" asked Mectar. "Another custom," he snorted with disdain.

"Water ritual?" asked Beth.

"I pray in the shower, Mectar," said Simon. "Generally accompanied by hymns."

"What?" Beth asked. "What are you talking about?"

"The water ritual, Grey. I'm surprised that you do not partake of it. Something humans must do," said Simon. "Mectar, we'll be out in a second. Why don't we meet you downstairs?"

"I'll wait," said Mectar.

"What's a water ritual?" asked Beth.

"I'll tell you later," said Simon. "How about you getting up and dressed?"

"With him here?" said Beth pointing at Mectar.

"Mectar," said Simon. "It's an Earth custom to allow Earth females privacy while they dress."

"Does that mean you leave too?" asked Mectar.

"No, because I'm familiar with her," said Simon.

"I will respect your privacy, Grey. Be downstairs in five minutes." Mectar turned and left.

Beth sat up. "What's a water ritual?"

"A water ritual is my shower. I like long showers. In a small spacecraft, water is at a premium. You sponge bath to use water sparingly. When I was in the Bendibast System—"

"The where?" asked Beth.

"It's a solar system out in deep space," said Simon. "Anyway, we had to install a weapons system on my space craft."

"You own your own spaceship?"

"Well, I did until it was shot down," said Simon.

"What was it named, the USS *Kathy*?" asked Beth with a hint of jealousy.

"No," said Simon. "It was named *The Good Ship Lollipop*."

"Seriously?" said Beth.

"Seriously," said Simon. "Mectar hated the name. He wanted to call the ship *Black Death* or *Kian Revenge*. The ship came from an Earth factory and I named it before he arrived. It had the prototype of the weapons system that should have been used in the Bendibast Battle." Simon paused and looked up thoughtfully. "Sort of lyrical," he said and then in a low voice, as though he were an announcer, he said, "Bendibast Battle, the battle at Bendibast." He then continued in a normal voice. "Anyway, I called it *The Good Ship Lollipop* because I knew that he would hate it."

"So what about the water ritual?" she asked.

"I like long showers. Mectar, of course, with his Spartan mentality, wouldn't allow or think of long showers until I explained that showering is a very important religious ritual I observe. I explained that Earth people partake daily in the water ritual and that it's generally accompanied by hymns."

"What kind of hymns?" asked Beth.

"I sing anything that comes to mind."

"My God, what have I gotten myself into?"

"Have you called Javic this morning?" said Simon to change the subject.

"No," she said petulantly.

"Try," encouraged Simon.

She pulled the phone off the nightstand and dialed. It rang many times. Finally, she extended the handset toward him and said, "See, no answer."

"How about Javic's daughter?"

After calling information for Judy Javic's phone number, Beth dialed it, but she received no answer. She left a message on the answering machine.

By that time, Simon was dressed. "Come on, let's go," he said.

"Benjamin, I've got to get dressed, and frankly I'd like a water ritual."

"All right," said Simon. "I'll give you fifteen minutes. Then Mectar and I are leaving."

"And then what am I supposed to do?"

"Beats the hell out of me, Grey," said Simon. "I say you should pass on your water ritual. Let's get a move on."

"Wait a minute, you son of a bitch. You're just not going to leave me here, are you?"

"That's pretty much the plan if you're going to sit in bed all day," said Simon.

"I'm coming, I'm coming," she said. "Give me five minutes to take a shower. I'll be quick."

Simon looked at his watch. "Go for it."

Passing him naked, with no hint of modesty, she muttered "bastard" under her breath. Smiling, he slapped her behind. She stopped at the bathroom doorway and said, "I'll get you, you know. I'll get you for all of this," she said playfully.

"Promises, promises, Grey," Simon said as she slammed the bathroom door. When she was done, a little more than five minutes later, she found Simon waiting in the bedroom and dressed without further comment.

Beth looked at his hand. Overnight it had healed remarkably. The two small fingers were gone but otherwise there was no indication of damage. "How could you stand the pain?" she said. "The trauma to the area?"

"I can produce chemicals to suppress the pain. Just like a camel."

"A camel?" she said.

"Never mind," he responded. "Call Javic."

"Not even a good morning kiss?" she said.

"Call Javic," he repeated flatly. She dialed. Again, no answer. "Where does Javic live? I want to go to his house."

"He lives in Watchung," she said. "Why don't I call Judy again?"

She dialed and received an answer. "Hello, is Leonard there? This is Beth Grey. Is Judy there? Hi Judy. This is Beth. I've been trying to reach you all week. Is the bris today? Oh." She looked at Simon. "Hang on, will you?" Addressing Simon, she said, "They moved the bris from her house to her father's house because her mother wanted it that way. Her father still hasn't been located." Again speaking into the phone, she said, "And you were trying to reach me? Yes,

I know there was an accident. A lot of people have been trying to find me."
Simon became interested.

"I'm fine. Yes, there was some trouble at my apartment," Beth said while rolling her eyes impatiently. "Well, what time is it? One? Oh, of course I'll be there.
May I bring a friend? Fine, I just wanted you to know. Thanks, see you at one."

Simon saw that it was eleven o'clock. "Let's go," he said.

Simon, Beth, and Mectar left the hotel. Beth saw Simon stop and look at a
device on his jump belt. He stopped and then took her by the hand and backed
into the building.

"We need another car," he said to Mectar.

"What's wrong?"

"That one's rigged to blow up the minute we start it."

They walked along the south side of the building and entered the side parking
lot. Mectar saw an unattended Ford Taurus and began to move toward it. "Stop,"
said Simon. "If we are going to steal a car, take a better one." Then he pointed to
a late-model black Cadillac. Simon took a device from his jump belt and placed it
on the door lock. The door popped open. Beth stared at him. He returned her
stare while saying, "Magic."

"You've got more gadgets than I've ever seen," she said. "Is that thing going to
start the car too?"

He nodded as they got in. He placed the device over the ignition and the car
started. He put the car into gear. Mectar, looking out the back window, said,
"We're not being followed."

"Oh yeah, we are," said Simon.

"Why didn't they chase us?" asked Beth.

"They haven't made their move because if we have the formula, and if Mectar
and I time jump they will lose us. They can't just leave us wandering around
here. Maybe they missed something. They have to be careful about how they
approach us. Time jumping makes us different from you. They can kill you. If
Mectar and I time jump right now, they lose our trail."

"Well, why not time jump and lose them totally?" asked Beth.

"Because," Simon said, "I don't want to lose them. Right now I know where
they are."

"Where?" said Beth. "Where?"

"Behind me," said Simon while keeping his eyes on the road. "Tell me how to
get to Javic's place."

Beth sat back and said, "Turn left and get on 287 West."

31

Swinging on the Gateless Gate

Javic lived in a small mansion, a million-dollar home in a beautifully styled, architecturally crafted development in the Watchung Hills, near Rahway. Simon parked across the street from Javic's home, behind a landscaping truck. A big, fit-looking black man in his mid-twenties stepped out of the truck, which bore the logo "Nature's Image Landscaping." As he stepped out and sauntered to the rear of the truck, two coffee cups fell to the ground behind him. He opened the rear door and took out an edge trimmer, then sauntered off to the back of a home across the street from Javic's. Simon cut the ignition.

Many would say Javic lived in splendor, if not opulence. Because of the importance and quality of his work, and because of his licensing fees, he was a millionaire many times over, but he was a millionaire in hiding. Despite his disappearance, life went on normally for the rest of Javic's family. On this day, they were having a bris for his newly born grandson.

"Mectar," said Simon. "I think you should stay in the car."

"Why is that?"

"The hostess is expecting a couple. She thinks I'm dating Beth. It's not acceptable to bring a third person, particularly one as formidable as you. This woman's husband has disappeared, she has a house full of people, and her grandson is about to have his foreskin removed. Your presence would be, I think, too intimidating."

"His foreskin removed?" asked Mectar.

"This is a bris, Mectar. It's part of the Jewish religion."

"Another religious rite?" Mectar asked.

"That's correct," said Simon.

"What does it entail?" asked Mectar.

"Well, a man called a moile cuts the foreskin off the end of the penis," said Simon.

"You mean you sacrifice body parts to your god?" asked Mectar incredulously. Beth was shocked at this new slant on an aspect of her religion. "Why the end of your penis?" Mectar continued. "Why not the end of your finger or the end of your nose?"

Simon feigned shock. "That's it," he said. "All these years we Jews have been doing it wrong. After all, we need all the total penis length we can get. And with our noses so big, we should have cut them off."

"Fuck you," said Beth. "You've got such a perverted mind."

"You agree to stay here and watch the car?" asked Simon.

"Wait" said Mectar. "Did not Grey say that you think with your penises? Do all Earth people lie or do you lose brain cells when this happens?" Simon dropped his head onto the steering wheel between his hands and moaned softly.

Beth, after an immediate little snort, composed herself. "There probably wasn't much there to begin with," she said.

"Still, two heads are better than one," reasoned Simon quietly without lifting his own head from the steering wheel.

"Are you now saying you have two heads?"

"Mectar, your questions are getting harder and harder. If I told you about this I would have to kill you" said Simon

"No," Mectar shouted angrily, "It will be I who will kill you."

"Stop!" screamed Beth with such force that both Mectar and Simon both stopped and looked at her.

"Mectar, Simon is kidding."

"What is kidding?"

"Joking, Simon is joking about killing you."

"I assure you, Grey, Simon wants me dead."

"Mectar, in this context Simon is totally joking and that is because when Earth men talk about their penises they are all morons, making claims that are either untrue or so exaggerated they border on the absurd. Don't try to understand it—Earth women have lived with earthmen for millennia, and we still don't understand it. Now Simon is going to apologize to you for being the stupid ass he is, and you are going to say, 'All right,' and then we are going to go. Isn't that right, Benjamin?"

"Whatever," said Ben. There followed a long silence.

"Well ..." said Beth.

"Mectar," mumbled Simon, "I am sorry for being ... uh ... stupid. I apologize."

Mectar looked at Beth with surprise and respect. "I did not realize Earth women could be so powerful."

"Your turn," said Beth, looking at Mectar.

"What was I supposed to say?" asked Mectar.

"Say, 'All right, I'll watch the car.'"

"All right, I'll watch the car," Mectar repeated. With that, Beth got out and slammed her door while shouting the word "morons."

"I like that girl," Simon said as he watched Beth walk around the front of the car. Simon opened his door and Beth turned the side-view mirror out to freshen her lipstick as Simon watched patiently.

"Do you know what they do with all the foreskins?" Simon asked Mectar, leaning into the car while he waited for Beth to finish applying her cosmetics.

"What?"

"They make wallets out of them."

"What?"

"That's right," said Simon. "The moiles collect the foreskins they've removed and make wallets out of them. Really, Mectar, it's true. That way if a moile wants to go on a trip, he rubs his wallet real hard. And just as a penis grows when you do that, the wallet grows into a suitcase."

Mectar glared at him and said, "Any decent religion would have burned you at the stake long ago." Simon just smiled. Beth was seething with anger. As they walked toward the house, she started in on him.

"Why do you do that?" she demanded. "There are times you are so wonderful … and then you do that." Becoming angrier, she said, "You're a fuck, you know that, Benjamin? There's nothing you won't take down. There's nothing you wouldn't insult or mock. Circumcision doesn't shorten the penis—"

"I know that," said Simon, "but Mectar doesn't. Why are you so upset?"

"How can you be that … that … sacrilegious?" Beth demanded angrily.

"You criticize me for poking fun at my religion?" Simon demanded indignantly. "Is religion some solemn sacred icon that should be revered? Religion fractionalizes God or fictionalizes him. Give me a concise reason why Catholics and Protestants are killing each other in Northern Ireland when Christ said to turn the other cheek and that murder is wrong. Explain the Near East, where Islamic and Jewish murder has gone on for centuries, even though the Arabs and Jews are brothers, descended from the same father. That fighting stopped not because of maturity and mutual regard but because a common enemy presented itself. It was either band together or die individually. An Arab maxim is 'The enemy of my enemy is my friend.' Arab and Jew are both enemies to the Kians.

"Extrapolate this further. Kians are to Earthmen in my time what Arabs are to the Jews in your time. I cannot be offended by Mectar's lack of regard for my culture. If I am, I violate my own ethic. If I kill him because he insulted me, my action is worse than his insult. How can I teach him this notion unless I am willing to laugh at myself? Who are you, Grey, to criticize the method I use to teach my student? I am searching for the method that best communicates the lesson.

"If Mectar is afraid I am going to destroy his empire, he is right. I can destroy it with an idea more easily than I can with a weapon. This doesn't mean I have to kill a single Kian. Do I not destroy my enemy if I make him my friend? Don't you think religion and philosophy are weapons? By infecting Mectar with religion and philosophy, do I not infect the entire Kian race? The overriding social imperative is to protect instead of attack. If I teach this to the Kians, what have I done to Kia's warlike culture?

"All religions speak of the soul and the spark of divinity. `Soul' is a word used to describe an electromagnetic phenomenon. It is a part of you that makes you part of the greater whole. Ditto for Mectar and the Cylots. I am more peace-maker than warrior. If you do what I do, you must deeply believe in God. Your God. My God. Mectar's God. Religion is about redemption. When will redemption come? It will come when we look upon others as we would have them look upon ourselves. It will come when we grant to every person the rights we claim for ourselves. Science offers a surer path than religion if you are searching for God, and religion offers a surer path than science for defeating the Kians. I want to defeat the Kians by making them my friends."

"You don't believe in God, do you?" said Beth. "You just believe in science."

"You're right. I don't believe in God," said Simon. "Belief implies doubt. I have knowledge. I know God exists. I know this beyond doubt. Did Galileo stop believing in God because he discovered the Earth revolves around the Sun? My humor just hides the pain, makes it easier for me not to kill the creature who wants me dead."

"You're a Jew and you mock your own religion?" said Beth. "I'm a Jew too, Simon, and I don't like you mocking Judaism."

"That's because you take a parochial view of religion, Grey. Scientifically, I can't be one religion," he said. "My roots are Jewish. But, scientifically, I must be a pantheist. How many sciences do you think there are, Grey? Do you think there is a different science for every religion? I have to follow my God, not your precepts."

"And what is your God?" asked Beth.

"My God is science. There is only one science, Grey. There is only one God. There is only one light. It's made of photons. No matter what your religion, when you run it through a prism it reveals many colors. I describe to you verifiable scientific proof of the existence of out-of-body consciousness. No matter what science says, the fact that your consciousness survives outside your body is proof of the soul."

"You know you're full of contradictions," shouted Beth. "You mock religion, yet you tell me that your work and Benveniste's locate the footprint of the human soul in the body's electromagnetism."

"Its as good as where you say the soul is."

"I didn't say the soul was anywhere," said Beth.

"You said you're a Jew," said Simon.

"That's right."

"Do Jews believe in the soul?" asked Simon.

"Of course we do."

"And where is it?"

"I don't know."

"Gimme a break, Grey," said Simon. "Did you ever read the Kaballah?"

"No. You have to be invited to read that. It's part of Jewish mysticism."

"Well, the Kaballah says that the soul is in the blood," said Simon. "That's why people keep kosher. Koshering involves removing the animal's blood and eating only the flesh. That way you don't ingest the animal's soul. What do you think religious rites will be like eight hundred or eight thousand years from now? Look at Neanderthal and Cro-Magnon man's rites. *Homo sapiens* have their own distinctive religious rites. But what about *Homo futuris*? Cro-Magnon man said God lived in thunder. You say he lives in spirit form. Well, I know where God lives," said Simon. He pushed the doorbell to Javic's home.

"Where, Ben, does God live?"

"Inside you, Grey. God lives inside you." His answer opened a door of understanding in the flash of an instant. Satori. No longer was Ben Simon a wisecracking, sarcastic son of a bitch but a man driven by deeply held moral values and beliefs. By choice, and at personal sacrifice, he had taken on the entire Kian race, not to defeat them but rather to befriend them. In the present, he had to begin with a single convert, his would-be assassin. Beth would never again feel as she had about Benjamin Simon. She now fully loved and understood him.

The door opened. "Beth, I'm so glad you could come," said Javic's daughter Judy.

"Oh, hi, Judy." Beth blinked, reorienting herself.

"My name is Ben Simon," said Simon, extending his hand and flashing a toothy grin. "I'm Beth's boyfriend."

Beth stepped forward, put her arm through Simon's, looked at him and said, "This is my boyfriend, Benjamin Simon." Judy smiled at the redundancy of the introduction. It was clear to the three of them that Ben and Beth were a couple for the first time and that Beth was staking a claim on Benjamin Simon.

"Pleased to meet you. Come on in," Judy said.

As Beth walked past Simon, she glared at him and said, "I hate you." Only he could hear her. He smiled in response.

After a butler took their coats, Beth and Simon mingled in the crowded living room. She was appropriately dressed for the occasion. He was underdressed in a sport shirt and slacks. His khaki slacks looked as if they hadn't been pressed in several days, and when she looked at his worn boots she just shuddered. She wished she could have dressed him better.

"Where's Judy's mother?" Simon whispered.

"I don't know. I don't see her," said Beth. While the guests greeted Beth, she continued to look for Judy's mother. Simon drank a can of beer while he stood behind Beth, smiling and meeting the other guests. "Where is she?" he demanded again.

"I don't know," Beth repeated. "She's probably with the baby and the moile."

As she said that, Lisa Javic, Leonard's wife, came out and asked for quiet. Simon and Beth could hear the baby crying in the next room.

Finally the moile carried the baby into view. He was followed by Javic's wife, Lisa. The crying baby was placed on a table in the center of the living room. The guests gathered around. Rabbi Liebowitz, the family rabbi, was present but graciously deferred to the moile, saying, "You're the rabbi here."

After chanting in Hebrew, the moile offered the baby a wine-dipped fingertip and resumed chanting. Finally, the moile fastened a clamp around the baby's penis, which he had previously anaesthetized. He then clipped the foreskin amid shrieks from the child and grimaces from every man in the room, including Simon. Congratulations were offered all around—to the parents, who couldn't watch the actual cutting, and to Grandmother Lisa, who did watch.

When the guests resumed their mingling, Simon and Beth accosted Lisa Javic, who they found talking with the butler back in the maid's quarters. "Lisa, can I have a minute of your time?" asked Beth.

"Certainly, dear," said Lisa.

"Lisa, this is Ben Simon."

"How do you do, Mrs. Javic? I'm sorry to hear about your husband," said Simon. "I think I can help."

"My husband is dead. I'm sure of it," Lisa said.

"And I'm sure of just the opposite, Mrs. Javic," said Simon. "I'm so sure of it, I'm willing to bet you know where he is."

"Listen, I have to go," she said brusquely, turning to walk away.

Simon grabbed her arm and pulled her around. "Mrs. Javic, I don't think you understand. You have to hear me out. I think your husband has the formula I need to stop these murders. There are beings who will stop at nothing to take it from him. He is in greater danger than you realize."

"How can that be? How can you know what he has and doesn't have? Besides, he's dead. Excuse me. I have to go," she said, walking into a bathroom. Simon followed her in. She stared at him, astonished at his audacity.

"If he were dead, he would have been found," said Simon. "Researchers have died because they have this formula. The creatures who want it don't play games. If they had found your husband, we would have found his body already. We haven't, which means he's hidden somewhere. If I can get the formula from him, I become the target instead of him."

"Why? Why you?" asked Lisa, her brow wrinkling.

"Because I'm from the future. These beings don't want the formula going back there," said Simon.

"Don't be ridiculous," said Lisa.

"It's true, Lisa," said Beth, who had joined them.

"You're both crazy," Lisa said, trying to leave again. Simon grabbed her arm again.

"Mectar, I need your help," said Simon.

"Who's Mectar?" asked Lisa.

"Mrs. Javic, do you love your husband?" asked Simon.

"Of course."

"Then, you have no way out but through me. I can save his life. Do you understand? But I can't do it unless I find him."

"You're insane," said Lisa.

"Listen. A friend of mine is going to come in here," said Simon. "I want you to relax and be very calm. We're going to ask a few more questions. Then we'll leave, whether you tell us what we want to know or not. Beth, could you meet Mectar at the front door?" Beth nodded and left.

Lisa glanced at the technical journals on the small wicker stool next to the toilet. She began to cry. "He was always reading his technical journals in here," she said, shaking her head. "He was always absorbed in his science." Then she looked at Simon angrily. "Do you think you'll find him? He's eluded types much tougher than you. When the Russians came to Hungary in 1956, he and his parents had to leave Budapest. They fled to Prague, to Vienna, and then to Switzerland. His mother died along the way. He was kept in safe houses. That's how he grew up—hiding. Between six and eight, he never went out like other children. He hid in basements with his father and read journals and anything else he could get his hands on. The memories have never left him. They went to England in 1958 and then to America. The people who employ him think he's just a doctor, but I know what he is made of."

"I'm glad he's tough, Mrs. Javic," Simon said gently. "He'll need to be."

Beth was on her way to meet Mectar when Judy Javic stopped her at the front door. Judy had questions about Beth, Simon, and recent events. As she began to speak to Beth, Mectar arrived at the front door. He paused at the top step and stared at the door as though it were a puzzle. "Knock," he said to himself. "Rap. Hit." His brow furrowed. He cocked his fist and hit the door.

On the other side of the door, Beth and Judy Javic were deep into a discussion. Mectar's fist crashed through the door, to the shock of everyone in the living room. He then pulled his fist back through the door and peered through the hole he had made. "Grey, Grey," he called, and then he saw her though the opening. "I am coming in." He then opened the door and entered the room.

Beth was furious. "What are you doing?" she shouted. "Are you out of your mind? Why did you destroy that door?"

Mectar became visibly angry. "I was keeping my promise to you to hit the door before I entered."

"I said knock, not hit," Beth screamed.

"You said knock, rap, or hit. You were not specific. I chose to hit. I do not understand the difference. They all seemed the same. I did this to satisfy your request that I respect your custom."

Beth threw back her head and exhaled the word *ohhh*. As she did, her breasts rose up and they pointed at Mectar.

"Do not shoot your guilt rays at me, Grey," said Mectar angrily, pointing at her. "I release myself from my promise to you. I will no longer respect your wishes about your customs. Now point your guilt transmitters elsewhere."

Beth thrust out her chest, pointing her breasts toward Mectar and shaking them.

"Mectar, dammit," Simon shouted form the bathroom. "Get in here." Mectar turned and walked toward the sound of Simon's voice. As he passed through the living room, the assembled guests went silent and stared at him. Oblivious to them, he glanced at the long buffet table laden with food.

"Oh God," said Beth to herself as Mectar walked away. "I'm becoming just like Benjamin. Mectar strode directly into the bathroom, where Lisa Javic gasped in shock and fear. He shut the door.

"Why do you need me?" Mectar asked Simon.

"Mrs. Javic, my friend here is going to touch your shoulder softly. Don't be afraid."

Lisa looked fearfully at Beth, who had followed Mectar into the bathroom. Beth patted her arm reassuringly and said, "Lisa, it's all right. Here." She lowered the toilet seat. "Sit down."

Lisa sat.

Mectar put his hand on Lisa's shoulder and Simon joined them in a Kian ankwar. Beth had seen Mectar and Simon in an ankwar only once before. "Hell," she said. "I was in an ankwar at Hoffman-LaRoche when Mectar touched my shoulder." She watched Lisa's eyes cloud over.

Images reeled in Lisa's mind: of space, of space-time, and of Simon. She saw her husband lying dead in their country cabin. Then she saw an alternative image forming, a different path, one that ended with her husband alive. At that instant, she knew that Mectar and Simon had absorbed from her mind knowledge of her husband's whereabouts. Also at that instant, she knew that Mectar, Simon, and Beth were there to help. Then the ankwar was broken. "My God," Lisa said.

"We have to go," said Simon. "We don't have a lot of time. Don't tell anyone we were here."

"How can I not?" Lisa asked in wonder.

"Because your husband's life depends on it." Lisa began to cry uncontrollably.

"Mectar, can you leave us alone with Lisa for a second?" asked Beth. "I don't want to leave her like this." Mectar nodded and walked out to the dining area. The people there seemed to melt away from him. Mectar then spied the dining room table laid out with food for the guests. He wandered over to inspect it. He surveyed the table and selected a brownie, choosing it because it was the same color as chocolate. He put it in his mouth, chewed it once, and stopped. He closed his eyes, his head tilted back, and he let the flavor melt in his mouth. He sighed.

Judy Javic's grandmother had been in the kitchen and had not heard the commotion. She was slightly hard of hearing and just a little "Out of touch". She exited the kitchen with a fresh plate of cut fruit to put on the dining room table when she saw Mectar for the first time, his head back, his eyes closed, chewing slowly, one of her homemade brownies in his hand.

"Do you like my brownie?" she asked.

Mectar opened his eyes and looked around. He saw no one and said nothing.

"Do you like my brownie?" she asked again. Mectar then looked down. At six feet five inches tall, he was nearly two feet taller than the white-haired woman asking the question.

"It is delicious," he said.

"I made them from scratch myself," she said with pride.

"What is scratch? Is that like an itch?" asked Mectar perplexed.

She smiled. "No. I have my own special recipe for brownies."

"What is a recipe?" asked Mectar.

"Well, I can see you don't cook. It's where you take all the ingredients and mix them and cook them to make that brownie. You're not from around here, are you? You're Beth's friend, aren't you? Judy said Beth would be coming with some friends."

"No, I come from far away. Recipe is like a formula, right?"

"I'm Maida," she said, putting down the dish and holding out her hand to shake, "but my family calls me Bubbe."

"Mectar." He gently took Maida's hand and pumped it once.

"Well, if you had a wife you would know what a recipe is."

"You have told me the recipe is the formula to make this wonderful food. Will you give me this formula, Bubbe Maida?"

"It's a family recipe, Mr. Mectar. I would really only give this to my daughter and granddaughters."

"Would your family give it to my family so upon my return to my home I may give it to my family."

"I suppose," said Maida. "Do you have anything to write with?"

Mectar produced from his jump belt a small electronic pad and stylus. "Go," he said.

"Well, first you need to grease the pan ..." Bubbe Maida began.

Meanwhile, Lisa Javic had finally settled down, and while she was still crying she told Beth she would be fine and that they should go.

Simon and Beth headed right for the door. Mectar was talking to Bubbe Maida. As Simon and Beth passed the living room on the way out, Simon saw Mectar talking to the old lady. "Mectar," Simon shouted, "let's move."

"Thank you, Bubbe Maida, for this formula. Your brownies are delicious."

"Mr. Mectar, I'm so sorry you have to leave. I would love for you to meet my granddaughters. One of them is single, you know."

"I can take one to go?" said Mectar, pointing at the brownies.

"Take as many as you like," said Bubbe Maida. Mectar produced a drawstring bag and emptied the contents of the brownie tray into it. He turned and saw Simon and Beth walking out the door. He turned back to Maida and said, "Thank you. I must go," then turned abruptly and followed Simon and Beth out the door. Maida turned to remove the empty tray, and when she turned her back, Mectar saw one last piece of brownie that had fallen on the table. From a distance of about eight feet, his tongue shot out, grabbed the piece of brownie, and then snapped it back into his mouth.

Maida then turned and joined Judy Javic her granddaughter. "That Mr. Mectar is sure a nice young man," she said to her granddaughter. "I wanted to introduce him to your sister. He sure liked my brownies."

"Bubbe," said Judy, putting her arm around her, "he's an alien."

"He'd convert for the right girl," said Maida knowingly. "He's a catch—look at his car."

Mectar walked out the door carrying the bag of brownies. Beth turned around and saw him chewing on them. "What are you doing?" she said.

"I got some food as I left."

"For God's sake. You're chewing on a pound of brownies. Do you know how many calories there are in that?"

"And a tasty brownies it is," said Mectar. "The food you have here is unbelievable. Do you know what I think would be fantastic? Chocolate meat."

Simon put his hand around Beth's arm as Beth rolled her eyes and said, "C'mon. Be grateful he didn't eat the linen."

Beth touched Simon's arm as they walked. "Ben, on the way in you said that technology continually redefines God. What did you mean?"

"As scientific thought evolves, it does not deny the existence of God. It just re-explains the mechanism by which God works," he said. "Try to separate your consciousness from your mind. If there is no God, then consciousness is simply a manifestation of chemical reactions. That's all you are, Ms. Grey, chemicals and matter."

"The old paradigm is that matter creates consciousness. I submit to you that consciousness creates matter. Consciousness does not reside in your chemicals. Apply the physics to the chemistry and the biochemistry and you'll find sub-atomic particles behaving intelligently. Now consider a species progressing along the evolutionary path, the phylogenetic spectrum. Regard a single-celled creature and move along the phylogenetic spectrum until its conclusion. The most advanced creature is located there. Is that advanced creature God? Certainly, if I apply basics of nature to God, God is in the process of procreation. Or are we just an integral part of nature, woven into it? Ms. Grey, we are God. The universe is conscious of itself. The struggle between humans and Kians is occurring at a greater depth than we know.

"We're all children of God, right, Ms. Grey? Jews are the children of God. When do they become the adolescents of God, or grown-up gods?" said Simon, raising an eyebrow. "I want to expand that awareness, because I don't like being saddled with this monkey." He pointed to Mectar.

"You see why he is a threat to me, Ms. Grey?" said the Kian. "You see why I'm going to kill him?"

When Mectar said "Ms. Grey," he mimicked Simon precisely. Beth realized Mectar could impersonate Simon any time he chose to.

"That's what I'm beginning to believe, Beth," Simon continued. "If consciousness exists separately from matter, then what is time/space except a sandbox? A poet once wrote, 'Gandolf brought me a goat's head that did not bleed and wanting to learn more has become my only need. A thousand keys tried and none of them fit. Perhaps one day upon a key I'll hit.'"

Beth saw a struggling scientist who was crashing through barriers and destroying icons. He was bringing a new dimension to science. She realized that in many ways, she played out this struggle in her own mind. She replied, "Then remember this: Great oafs from little icons grow."

Simon laughed aloud. "You mean great oaks from little acorns grow," Simon chuckled.

Beth's eyes twinkled in response.

"I like you, Grey," Simon said. "I see why Javic kept you around for so long."

Beth exploded again. "Like! You *like* me?" She stomped to the car, seething with anger. "You ... you ... you ... are obtuse," she shouted. Then she got in the car and slammed the door shut. Simon had missed her point entirely.

Mectar, still eating, watched Beth explode. "What did I miss?" he asked calmly between bites.

"I'm not sure," said Simon, puzzled, but he was beginning to discern what Judy Javic had recognized from her front porch: a summer squall, a lovers' argument.

"Where are we going?" asked Mectar.

"To Javic's country house," said Simon.

He and Mectar got in the car. As the trio drove off, another car followed, keeping out of sight. Mueller drove it. Beside him sat Heinrich.

32

The Chance of a Lifetime in a Lifetime of Chance

While Mectar waited near the car, Beth and Simon approached the front door of Javic's Bucks County, Pennsylvania, country house. Simon knocked and received no answer. He turned the knob. The door was unlocked. He drew a phaser from his belt. He and Beth walked cautiously into the empty living room.

They inched their way toward the bedrooms. The door to one of them opened slightly and a double-barreled shotgun appeared. "Leonard?" Beth asked.

"Who is he?" Javic demanded from behind the door.

Simon lowered the phaser.

"A friend, Leonard," Beth responded.

"You shouldn't have brought him."

"Leonard, he's here to help," said Beth.

"Tell him to go away."

Simon became impatient. "Javic, I'm your only hope of living. You god-damned well better get your ass out here, because if I turn away and walk out, you're dead."

Beth, surprised by his bluntness, looked at Simon.

"How can I be sure?" Javic asked.

"If I wasn't your friend, you'd be dead already."

Javic emerged from the bedroom, aiming the shotgun at Simon.

"Put that down before you hurt somebody," Simon ordered.

"No."

Leonard Javic was tall and thin, with brownish gray hair on the sides and back of his head. When Simon, Mectar, and Beth reached him, he looked haggard and tired. A tic under his right eye made him wink continually.

"Fine. Then keep it aimed at me. Do you have the formula?"

"Who told you about the formula? Who are you?" Javic demanded.

"He's from the future, Leonard," said Beth.

"The future?" asked Javic.

"He can time travel."

"Javic, I need the formula," said Simon.

"You get out of here before I blow your head off," shouted Javic, aiming the gun at Simon's head.

Beth stepped in front of the gun to face Javic.

"Beth, stop," said Simon.

"Shut up!" she commanded. "You listen to me, Leonard Javic. We didn't come all this way for you to threaten us with a shotgun and tell us to get lost. We need the formula and we need it now. Don't think we're going anywhere without it. Is that clear? If Benjamin says he's from the future, then you better believe him. Now we need that formula."

Javic lowered the gun. "She's just like her mother. So help me, God, when her mother worked with me, she wouldn't tolerate anyone's opinion. She had to see everything for herself. It's one of the reasons I hired her daughter. Beth's pretty good, isn't she?"

Simon smiled broadly and genuinely. "She is that, Leonard. She is that. Now look. The creatures that are killing all the researchers are here because Yugen was actually from the future. He came back to your present to work on the formula in safety, but they tracked him down, and once he made the formula work, they had to stop him. Did you get any of the formula on you?"

"No," said Javic.

"If you've written out the formula, give it to me now, before they find you. Once someone else has the formula, namely me, you will become irrelevant. Giving me the formula makes you safe."

"Leonard," said Beth, "you knew my mother for many years. I've worked with you for a long time. You can trust what I say. Give him the formula."

"It's in the bedroom," said Javic. "In the top drawer, near the belt Yugen gave me."

Simon looked puzzled. "What belt?"

"The one Yugen gave me."

"You knew Yugen?" asked Simon.

"Yes. That's how I got the formula."

"Then you weren't on the list?" asked Beth.

"What list?" asked Javic.

"The list of researchers Varley made up," said Beth. "He sent a letter to everyone on the list, along with a copy of the formula."

"No, I didn't get any list, or any letter from a guy named Varley. Yugen gave me a package. He told me it contained a belt and a formula that I had to keep safe. He said someone would come for the package. He also—"

"Someone has come for the package," said Simon. "Do you have it?"

"Are you sure I'll be safe?" asked Javic.

"Oh, yeah," said Simon. "You'll be very safe."

Simon picked up a telepathic communication from Mectar: *Something's coming. My sensor is reading that Cylots are approaching.*

"Mectar says the Cylots have trailed us here," Simon said. "Javic, you and Beth can live if you listen to me very carefully."

"You should have thrown away the tracking device," said Beth.

"Who's Mectar?" asked Javic suspiciously. He again pointed the shotgun at Simon.

"It doesn't matter. If you give me the damn belt and formula, you will literally become irrelevant. I'll let them know I've got it. They won't bother you anymore. They'll want me."

"How will you let them know you've got it?" said Javic.

"By walking out the door and telling them."

"But they'll kill you," said Beth.

"If they can," said Simon.

"Leonard," said Beth. "He's fought them before. I saw him do it at Merck. He knows what he's talking about."

Javic removed a package from his bedroom dresser wrapped in brown paper. Simon put it on the dining room table and ripped it open. He smiled and lovingly took out the belt. He ran his hand across it softly. "I'll be damned," he said to himself. "Yugen bless you."

"There is something else I need to tell you—" said Javic.

"Simon, the Cylots are here," shouted Mectar while firing his phaser. They could hear his phaser fire being returned by the Cylots.

"What's that?" Beth asked. "Another jump belt?"

"It's an unregistered jump belt," said Simon.

"Unregistered. Can you use it to return to Kathy?" said Beth.

"I can use it to go anywhere."

"But what about the formula?" Beth asked.

"Mectar can take it back."

"Benjamin, I've got to tell you something about Mectar and Kathy," said Beth.

Mectar yelled, "I can't hold them too much longer."

"Benjamin," shouted Beth. "Mectar can—"

A Cylot grenade exploded ten yards in front of the house. Shards of broken window glass flew across the room. Simon, Javic, and Beth dove to the floor. Simon snatched the formula and the unregistered jump belt from the table and began to work on it. "Mectar, I'm trying to get the formula," he yelled.

"Do it fast," Mectar shouted, firing at the Cylots.

"Oh God. We're going to die," said Javic. He stood up and pointed his shotgun out the window.

"Put that thing down," said Simon, "and do as I tell you."

Beth realized that she was about to lose Simon. In a moment, he would be either dead or gone. "Benjamin, will you come back?" she asked. "If you can't find Kathy, will you come back?"

"Benjamin?"

"What?" he said impatiently. He had begun to do something to Yugen's jump belt.

"I love you."

"Don't say that," he said.

"It's true. I didn't realize it before, but all my life I've been looking for a man like you. I don't want to lose you. Take me with you," she begged.

A pain shot through Beth Grey. "Benjamin, I want to come with you," she pleaded. "You have two jump belts."

"You don't know what you are asking," said Simon.

"Throughout my life, men have either run from me or I've chased them away," said Beth. "I realize that now. I finally know what I want. I want to be with you. Take me with you."

The phaser shots were getting closer. Mectar shouted, "Get out of the house, now!"

"Time. Buy me time," Simon yelled to Mectar. An explosion outside near the Cylot vehicle was his answer.

As the shooting continued, Simon worked furiously on the unregistered jump belt. "Listen, Beth," he said. "I love you too, but your life would be drastically shortened. I couldn't give you the education you'd need to survive in the places I've got to go."

"It's Kathy, isn't it? After all this time, you're still trying to get back to her. Why don't you just give her up? She's dead."

"There never was a Kathy. Mectar was set up."

"You mean Kathy never existed?"

"No, she did. Look, it's a long story. It's not what you think."

"Why are you telling me now?" she asked with hope in her eyes, wanting to believe him.

"Because it doesn't matter anymore if he knows. I've got what I need," he said, motioning to the belt.

"How will he find out?"

"He will get the information from you."

"No he won't."

"Beth, don't fight him. Let him have any information he wants."

"The Cylots are coming for me, not you.

"You are going back to Kathy."

Simon's eyes flashed angrily. "It's not just Kathy. Kathy and I were never in love. When I say I love her, I don't mean as a life partner. She was an operative who ultimately gave her life while protecting mine. She did it because I was valuable to the war effort. We weren't lovers. My obligation does not involve love ... but I do love her. Am I making sense?" asked Simon while working furiously on the jump belt.

"There's more. More I haven't said, but I have to do what I have to do, and I'm going to do it in spite of you, in spite of that asshole Kian outside, in spite of Heinrich. Everyone acts according to his own imperatives. They don't give a shit about anyone else. All they ask is that you do whatever they want. I've been everybody's pawn long enough. I'm going where I want to go. I'm sorry, Beth. If I can get back here, I will. If we'd had the time and the space, something might have happened between us."

"Something *has* happened between us," she said bitterly. "Goddamn it. I love you," she said. "Is that clear? I've fallen in love with you. You're what I want!"

"I can't let any more happen," said Simon. "I can't ask you to wait, Beth ..." Simon stopped and looked up. "I love you, but that means I want you safe. You can't be safe with me." He returned to his work on the jump belt. He removed his jump belt and clipped on the unregistered one in its place. He hit some buttons on the belt and his image seemed to fade, then grow stronger.

"Wait a minute," said Beth. "You said your jump belt couldn't come off."

"I lied."

"What else did you lie about?" she demanded.

"Don't really have time to discuss it," said Simon. Stepping near her, he slipped the flashing bracelet off her wrist. Then, with a few deft motions, he connected it to the registered jump belt he had just removed. Sparks jumped from the belt as he made this connection, as though he had short-circuited it.

"I'm no use to you now?" asked Beth. "Is that it? You've got your formula, so now you can take that bracelet off me and let them kill me?" She seemed resigned to her fate.

Simon, looking straight into her eyes, said, "Honey, I'm trying to fix it so they don't kill any of us—me included." He walked to a shattered window, holding the jump belt with Beth's bracelet attached. She pulled him away from the window and pressed her body against his. "Then this is our agreement. I'll wait for you for a year. After that, don't come back. When this ends, you can jump to any period you want. Jump back to me in that one-year period and I'll be yours. Do you agree?"

He smiled with pride as he stared into her eyes. "Not only do I agree," he said. "I promise. I promise to return to you sooner than a year. If I can I will be right back." Then he kissed her hard on the lips. He pulled away and said, "I … love … you."

Then he said, "Mectar, I have Yugen's jump belt and have short-circuited my own. Our belts are no longer connected."

"The formula," Mectar shouted. "The—"

"Beth has it. It's yours, asshole. I have a way to take out the Cylots," said Simon. Although he shouted, his words reached the Kian telepathically. "When I come out the front door, lay down covering fire."

"Too late," said Mectar. "They're going to blow down the house. Get out the back. Now!"

"Come on!" said Simon, grabbing Beth's arm. "Run!" With Javic close behind, they raced out the back door. Just as they jumped behind a large boulder behind the house, the house burst into flames.

"Oh, God!" said Javic, suddenly standing up. "My equipment is in the cellar!" A phaser shot barely missed him. Simon grabbed his collar and pulled him down. "The equipment!" shouted Javic. "It's lost."

"Shut up!" said Simon.

"No. You don't understand."

Simon crouched and held his original, registered jump belt. Leaning against the boulder, he pointed to another boulder and said, "I'm going to try to make it there. Stay on the ground and cover your heads. Is that clear? Mectar can't keep them pinned down much longer. He's running out of ammo."

He handed the written formula to Beth. "Give this to Mectar," he said. The Cylot control device he had taken out of his shoulder that morning was taped to the formula. "See you soon," he said, "I promise."

She put both hands on his outstretched arm and rubbed her cheek against his hand. "Be careful," she said, and then she kissed his palm.

An exploding Cylot grenade leveled what remained of Javic's house. A shower of flaming debris ignited small brush fires. Simon saw the Cylots' car through the newly destroyed walls. Heinrich and Mueller, trading shots with Mectar, were pinned behind it.

Beth clung to Simon's hand, not wanting to let go. "I'm sorry," he said again, but you should be okay after this." He pulled away. "Covering fire! Now!" he shouted to Mectar. The Kian lay down a sustained covering fire. Simon ran to the other boulder and dove behind it.

Beth now saw the action unfold in slow motion. Simon rose to his knees and threw the registered jump belt toward the Cylots. As a Cylot shot vaporized his sheltering boulder, Simon began to disappear in a time jump. Another Cylot shot actually passed through Simon's fading image. Blood burst out of Simon's back. A third Cylot shot seemed to sever his legs from his torso. Since the jump belt he had thrown was on a feedback loop, it immediately exploded upon landing. The exploding jump belt created a time vortex and sucked the two Cylots into it. The suction literally sucked Simon's torso into the vortex. His legs, the boots still attached, fell forward to the ground.

The temporary time vacuum the explosion created extinguished the fires in the woods and in what remained of Javic's house. Beth gasped for breath as air rushed by her into the vortex. Then, as she regarded the eerie scene around her, she was struck by one thing: silence. The silence was complete, still, and calm.

Simon and the Cylots were gone. Beth screamed and ran to the spot where she had seen Simon fall. Blood and bone covered the ground. Simon's legs had been severed at the knees. His weathered boots were still on his feet. His jump belt had carried the rest of his body through the time jump. Mectar walked toward Beth, who stepped out from behind her boulder. "You have the formula," said the Kian, pointing his phaser at her. She nodded and handed it to him. He stared and began to probe her mind. She felt the penetration and fought back.

She tried to run. He grabbed her by her arm and, looking deep into her eyes, established a telepathic bond. She remembered Simon telling her not to fight.

The information Mectar received surprised him. "Simon has Yugen's unregistered jump belt," he said. "His romance with Kathy was a lie. You have fallen in love with him and he promised to come back to you." Mectar smirked. "He lies, Beth. Why should he?" Surprise registered on Mectar's face. "You carry his child."

Beth looked at Mectar, startled. "It's true, Grey. You carry his child and I will be sure he knows. I know Simon. If he is alive he will return to you. You, Grey, are my bait, and though I once missed him, now I will kill Simon, you, and your child upon his return."

"You saw him die like I did," she said.

Mectar let her go as a menacing smile contorted his face. "So it would appear," he said. "I have to leave now. There are some things I need to settle on Kia. Some will not be pleased to see me, but the ones who sent those to kill me will not live long. After that, I will deal with you and Simon, if he is still alive.

"Look," she screamed at Mectar, "there, take what's left of his body."

Mectar looked at the blood and bone fragments. "So I will." Throwing the same type of sheet Razqual had used previously Mectar threw the sheet over the body parts. He pointed something at the sheet and it disappeared into what Grey could only guess was its own time jump. Then Mectar disappeared into time.

Beth fell to the ground and began to sob. Javic came up behind her and put his hand on her shoulder. Suddenly the sky lit up with a disruption field the size of which Beth had never imagined. She had seen the flashing display of color around the disruption fields that Mectar and Simon had used, but whereas those were the size of a car, this was as big as an aircraft carrier.

More than a hundred helmeted soldiers appeared around them, goggles covering their eyes and weapons at the ready, securing the area around Beth and Javic, who stood frozen. They were silhouetted by Javic's burning home, they moved ghostlike through the smoke. They moved past Javic and Beth, who stood at the center of their protective ring. Overhead craft hovered and flew in a protective cap.

A moment later, Razqual arrived out of a jump in full military combat gear. He stood a little more than four feet tall. He surveyed the area, his bearing exuding full command. Then he walked slowly to Beth. His eyes were narrow and threatening, but he said nothing, scrutinizing her for a long time.

A burst of light fired above her, and Beth in a flash saw some type of craft fly overhead. She looked up and then at Razqual. "Is Ben alive?"

Razqual stared a moment more and then answered. "Selfridge wanted to come here to talk to you. A man jumped into her presence behind Razqual. Razqual stepped aside as the man walked toward her while removing his helmet. "As quickly as you can, please; we are exposed here," said Razqual to the new arrival. On his black shirt, embroidered over the left pocket, was the name Selfridge. She looked back at Razqual and saw that he wore the same name over the top of his left pocket.

She didn't recognize him as the man approached, and then, as a tear fell from her eye, she said softly, "Ben?"

The Ben Simon who had left her moments ago as a twenty-seven-year-old had returned years older. She could see they had been hard years.

"I'm sorry to tell you Ben Simon is dead. My name is Selfridge."

"Ben?" she ask again. "You're Ben, aren't you?"

"Beth, you have to understand a lot quickly: Ben is gone forever. Cylots killed him in front of you. Because of your contact with him, your life is danger here."

"You're Ben. Say you're Ben."

"I can't, Beth, I am Selfridge, and I have come to ask you a question."

Another individual arrived in a time jump behind Selfridge. Slighter than the others, this trooper arrived weaponless. As this trooper entered the time space, Razqual's hand reached for the blaster at his side, and upon recognizing the individual he snorted disdainfully. As Selfridge turned, the trooper pulled off her helmet revealing a beautiful woman with long hair in her early twenties. Her uniform tight against her well-figured body, she looked upon Selfridge and Beth with a smile of giddy excitement. Selfridge turned in anger and strode back to the individual. While Beth could not hear their muted one-sided conversation, it was clear Selfridge was angrily addressing the woman. Pumping his fist and then pointing at the ground, his face up against the woman's, it looked to Beth as if Selfridge was ready to kill her. Yet through his tirade, the woman's smile would not leave and she kept looking over Selfridge's shoulder at Beth and smiling.

"Who is that, Razqual?' asked Beth

Razqual was enjoying Selfridge's outburst. Without taking his eyes of the scene in front of them, he said to Beth, "You are going to have an interesting life."

Beth looked up at Razqual and then back at Selfridge, who had now stopped and was apparently waiting for the young woman to do something. She then placed both her hands on either of Selfridge's face and kissed him softly on the cheek. Selfridge's head slumped forward and his shoulders dropped in defeat—his burst of anger had been ineffective. The woman looked at Beth one more time, smiling, and waved to Razqual. He stiffened and then discretely acknowledged the wave. Then the woman put on her helmet and disappeared in to her departure jump.

Selfridge turned and came back to toward Beth, now appearing more comfortable.

"I've come here to ask you to marry me."

"What?" said Beth. "You won't even admit you're Ben—if you are—and now you ask me to marry you. And who was that woman?"

Selfridge pointed his finger in her face and spat angrily, "That is your daughter, and it's about time you began to control her. She won't listen to me. You are the only one who seems to have any effect on her, and you had better ..."

As quickly as the torrent of words began it stopped, as Selfridge saw Beth's perplexed look and Razqual's smirk.

"Nice job, asshole. You're a real romantic," said Razqual under his breath. "I have seen Dinnic sea squids do a better job than you."

Selfridge brought both his hands up to his face as if to hide.

"My daughter?"

"Your daughter, Lerri," said Razqual motioning with his head to both Beth and Selfridge.

"I have a daughter named Larry?" demanded Beth, her brow contorted in confusion.

"Fuck," said Selfridge in exasperation. "Look, if you could name your daughter any name you could, it would be ...?"

"Lori. I would name my daughter Lori, after—"

"Your mother, which I totally agree with," Selfridge said, but if you agree to marry me then our first stop right now is to go to Lalia. My work is there. You will love Lalia—it is a beautiful planet, and we will be there for a few years before we get back to Earth. Moreover, the Lalians will love your ... our daughter. Their pronunciation of Lori is Lerri. It is they who will give her that nickname, a nickname she will be proud of."

"Our daughter," said Selfridge, putting his hands on Beth's shoulders. "I've come here to ask you to please marry me."

"And Mectar doesn't want to kill you anymore?

"Mectar has announced on Kia that he saw Simon die. They have the body, and it has been confirmed that Simon is dead. The Cylot advance has also been stopped. On Kia, Mectar is a hero. He has become one of the most powerful citizens on Kia—if not the most powerful."

"Wait. I thought you said Selfridge was married to Lynth."

"I was for a while, but—" said Selfridge.

Before Selfridge could finish, a tall trooper removed her helmet. Before Beth stood a six-foot beauty with blue skin, six arms, and beautiful long flowing blue hair. She was thin, with an almost human face, but with three slit openings above her mouth instead of a nose. Her eyes were like cat's eyes. They were yellow like the sun. Her hair was dark blue, heavy, and braided. They were more like tubules

than strands of hair, hollow and the thickness of spaghetti. Beth marveled at the
alien before her. Lynth softly put one hand on Beth's shoulder and held Beth's
left hand in two of hers. With her other three hands she held her cloak about her.

"I married him because he saved me and my people. I married him because by
doing so I thought I could keep him. He married me for the position. As my husband, he commanded the Lalian forces. It took several years, but I fell in love
with Linge. I will never stop loving Liud, but I love your man as well. A queen
needs a husband if the line is to be carried on, and Selfridge and I agreed to
divorce. He loved you. I always told him to come back to you. You are a strong-
willed woman, like your daughter. I think you understand. There was nothing
physical between Selfridge and me."

"How do you know what I am?" demanded Beth.

"I am your daughter's godmother and I am an old woman now. I have spoken
to my younger self, who awaits you. You are dear to me, as is your daughter. As a
child, she spent much time in my court. It was I who gave her permission to
come here and it was I who escorted her here."

"Bitch," he said under his breath, but loud enough for all to hear.

Lynth only smiled. "As a young queen I was trapped on Gongrn. Liud was
dead. The Cylot fleet was approaching and this young man, this brash alien,
came and said 'I will save you. I alone will get you to safety.' What choice did I
have? The Cylots had destroyed my troops. I had only a few guards left, and they
were prepared to die with me. I was an emotional wreck. At that moment, I could
not think clearly and had resigned myself to my death.

"What was left except this man, who said upon his life my life would be saved
and with my life, my peoples? When he had defeated the Cylot force that had me
trapped, he broadcast that I had been victorious. He rallied my people and gave
us a technology we had never dreamed of.

"The Lalian nickname for Selfridge is Burbak. The joke is, 'Where does Burbak sit?' The answer is, 'Anywhere he damn well pleases.' After he saved my life
and pulled the Lalian forces together, he took command. I was a wreck and was
grateful to have him take that command. Everything he did strengthened our
people, our military, and our research. He was a taskmaster, but under him we
regained our planet and were able to hold it.

"I constantly asked him what he demanded for the service he provided. He
said he would let me know. While I lived in the palace and we rebuilt our homes,
he lived in three sparse rooms. One day, he said there was something he wanted.
I wondered, would it be jewels, precious metals, wealth? No—he said he wanted
a good hamburger."

Beth looked at Selfridge and said, "Hamburger?"

"Beth, do you think I can make this up? I have been told reality is stranger than fiction. I tell you the truth. He was tireless. We fought battle after battle, and we were stronger after each fight than we were going in. The Cylot advance moved past us toward Earth and Kia and those planets expected the same fate as all planets the Cylots had faced."

"So what happened?" asked Beth.

"We fought some more. The Cylots moving past us did not mean the fight was over. There was too much to do. While my military leaders at first resented him, they came to revere him and then emulate him. The troops came first; he never abandoned anyone; he had the values of my beloved Liud, but he was so much stronger. When he left I cried—I had been restored to my throne, I had gotten past the death of Liud, my people had regained our world, and we no longer lived in fear of Cylot attack.

"Beth, the Lalian military would go to war on his word and I would command it to be so. You could do so very much worse. But you need to answer his question," said Lynth.

"So what difference is there in a name? What is so important about the name Selfridge?" demanded Beth.

"If Ben Simon had lived, he would have been a target forever—if not the Cylots then the Kians, if not the Kians then the Dard. If not the Dard then the bounty hunters and so very many more. The less there is of Ben Simon, the better it will be for all. I think his death was genius."

"Does Selfridge have a first name?" Beth asked.

"No, Beth. I just have one name. Selfridge."

"So then I would be Mrs. Selfridge?"

"I guess."

"Then," she said, hugging and kissing him, "I'm going to be Mrs. Selfridge."

"We'll take that as a yes, said Razqual, signaling the troops to move as he clicked a jump bracelet around Beth's wrist.

Beth and Selfridge disappeared into their time jump still in their embrace. One by one, the troopers disappeared into the jump. Lynth too disappeared. Razqual turned to Javic, who towered above him. He reached into his pocket, took out a sheet of paper, and handed it to Javic. Razqual then disappeared into his own time jump, leaving Javic totally alone.

By the remaining light from the fire of his burning home, Javic opened the sheet of paper. It was a hand-scrawled diagram of a machine, and under the diagram were just two words: *Build this.*

The End

Epilogue

by Mectar

My arrival back on Kia was not welcomed by all. Some of the powerful who had sent assassins after me became some of the dead after I was done. Then I killed those who sent the assassins. What I did not anticipate was being sucked into the power vacuum I created by killing them. When the killing was done, I found myself given the title of Selfridge, that way Kia would be given the technology that was offered. While I accepted this because it helped Kia, it gave me great personal power. Yet I saw Simon's hand in the movement. Yes, I saw Simon die.

It was then that I was given this book and told to write the epilogue and have it published on Earth. For one moment I see the playing field as Simon did and am able to state clearly how I feel. Not as in the foreword when I was given an order to write a forword, not knowing the situation I was going into. Now I am given an order to get this book published in your time.

A comment on the foreword. It is not in the book you hold. The publisher has chosen to remove it from the edition published on Earth. It is in the Kian version of this book. On Earth, they slant the truth to their own ends.

I have already mentioned in the foreword (which you do not have) that I am not a writer. I will distill for you the debriefing report I gave to my military superiors after the mission, along with the risk assessment analysis I prepared to assess threat levels to Kia. My debriefing report forms the basis of this epilogue.

So let me dispose of this episode in my life and tell you what I think. Do not think you know the one called Simon, or even the person who wrote this book. The name of the author is owned by a corporation. That corporation is represented by an individual who claims authorship. What has this person published before? What does that tell you? It was Simon who wrote this book and attributed the authorship to someone in your time period. What you are reading in your time is called "fiction." In my time, the blood of my fallen comrades makes it a fact. Simon became Selfridge and Selfridge has become lost in the mass of Selfridges. Then he published this in your period, using an alias. I cannot prove that, but I believe that. I hate him for what he has done.

I met him when he had the name Simon. Simon was quantifiable. He was a person in space-time, like a particle. A particle moves in and out of your time space—sometimes it is there and sometimes it is not—but it is a definable object. It is subject to the laws of quantum mechanics.

He then adopted the name Selfridge—which amused him I think—and then conferred that name on whatever group became an ally. Suddenly there were many Selfridges—Selfridge was not a particle but a wave. Those of you who understand physics will understand the subtle difference and the insidious nature of the change. It is a change only a twisted physicist could effect.

While I was with Simon, Selfridge came to Kia. At that point, we were preparing to fight the superior Cylot force. He arrived in our midst having gotten through our defenses undetected. Selfridge parked his spacecraft in our main spaceport unguarded and checked in to the best suite at the best hotel. We immediately went to arrest him, whereupon he told us this was where he would be staying during what we considered his incarceration. He then demanded an epicure's diet, a limousine, and a chauffeur to take him where he had to go. He told the Kian authorities that as far as he was concerned, he was free to come and go as he pleased. We could provide a guard if we wished. We waited to see his next move. If we didn't meet his demands he asked us which one of our cities we would like to see destroyed. He gave us his first written message with his dinner order.

Then he set up meetings with our *droggberg* (our leader), addressed our parliament, and met with our leading scientists and generals. He gave us the technology that he had given the Lalians that had allowed them to defeat the Cylots. He had but a few demands. First, when he left, the title of the commander of this new technology was to be called a "Selfridge." The rank was to be the highest in our military. All we had to do was add one more rank in our military hierarchy and all the technology would be ours. How could we not agree to such stupidity if that was his only demand? Then for Kia and for me came a second demand. I would become the first Kian Selfridge. His last demand was that I write this epilogue and deliver it to his representative on Earth.

One day he was gone without announcement, leaving no trace. I was left as Selfridge. His technology was at my disposal; I was fully armed and capable of defeating any Cylot attack, with other Selfridges to call on if I needed.

When the Lalians fought the Cylots there was one Selfridge; by the time he got to us there were two. The second title fell to Razqual. When he left us, there were three. I was the third. There are more than fifty now. By making me a Selfridge, he conferred on me the responsibility of protecting not just Kia but also Earth. Do you see the insult? Do you understand my situation? I hate him.

Every Selfridge protects multiple systems. We already know Simon is dead, killed by the Cylots. I saw him die myself. I have his bones. DNA tests prove they are his. Simon used to ask me, "Who are you going to believe, me or your own eyes?" I don't even trust my own eyes when it comes to him. For that matter, how do you, reader, even know this story hasn't been tampered with?

I saw him die. I identified the remains of the body. I brought it to Kia and the DNA checked out. Before he is done, everyone except the Cylots will be armed with new weapons. He will have created parity in the known galaxy and removed the Cylot threat. Those who were weak are now strong. Those who were strong are merely our equals now. Those who are attacked can call upon Selfridge, one of the fifty or so, to come to their aid. And maybe inside of that fifty, the real one may come, or not. Perhaps he has simply disappeared. This is simply where the story of Selfridge ends, or the trail goes cold.

The Lalians were the first to have a Selfridge leader. Some say Simon was at those early fights, but there is no proof. Some say it was there that Simon's stealth technology was first deployed and that is why we can't find him still. Only Lalian legends and stories remain, and they purposefully conflict so the truth is known to very few, and perhaps not even to them. I sense falsehoods in the story you have read, not because I know but because of how I was duped before. What you have read is a Lalian version of the events. The ending suits the Lalians, but my evidence says that it is false.

The Kian version of this book, which I wrote, ends with my return to Kia, along with part of Simon's body and the science we needed to fight the Cylots. My mission was successful. My version ends with Simon dead, the formula here (as well as the new technology that Selfridge had delivered), and me a hero.

While I got his bones, the Cylots got his head and eyes, so I suppose they got to "see what he sees and know what he knows." His blood soaks the soil of Earth. On your planet when someone dies they say he rests in peace. Simon rests in pieces.

When Simon said he was the disease, he must have been speaking the truth. Once the Cylots brought Simon's body back to their ship, their advance, which was headed toward Kia, stopped and headed toward Earth. Simon's body seemed to have infected them with a disease. It was then that Selfridge's force hit them just outside the Earth solar system. It was there that the Cylot force was destroyed. Kia was unscathed.

The Lalians did not stop the Cylots. They simply reclaimed their planet after the Cylot advance moved through their sector of space. The Kians did not stop the Cylots; our fleet was not there at that battle. Earth did not stop the Cylots either; the fleet was simply destroyed outside their solar system. Simon was dead. Yet the question remains: Was Simon's death simply convenient for Simon?

Let us now follow the trail of Beth Grey. She agreed to marry Selfridge, but he had disappeared into a maze of Selfridges of which I am one. She spent many years in the Lalian court, to which Kians have little access. Then she wasn't there. It is said she divorced Selfridge and returned to Earth. It is said that she grew tired of Lalia and wanted to return home. To compound the confusion, Linge is called Selfridge. It is a maze of mirrors.

Some say she lives in the past on Earth near her parents in a place called Sedona, Arizona. There are even stories that Simon is there with her and that he hides in plain sight.

Razqual has become the Paradorian Selfridge, and Parador has developed its own sphere of influence. They are not a threat to Kia, but the dwarves should be watched, as they have developed an inflated sense of importance. I am told there is a Paradorian version of this book—which Razqual wrote, of course—in which Razqual plays a much larger role than he does in the Earth version. There is also a Lalian version of this book. Imagine my surprise.

Due to their lack of involvement, the Kaf are on the decline, having lost prestige and importance to the Paradorians. The Dard are now in the Paradorian sphere, much to their chagrin.

The Lalians have become something they never were, a research center. But even as they grow more powerful, they grow more benign. In that way they are becoming increasingly like the Barcini. Instead of expanding their sphere of influence, they are contracting it, allowing planets in their sphere more independence. But they have done something strange. They have claimed Earth to be in their sphere. That is not possible. They are too far from Earth and could never defend it. Earth lies in the Kian sphere of influence. Yet they have made it clear that if Earth is attacked, they will go to war to protect it. Once they said that, the Paradorians said they would as well. Some say Selfridge was human. Some say they did this because Simon was a friend to Lynth.

I was not on Kia when Selfridge came to Kia, but after I returned to Kia I jumped back in time to meet him. I can tell you he was not human. He was an alien whose form was much different from a human's. Years later after that week period had been locked out to prevent more time travel to it to protect Selfridge I had this thought: Was that Simon wearing a holocloak? I am prevented now from finding that out.

Earth is as strange a planet as there is. They are tough to assess. They have a veneer of importance but have no sphere of influence and just a few mining colonies. Yet around Earth a ruined Cylot fleet stands in mute testimony that any who try to attack Earth will suffer a similar result. The wreckage of an unstoppable scourge, the Cylots, speak of the danger of attacking Earth——a moron of a planet on the surface, as though two separate species live there. Every time Earth forces fought the Cylots, they beat them. How did this happen? Was it mere luck? My advice to my superiors was to use caution in dealing with Earth. I also made note that their food is delicious.

There are other issues I need to dispose of for you. Apparently the time belt that Simon threw at the two Cylots came with a disease. Simon once said to me, "I am the disease." The Cylots were uninjured and returned to their fleet thinking they had killed Simon and had escaped. They became the path of their own infection. It wiped out the Cylots in their ships as they approached Earth. Selfridge's force did the rest, fighting ships filled with Cylots already dead from the disease. Simon was indeed the disease.

And what of me, you may wonder? I have become more powerful and wealthy than I ever imagined. I was a simply a soldier, a good soldier. When I got back to Kia, I found out Selfridge had been there and had chosen me to be the lone Kian Selfridge. This honor gave me much power. I would be the recipient of the new technologies the Selfridges shared. I ceased being a soldier and became, much to my horror, politically involved. It is much harder to be a politician than it is to be a soldier—things are much less clear. But there are benefits. I was able to marry, to use an Earth term. I took a mate—a female from a noble family, a rich family whose wealth lay in commerce. I told her of my experiences and gave her some of the remaining brownies I had been given by Bubbe Maida. It was my mate, my *liat*, Ulkar by name, who told me what I should do.

The *liat*, the wife, needs to be trusted. While the *znec*, me, the father, raises the Kian family, the *liat*'s instincts are supreme. Logic need not support a *liat*'s instincts. My *liat*—to whom I had brought some chocolate brownies—told me to import and control chocolate. I told her I would do it but she and she alone was to control this endeavor as she regained her adulthood. It produced wealth for my family beyond my conception. I became the oligarch of chocolate. I became what I hated most: a wealthy politician who also ran a monopolistic oligarchy.

Now I am in politics. Simon once spoke to me about politics. On Earth, he said the word was derived from the ancient Earth words *poli*, meaning many, and *tics*, meaning bloodsuckers. I think this is one of his many lies, but there is truth in that explanation regardless.

My wife and I have had many children, and our children have had children. They constantly ask me what Simon was like. I say if he were alive today, he would be hunted. He empowered some and disempowered others. The Cylots would hunt him. Some Kians would hunt him. The Dard hate him. There are others on a multitude of worlds that he disempowered by giving their enemies parity with them. There are bounty hunters who could sell him to the highest bidder. But how do you hunt the dead?

By explaining the particle–wave duality of physics, I hope to show I was not the dolt Simon has portrayed me to be. I challenge any reader to enter Kian society and do as well as I did with Simon. We live in a time now called Simon's Peace; some call it Selfridges's Peace. The remnants of the Cylots have fled or been destroyed. Local wars have ceased, lest a Selfridge force show up and decide the outcome. Still, for all of that, he is hated.

I have heard that this book was published in your time to put one sentence into your cultural consciousness. I got this from Razqual, who got it from Linge, who got it from Lynth, who got it from Beth's daughter, Lerri, when she was eighteen and drunk at a Lalian party.

Years later, I met Razqual for a drink and do you know what that fuck—yes, I can now curse in Simon's language—told me? He said Selfridge told him our chase with Simon was never about the formula; it was to trap the two Cylots. When the formula was sent out, we needed to sanitize the time period. Millions died. But Kia and Earth and our part of the galaxy are now safe. You do the math, reader. Was he right?

Simon is dead, yet I have doubts. Years have passed and there are nights I think: What if the Lalian legends are true? Earth is safe and no one dares attack it. The Cylot fleet lies in mute testimony that. I am sworn to defend it, as would the Lalians and the Paradorians. That would bring all the Selfridges. And who looks for Simon? He is dead to all.

There are some who say he lives with Beth in Sedona, Arizona, in your period. They say he goes to work in the future and returns home at night to the past. It would be an interesting commute. There is golf, which he loved, and skiing nearby. She is near her parents, if she lives. Area 17, the secret base in North America, is near him as well as White Sands in New Mexico. Both are preeminent Earth military test facilities. He would be hiding in plain sight with his family and his work nearby. If it is true, he must laugh.

I have heard it told Simon once said he could negotiate with the Kians but not with a species that regarded him as a food source. Simon simply became indigestible. And in that instant, so did Earth, a stupid planet.

Finally, I went to Earth and met with the author of this book, that friend of Beth Grey's. He cleaned up the story so it could be published in your time, so he claims the title of author in your time. I spent a few days with him before I returned to Kia. He gave me fudge. I mention that to let you know that importing fudge alone would have made me wealthy on Kia.

I have been told this story is like an onion—an expression in your society to mean it has many layers. I also agree because it stinks, it leaves you in tears, and you can't wash it off your hands. It fouls you.

Wherever he is and whoever he is, he must laugh that I, who once vowed to destroy Earth, am now its defender, along with forty-nine other Selfridges who would devour me if I acted against Earth or any one of my protectorates. The political configuration he left is a stable structure, like a molecule; that is how he thinks. Can you not see his deviousness in it?

I must say one last thing to the readers of this epilogue: Simon is currently dead. He had better stay dead, or I will kill him myself.

978-0-595-70047-9
0-595-70047-0

LaVergne, TN USA
23 November 2009
164998LV00002B/14/A